Praise for *The Lo*

"*The Lost Portal* is like the biggest, baddest, and boldest roller coaster at the amusement park. From dizzying heights to heart-stopping plunges, the thrilling ride through Hadley's world of mystery, magic, and mayhem is a journey readers won't soon forget. Fans of adventure, sisterhood, and the supernatural will find a home in the Mirror Realm series. A must-read!"
—TURNEY DUFF, *New York Times* best-selling
author of *The Buy Side*

"A perfect mix of history and mystery, *The Lost Portal* is an entertaining sequel well worth a read. The female friendships at the center of this story are as delightful as the first time around and they remind us of the importance of our chosen family."
—KELLY SCHUMANN, actor from
NBC's *Superstore*

"An intriguing combination of Greek mythology and adventure that will leave you wanting more!"
—A. F. PRESSON, author of
the Trust series

"This next book in the Mirror Realm Series preserves the heart-warming themes of sisterhood and magic from the first book, but also cranks up the action and mystery. *The Lost Portal* will keep you eagerly turning pages until the very end."
—KATY FORAKER, author of
Memories, Lies, and Other Binds

"Brilliant and creative; Lenore Borja's imagination is as endless as the Mirror Realm itself."
—JEN BRAAKSMA, author of *Amaranth*

"Loaded with adventure, Greek and Egyptian mythology, and the magic of sisterhood; Borja has crafted a unique tale you won't want to miss."

—JODY HADLOCK, author of
The Lives of Diamond Bessie

"Borja expertly weaves ancient myths into the modern world in this intoxicating story of found family, the power of secrets, and the risks we're willing to take for those we love."

—KATIE KERIDAN, author of
The Felserpent Chronicles

"The girls are back in town! *The Lost Portal* is a thrilling adventure full of action, mystery, and the unique bonds of female friendship."

—ALISON LEVY, author of
Magic by Any Other Name

the lost
portal

Published by SparkPress, a BookSparks imprint,
A division of SparkPoint Studio, LLC
Phoenix, Arizona, USA, 85007
www.gosparkpress.com

Published 2024
Printed in the United States of America
Print ISBN: 978-1-68463-260-2
E-ISBN: 978-1-68463-261-9
Library of Congress Control Number: 2024911050

Interior design by Tabitha Lahr

MIRROR REALM SERIES BOOK II

the lost portal

LENORE BORJA

SPARKPRESS

HADLEY—AGE THIRTEEN

Hadley awoke to the sound of glass breaking. She shot up like a catapult, eyes wide and heart racing. Was that a window? Was someone trying to break in? She quickly kicked the covers aside and reached under her bed. With her gaze fixed on the door, she patted the carpet, searching until her fingers brushed the smooth wood of her baseball bat. She grabbed it and swung it above her shoulder, ready. Then she slid off the bed and tiptoed toward the door, stopping when she heard voices down the hall.

" . . . don't care what you think. I'm almost seventeen. I can make my own decisions!"

"You're making the wrong ones!"

She let out the breath she held and dropped the bat to her side. It wasn't a break-in—it was just her dad and brother at it again. She crossed back to the bed and plucked her phone off the nightstand, groaning when she saw the time.

Why did they always have to do this in the middle of the night? Did they not realize how laughably thin the walls of this house were? She set her phone back down and spun around, seething. Their voices carried down the hall and through her bedroom door like it was made of rice paper.

"What, so I can sell used cars for the rest of my life? No thanks, Dad."

"I've been down this road, Caleb. Trust me, it only leads to prison!"

She winced as something else was broken. She'd put money on it being a beer bottle.

"Yeah, maybe for *you*," her brother's voice sneered. "Ever think I might be smarter than you? Frank sure as hell is!"

"Your grandfather is a lying, scheming—"

She'd had enough. With a loud grunt, she leaped up and swung her bat against the wall. It punched through the drywall and left a hole the size of a grapefruit.

"Some of us are trying to sleep!" she yelled.

Her dad's voice silenced. She waited a few seconds, bat at the ready in case she needed to put another hole through the wall, but the silence resumed. Either they'd taken the argument outside, or they were whispering. She didn't care as long as she didn't have to listen to them anymore.

With a yawn, she tossed the bat aside and headed to her bathroom. On the way, she threw a fist into her punching bag, halfway wishing it was her brother's mouth. It was a good thing she had to pee; otherwise, she really would have let them have it.

She didn't bother with the light and instead sat down in the dark. Eyes closed, she let herself relax and relieve herself, grateful as always for her own bathroom. Being the only girl in the house sucked, but at least she had her privacy. She could sit on this toilet all night if she wanted to. Her head lolled forward just as a sound in her bedroom snapped her spine straight. Her eyes flew open.

"Hadley?" her brother whispered through the door.

She clenched her teeth and fumed. "Do you mind? Get out of my room!"

"I'm leaving, Haddy. I can't stay here anymore."

His voice sounded distant and hollow, and a strange unease settled in her stomach. She quickly finished her business and stood, pulling her pajama bottoms up with an angry snap.

"Shut up, Caleb," she said with a bitter laugh. "You are not."

She waited several seconds for him to respond. When he didn't, she flung the door open. He was sitting on the edge of the bed, her Taekwondo junior black belt folded neatly in his hand. She lunged for it, but he scooted away, holding it just out of reach.

Without hesitating, she tumbled on top of him and wrestled him to the ground. But he was bigger and faster than she was, and he had her pinned in less than five seconds. She growled in frustration.

"You're good, Haddy Bear," he said, shaking his head. "But not that good."

Exterior security lights shined through her bedroom window, illuminating his eyes. It irked her that his were a shade darker than her own and hence more like their mother's. But that was where the resemblance ended. In pictures Hadley had seen, her mom had soft features and a warm, radiant smile. Caleb, on the other hand, had a face full of sharp angles and a crooked nose, thanks to a street fight gone bad. Sometimes he reminded her of a crow. Smart, cunning, and resourceful, but not exactly cuddly. He relished his hard exterior because he wanted people to be afraid of him. But Hadley would never be afraid of her brother.

She sighed and pretended to concede. When his grip loosened, she arched her back, brought her leg up, and kneed him in the gut. Not hard, but enough to get his attention.

He made a garbled sound and rolled onto his side, clutching his midsection. She snatched the belt from his hand and jumped to her feet.

"I earned this," she said triumphantly, lifting the red-and-black belt above her head. "What have you ever earned, besides six months in juvie? And quit pretending you're hurt. I barely touched you."

He let out a strained laugh and slowly peeled himself off the floor. "You're stronger than you think, Haddy."

She was about to protest when she noticed the duffel bag at his feet. Her throat tightened, and the air nearly went out of her.

"Wait," she whispered. "You're really leaving?"

He exhaled slowly, resting his hands on his thighs before standing to his full height, just shy of six feet. At five foot nine, she was catching up to him fast. But clearly not fast enough. She shoved him, hard. He stumbled back but kept his footing.

"So that's it?" she demanded. "You're just gonna leave me here with Dad?"

He hung his head, refusing to look at her. "Dad's making me choose. At least with Frank, I can do something with my life. There's nothing for me here."

"Grandpa Frank is bad news, Caleb. You know that. He's a *criminal*."

Caleb looked up sharply, eyes blazing. Then he grabbed her arm and pulled her across the room until they stood in front of her full-length mirror.

"Look at us," he ordered her. "What do you see?"

She tried pulling away, but he held her tight and grabbed her by the chin, forcing her to meet his gaze in the glass. His expression was pained but determined.

"That's right," he answered for her. "I'm a high school dropout with a record. I'm a lost cause with no future. We're not the same, sis. We never were."

His words burned. "Caleb, don't say that, it's—"

"You said it yourself," he cut in. "What have I ever earned besides trouble? Now you," he paused, softening his grip on her chin, "you actually have a future. You're strong, and whatever you want, I know you'll get it."

Her eyes stung, but she bit back the tears. "I want a family, Caleb. That's what I want. If you leave, then what?"

He seemed to wilt in front of her. "I'm sorry. I know he's never gonna win any Father of the Year awards, but he does his best. Dad's a decent man."

"So are you."

"No, Haddy. I'm not."

She stared at her brother, unable to imagine her life without him in it. She knew what leaving meant—what committing to their grandfather meant. But Caleb was stubborn. If he'd made his decision, there was nothing she could do to change it. So she squared her shoulders and swallowed her tears, too angry to give in to the pain.

"You're right," she said, her voice hardening. "You're not decent. You're a coward."

His eyes flared with anger, and his face turned to stone. Before she could react, he grabbed his bag from the floor and stood. When he slung it over his shoulder, he looked at her in a way he'd never looked at her before—like he was relieved to be done with her.

"Go to hell, Hadley," he said flatly. Then he shoved her aside and turned to leave.

Her hands curled into fists even as her heart threatened to rip in two. She wanted to leap on his back and pummel him until he bled, until he hurt as much as she did. Instead, she just stood there as he quietly walked out of her room and closed the door behind him.

She listened as his footsteps receded down the hall, the security system eventually beeping when he opened the door to the garage. Chills took over her body, and she shook as reality sank in. But she wasn't going to chase him. She'd never give him the satisfaction. He left because he wanted to leave—because he didn't care enough about her to stay.

She turned around and looked at her reflection in the mirror. A sad-looking girl with messy blond hair and a boyish frame stared back at her. She didn't mind that her chest was flat or that she had no real curves to speak of because being a girl in her family was nothing but a liability. Looking like one only made it worse.

"I hate you," she whispered, the words raw and unexpected. But it was true, wasn't it? She hated who she was, this pathetic girl without a mother, who other kids felt sorry for. And now she was a girl without a brother, too.

A feeling she couldn't describe suddenly sliced through her core, bringing with it a longing so intense it was difficult to breathe. Her vision blurred, and with it, her image in the mirror.

"No, Hadley," her reflection said. "Hate is but fear in disguise. Do not fear what you are."

She gasped and leaped back, taking a defensive stance. But her reflection did not move with her. It stayed where it was, as if it were a separate Hadley, just standing there, casually speaking to her through the glass.

"What—who are you?" she heard herself say. Blood pounded in her ears, but her vision was now crystal clear. There was no mistaking that something very bizarre was happening. She didn't question if it was real, only if it was a threat.

Her image regarded her curiously. "I'm you. You're me. Don't you see?"

"No," Hadley responded, shaking her head. Was she really talking to her reflection? What the hell was going on?

Her reflection stepped forward and pressed a palm to the glass. At that moment, a sudden calm came over Hadley, and without thinking, she stepped forward and did the same. The second her hand made contact with the mirror, her image flashed her a kind and knowing smile.

"The question is not who are you," it said. "The question is, who are *we*."

Hadley swallowed, not daring to blink. The words felt right in a way she'd never known words could feel. And all she had to do was say them. Three little words, and she'd never be alone again.

Her eyes flickered to the door behind her. If Caleb could choose a new life, well, she could, too.

So she did.

chapter 1

Six years later

Hadley rushed through the door of the bridal shop, anxious to be running so late. The woman behind the clear acrylic desk looked up, then nodded toward the back of the store.

"Don't worry, she hasn't come out yet."

Hadley breathed a quick "thank you" and zigzagged through a gauntlet of faceless mannequins in floor-length gowns. When she rounded the corner to the fitting rooms, she was already halfway through her excuse.

"Guys, sorry I'm late, traffic was crazy, and you wouldn't believe what my dad—"

Her words stuck in her throat as she looked up. Her friend Alice was just stepping onto a platform that faced a wall of mirrors. Their eyes met in the glass, and Hadley's heart nearly melted into a puddle at her feet.

Alice smiled, and her brown eyes glistened, complementing her snowy-white hair. Hadley barely noticed the dress. It was white, elegant, and pretty, but nothing compared to her friend.

"Oh, honey," she said, placing a hand over her heart. "You take my breath away."

"She does, doesn't she?"

Hadley turned toward the voice. Alice's mom, Judy, sat on one of the plush velvet couches in the middle of the room, staring at her daughter with pure adoration. It was the kind of look that gave Hadley a small pang of jealousy—the kind reserved for mothers looking at their daughters.

"Nice of you to join us," said another voice, this one raspy and deep. Hadley smiled as a curvy redhead sidled up next to her. As usual, Soxie was dressed to the nines in high heels and a green designer dress that matched her eyes and showcased her fiery curls. She held two glasses of champagne and pressed one into Hadley's hand.

"Aren't you girls too young to be drinking?" said Judy, the accusation in her voice belying the innocent look on her face.

"Mom, it's fine," Alice insisted. "It's just sparkling cider."

Hadley glanced at Soxie, who subtly shook her head.

Judy made a *tsk* sound but didn't press the issue. Instead, she stood and began to fluff the bottom of Alice's gown, much to the seamstress's chagrin. Alice mouthed "sorry" to the woman and shot her mother an exasperated look.

"Mom. She just finished pinning that."

Judy kept fluffing, oblivious. "Well, I think this is just about perfect. Don't you agree, girls?"

"Not yet."

All heads in the room turned. Olivia stood in the doorway, her black hair, black dress, black tights, and dark makeup making her stand out like a human exclamation point. Draped across her arms was a delicate antique lace veil.

"Sweetheart," said Judy, her face pinched. "I thought we talked about this."

Alice looked at her mother and then at the seamstress. The woman took the hint and elegantly shuffled out of the room. Once they were alone, Alice lifted her dress skirt and stepped off the platform.

"Molly left it to me, Mom. I want to wear it."

"But—"

"She'll just wear it for the ceremony, Judy," Olivia added quickly. "Then we'll pack it up safe with the rest of Molly's things."

"It's not that," she objected. "I just thought it looked a little old-fashioned. You know, for a *nineteen-year-old*."

Hadley winced at the obvious barb. It's not like she didn't agree—nineteen *was* kind of young to get married—but this was what Alice wanted. Besides, age didn't really mean anything for this particular coupling. The groom might be nineteen, but he'd already *been* nineteen dozens of times. If Judy knew that little nugget, she'd probably spontaneously combust.

Olivia let out a startled laugh.

"I'm sorry, is something funny?" Judy asked.

Hadley glanced at Olivia, whose face turned beet red. If she was reacting to Hadley's thought, she'd slipped by laughing out loud. It was rare for her to make that mistake, but even perfectionists weren't perfect.

Judy's lips drew into a thin line. Before the situation escalated, Alice stepped in and herded her mom toward the door.

"It's nothing, Mom—inside joke. Why don't you take off? Didn't you want to get to the store before dinner? We're just narrowing down bridesmaid dress options, so we can take it from here. We'll see you at home."

After a flurry of protests, Judy reluctantly took her leave. Once she was gone, Hadley kicked her legs over the back of the couch and slid down into the soft seat, her motorcycle boots making a loud *thud* as they hit the floor. She took a swig of ice-cold brut.

"Sparkling cider never tasted so good."

Alice walked over and took the glass from her, downing the rest of its contents in one go.

"Thirsty?" Soxie asked her.

"You guys, she's driving me crazy," she burst out. "Seriously. Every five seconds, she makes a comment about how I'm too young, how we barely know each other, or worse, she drops little hints about how different David is from Colin. Can you imagine? It's making my head spin. We either need to bring her in the loop or kill her."

Hadley snorted despite how wrong the joke was. "Honey, you're stressed. That's normal, I think."

The truth was she didn't know what normal was anymore. None of them did—certainly not Alice. She was marrying her soulmate of two thousand years, who now resided in a different person's body. That had to be the holy grail of abnormal. Hadley only wondered why her friend wasn't *more* stressed.

Alice planted her hands on her hips and sighed. "Maybe we should have eloped."

"And leave us to deal with Judy's wrath? No thanks," Soxie said. "I'd rather deal with the gods."

"We already are," Alice reminded her.

"Well, there you go. We don't need to deal with both."

Hadley shook her head and chuckled. Soxie had a point. Alice's mom was a bit of a force, and they already had their hands full with the gods. Keeping *them* happy was hard enough.

"Happy?" Olivia scoffed. "I don't think that's the right word, Hadz. Let's just see if we can keep them occupied. I'll settle for that."

"What are you talking about?" Soxie asked, her gaze flitting between them. Then her eyes narrowed. "Dammit, Diaz. Give us some context before you reply to someone's thoughts. You know I hate when you do that."

Olivia responded with a bored shrug.

"Sorry, Sox," Hadley intervened. "I was just thinking about our god problem. You know, the usual."

Soxie gave her curls an irritated flip. "Whatever. It's not a problem if they stick to our dreams."

"*If* being the operative word," said Olivia.

"If?" Alice repeated, looking suddenly anxious. "You think they're no longer interested in our dreams?"

The conversation had derailed, and even though Hadley didn't technically start it, she felt responsible. "Listen, I'm sorry I brought it up. Maybe we shouldn't worry about the gods until they give us something to worry about."

Rather, let's not worry about something we have zero control over, she really wanted to say.

Olivia gave her a pointed look but chose to stay silent this time. Hadley couldn't read *her* mind, but she knew what she was thinking. Today wasn't about their god problem. Today was about Alice.

Hadley quickly rearranged her face, attempting to look more like a doting bridesmaid, and her friends did the same. Soxie joined her on the couch, and together, they watched as Olivia pinned the delicate veil to Alice's hair. The white of the lace blended with her white locks, giving her an angelic appearance. When she finished, Olivia rested her hands on Alice's shoulders and spoke to her reflection.

"Persephone knew," she said softly. "She knew all along you'd end up together, that Cithaeron would find you. She planned for this. I think it's her way of saying she's sorry."

A sad, almost invisible smile appeared on Alice's face. "You're probably right," she said, pausing to finger the wispy lace. "It just makes me sad to think of her buying this, knowing she'd never get to see me wear it."

Hadley looked down. This had to be hard for Alice. Her Aunt Molly—who was really the goddess Persephone—had given up her existence to save Alice and destroy the Mirror Realm. They'd all believed it had been a split-second decision, but being the goddess she was, maybe she'd known all along it would end up the way it did. Hadley noticed Olivia nod solemnly in agreement and decided it was time to change the subject.

"Well, I think the veil is perfect and timeless," she declared, sitting up. "You look beautiful, Alice. The groom won't know what to do with himself."

Alice's face lit up. Then she turned around, her gown's skirt billowing as she moved. "It's not too ice princess or snow queen?"

"Don't be silly. You look like an angel."

"I do not," she laughed, fiddling with a strand of white hair. It was only last year that it had turned white—thanks to all the demons she ashed—but Hadley could barely remember what she looked like before. As far as she was concerned, Alice was born with white hair, and it suited her.

"But the dress," Alice continued. "You think he'll like it?"

"Ali, you could walk down the aisle in a bright green elf costume," joked Soxie. "All that lucky bastard will see is you."

Alice dipped her head. "Thank you. I love you guys."

"Yeah, yeah," Soxie said. "We know." Then she stood and made her way to Alice, her stiletto heels click-clacking as usual as she crossed the floor. She grabbed hold of Alice's heart-shaped face and gave her a big smooch on the lips.

"Just remember," she said with a knowing smirk. "You promised no babies for a while. None of us is ready for that."

They all laughed, and on cue, the seamstress entered the room, no doubt having waited until it sounded safe to do so. Soxie and Olivia took seats on the opposite couch from Hadley, and the scene turned into a typical bridal fitting, the conversation moving to safer topics like cake, party favors, and band choices.

Instead of participating, Hadley found her mind drifting. Once she got a better look at Alice's dress, she couldn't stop staring at it. The design was more modern, but it reminded her of another dress, one she had tried on when she was seven years old. She'd been playing in the attic when she came across it. Not a fan of dresses, she normally avoided them. But this had been her mother's, so she'd felt compelled to try it on. Caleb, ten at the time, had come looking for her and found her crying on the floor in a heap of white silk.

"What's wrong, Haddy Bear?" he'd asked.

She'd wiped her snotty nose with the sleeve of the dress and looked up. "Do I have to wear a dress when I get married?"

Caleb had laughed. "Don't be stupid. What makes you think you're ever getting married?"

A familiar ache gripped her chest, and she quickly cut the memory short. She was usually better at keeping intrusive memories at bay, but seeing Alice in her wedding dress wreaked havoc on her emotions. Her leather leggings squeaked subtly as she stood to excuse herself.

"I'll be right back," she announced, not waiting for a response before hastily exiting the room.

She darted through the maze of mannequins and pushed the front doors open, eager for some fresh air. A mid-winter chill greeted her despite the unrelenting desert sun. She squinted as her eyes adjusted to the brightness. The bridal shop was located in a posh outdoor shopping mall, the kind that sold three-hundred-dollar jeans and handbags with certificates of authenticity. It wasn't her jam, but she appreciated the ambiance. Flowering desert plants lined the walkways, and cool jazz pumped through hidden speakers. She dodged a group of chatty shoppers and looked for a place to sit down. She spotted a pair of teak lounge chairs in the shade, but one of them was occupied. Before she could make her escape, its occupant spotted her and waved. She reluctantly lifted her hand and walked over.

"You're not supposed to be here," she said as she fell into the seat next to him. "Did Judy see you?"

"No, thank god. And I won't tell if you won't."

She leaned her head back and closed her eyes. "Deal. But you might want to think about giving your bride-to-be some space, Colin. This whole stalker thing is getting old."

"I'm picking up my tuxedo, thank you very much. And it's *David*," he corrected her, lowering his voice. "You have to start calling me David. It's been almost a year, Hadz."

She bit the inside of her cheek and opened her eyes. Sun peeked through the fronds of the palm leaves above. They swayed gently in the breeze, helping calm her frayed nerves. Too bad the guy next to her had the opposite effect.

"I thought we agreed we could still call you Colin in private."

"If you haven't noticed, this is a public place."

She rolled her head to the side and glared at him. David's green eyes stared back at her. No matter how many times she looked at him, she still saw the old David. The one whose soul was probably annoying the crap out of Hades in The Underworld this very second.

"Whatever you say, *Cithaeron.*"

She watched with satisfaction as his eyes clouded dark, the way they always did when he heard his true name spoken.

He blinked a few times until they were green again, then gave her a withering look. "Thanks for that. It's not a parlor trick, by the way."

"I enjoyed it," she shrugged.

He let out a frustrated sigh and leaned back. "As much as I hate to ruin your fun, it's better if you call me David from now on. If Alice can do it, so can you."

She smiled sideways, amused by his naivete. "There are a lot of things Alice can do that I can't do. That none of us can do."

"Can we please not talk about it? Let me marry her first. Then we can worry about stolen souls and restless gods."

Her hands gripped the armrests. It was the elephant in the room, the one they had all been ignoring for months, ever since Cithaeron showed up in David's body. The gods had given them a gift. It was only a matter of time before they expected something in return.

Hadley closed her eyes again, trying to empty her mind of all things god- or goddess-related. But all she could picture was the Realm, that impossible, beautiful place they once called their second home. She missed those mirrors, the feeling of flipping and flying through space and fighting evil, one demon at a time. They'd had a common goal then. A purpose. With the Realm gone, it was hard to know what that purpose was now, other than being a direct conduit for the gods. Luckily, and at least for now, it was only through their dreams. But restless gods sometimes made for restless nights.

"What are you thinking about?" the man she now had to call David asked.

"Like you care," she laughed. "I'll let you know if it has anything to do with Alice, though."

She heard him slap the side of his chair and stand. "That's not fair, and you know it."

Her eyes popped open, and she jumped to her feet, eager for a fight. *This* fight. "What's not fair?" she snapped. "That since day one, you've treated us like a chore you got stuck with? That no matter what we did, it was never enough? If it weren't for that girl in there," she stopped to point to the bridal shop, "I guarantee you wouldn't be here. Now that the Realm is gone, you'd have left us. And you know what? That's fine. But don't pretend we're best friends. You treated us like a job because that's what we were to you. A job."

"Hadley, I—"

She put her palm up, signaling for him to be quiet. "Save it. I had a brother, and he already let me down. I was never going to give you that option." And then, as she walked away, she couldn't help but stop and say over her shoulder, "I buried you in that desert too, you know. It wasn't exactly the highlight of my life. But I guess you wouldn't know anything about it because you never bothered to ask."

A passerby stopped and gaped, but Hadley didn't care. She'd said what she needed to say, and she was done with this conversation.

"I'll see you back home, *David*." Then she turned, plastered a smile on her face, and walked back into the store to try on some bridesmaid dresses.

chapter 2

By the time they got home, the sun had begun its descent behind the mountains, casting the Roxland mansion in all its sprawling, golden glory. As Hadley maneuvered her car down the drive, she let her eyes wander to the barn where the horses were now tucked into their stalls, then to the pool where she and the girls had spent many a summer's night staring at the sky. Out here, near the mountains, there was less light pollution, so the stars were brighter. But never quite as bright as those they used to encounter in the Realm. She frowned, irritated with her rambling thoughts. First her brother, and now the Realm. What was with her today?

"Your brother?" asked Olivia from the back seat. "That's why you were late today. Your dad is giving you grief about him again, isn't he?"

Hadley's knuckles turned white as she gripped the steering wheel. She wasn't in the mood to get into it.

Not now, O.

Olivia acknowledged her by giving her shoulder a quick squeeze. Meanwhile, Alice and Soxie were too busy chattering away to catch on. Despite it not belonging to her, Soxie was offering her uncle's private jet for Alice to use on her honeymoon.

"We can't possibly," Alice demurred.

"What are you, a nineteenth-century debutante? *We can't possibly*," Soxie teased. "Of course you can, Miss Daniels, right after the Netherfield Ball."

Alice reached back to slap Soxie's arm. "You know what I mean. We don't need a fancy vacation, and we certainly don't need to bother Mayron for his jet. Plus, I don't think he's warmed up to the whole David thing yet."

"Have any of us?" asked Soxie.

Hadley giggled. "Not me. He was hard enough to like when he was Colin."

"Well, the dogs don't mind him," Olivia piled on. "But they might be the only ones."

Everyone laughed except for Alice. Hadley glanced over and tapped her on the arm.

"Hey, you know we're just kidding, right?"

Instead of answering, she turned to look out the window, fingering the ring on her left hand—a simple gold band with a delicate mother-of-pearl butterfly. It wasn't a traditional engagement ring, but then again, Alice and David weren't a traditional couple. Hadley watched her twist the little butterfly back and forth as an uncomfortable silence descended on the car.

She turned into the circular drive and caught Olivia's eye in the rearview mirror.

I think we went too far.

Olivia made a face and leaned forward. "Alice, is everything okay? We *were* joking."

"No, you weren't."

Hadley pulled to a stop and put the car in park. Alice immediately unbuckled her seatbelt and gathered her things. It was uncharacteristic of her to shut down like this. Something was up. Before she could exit the car, Hadley took a firm hold of her wrist.

"Honey, what's going on?"

Alice refused to look at her. "Nothing. Everything's perfect."

"It's not, though. You're obviously upset."

"Yeah," agreed Soxie. "Talk, Daniels."

With a heavy sigh, Alice closed her eyes and slumped back in her seat. "I'm not upset. I promise."

Hadley shot a worried look at the back seat. If only Olivia could read Alice's mind—or even David's—they wouldn't have to go through this song and dance.

"Whatever it is, you can talk to us," she said, loosening her grip. "About anything."

Alice opened her eyes and twisted around. "Even David?"

"If you insist," Soxie groused.

"See, this is what I'm talking about," Alice said with a huff. "He's trying, Sox. I just wish you guys could cut him a little slack."

"That's asking a lot."

"Fine," she relented, throwing her hands up. "I get it. He's the worst, and you'll never think otherwise."

Hadley would love to agree, but instead, she moved her hand to Alice's shoulder. "Why are you worried about Coli—" She stopped, catching herself. "I mean David. Why are you worried about him? Did something happen?"

Her gaze lowered. "No. Nothing like that. It's just, sometimes I feel like I'm in the middle. I know you've had your issues with him, and I know it's not easy accepting him as David. But imagine what it's like for him."

"Alice, Cithaeron's lived at least forty, maybe fifty lives," said Olivia. "He knows how to acclimate to a new body. Why do you think this one is any different?"

Alice shrugged and fidgeted with the straps of her bag. "I'm not sure. He hasn't said anything, but I get the feeling he struggles with it sometimes. And believe it or not, he does care what you guys think."

Soxie sat back and blew an errant curl from her face. "So you want us to be nice to him."

Alice gave her a sheepish look. "Could you? Just until the wedding. Then you'll only have to see him when you visit us in Sedona."

Hadley resisted the urge to object. She hated it when the subject of Sedona came up. They all did. But they also wanted Alice to be happy, even if it meant her moving two hours away.

"Sure thing," she forced herself to say. "We'll do our best."

Alice gave her a grateful smile and looked to the back seat for confirmation. She received two unenthusiastic grunts of assent.

"Thanks, guys," she gushed. "I appreciate it."

Hadley gave her a loving pat on the cheek. "Consider it your wedding present."

Everyone laughed, and the mood lifted. Then Hadley quickly shooed them out of the car just as the front doors of the main house opened. Three frenzied Dobermans flew down the granite steps like racehorses clearing the starting gate. They barked and howled and spun in circles as if their humans were coming home from war and not a three-hour trip to the mall.

David stood at the top of the stairs, eyes trained on his bride-to-be—his soulmate. Hadley watched as Alice stepped into his arms. He didn't look like a man struggling. He looked like David. Tall, dark, and—Hadley was loath to admit—handsome, with sixteen hundred years of knowledge crammed into his brain. Not to mention a fiancée who worshipped the ground he walked on.

Hadley studied his chiseled face, feeling more than a little annoyed. How exactly was he the victim here? As far as she was concerned, he'd won the lottery. He got his life back, *and* he got the girl. What more did he want? But she'd promised she'd play nice, so when he looked in her direction and waved, she put a fake smile on her face and waved back.

"Hi, you lucky jerk," she said through her teeth.

A dog's head suddenly popped up in the window, obscuring her view. She winced as paws scraped her car door. "Get down!" she yelled, hitting the horn.

Schlemmer—or Fred or Ginger, she couldn't always tell them apart—just barked and slobbered at her through the glass. The other two ran loops around the car while Soxie and Olivia attempted to get them under control.

Hadley dropped her head onto the steering wheel, waiting for the chaos to subside. Eventually, the dogs followed everyone inside, allowing her to circle back toward the garage.

After pulling into her spot, she turned off the ignition and waited as the heavy doors rolled down behind her. They screeched like banshees, in desperate need of some WD-40. Normally, she'd take care of it, but ever since David moved in, she'd made a point not to fix them. It gave her a certain amount of joy knowing the sound traveled through the floorboards to his room above the garage.

She glanced at the ceiling. Crap. That qualified as mean, didn't it?

With a resigned sigh, she got out, grabbed a can of WD-40 from the workbench, and spent the next ten minutes dealing with the garage doors.

"You're welcome," she muttered at the ceiling.

When she finished, she made her way to the other end of the garage, aka the showroom. A sitting area in the center boasted four sleek leather chairs and a coffee table overflowing with automotive magazines. Surrounding the sitting area, each with its own spotlight, was Mayron's collection of classic cars. They were in mint condition and made her dinged-up Volkswagen convertible feel like a junker in comparison. There was a '63 Aston Martin DB5, a '61 Austin-Healey 3000, a '64 Jaguar XKE, and Hadley's least favorite, a '67 Ford Mustang Shelby GT500, dark blue with white racing stripes. It was a gorgeous car, but she could barely bring herself to look at it. It reminded her too much of her mother.

Taking a seat facing away from the Shelby, she took out her phone and stared at the lock-screen photo of her and the girls. It helped psych her up for the thing she'd been avoiding all day. With a deep breath, she unlocked the phone and brought up the latest text from her dad.

Dad: *Caleb was sentenced today. The judge gave him ten years. Thought you should know.*

Her eyes slitted. She hadn't spoken to her brother in years. What did her dad expect her to do with this information? Send him a cake with a file baked in? She furiously typed a response.

Hadley: *Why are you telling me this? I don't want to know.*

She hit send, enjoying the *whoosh* sound her phone made as her words flew through the ether. Knowing her dad, he'd wait a couple of days before responding. He usually did when he didn't like a message. Well, let him chew on that one for a while.

Happy to have checked that chore off her to-do list, she settled in and quickly fell into a social media black hole. The mindless scrolling helped override all the heavier thoughts rattling around in her brain.

"There she is, on her phone again."

Hadley jumped in surprise and looked up. Barry, the former chauffeur, had snuck up on her from who-knows-where, wearing coveralls and holding a socket wrench in one hand and a car manual in the other. She quickly shoved her phone into her back pocket and stood.

"Hi, Barry. Sorry, I didn't hear you come in."

"I gathered," he said, his Scottish accent stronger than ever. "A grizzly bear coulda snuck up on ye." Then he pointed the manual at her. "Ye better be careful, or the FaceTok will rot your brain!"

She laughed. "Nice try, Barry. But even you posted your wedding pictures on Facebook. Speaking of, shouldn't you be helping Judy with dinner?"

He pretended to look behind him, then put a finger to his mouth in a "shhh" gesture. "My wife dunna like me foolin' around with her recipes. I thought I'd tinker with the Beast instead."

Hadley followed his gaze to the corner where a 2009 Bentley Arnage sat hidden under a cloth tarp. The car was retired last year when Barry married Alice's mom and retired himself.

She eyed the socket wrench. "Need some help?"

Over the years, Barry had come to rely on her help in the garage. Spending part of her childhood in her grandfather's chop shop had taught her a thing or two about cars.

He smiled wide. "Was hopin' you'd ask."

An hour later, she made her way upstairs to clean up before dinner. Morgan, the house manager, passed her on the second-floor landing as he headed home for the night. He took one look at her, shook his head, and laughed. She threw him a sarcastic nod and continued up the stairs.

Pots and pans clanged in the kitchen below as Judy prepared dinner. A suspicious smell traveled up the stairs, making Hadley wonder what was on tonight's menu. Alice's mom tried her best, but they'd all have been better off if she'd let her husband do the cooking.

Hadley skipped up the last few steps and turned toward her bedroom on the third floor, stopping when she caught a glimpse of herself in the hallway mirror. Her face was smudged, and she'd managed to get grease in her hair. She wrinkled her nose. No wonder Morgan had laughed. She was a mess.

With a sigh, she pushed her hair back, wondering if it was time for a change. Every year, it turned a darker shade of blond. Compared to Alice's white hair, Hadley was practically a brunette. Not that she cared. Being blond had never been the fun it was advertised to be. Plus, hers was getting too long to deal with, almost to the middle of her back now. She looked down to search for split ends when she noticed a big grease stain that slashed right across the middle of her T-shirt.

"Damn," she said to herself. "I just bought this." With a frown, she grabbed the bottom of her shirt and pulled it over her head.

Her reflection, however, did not.

She froze, staring at her image in the glass. The same image that should have taken off its T-shirt. But instead of standing there in a sports bra holding a greasy shirt, the Hadley in the mirror was still *wearing* it.

She blinked and stepped back. Her image just stared at her, like it was waiting for her to do something. Seconds ticked by as she held its gaze. Surprisingly, she didn't feel scared. Whatever this was, it didn't have a demon vibe. She'd chased down enough demons in the Realm to know what that felt like.

But she was definitely confused.

The Realm was gone, and the only person who still had the ability to manipulate mirrors was Alice. So what was going on? She timidly leaned forward.

"Hello?" she whispered. Her reflection didn't react. It just stood there, looking like it wanted to take off its T-shirt but couldn't. Hadley scowled. This shouldn't be happening. She glanced to her right and left, confirming no one was around. Then she stuck her thumbs in her ears, wiggled her fingers, and pushed out her tongue. It was childish, but if something was watching her on the other side, she figured this was better than flipping it the bird.

Her image didn't move. She leaned back and folded her arms. Now what?

A loud meow rang out behind her, and she whirled around. Alice's cat, Boop, sat at her feet, eyeing her with his usual feline disdain. Her eyes immediately began watering.

"Go away. You know I can't pet you."

He glared at her, then leaped forward and wrapped himself around her ankle like a furry black snake. She yelped and hopped back, pressing her hand into the mirror for balance. Before she could scold him, he let go and darted down the hall into the safety of Alice's bedroom.

"Yeah, that's right," she called after him. "You'd better run!" Despite being allergic, she used to love cats. Until she met that one.

She turned back to the mirror just in time to watch herself sneeze into it. Droplets sprayed the glass, distorting her image. But at least it was the *right* image. She hurriedly wiped the mirror with her T-shirt, confirming her reflection did the same. Then she turned her head from side to side and made a funny face, just to be sure. Frozen Hadley was gone, and the mirror was working properly. All was well.

Except it wasn't. She knew better than that.

Olivia, where are you? Something just happened.

Olivia didn't always hear her telepathically. It depended on how far away she was and what she was doing. But Hadley figured it was worth a try.

The house PA system suddenly crackled to life, startling her. "Hadley, I'm in the kitchen. I'll be right up."

Hadley nodded to herself, then slung her T-shirt over her shoulder and headed to her bedroom. When she got there, she shut the door behind her and leaned against it, rubbing her nose. As she waited for Olivia, she stared at the bedroom she now called her own. The furniture was clunky and claw-footed, and the floral wallpaper gave off Regency-period vibes. It wasn't her style, but the fireplace made it cozy, and the en suite bath was a white marble Shangri-La—a far cry from the bachelor pad she grew up in. More importantly, she liked knowing Olivia was next door, and Soxie and Alice were across the hall. It made it easier to close her eyes at night.

A loud knock behind her head startled her.

"Hadz, it's me. Open up."

She pushed off the door and turned around to open it. Olivia stood on the other side, her olive complexion somewhat pale.

"This is not good," she said, shouldering past.

Hadley swept her arm in an exaggerated gesture. "Please, do come in."

Olivia walked to the fireplace and flipped it on. Then she stepped back and stared into the flames. Hadley watched her begin to chew on her thumbnail.

"O?"

"My reflection just did something weird, too."

Hadley tossed her T-shirt aside and pulled her hands down her face. "Ugh. What did it do?"

"Same as yours," she replied. "It got stuck."

Hadley sank onto her bed and fell back. "What about Soxie and Alice?" she asked the ceiling.

"If it happened to us, I'm sure it'll happen to them. Something's going on."

"I figured," Hadley said dryly. "But I don't think it's necessarily bad. At least, I didn't get a bad feeling from it. Did you?"

"No, but it shouldn't be happening. Not with the Realm gone."

Hadley lifted her head. "So I guess this means we'll be putting school on hold for another semester." They were already a year behind their peers, but after the events of last year, they'd needed a break. Now, it would seem, they might be getting a longer one. Hadley didn't mind. She'd been thirteen years old when the demi-goddess Philautia made her a huntress. It was part of her identity now. She'd never put much thought into being anything else.

Olivia ignored her and continued staring into the fireplace as if the answers lay in its flames.

Hadley rolled off the bed and grabbed her robe. "I was kidding, by the way. I wasn't planning on registering, anyway. Was thinking I'll go into the family business. Any interest in joining?"

Olivia nodded, muttering to herself as her brilliant mind attempted to solve the puzzle of the frozen mirrors. When she got like this, Hadley could press a bullhorn to her ear, and she wouldn't hear it, let alone read her mind.

"Okay, then. Good talk," she said before leaving her friend to her thoughts and closing the bathroom door behind her.

chapter 3

Olivia was gone by the time Hadley finished showering. Hair still damp, she threw on some cargo pants and a tank top, shoved her feet into a pair of flip-flops, and headed downstairs.

When she got to the first floor, the old grandfather clock in the foyer gonged, and all three dogs sat on the marble tile, staring at the entrance to the parlor room. Hadley paused at the bottom of the stairs. Why were the doors to the parlor room open? It was everyone's least favorite room in the house. Not just because it was pretentious and stuffy but because of what happened there last year. Nobody wanted to spend time in a place where a man, possessed by a god, tried killing his own daughter. Hadley shivered, reliving the awful moment. She'd been sitting in the library across the way when she'd heard the dogs snarling and a terrifying scream—

"Whoever you are, you're early. I'm told dinner isn't quite ready."

Hadley's breath caught as she recognized the voice. Of course. There was only one person who spent time in that room, because nothing phased him. A herd of *Jumanji* rhinos could stampede through the hall, and he'd probably just step aside and carry on. She'd seen a thing or two in her nineteen years. But she'd never seen a human quite like Soxie's mysterious uncle, Mayron Roxland III.

She heard what sounded like ice tinkling in a glass, then, "For heaven's sake, don't just stand out there like a moron. Come in. I'd like to have a word with you."

The hairs on the back of her neck stood up. It irked her that she'd encountered demons—actual Underworld demons—for years yet was still more scared of Uncle May. She steeled herself and tucked wet hair behind her ears. Then she hopped down, patted one of the dogs on the head, and joined Mayron in the parlor room.

He sat on a chair in front of the fireplace, sifting through a stack of mail. She stepped further into the drafty room, hugging herself for warmth.

"Hi, Mayron," she said as politely as she could. "I didn't know you were home. When did you get back?"

"I wasn't aware my arrival required an announcement," he answered smoothly. "I will be sure to alert you going forward."

She coughed and cleared her throat. "No, no, of course not. You don't have to—I mean, this is your house. You can do whatever you want."

"That's very generous of you."

Her cheeks flamed as she searched her brain for something to say. A dog whimpered behind her, and another sneezed.

"So, you said you wanted to talk—how did you know it was me?"

He set the pile of letters on the table next to him and picked up his drink. "I didn't. Any of you will do."

She winced. "Understood. So, what can *any of us* do for you?"

His head flew up, and cold eyes regarded her. His dark hair and features complemented his tailored blue suit. Hadley didn't think of him as handsome—she tried not to think of him at all—but in the few times she'd been in his presence, she definitely found him striking. Like a scorpion, or a viper.

"For starters," he said, his voice low and menacing, "you can explain to me what that woman is cooking in there. It smells like death."

A laugh escaped her. "Don't worry. Judy only cooks one night a week. Unfortunately, that's tonight."

"Lucky me," he mused as he took a sip of his drink. "I must remember to make myself scarce on Wednesdays."

Hadley nodded, wondering if that meant he was planning to be here the other six nights of the week. The thought did not sit well. She took a step back and regrouped.

"Well, if that's all—"

"It is not."

The dogs chose that moment to hightail it down the hall toward the kitchen. She glanced over her shoulder, sad to see them go.

"At some point," he began, "we will need to discuss the extent of my involvement in your various . . . activities."

Her stomach knotted. "I thought you spoke with David about that stuff."

He chuckled and moved his glass to mix the ice. "Ah yes, David. He does have all the answers, doesn't he? Smart and charming young man too. One might say he's just as charming as his predecessor, Colin. You remember Colin, don't you? I believe I helped you and my niece cover up his unfortunate demise."

Her mouth suddenly felt dry, just like the desert they'd buried Colin's body in. Sure, she could tell him they'd really sent a god back to The Underworld, but it wasn't her place to divulge that information. "It's complicated. I wish I could explain, but I can't."

He flicked his hand dismissively. "I'm not interested in your explanation. I have a responsibility to my niece, and as long as I believe you and the others—David included—have her best interests at heart, I will continue supporting you in your endeavors, and look the other way. But there are limits to my generosity."

Hadley couldn't believe she was standing here having this conversation. It felt way above her pay grade. "I really think you should talk to Soxie or David about this. I'm just—"

"Just what?" he cut in. "An innocent bystander who knows

nothing about it? I'll have you know, I went to great lengths to have your presence scrubbed from CCTV cameras all over Lyon. My Interpol contacts still have questions I cannot answer, and I lost two of my best people after a woman in my custody disappeared into thin air. So please do me the courtesy of dropping the act, Hadley."

Hadley blanched. She wasn't sure she'd ever heard him say her name. He knew who she was, of course. This had basically been her and Olivia's second home since the day they became huntresses. But Mayron had never been more than a spectral figure, appearing once in a blue moon to pay the bills or get them out of a sticky situation. So why was he suddenly asking questions?

And then his words hit home.

A woman in my custody.

"Molly!" she blurted out. "You're talking about Molly. That's what this is about, isn't it?"

His eyes flashed with surprise. But before he could answer, Judy's voice screamed through the home's PA system, announcing that dinner was ready.

They looked at each other, and Mayron did something she'd never seen him do. He smiled. It wasn't scary, but it wasn't warm either. It felt like the kind of smile you'd get from an android.

"Perhaps we'll continue this conversation another time," he said, his tone curt. "Our dreadful meal awaits."

Then he stood, buttoned his jacket, and strode out of the room. She waited until he turned the corner before falling into the chair he'd vacated. She looked at his half-drunk scotch and considered tossing it back. Instead, she slowly rose and headed for the dining room, making a mental note to take the back stairs from now on.

Dinner was as expected. Bland and burnt. But they all pretended to like it, even Mayron. Hadley kept her eye on him throughout the meal, but he never once looked in her direction. It made her think he'd already forgotten their conversation, which was unfortunate, because it would stick with her for a while.

After the dishes were washed, and the leftovers were "accidentally" dropped on the floor, Judy and Barry retired to their quarters in the guest house, and Mayron disappeared into his rooms in the east wing. Still hungry, Hadley grabbed a stale baguette and a block of cheese before heading to the library.

Unlike the parlor room, the library was cozy and comfortable, and easily Hadley's favorite room in the house. It was old school, with floor-to-ceiling bookcases, a rolling ladder, heavy brass lamps, and of course, a fireplace, because whoever designed this place must have been perpetually cold.

When she walked in, Alice and David were sitting on one of the two leather couches in the middle of the room, Soxie and Olivia on the other. She took a bite of cheese, then a bite of bread, and made her way to her usual chair by the fire. The dogs were lined up in front of it, toasting themselves like fat seals on a beach. She nudged one of them aside and sat down.

"Classy," Soxie said, nodding at her snack choice.

"Wha—?" she said, chewing. "I'm still hungry."

Soxie raised an eyebrow in disapproval, but Alice eyed the bread and cheese like it was made of gold. Hadley broke off a hunk of each and tossed them to her.

"Thank you," she said, sighing with delight as she snarfed them down. David watched his fiancée with an amused, starry-eyed look on his face. When she was finished, he reached up to brush a stray crumb from the corner of her mouth. Hadley couldn't argue that it was a touching moment, if maybe a little saccharine for her taste. After taking one last bite of her own, she tossed the rest of her makeshift meal on the floor. The dogs devoured it in less than a second.

"Hadley, that's not good for them," scolded Olivia.

"Don't tell me they're lactose intolerant."

"I bet you fifty bucks Schlemmer is," said Soxie.

At the sound of her name, Schlemmer's head popped up, nubby tail wagging and floppy ears at attention.

"You know Schlemmer has allergy issues," said Olivia, calling the dog to her. Schlemmer jumped onto her lap like she was a Pomeranian and not a muscly, eighty-pound guard dog. Olivia grunted at the weight but allowed the dog to settle in.

"She definitely has issues," agreed Soxie. "At least Fred and Ginger don't sneeze when someone closes a door too hard."

"We're not here to talk about the dogs."

Hadley bristled at David's snippy, authoritative tone. But he was right. This wasn't a social gathering. She sat up and leaned over the arm of her chair.

"Sox, Alice, your reflections got stuck too?"

They nodded.

David sat forward and rested his elbows on his knees. "Theories?"

They all looked at each other, waiting for someone to speak up. When no one did, he stood and moved to the game table by the window, his thinking spot. He folded his arms and stared into the night. The voice and body might be different, but his mannerisms were the same. Hadley could almost see the old Colin standing there in the same black T-shirt and slim-fit jeans, ready to read them the riot act.

He turned his head to the side. "And how long before your reflections returned to normal?"

"Not until I made physical contact," answered Olivia.

"Same," Soxie and Alice said in unison.

Hadley perked up. Physical contact? She replayed the mirror event in her mind, and recalled how she'd leaned into the glass when Boop attacked her. She'd fixed the glitch without even knowing.

"I think it's more than a glitch, Hadz," Olivia remarked.

Hadley kicked her feet up to rest them on Fred's rump. "But we all agree it didn't feel threatening," she countered. "Maybe it *is* some kind of glitch, or malfunction. What if it's because of something we're doing?"

"Or not doing," added Alice.

David spun around, his face taut. "Meaning?"

Alice nodded toward the fireplace. They followed her gaze to the mirror that hung above it.

"No," said David. "This has nothing to do with the dagger."

"How do you know?"

"I just do."

Hadley narrowed her eyes. David had always been cryptic when it came to the dagger. No one argued it wasn't dangerous. It once belonged to a goddess of vengeance—a Fury. A weapon like that needed to be handled with care. But his insistence that it remain locked up had always felt suspect.

"Philautia used the dagger to create the Realm," she said pointedly. "Don't you think that means it could have something to do with our reflections getting stuck?"

David gave her a stern look and gestured to the mirror above the fireplace. Or rather, what lay hidden behind it. "It stays in the wall safe. That's final."

Her jaw tightened. "Fine. Then what about the compasses?"

"What about them?"

"They belong to us. Why do they have to be in the safe too?"

"If you're not using them, they're better off locked away."

"He's right," Olivia chimed in. "They might not have any use outside the Realm, but we can't risk losing them just because we want them around as keepsakes."

Hadley reluctantly agreed. The idea of losing her compass was unimaginable. But she hated not having it with her all the time. It was more a part of her than her iPhone. And that was saying a lot.

"Okay, so what are our options?" Soxie asked the room. "Do we assume it's a glitch and just wait for it to fix itself? Or do we take action?"

"What kind of action?" asked Alice.

"Well, like you said, maybe the mirrors are getting stuck because of something we're not doing," she said, pausing to address the room again. "So, what have we *not* been doing?"

Hadley considered their lives for the past few months. They'd been hosting the gods in their dreams, and so far it was manageable—depending on the god. It wasn't hunting demons and saving the world, but it was something. So what was the glitch telling them? What were they missing?

Olivia suddenly leaned forward, startling the dog in her lap. "Alice, when was the last time you practiced projecting an image onto a mirror?"

Alice sat at attention and began absently pulling on the ends of her snow-white hair. She glanced at David before answering. "I thought we decided I shouldn't do it anymore—that it was a waste of time."

"*We* never decided that," Olivia clapped back. "That sounds more like a David decision."

Hadley watched the color fade from Alice's cheeks. Her ability to project images onto mirrors had never amounted to more than a fun magic trick, but it was a mystery they'd been working hard to solve. At least they had been, until wedding planning and normal life got in the way.

"It wasn't just David," Alice said defensively. "We decided together."

Soxie made a loud *pfft* sound. "I see, so the two of you decided something that concerns all of us, without consulting us first."

"That's right," confirmed David, doubling down. "And I stand by our decision. The Realm is gone, and the gods are happy. I didn't see any reason to keep messing around with something we don't understand. Ever heard the phrase, 'Don't wake a sleeping dragon?'"

Soxie smacked the back of the couch, making Schlemmer sneeze. "And who says the dragon isn't already awake? Listen, I know you want to get married and live happily ever after, but just because the gods are happy now, doesn't mean it'll stay that way. What if they want more? What then? We've been sitting on a ticking time bomb, and Alice's power might be the only way of defusing it." She stopped and turned to Alice. "I'm sorry, Ali, but keeping us out of the loop was wrong."

Alice dropped her head in shame. "I'm sorry. It's just, once we started planning the wedding, I didn't see any reason to keep practicing. All I ever did was throw a moving image onto a mirror. We have televisions for that. What's the point?"

"I think what happened today is the point," said Olivia.

Alice was visibly upset, and David's face turned redder by the second. Even the dogs were agitated, occasionally growling from their warm spots by the fire. The energy in the room had grown too intense.

Hadley pulled her feet off her canine ottoman and moved to the couch next to Alice. She put an arm around her shoulders and pulled her close. "Listen, we're not mad. We're just surprised."

"Speak for yourself," snapped Soxie.

"That's enough!" shouted David. "It's her power, and if she doesn't want to use it, that's her choice!"

All three dogs leaped to their feet and flew out of the room, spooked by his sudden outburst.

"Baby, don't yell at them," Alice pleaded. "You're just making it worse."

David clamped his mouth shut, though it was obvious he had more to say. But when Alice asked him for something, he always gave in. If David had a kryptonite, she was it.

"This isn't productive," announced Olivia. Then she turned to Alice, frowning. "You never answered my question. When was the last time you projected an image?"

Alice looked like she'd rather disappear into the couch than answer. "It's been almost six months," she said at last.

They all hushed. Six months? Had it really been that long? They used to keep her company in the ballet studio when she practiced, but after a while it got boring. There were only so many images of Boop chasing a toy mouse that Hadley could stomach. So she'd stopped going, and apparently so had Olivia and Soxie. They'd assumed Alice would continue on her own. To be fair, this was as much their fault as it was hers.

"All right then," said Olivia, nodding to the mirror above the fireplace. "Do it now. Project an image onto that mirror."

David stepped forward, but she threw an arm out to stop him. "Let her do it."

Alice looked around the room. Her tiny body felt colder than usual. Hadley ran her hands up and down her arms to warm her up. "It's okay, honey. You got this."

With a weak smile, Alice slowly stood to face the mirror.

"You don't have to do this," David told her.

"Yes. She does," said Soxie.

His expression darkened, but he didn't argue any further. For once, he accepted that he was outnumbered. Alice offered him a reassuring smile, then raised her hand toward the glass.

They all turned toward the mirror, waiting for an image of Boop to appear, or one of the Roxland horses—images Alice normally practiced on. Instead, the mirror reflected nothing but the library and its collection of valuable books. Alice blinked a few times before dropping her hand. From the look on her face, it was clear she was as shocked as they were. Even David seemed alarmed.

"What happened?" asked Hadley.

"Nothing," Olivia answered. "That's the problem."

chapter 4

Hadley sat in the third-floor window seat across from Soxie, Olivia curled up between them. It was a spacious but cozy nook, with soft pillows and a mountain view to rival any luxury resort. Usually, Alice and David claimed it first, but after what happened in the library, they'd gone to his room above the garage to talk. Hadley glanced out the window toward said garage.

"What do you think they're talking about?"

Soxie twined a curl around her finger and yawned. "If only Diaz here could read their minds. My guess, though? They're probably not talking."

"Thanks for the visual," Hadley deadpanned.

Olivia pulled her knees to her chest and leaned back against the window. Her dark hair and signature black clothing blended with the nighttime sky behind her. "I wish I *could* read them. Then maybe we wouldn't be in this situation."

"But seriously," Hadley began. "Do we really think this glitch happened because Alice hasn't been projecting cats onto mirrors?"

"Not sure the cat part is relevant, but yes—they must be related," Olivia concluded.

"Then why can't she do it now?"

Olivia twisted her mouth to the side, thinking. "Maybe it's as simple as forgetting a foreign language when you haven't spoken it in a while. She just needs to relearn how to do it."

"No problem. I'm sure there's a copy of *Mirrors for Dummies* somewhere in May's library," Soxie wisecracked.

Hadley's laugh turned into a yawn. She stretched her arms over her head and glanced at her diver's watch. It was closing in on midnight. The grandfather clock in the foyer would be announcing the hour with its melancholic gongs any second. She slid out of the window seat and bent down to retrieve her flip-flops from where she'd kicked them off earlier.

"We're not going to figure it out tonight," she said, stifling another yawn. "Besides, we need to get to sleep in case we have visitors."

Soxie leaned over to scoop her heels off the floor and stood, pointing them at Hadley. "Don't remind me. I can't remember the last time I got a decent night's sleep, especially when I get Circe. She's always asking me to insult her just so she can turn me into a three-headed chicken or something."

"Ha. At least she asks," Olivia weighed in. "Unlike Hera. She waltzes into my dreams like she owns the place."

"Well, she is a queen."

"So was Persephone, but I don't remember her ever bossing us around."

Hadley offered a hand to Olivia and pulled her up. "Speaking of Persephone, I'm just glad her ex hasn't shown up. Can you imagine? What would we say?"

"'Sorry we stabbed your evil ass and sent you back to The Underworld'?" said Soxie.

Hadley snickered. "I'm sure that would go over well."

"You guys, it's not funny," Olivia said soberly. "If Hades could access our dreams, I'm sure he would. Let's just be thankful he hasn't."

The clock downstairs began gonging the hour. The timing sent shivers up Hadley's spine. They listened as it echoed throughout the otherwise silent house. She hated the thing, and on more than one occasion had tried disabling it. Morgan thwarted her efforts every time.

After the last dreadful gong played out, they hugged their good-nights and retired to their rooms. Hadley quickly changed into her pajamas and headed to the bathroom, flipping on the light before entering. She peeked around the door, hesitant to look at her reflection.

Her own face peeked back at her, blue eyes a little rounder than usual. She inched further in, holding her breath as she waited for her image to get stuck. When it didn't, she breathed a sigh of relief and hurried through her nighttime face washing, moisturizing, and teeth brushing routine. When she finished, she darted out of the bathroom and hopped into her bed, immediately soothed by the weight of her heavy blankets. She turned out the lights and stared into the darkness while she relived the events of the day. It was interesting, that's for sure. Frozen mirrors. Her conversation with Mayron. The text from her dad. Her brother.

She pushed herself up onto her elbow and punched her pillow, fluffing it before falling back on her side and hugging it tight. There was too much to unpack in her brain right now, and she was too tired to try.

Besides, the gods were waiting.

She awoke to the sound of glass breaking. She sat up and reached for the bat under her bed. As her fingers wrapped around the wood, she had a strange sense of déjà vu. She froze, listening.

" . . . don't care what you think. I'm almost seventeen. I can make my own decisions!"

"You're making the wrong ones!"

She looked around. It was dark, but the security light outside her bedroom window made it easy enough to see. There was her old punching bag, silent and still, awaiting its next sparring session. Her bookshelf, lined with dusty old padlocks, doorknobs, and deadbolts—locks she'd learned how to pick by the age of ten. And Scotch-taped to her bedroom door, a poster of one of her favorite movies, *Mad Max: Fury Road.*

She let out a loud sigh and fell back on her childhood bed. Her dad and brother were still yelling, but the argument would come to an abrupt stop soon. She waited for it.

"Ever think I might be smarter than you? Frank sure as hell is!"

"Your grandfather is a lying, scheming—"

Silence. She stared at the ceiling, wishing she was able to hear what would come next. Your grandfather is a lying, scheming . . . what? Car thief? Sonofabitch? Waffle maker?

She laughed, despite her disappointment. Nothing would ever come next, because she had ended that argument when she swung her bat into the wall—when she was thirteen years old.

With a frown, she pushed herself onto her elbows and looked around again. Her room was exactly as she remembered it, right down to the pile of dirty laundry and old candy bar wrappers dotting the floor.

"What kind of dream is this?" she wondered aloud.

"Perhaps this is more than just a dream."

Hadley twisted around. A dark figure leaned against the wall by her window, hidden in shadow. With a weary sigh, Hadley sat up and rubbed her eyes.

"If you're here, then it's definitely a dream," she said, yawning. It was odd to feel tired *while* she was sleeping, but with all the dream hosting she'd been doing lately, she felt like she needed a rest from resting.

"If you prefer, I can return in a different dream. I am uncomfortable in this one."

Hadley let out a small snort, then leaned over to turn on her bedside lamp. The room was suddenly bathed in light, revealing tonight's mystery guest. Hadley suppressed a smile. The woman standing by the window had Adriatic features, violet eyes, and long, dark hair. According to myth, she should have been wearing a white tunic, gathered at the waist with gold leaf, and sandals laced to the knee. Instead, she was wearing a leather bodysuit that made her look like a badass motocross champion. Despite the modern ensemble, the wooden bow and quiver slung across her back gave her away.

"Artemis, it's nice to see you. Love the outfit."

The goddess looked down, as if noticing her clothing for the first time. Then she walked over to the wall mirror. Hadley flopped on her stomach and rested her chin in her hands. She always enjoyed this part.

Artemis studied her image, pivoting to see her outfit from different angles. "Mortals are odd creatures," she said, even though there was a slight smile on her face.

Hadley rolled her eyes. "Admit it. You like it. Besides—my dream, my clothes. If we're going hunting, I'm not doing it in a bedsheet."

Artemis met her gaze in the mirror. "You will abandon this dream and embark on a new one?"

Hadley heard a noise in the hall and suddenly remembered where they were. Caleb would be walking through her bedroom door any second. He'd be coming to say goodbye, and the thought of reliving that, especially in front of her favorite goddess, was too horrible to bear.

She scrambled off the bed and hurried to the window. After forcing it open, she swung her legs through and waved Artemis over.

"Come on, hurry!" she yelled.

Artemis joined her, and together they dropped onto the ground of a new dream.

It felt like they'd been hunting for hours. The forest was thick and full of undergrowth, with the occasional nymph or sprite appearing to point them in the direction of game. Hadley had no desire to kill animals, even in a dream, but she appreciated that this was what Artemis needed. Her world was dying, and if Hadley was able to provide her with a little hunting to give her purpose—and keep her occupied—then that was what she would do.

She stopped to rest in a small clearing, one her dream had conveniently provided. Artemis flew past her in a blur of black leather, arrow poised to fly as she chased down a majestic white stag. The thunder of the creature's hooves shook the forest floor, making the leaves on the trees rain down in spirals. Hadley tossed her unused bow aside and sat down on a mossy rock. Artemis would eventually get the stag, and Hadley would have to manifest another. It made her miss when she was the one hopping into other people's dreams. Dream hopping had been one of the better perks of being a huntress. And visiting someone else's world was a lot easier than creating it.

A flock of sprites suddenly buzzed through the clearing, chasing after Artemis. One of them stopped, hovering in front of Hadley, like a curious hummingbird. Her wings were translucent, and she wore the hell out of her skimpy green dress. She trilled like a bird and blew a pile of glitter in Hadley's face. Then the mischievous little twit giggled and zoomed out of sight.

Hadley huffed as she wiped away the glitter. She was pretty sure that version of Tinkerbell was not an accurate depiction of a woodland sprite, but her dream only had access to her mind, not the internet.

A twig snapped behind her, and she spun around. A man stood at the edge of the clearing, holding a large box. Sunlight peeked through the forest canopy, spotlighting him in a yellow circle. His shirt and shorts were the color of mud, and the words *This Side Up* were printed on the side of his box. He stepped forward, his expression neutral.

"Greetings, huntress."

Hadley couldn't help but snicker. "Hi, Hermes."

The messenger god stepped further into the clearing. Then he stopped to study his clothing. His confusion made her feel bad about dressing him up as the UPS guy, even if it wasn't a conscious decision. She scooted over and patted the rock next to her. He set his box down and accepted her invitation.

For a moment they sat, listening to the sound of her dream forest. The trees swayed in the breeze, sending leaves dancing through the air. Hadley inhaled, breathing in the sweet scent of gardenia and honeysuckle. It was a good dream. She hoped Hermes's arrival didn't turn it into a bad one.

"So, I assume you have a message to deliver?" she muttered, hoping she was wrong.

He nodded. "I do."

The gravity of his tone made her nervous. On cue, the light around them dimmed. Storm clouds rolled in, blocking out the sun, and a burst of cold wind blew through the clearing. Then the forest grew quiet. Hadley swallowed hard, wondering how far she was into this dream. She stood and walked over to the box. Then she knelt down, reaching for the switchblade she kept tucked in her boot, right next to her trusty lock pick. She flipped the blade open and looked to Hermes for permission. He nodded again.

She turned back to the box and sliced it open. But instead of lifting the cardboard flaps, she hesitated. Something about this didn't feel right, and it made her wonder if the gongs of Mayron's old grand-father clock had been portending doom.

She glanced at Hermes, and he gestured to the box. "Your mes-sage awaits, huntress. It will not open itself."

"I know, I know," she griped. She had to open the box. It was a message from the gods. But it was just like Hermes to ruin a per-fectly good dream. Well, maybe not the dream she was having before Artemis showed up, but her brother was a whole other box of issues. Unable to stall any longer, she cleared her mind, stepped forward, and pulled back the cardboard flaps.

A swarm of black crows burst forth, surrounding her in a cyclone of flapping wings and ear-splitting caws. She shrieked, hopping back and forth, and swatting at the air until they dispersed into a pile of black ash. Gasping and enraged, she stumbled backward and pointed the business end of her knife at Hermes.

"What kind of message was that?" she roared.

He calmly motioned to the box. "There is more."

She shoved the hair from her face and tried to calm her breathing. Crows turning to ash was not a visual she wanted in her brain. Did she really want to know what else was inside?

"Somebody wake me up, please!" she screamed into the trees. "Olivia? Alice? Boop?"

"Please, huntress. I have other deliveries to make."

Her eyes fell back on Hermes. She noticed little wings on his Timberland boots, and an electronic pad had appeared in his hand. Wait, was she supposed to *sign* for this?

He noticed her staring, glanced at the electronic gadget, and quickly tossed it aside. "Do not underestimate me," he warned. "My patience is not infinite."

She ignored his veiled threat. After all, this was still *her* dream.

"Fine," she said, ready to get this over with. She inched forward and leaned over the box. When she peeked inside, she saw something familiar.

"What the—" she exclaimed as she reached into the box. She pulled out a small round mirror, about a foot in diameter. Her eyes went wide.

"The *map*? But, why?"

Hermes smiled. "Dear child, what you hold in your hand is far more powerful than a simple map."

Hadley was stunned. She stared at the mirror, remembering all the times they'd used it to travel to exotic locations around the globe. It was Philautia's reward to them for hunting and banishing demons, allowing them access to any mirror in the world. But was this real? The map had disappeared with the Realm. Why were the gods showing this to her now? She put the question to Hermes.

He lifted his shoulders. "Your dream was the most welcoming. Your fellow huntresses have less ideal dream environments."

"I don't mean why *my dream*," she said, curbing her frustration. "I mean why are you showing me the map? Are you saying it still exists?"

"Yes."

Her brain short-circuited. "But . . . how?"

He took a quick breath and glanced at the gray sky. "Your dream cycle will end soon. We do not have much time."

"Then just tell me!"

He stood and dusted off his shorts. "The Portal of Osiris has existed since the beginning of time. It is older and more powerful than even the gods."

Hadley felt the blood draining from her face, and the sky turned black. Another flock of crows burst from the trees, cawing into the night. Her grip on the mirror tightened. She didn't like where this was going.

Hermes continued, unaffected by the changing dreamscape. "The gods believe the Portal holds the key to our salvation."

She blinked, waiting for him to go on. When he didn't, she looked at the mirror—the Portal—in her hand. As she did, it cracked down the middle and began disintegrating into another pile of ash, reminding her that this was only a message. This was still just a dream.

"So where is it now?" she asked. "Where's the real one?"

"Ah," he said, pointing his index finger in the air. "We come to the crux of my message. When your Realm disappeared, so did the Portal of Osiris. It cannot be destroyed, but it can be . . . misplaced. You must find it for us."

Her world began to unravel. "Find it? How would we even know where to start?"

"I am but a messenger," he said, giving her a courtesy bow. "It is not my place to guide you."

She gave him a sardonic look. "And if we refuse?"

"Refusal is not an option. Do what we ask, or we will destroy your minds." He paused to gesture grandly around him. "We will destroy *you*, through your dreams."

A loud crack of thunder rocked the forest, causing the entire world to tilt. Hadley fell to the ground, dropping her knife. Rain fell in sheets.

She clawed through mud, searching for the blade so she could sink it into Hermes's neck. Her hand found the handle, and she leaped to her feet with a loud battle cry. Water pelted her face, and lightning flashed, splitting a nearby tree in two. She pushed the hair from her eyes and turned in circles, squinting through the rain in search of her target.

"Huntress, what is going on?"

She twisted around and let her knife fly. Artemis caught it by the blade, an inch from her face. Hadley gasped.

"I'm sorry!" she yelled. "I thought you were Hermes!"

Artemis flipped the blade closed and tossed it in the mud at Hadley's feet. Then she walked around the clearing, taking in the raging rainstorm.

"I see he has delivered his message," she said, her voice tinged with excitement.

The rain stopped, and Hadley stood rooted to the spot, sopping wet, her clothing stuck to her skin. But Artemis looked dry, fresh, and exhilarated. As goddess of the hunt, she was an expert at hunting game, but she also honored and protected it. Hadley admired her talent and strength and had always thought of her as one of the good ones. After months hunting together, she'd even started to think of her as a friend.

"You—you knew?" she blustered.

Artemis tilted her head to the side. "I am a goddess. An Olympian. Of course I knew."

Hadley couldn't mask the hurt in her voice. She felt betrayed. "I've created so many dreams for you. How could you do this?"

Artemis turned to the sky. Sun poked back through the forest canopy. She smiled, letting its golden rays warm her regal face. Then she moved her attention back to Hadley, violet eyes glowing and fierce.

"You silly mortal," she almost cackled. "Why do you think I am here?"

Hadley could barely breathe.

"To destroy me?" she whispered.

"Only if you fail."

chapter 5

Hadley's eyes popped open, and oxygen flooded her lungs. She kicked the covers off and sat up, staring into the darkness of her bedroom. Then she looked around, taking a quick inventory to ensure this was the *right* bedroom—that she wasn't still dreaming. Fireplace, check. Four-poster bed, check. Claw-foot tables and antique lamps, check and check. Satisfied, she pressed the heels of her hands into her eyes and sat for a moment, collecting herself. As much as she hated to be the receiver of Hermes's message, she was glad it was her. But the thought of relaying the message to the rest of the girls made her head throb.

She dropped her hands and stood, grabbing her phone off the nightstand to check the time. 3:12 a.m. Of course. The witching hour. She shook off the shivers and went to the bathroom to pop some Advil and splash water on her face, all the while keeping her eyes down to avoid the mirror. She didn't have the mental bandwidth to deal with a stuck reflection right now.

As cozy as her bed was, she wasn't about to get back in it tonight. So she threw on her robe and slippers and headed downstairs to raid the kitchen.

She was just pulling a pint of ice cream from the freezer when Soxie shuffled in. In her fluffy white slippers and silk robe, she looked like a Hollywood starlet from the 1940s. Hadley popped the lid off the ice cream and reached behind her for two spoons.

"You look smashing for three a.m.," she said.

Soxie ignored her and took a seat at the kitchen island. Hadley slid a spoon across and leaned her elbows on the counter, moving the pint so they could both reach it. They spent the next few minutes eating ice cream and staring off into space.

When they'd scraped the bottom of the pint clean, Hadley pushed it aside and walked around the island. The sugar was kicking in, and she had a sudden urge to hug her friend.

"What's this for?" Soxie asked.

"Nothing. I just needed a hug."

Soxie pulled away and took hold of Hadley's face, studying her. "What's going on, Caldwell?"

"Boy, if that isn't a loaded question."

"Fair enough," she conceded. "Then tell me what isn't going on."

Hadley gave her an impish grin. It was a game they'd played for years. Whenever things got too intense, they'd spend a few minutes brainstorming about things that *weren't* happening. It helped put their own problems in perspective.

"I'll start," Soxie continued, rotating her stool back and forth. "I am not eating a second pint of ice cream."

Hadley smirked. "I am not *sharing* my second pint of ice cream."

"Show-off. Okay, I am not a convicted murderer."

"Well, technically—"

"I said convicted!"

"Right. I guess that's fair," Hadley agreed, taking a seat on the other stool. She propped her chin in her hand, thinking. "I am not developing weapons of mass destruction."

"Good one," Soxie acknowledged. "I am not dumping oil in the Gulf of Mexico."

Hadley wrinkled her nose. "I am not clubbing baby seals."

"Dark, but okay. I am not dealing drugs."

"I'm not taking drugs."

Soxie gave her a look. "I'm not either."

"I didn't say you were."

A brief, uncomfortable silence followed. Hadley's spine straightened as she realized her mistake. Before she could take it back, Soxie sucked in her cheeks and said, "I'm not abandoning my brother in prison."

Hadley reared back as if she'd been slapped. "That's not fair."

"Yeah, well it's not fair to throw my past in my face either."

They glared at each other. Hadley hadn't meant anything by the drug comment, but she should have known better. It was a sensitive subject. But so was her brother. She looked down.

"I'm not abandoning him. He abandoned me."

Soxie sighed and reached over to take hold of her hand. "He's your brother, Hadz. He's your family."

She looked up. "No," she croaked. "You're my family."

Soxie's eyes glistened. "I swear to god, Caldwell. If you make me cry . . ."

The tension between them dissipated, and Hadley threw her arms around her friend's neck. "I'm sorry," she whispered.

"Me too," Soxie replied. Then she pulled away and nodded at the refrigerator. "Well, what are you waiting for? Grab a second pint and tell me what's really going on."

Olivia showed up around 6:30 a.m., Alice shortly after. It had taken two hours, a second pint of ice cream, and a bag of popcorn for Hadley to bring Soxie up to speed—about the dream, her conversation with Mayron, everything. Olivia relived all the fun in Hadley's head and was kind enough to relay it to Alice when she arrived.

"Don't worry about May," Soxie said as she poured herself a cup of coffee. "He's only here for a couple of weeks. Then we probably won't see him for a month."

Hadley's lip curled. "Easy for you to say. I felt like I was in an interrogation room instead of the parlor room."

"Don't be so dramatic. It's just Mayron. He's harmless."

"Sox, your uncle is a lot of things, but I don't think harmless is one of them," interjected Alice. Then she turned to Hadley and added, "He really mentioned Molly?"

"Not directly. But it was implied."

Alice nodded, then turned back to her oatmeal, stirring it slowly. "I guess it doesn't matter."

"Wrong," Olivia objected. She was sitting at the kitchen table in front of her laptop, eyes glued to the screen. "If we've learned anything in the past twenty-four hours, it's that everything matters."

"What's that supposed to mean?" asked Hadley.

Olivia's hands flew over the keys. "Alice's power with mirrors. The gods connecting to us through our dreams. We stopped asking questions and assumed it didn't matter—that it was just the new normal. But we were wrong. I should have known better."

"Hang on, Captain America," said Soxie, her mouth full as she chewed on a piece of toast. "*We* should have known better. Share the blame once in a while."

Olivia rolled her eyes but didn't argue.

"I'm the one who chose to stop using my power," Alice said, staring at her breakfast. "I got caught up planning a wedding and pretending I could just marry my soulmate and be happy. And now look where we are."

Hadley placed a hand on her shoulder. "Honey, it's nobody's fault. This is new territory for all of us. And you're still going to marry your soulmate. I'll even drive you to Vegas if I have to."

"The wedding's off."

Soxie coughed on her toast, and Olivia's head popped up from her screen.

"I'll kill him," Soxie seethed. "If that sonofa—"

"It wasn't him. It was me."

"Honey—"

Alice slammed her hands on the counter. "Please, Hadley. Don't call me 'honey' right now. I need you to be mean to me. I need to get angry."

Hadley didn't know what to say. She glanced at the others, hoping one of them knew the magic words. Olivia pushed her chair back and stood. The dogs, who had been lying at her feet, lifted their heads.

"Alice, you don't have to do this," she said. "We've been through worse, remember? We'll get through this."

Hadley watched a tear roll down Alice's nose and drop into her bowl. Her instinct was to embrace her and say, "Honey, everything's going to be okay." But she didn't because that wasn't what Alice needed right now. She turned to Soxie.

"She wants someone to be mean to her. Pretty sure that's your department."

Soxie's eyes flared. "You're hilarious, Caldwell."

Hadley gave her a pleading look.

"Fine," she glowered, downing the rest of her coffee like a shot of tequila. "Alice, get your skinny ass up and stop your whining. There's plenty of time to get married. For now, this Portal of Osiris isn't going to find itself."

They spent the next two days at the public library, poring over every text they could find that pertained to Osiris. It was painstaking, monotonous research, and so far all they had to show for their efforts was a lot of bad moods and missed meals.

"This is pointless," said Soxie, snapping the book she was reading shut. "If David doesn't know anything about the Portal, how are we supposed to find it? We're not going to learn anything in here. We have to try something else."

"Keep your voice down," shushed Olivia. "And what else do you suggest we try? David only knew what Philautia told him, and clearly she never told him about this. Our only lead right now is Osiris, and most of these older texts are only available in print. We have to be here."

"I guess," Soxie huffed, shoving her stack of books aside. "I just don't understand why Greek gods want something named after an Egyptian god."

Olivia took a deep breath, then resumed her laptop scrolling. "That's what we're trying to find out, Sox. We're exhausting all options."

"No, we're exhausting *ourselves*," Soxie complained. Then she pushed her chair back and stood. "I'm going to get some coffee."

Hadley watched her click-clack down the long hall, getting a look from a librarian as he pushed by with a cart of books. It was 11:00 a.m. on a Friday, and other than a couple browsing the travel section, they had the cavernous place to themselves.

"She kind of has a point," Hadley said, turning back to her own book. "It says here that Osiris was the god of vegetation and The Underworld." She stopped and slid another book over, flipping to a page she'd already bookmarked. "But this one says god of the dead and fertility, which I'm assuming is the same thing? Then there's a lot about him getting torn into pieces and his wife, Isis, putting him back together. I doubt it's relevant, but how can we know when we don't even know what we're looking for? There are just too many threads to pull."

Olivia's eyes remained glued to her laptop. "I think we'll just know when we know."

Hadley let her head fall forward onto the book, wishing she'd gone with Soxie to get coffee. She was going cross-eyed with all the useless information she'd ingested.

"It's not all useless," said Olivia. Hadley lifted her head and watched as Olivia made a note on a pad of paper. She leaned over to see what she was scribbling.

"Hieroglyphs?" she asked, tilting her head to better see the drawings. "Do you even know what those mean?"

Olivia looked up and gave her a knowing smile. "Not exactly. But I know the map when I see it."

Hadley blinked once, then grabbed hold of Olivia's laptop and spun it around. On the screen was a photograph of a statue depicting the Egyptian god Osiris. He was seated, wearing a tall headdress with two canes crossed in his arms.

"They're not canes. They're called the crook and flail."

"Right," said Hadley, as if she'd ever had a reason to know that. But the crook and flail didn't interest her. It was the symbols carved at the base of the statue that did, one set in particular. Her eyes alighted with recognition.

"You see it?" asked Olivia.

Hadley leaned closer until her nose nearly touched the screen. She nodded, too excited to speak. Hieroglyphs covered the base of the statue, which, for the most part, all looked the same. Just a bunch of symbols she couldn't decipher. But in the corner, at the very bottom, she spotted a group of carvings that, when put together, could very well be the clue they'd been searching for.

The first carving, a figure of a man, stood next to a line of symbols, one on top of the other. A half-moon, a circle, and an ankh. Hadley sat up and tapped the keys to enlarge the photo. In the Realm, the map—or Portal as they now knew it—was a curved mirror that expanded into a sphere. She'd never seen an ankh in the Realm, but it was the Egyptian symbol for eternal life. It stood to reason it might point them to something as old as time. Just past the ankh, she saw what looked like a bird, but it disappeared around the corner of the base. She glanced at the web address. It was the website for the Egyptian Museum of Cairo. She quickly scrolled through to find additional images of the statue.

"There aren't any," Olivia informed her. "Trust me. I've looked everywhere, even on socials. It's not exactly a main attraction."

Hadley sat back and stared at the screen, willing the image to spin around so she could see the back side.

"It's a stretch," she finally said, "but it's better than what we've found so far. Though, don't you think Egyptian scholars would have deciphered this by now?"

Olivia shook her head. "How? They'd have to know what they were looking for. The ability to read hieroglyphs was lost for centuries until the discovery of the Rosetta Stone. I'm sure an Egyptologist would have a different interpretation, but what if there's more than one way to interpret them? We're talking about images carved thousands of years ago. For all we know, this is a hidden message only meant for those who *know* what they're looking for."

"I guess," mumbled Hadley as she leaned forward again. "It's worth investigating, but we need to see what's on the other side of that base."

"I've been searching for the last two days. This is all we have to work with."

Hadley blew the hair from her face. "You're not saying what I think you're saying, are you?"

"I'm afraid so," Olivia said, spinning the laptop back around. "And I doubt Mayron is loaning his jet for this kind of trip. I better start looking up flights."

Hadley weaved her way through a maze of library stacks as she searched for Alice. Ever since her announcement that the wedding was off, she'd been more quiet than usual, spending all her spare time trying to conjure images onto mirrors. David kept to himself in his apartment above the garage, and every time they asked Alice about it, she shut down or changed the subject. Granted, they had other things to focus on at the moment, but Hadley knew Alice was hurting, and her brave face would only last so long.

She rounded the corner and found Alice sitting on the floor next to a stack of books, her nose buried in one of them.

"There you are."

Alice looked up. Her complexion was on the pale side, and with her white hair, she looked almost ghostly. "Hey," she said tiredly.

Hadley took a seat on the floor next to her and leaned over to see what she was reading. On the page was a colorful painting of the Greek god Hades. He was sitting on a throne of skulls, and at his feet was a three-headed dog. His wife, Persephone, stood beside him with a bright red pomegranate held in her hand.

"That doesn't look like her at all."

Alice's eyes moved back to the page. "We only knew her as Molly."

"Yeah, but that woman," Hadley pointed at the book, "doesn't have her vibe. She looks too meek and docile. Persephone had more fire than that."

Alice traced her finger over the glossy image and smiled. "She did."

They lapsed into silence, giving the memory of Persephone the moment it deserved.

"It's funny," Alice suddenly said, still gazing at the image. "I didn't really miss her that much until now."

"Why do you think that is?"

"I don't know. Maybe because I knew that wasn't what she wanted. She wanted me to be happy."

Hadley nodded casually, eager to keep her talking. "And now?"

"Now everything is different," she said, fidgeting with her butterfly ring. "She gave up her existence to save me—to save all of us. But what good is that sacrifice if we're still in danger? The gods aren't done with us yet. We're not getting our happily ever after. We never were."

Hadley stiffened, nodding at the ring. "Is that why you called off the wedding?"

"I don't want to talk about it," she said, slamming the book shut. Then her voice softened. "I'm sorry. Is that okay? I'm just, I'm not ready to talk about it."

Hadley reached out to cup her cheek. "Of course. I'm just worried about you."

Alice shook her head and smiled. "Don't be. We have enough to worry about as it is. I haven't found anything in these books about the Portal."

"That's why I came to get you," Hadley said, standing. She reached down and helped Alice to her feet. "Olivia found something. It's not definitive, but it's a start."

Alice dusted the library floor off her backside. "What is it?"

"A trip to Egypt."

chapter 6

When they got home, Soxie went straight into the parlor to speak to her uncle, and the rest of them adjourned to the library. Hadley took her seat by the fire and pulled out her phone, only halfway listening to Olivia and Alice's conversation as she scrolled through her missed texts.

"I thought it was her money. Why does she have to ask her uncle for permission?"

"It's a trust fund. She only has access to a certain amount every month. Anything more, and he has to authorize it."

"How much are four round-trip tickets to Cairo?"

"A lot."

Hadley read the latest text from her dad and looked up. "When do you think we'll leave?" she asked Olivia.

"Assuming Mayron agrees, we might be able to catch a red-eye flight to New York tonight, and a flight from there to Cairo in the morning."

"Oh," Hadley said, glancing at the time. It was just after 1:00 p.m. She looked at her dad's text again.

Dad: *They're clearing out the Boneyard next week. I'll be there later today if there's anything you want. Otherwise, it's going in the trash.*

Her hackles rose. Anything of value in her grandfather's old warehouse would have been confiscated after her brother's arrest. Whatever was left was worthless, and she wanted nothing to do with it. Well, most of it, anyway. Her dad knew that. He was just trying to bait her with some weird, manipulative guilt trip.

"Maybe you should go," suggested Olivia. "There's plenty of time." Then to Alice, she added, "She just got a text from her dad. He's asking if she wants anything from her brother's chop shop."

Hadley gripped her phone. "You know, if I wanted to share my *private* texts with the room, I would read them aloud."

"Relax," said Olivia as she kicked her Doc Martens onto the coffee table. "You would have told us eventually."

"Of course, I would have. But that's not the point."

Alice twisted around on the couch. "When was the last time you saw your brother?"

Hadley closed out her dad's text and dropped the phone in her lap. "At my grandfather's funeral. I was fifteen."

"How old was he?"

"Eighteen," she said, her patience waning. "Hey, remember when you said you didn't want to talk about you and David? Well, I feel the same way about this subject."

Alice frowned. "Hadz, he's your brother."

"So?" she said, laughing. "David's your soulmate, and I don't see you running to the garage to visit him right now."

As the words were coming out of her mouth, she immediately regretted them. Alice's expression crumpled into misery, making Hadley feel even worse.

"I'm so sorry," she said, backpedaling. "I didn't mean it."

"It's okay," Alice assured her. "You're right. Your brother is your business, just like my relationship with David is mine. But just so you know, he isn't living over the garage anymore. He moved out yesterday."

"What?" Hadley and Olivia said at the same time.

Alice stood quickly. "It's not forever. But with everything going on right now . . . it's for the best. At least until my power returns."

Hadley was sure she heard that wrong. David moved out? She had her issues with him, but this was next level. "And this is what you want?" she confirmed.

Alice walked to the chessboard by the window and fiddled with one of the pieces. "No. But he seems to think I need it."

"He? So this was his decision?"

Hadley watched her flick the chess piece onto its side, as if conceding a game she hadn't yet played. Then she turned around to face them.

"Please don't blame him," she said. "It's not like that. He's trying to do the right thing. Not just for me, but for all of us."

"He thinks he's getting in the way," Olivia deduced. "Of your power. That's what this is about."

Alice nodded. "Maybe he's right."

"Or maybe he's not," said Hadley. "What is he basing this on? A stupid hunch?"

She let out a soft laugh. "Even if he is, I want to respect his decision. He would do the same for me."

Hadley and Olivia exchanged worried looks.

"Guys, it's okay," she went on. "Honestly. I'm fine. But, can I ask you for a favor?"

Hadley admired her strength. She seemed awfully calm and poised, considering. "Of course, honey. Anything."

Alice licked her lips and swallowed. "He's staying at his parents' house. I don't want to tell him what's going on over the phone, but I can't see him right now. I just . . . can't."

"You want one of us to go for you," guessed Olivia. Then she turned to Hadley. "You're the one with the car."

Hadley cursed under her breath. She'd rather go see her brother in jail. But she didn't want to make this any harder on Alice than it already was. "Sure," she said, her smile strained. "I'll go."

Alice gave her an apologetic look. "Do you mind? I promised him we'd keep him updated."

"Don't be silly. I'd love to tell your ex-fiancé-slash-soulmate that we're headed to Africa in a few hours. I'm sure he'll be over the moon."

Hadley ran upstairs to grab her jacket. As she turned to put it on, the reflection in her closet mirror froze. She did a double take, then stepped forward for a better look. She studied herself, curious. One arm was pushing through a sleeve as the second reached back to find the other sleeve. Her hair defied gravity, rising off her back mid-turn.

She lifted her hand and tapped the glass. The image immediately fast-forwarded to catch up, and a second later her reflection was back where it should be. At this point it had gotten stuck about six or seven times, which wasn't that often considering how many mirrors she passed in a given day. It bugged her, but she was getting used to it. If it didn't feel like a threat, she wasn't going to treat it like one.

On the drive to David's house, the mirror problem faded to the back of her mind, and instead she thought about the last time she'd made this drive. It was right before senior year. They'd been at a back-to-school party at Remington Carver's house when Olivia overheard someone's thoughts. That someone didn't seem relevant at the time. It was just some new girl from Colorado. But she'd seen David's eyes—the *old* David's eyes—turn black, which meant there was a demon hiding inside him. It was their job to get it out.

Little did they know that the girl from Colorado was Alice, and she'd end up playing a much bigger role in their lives than they could ever imagine.

Twenty minutes later, Hadley pulled up in front of the large Tuscan-style house. David's black Porsche was parked at the top of the drive, confirming he was home. She turned off the ignition and pulled her phone from her pocket, texting him that she was outside and needed to talk. She wanted to avoid his parents if possible. This version of their son was the better one—no question about it—but they didn't even know their real son was gone. It made her feel guilty and awkward in their presence.

Her phone dinged with an incoming text.

David: *be right there*

She texted back "k" and took a long drink from her water bottle. Then she turned the car back on and lowered the windows to put the top down. She needed air. And maybe a quick escape if things went the way she feared they would.

The front door opened, and David jogged out in sweatpants and a black hoodie. He cut across the lawn and opened the door to her passenger seat.

"It's cold out here, Hadley. Don't you want to come inside?"

She shook her head no. He sighed, then climbed in. "At least put the top up."

Rather than answer, she leaned over and grabbed a pair of leather driving gloves from her glove box. "Here," she said, tossing them in his lap.

"Gee, thanks. These'll really help," he said, even as he pulled them on. Then he crossed his arms over his chest and gave her an expectant look.

"Well, what's this about?" he said, shivering.

She stared at him for a moment. His cheeks were red from the brisk weather, and his hair was disheveled, but otherwise he looked fine. She'd expected him to be distraught or strung out. The last time he'd been separated from Alice, it nearly ended him. But right now he looked well. Maybe not *happy*, but in good physical condition, anyway.

"You look well," she said, unable to disguise the accusation in her voice.

"Does this bother you?"

"Shouldn't it?" she challenged him. "Why are you here, David?"

She didn't expect to go off script so quickly, but seeing him here, in the old David's house . . . it bothered her.

He averted his gaze, choosing instead to look out the front window. "I'm giving her some space, Hadz. It's what she needs."

She couldn't help but laugh. "Seriously? This coming from the guy who once drugged her to keep her from doing what she *needed* to do."

He glanced at her, his face a stony mask. "And I'll regret that for the rest of my life."

"Then why did you do it in the first place?"

He closed his eyes briefly before responding. "In all my lifetimes, do you know how many huntresses I've vowed to protect? One hundred and thirty-two," he rushed ahead, not waiting for an answer. "And of those, ninety-one outlived me. Are you doing the math? That means I failed forty-one of them. Forty-one, Hadley. And I grieved every single one of them. I still do. I'm not defending the choices I've made, but sometimes the guilt takes over, and I would do *anything* to prevent another loss. I know it doesn't excuse my behavior, but I can't change it either. I regret a lot of things, but nothing more than what I did to Alice."

She stared at him, surprised by his sudden confession. In all the time she'd known him, he'd never opened up like that. Other than Margot and Janie, the huntresses from his previous life who were still alive, he'd never even mentioned his other huntresses. She'd always assumed they were just a job to him. Regardless, she wasn't here to dissect his past lives.

"I get that you have regrets," she began. "We all do. But won't you regret abandoning Alice now, when she needs you the most?"

He sagged into his seat. "She doesn't need me right now. She needs you. And Soxie. And Olivia. That's what she needs. I'm just in the way."

"So you say. But that girl loves you, David. If you hurt her, I swear to god, I'll never forgive you."

The corners of his mouth turned up, and a dimple appeared in his right cheek. Then a huge smile stretched across his face, the same one that survived his move from Colin's body. Alice referred to it as his "megawatt" smile. Hadley never paid his smiles much attention, but she had to admit that even on his best day, the real David never looked this good.

She frowned and punched him in the arm. "What are you smiling at? Stop it."

He turned away, absently rubbing his arm. "I'm smiling because you just proved why she needs you. What happened the other night . . . I'm worried that might be my fault."

"That's reaching. What makes you think it has anything to do with you?"

He chuckled and looked down, clasping his gloved hands together. "Call it sixteen hundred years of intuition."

She shook her head, frustrated by his nonsensical answer. "It's got to be more than that. I feel like there's something you're not telling me."

"Hadley, just trust me on this, okay? Alice is better off with you right now, focusing on recovering her power and helping you find the Portal. She needs to focus, and I need to let her do that."

"But—"

"I'm not finished," he interrupted. "This is not forever. The timing . . . it's off right now. I feel it. Our souls may have been mated two thousand years ago, but we've only known each other for one. Sure, I dreamt about her in every life I lived for sixteen hundred years, but she wasn't real until this one. If we need to wait a little longer, we'll wait."

Relief she hadn't counted on washed over her. "So the wedding isn't off? It's just postponed?"

"I don't need to marry her to know she's my future. I just need to know we have a future. So I'm going to need you to do what you do best. Protect each other."

"What about you?"

He sniffed, and she noticed the tip of his nose was now red. "I'll be fine. I'm here if you need me. And listen, Hadley. I know we haven't always seen eye to eye, and probably rarely will. If I was hard on you, I had my reasons."

"Okay," she said, unsure of what else to say.

"For what it's worth, I'm sorry."

She leaned back and appraised him. "Wow. I think that's the first time you've ever apologized to me." Then she pressed the back of her hand against his forehead. "Are you feeling okay?"

"Funny," he scowled, slapping her hand away. "Now, what was it you came here to tell me?"

Hadley merged onto the freeway, marveling at how well David had taken the news. She'd expected him to object to their trip, or at least demand to go with them. But he'd just pressed his lips together and nodded. Then, with nothing more than a quick "thank you," he exited the car and jogged back up to the house, taking her gloves with him.

A car sped past and honked, tearing her away from her thoughts. She stuck her middle finger in the air, hoping they got the message in their rearview. Plenty to see with the top down. It wasn't exactly convertible weather, but she needed some wind in her hair. She needed to be alone, and just drive.

The exit to Wayward Palms appeared faster than she wanted, so instead of heading home, she passed it and kept going. Soon the traffic got lighter, and the buildings fewer and farther between. She drove past the old juvenile detention center where Caleb spent six months of his fourteenth year. It was shuttered long ago due to budget cuts, but the damage it inflicted remained. He went in angry and came out angrier.

She pressed her foot into the accelerator, eager to outrun the memory. Strands of hair slapped at her face, and her cheeks were numb from the cold. But she didn't care. It was nice to feel in control for a change. Out here, on the road, neither the gods nor her memories could harm her.

And then she saw it—exit 581. Before she knew it, she was merging onto it. After navigating a deserted intersection and a few more stop signs, she turned onto a long gravel road. Her car bounced along, kicking up rocks and covering her sunglasses in a thin layer of dust. She hadn't been down this road in years, but everything looked the same. Dilapidated barbed-wire fence on one side, vacant dirt fields on the other. She passed signs that read "Private Property" and "Trespassers will be shot," each of them riddled with bullet holes and barely hanging on.

The road dipped and suddenly dead-ended at a gnarly old acacia tree. She slowed down and made a sharp right turn. The large metal gate was open, already rusting on its hinges. She rolled past it, peering into the abandoned guard hut. It leaned to one side and swarmed with hornets. The sight made her sad, if only because it was wasting away, just like the people who used to work in it.

The road turned curvy, and the carcasses of old cars appeared, increasing in number until they formed a makeshift barrier on either side. Every now and then, the road forked, forcing her to make a choice. It was a maze that she could easily get lost in if she didn't know where she was going. But she knew. She and Caleb used to play hide and seek in this old labyrinth of dead cars.

The last turn brought her to the middle of the maze—the heart of the operation. Her grandfather's old warehouse. The Boneyard, as it had always been known.

She parked her car next to a rusting Pontiac and sat for a minute, staring at the metal building. It was the size of a small gymnasium, with tilting garage doors that were propped open, one of them seesawing in the wind. It made an eerie creaking sound that disturbed the desert silence. Her eyes moved to the east, to Tire Mountain and the old school bus where she and Caleb used to hide. It was just a pile of old tires, and a bus that her grandfather inherited when he purchased the land. But it had been their secret escape. The place Caleb would take her when things around the yard got a little too intense.

She removed her sunglasses and exited the car, taking a moment to wipe the highway grit from her face. Gravel crunched beneath her boots as she made her way into the warehouse. The temperature dropped the second she stepped inside. As expected, the place had been cleared out. The cars, the tools—even the lifts—were gone. It had been stripped to its bare bones, and all that remained were grease stains, broken glass, some filthy rags, a forgotten office chair, and an old pizza box with something inside that no longer resembled food.

Her eyes moved to the windows in the back, where her grandfather used to survey his precious operation. The door to his office was open. She walked across the empty warehouse, kicking aside an old beer bottle. It rolled away loudly, the sound of glass on concrete echoing against the metal walls. When she got to the office, she stepped inside.

It was like stepping back in time. Everything was just as she remembered it. The desk. The filing cabinet. The stack of old rims in the corner. The computer was gone, but the monitor was still there, lying on its side with wires dangling out the back.

She crossed to the filing cabinet and opened the drawer labeled "Dashboard Junk." It was empty. Tilting her head, she peered deeper inside, bracing herself for disappointment.

"Looking for this?"

She jumped back and spun around. Her dad leaned against the door, holding a small bobble-headed angel. Its wings were made of real feathers and the halo, though crooked, was encrusted in rhinestones.

Hadley quickly slammed the drawer shut. "No. I told you, I don't want any of this stuff."

He pushed his bottom lip out and nodded. Then he gently placed the figurine on the edge of the desk. Its wings fluttered and its head bobbed up and down.

"Your back tire is low," he said, pointing his thumb behind him. "Make sure you take care of that soon."

She cringed internally. "My tire pressure stopped being your concern when I moved out, remember? I can handle my own car."

He placed his hands on his hips and chuckled. He was taller than she was, but only by an inch. Other than the slight paunch of his belly and a few gray hairs at his temples, age hadn't altered his appearance much. Even in his oil-stained jeans and wrinkly shirt, Jack Caldwell had always been a looker. In fact, he had a reputation at his car dealership for being a ladies' man. Apparently, the gals couldn't get enough of his devilish personality and baby blues.

"Sorry," he said, putting his hands up in mock surrender. "My mistake. Your tire pressure, your business."

She rolled her eyes and stepped forward to give him a hug. With the Caldwell men, it was always more of a half hug/half pat, as if they didn't know how to physically handle her.

"Hi, Dad," she said, stepping away. "Sorry I haven't been to the house in a while. I've been busy."

He shoved his hands in his pockets and looked around. "Don't worry about it, kid. I knew I'd see you here."

"Yeah, well, I didn't," she admitted, following his gaze around the old office. "I can't believe Caleb never changed it. This place looks exactly like it did when we were kids, when you were . . ." She hesitated, unable to say it. "You know. Away."

"You mean when I was in jail," he clarified. "You don't have to sugarcoat it for me, honey. I know where I was, and I know what it cost me."

Her jaw dropped. "What it cost *you*? Are you kidding me?"

He gave her a wounded look. "I'm talking about you and your brother. I know what that year with Frank did to you—to us—and I wish to god I could take it back. But I can't."

She wanted to laugh, but the lump forming in her throat prevented it. "Whatever," she said, attempting to brush him off. "I'm fine."

"No, Hadley. I don't think you are. Your brother sure as hell isn't."

His words cut deep, but she did her best not to show it. Keeping everything locked inside was exactly how she managed to *be* fine.

"Believe it or not," she began coolly, "I have a life now that has nothing to do with any of this." She paused, gesturing around her. "So it's really cute that you feel the need to fix me, but I don't need fixing. Save it for Caleb."

His face fell. "I never said you needed fixing. I just worry about you, kiddo. You can't hide from your past forever."

Wanna bet? she wanted to say. Instead, she made a show of checking the time on her watch and moved to step past him. "Well, this has been loads of fun, but I need to get going."

"Haddy, wait."

She stopped and turned around. He plucked the angel off the desk and handed it to her.

"It was your mom's favorite," he said. "She'd want you to have it."

Her heart thumped as she stared at the figurine. The paint had worn off its face, and the feathers had thinned a bit, but otherwise, it looked the same. Hadley used to pretend her mom had sent the little angel from heaven to watch over her. She'd nicknamed it Honey, because she always assumed if her mom had lived, she would have called her that, the same way her dad sometimes did. But now that she had three *real* guardian angels in Soxie, Olivia, and Alice, the trinket seemed a little silly.

She still wanted it, though.

"Please," he implored, shoving it at her. "Take it."

She cracked a half smile and begrudgingly took it, as if it wasn't the whole reason she'd come here. Then her eyes suddenly flew up, and she glanced at the empty warehouse behind her, remembering what was really missing.

"Where is it?" she demanded. "Where's the Shelby?"

He ran his fingers through his hair. She noticed his hands were dry, cracked, and full of calluses. The result of years working in this very garage.

"The Shelby is long gone. Caleb sold it after inheriting the business."

She rounded her eyes, stunned. "He *sold* it? He sold Mom's car?"

"It was just a car, Hadley."

Her anger flared. "But he had no right!" she shouted. "It didn't belong to him. It belonged to us!"

He shrugged, walking past her to survey the broken-down warehouse. "It didn't really belong to us either. It didn't even belong to her. Where do you think I got the money to buy it? Your grandfather didn't exactly pay me the big bucks back then."

"It was stolen? But I thought she hated all of this. Why would she accept a stolen car?"

"Because I never told her it was stolen."

Hadley's mouth fell open. She'd seen the video at least a hundred times. Her mom, pregnant with Hadley, opening a box with a key inside. She looks at the camera, and her smile is so bright it nearly breaks the lens. Then she runs outside to find a pristine white 1969 Ford Mustang Shelby convertible waiting for her in the driveway, a giant red bow fastened to its hood. She holds her growing baby bump as she jumps up and down, then runs toward whoever is filming, knocking the camera to the ground. The last frames of the video show a couple in love, embracing against the backdrop of a robin's-egg-blue sky. It was a memory Hadley liked to think was her own. After all, she'd been there, in a way. But it wasn't the wholesome memory she thought it was. It was just one more thing about her family that turned out to be a lie.

"How could you?" she cried. "You betrayed her trust!"

"Oh, please. Even if I did buy it, Johanna knew where the money came from. She wasn't as innocent as you think."

Hadley shook her head in disgust. Her dad could justify his actions all he wanted, but she wasn't going to stand there and listen to him drag her mother's memory down with him. With an angry sigh, she dug her keys out of her pocket, and marched toward the creaking garage doors. Then she turned around and threw the angel at her dad's feet. He dodged it like it was a poisonous snake.

"I told you, I don't want any of this crap," she hissed, then stormed to her car, eager to leave this place once and for all. Her dad caught up to her as she was buckling her seatbelt. He leaned over the side and tossed the angel on the seat next to her.

"I love you, Haddy," he said. "But sometimes you're as stubborn as Caleb. Don't punish yourself to punish me. I've made my peace with my past, and that includes your brother. I think it's time you do the same."

She put on her sunglasses and stared straight ahead. "Step away from my car, please."

He lifted his hands and backed away. Then she hit the gas and peeled off, kicking up gravel behind her. As she drove away, she spared one last glance in her rearview mirror. Her dad still stood there, watching as she turned the corner and disappeared.

When she got home, she took her mom's angel and placed it carefully on the dash of Mayron's Shelby.

"Here you go, Mom," she whispered. "This one isn't stolen."

Then she headed into the house to pack for a trip to North Africa.

chapter 7

Five hours later, they boarded a flight to New York. Having grown up like normal people, Hadley, Alice, and Olivia had no problem with the cramped seating and tiny bags of pretzels or shortbread cookies that qualified as in-flight snacks. Soxie, however, was having a rough go of it.

"What is with this seat? I feel like it's pitching me forward."

"It's called coach, honey."

Soxie pressed her back into the chair, as if brute force alone would give her a lie-flat bed. "This can't be normal. Are my knees supposed to be crammed in like this?"

Hadley turned to her friends across the aisle for help. But Alice was already asleep by the window and Olivia just gave her the side-eye as she put in her earbuds. The message was clear. Hadley was the one sitting next to Soxie, so Soxie was her responsibility.

"Try to get some sleep," she told her as she twisted back around. "It'll go by much faster. At least you have the window."

"Yeah. It's a regular Ritz-Carlton."

Hadley leaned over and pulled her sleep mask out of her carry-on. "Here. This will help."

"Thanks," Soxie grumbled as she slipped it over her head, flattening her unruly curls. "Just hope this trip ends better than it's starting. Speaking of, how did David take the news?"

"Surprisingly well, actually," Hadley replied, lowering her voice. "Part of me thinks he was happy about it."

"Happy?" Soxie repeated, stopping just short of slipping the mask over her eyes. "You did tell him we're going to Egypt, right?"

Hadley lifted her shoulders. "Okay, maybe he wasn't *happy*," she whispered, glancing across the aisle to ensure Alice was still asleep. "But he definitely didn't seem upset, which alone is suspect, don't you think?"

Soxie pulled the mask down and leaned against the window. "Maybe he's finally growing up."

"He's sixteen hundred years old."

"Yeah, but he is a man," Soxie chortled. "Doesn't that translate to like sixteen years?"

"Ha, ha," Hadley said, nudging her in the shoulder. "But seriously, I just hope they know what they're doing."

Soxie wriggled around, trying to get comfortable. "They're soulmates. They'll figure it out."

"I guess," she semi-agreed. There was no denying Alice and David were connected spiritually, but who said they were always going to connect otherwise? The same went for family. Hadley loved her dad, but she didn't always have to like him, especially if he didn't stop badgering her about making amends with her brother. The thought alone made her blood pressure rise.

"Maybe he's right," Olivia said from across the aisle. Hadley swiveled her head around as her friend pulled out her earbuds. "It's been four years, Hadz," she went on. "He's doing his time now, and he's paying for his mistakes. What are you so afraid of?"

Hadley turned off the overhead light and leaned back.

"I don't know, O," she sighed. "There's a lot to be afraid of right now. Is my brother really a priority?"

Olivia leaned her elbow on the armrest. "Isn't that reason enough to make him one?"

"It's not that simple."

"Yes, it is."

The cold cabin suddenly got colder. Hadley grabbed a sweatshirt from her bag and covered herself with it like a blanket.

"When you start spending more time with *your* family, we can talk."

"I knew you were going to say that."

"Gee. I wonder how."

Olivia gave her a scathing look. "My situation is different, and you know it. At least you'll never actually *know* what your brother thinks about you. Try hearing your own father think you're some kind of freak, or your mother tell you she's happy to see you, but in her mind she's counting the seconds until you leave. Or worse, wishing she'd never had you. Try dealing with that."

Hadley noticed the man in front of Olivia turn his head. Whether he meant to eavesdrop or not, it didn't change the fact that he was listening to their private conversation. She leaned further across the aisle and lowered her voice.

"I'm sorry, O. You're right. I know it's different." She took hold of her hand and linked her fingers through it. "I wish it wasn't."

Olivia glanced at their clasped hands and nodded. "Me too."

Hadley smiled sadly, wishing there was a way to take away Olivia's gift. Or, as she sometimes thought of it, a curse. Olivia gave her hand a quick squeeze and let go. Then she nodded to her left where Alice's head had just fallen on her shoulder.

"We should get some sleep too," she said. "Tomorrow's a long travel day."

Hadley nodded and looked around at the dark cabin. A few passengers were reading or watching movies on personal tablets, but most of them were asleep. She bent the sides of her headrest forward and settled in, closing her eyes.

"Sweet dreams, O," she said.

"We'll see."

Hadley stood in the back pew, watching the proceedings from afar. Her dad was at the lectern, reading a passage from the Bible. Next to him, on an easel, was a large picture of a man in his late thirties, maybe early forties. He had sideburns and wavy blond hair, and a smile that was both arrogant and charming. If the eyes were blue instead of hazel, Hadley would think she was looking at a picture of her brother, not a vintage photograph of her grandfather.

She glanced at the back of her brother's head. He was sitting in the front row, hands clasped solemnly in front of him. She followed his gaze to the black casket. It was covered in a mound of white flowers, some of them trailing over the edges. They were beautiful, representing purity and innocence, two things the dead man below them was never destined to have.

"And what do we have here?" said a curious voice.

Hadley's body stiffened. The gods had been quiet since Hermes delivered his message. Hadley assumed they were giving them time to find the Portal, but it would appear that time was already up.

She turned to see who was invading her dream tonight. A very tall and muscular man stood next to her in full snorkel gear—wetsuit, mask, and flippers. In one hand he held a program. In the other, a trident. He looked so out of place and ridiculous that she couldn't have suppressed a laugh if she tried.

Poseidon responded by giving her a quizzical look, which, through his mask, made him look cross-eyed. Hadley bit the inside of her cheek to stop from laughing again. Her subconscious had out-done itself this time. But as funny as it was, it also felt disrespectful, considering the occasion. She stepped onto the seat to reach his head and pulled the mask off.

"There," she said, hopping down. "Pretty sure you don't need that."

He looked at the giant mask in her hands and blinked. "What is it?"

"Forget it," she said, tossing it aside. "It would take me too long to explain."

"Then explain this," he said, waving his trident at the funeral proceedings. "I wish to know the meaning of your dream."

Hadley noticed his long blue hair dripping in saltwater and seaweed. Little crablike creatures darted in and out of its locks as if playing games of hide and seek. Her nose tingled with the scent of fish and brine. She took a subtle step to the side, eager for some fresh air.

He lifted his eyebrow. It was pierced with a silver starfish. "I do not like what I am seeing," he added. His tone was accusatory, as if she'd generated this particular dream on purpose.

She fell into her seat with a thud. "I don't like it either."

Poseidon took an awkward seat next to her. Water pooled beneath him, and he had to sit sideways to fit, but he seemed intent on learning more about her dream. She sighed.

"It's more of a memory," she attempted to explain. "I've been dreaming a lot of those lately."

A sound up front caught their attention. Her brother had just stepped up to the lectern. Hadley glanced at her younger self, sitting in the pew opposite. Next to her was a girl with black hair, another with curly red hair. At fifteen, she'd become inseparable from Soxie and Olivia, and even though this was a memory, it was nice to know they still made it. Their support had gotten her through.

"What is happening?" inquired Poseidon, leaning forward.

"My brother is about to blame my father for my grandfather's death. Then he's going to blame me for my mother's."

Poseidon didn't seem fazed. Where he came from, children killed their parents all the time, if they weren't getting killed by them first.

Caleb stepped up to the podium and began having a heated exchange with her dad. Behind them, the priest looked concerned, scanning the crowd in search of help. Poseidon flinched as her brother shoved her dad, knocking him and the lectern over. The heavy Bible hit the floor with a loud smack. Her dad scrambled to his feet and struck Caleb in the face. He fell against the casket, bringing a collective gasp to the mourners. It rocked precariously on its stand, sending a blanket of white flowers sliding to the floor. Hadley watched her younger self jump up and attempt to tackle Caleb, but Soxie and Olivia held her back.

"Leave us alone. You're not my brother! You're dead to me!" she screamed.

Caleb used the casket to push himself up, then dabbed the blood trickling from the side of his mouth. He spit a gob of red on the floor at her dad's feet, then gave young Hadley a hard, cold look.

"I'm dead to you, Haddy? Like Mom? Oh, wait. She's already dead."

Fifteen-year-old Hadley struggled against her friends' arms, desperate to hurt her brother—to kill him if she had to. But he just laughed and turned to the casket, giving it a quick rap with his knuckles.

"See ya, Frank," he said. Then he sauntered out, cocksure and full of swagger, leaving the rest of them to deal with the fallout.

Hadley watched the scene unfold with a detached heart. Compartmentalizing was a talent she possessed in spades, and keeping memories like these buried was crucial to her mental health. But if Poseidon wanted to watch, she didn't have much choice but to let it play out. Angering a god was never a good idea, even in a dream.

Her younger self sat down with Soxie and Olivia on either side whispering supporting words in her ears. She'd never cried. She'd been too angry to cry. And as time went on, she quickly put it behind her, choosing instead to focus on being a huntress. As a huntress, she made a difference, fighting evil one demon at a time. Caleb wasn't evil. He was just a waste of time.

Poseidon fidgeted next to her, planting the base of his trident firmly into the floor. "I did not hear the mortal accuse you of matricide. You are mistaken."

Hadley closed her eyes for a moment. "My mother died from complications in childbirth. She died an hour after I was born. That's why he said what he said. To hurt me."

Poseidon looked annoyed. "How can words cause pain? This I do not understand."

"Fair question. Sometimes they just do."

He suddenly stood. Water cascaded down his body, making all the little sea creatures in his hair skitter about. "Very well. I wish to adjourn to the sea now. The melancholy of this place displeases me."

With a roll of her eyes, she pulled herself up and grabbed hold of Poseidon's meaty hand. His flippers made huge slapping noises as she dragged him out of the church.

"Whatever you say, Lord of the Sea."

The sun felt nice on her skin, even if it wasn't real. Her dream had provided her with a bikini and a small sailboat to lounge on while Poseidon sang with the fish or swam with the mermaids, whatever it was he was doing beneath the waves. She just hoped he stayed occupied. The longer they kept the gods happy in their sleep, the longer they had in their waking hours to find the Portal.

She closed her eyes and listened to the sound of water lapping against the boat. It felt lazy, as if her dream ocean was too tired to generate anything more. If she wasn't already sleeping, she'd love to fall asleep, but she knew her dreams too well at this point. When the gods were present, nothing stayed calm for long.

On cue, a seagull cried in the distance. She opened her eyes and lifted her head, squinting into the bright horizon. A flock of them circled a dark mass just beneath the surface. She sat up and double-knotted the ties on her bikini top. If she was going swimming, she wanted to make sure her suit stayed on.

The little sailboat stopped rocking, and the surface of the water turned to glass. She grabbed hold of the mast and leaned over the side to get a better look. All she saw was herself and the blue sky behind her reflected in the dead calm water. She knelt and reached her hand toward her reflection. When her finger made contact, another hand suddenly broke through and grabbed hold of her wrist, pulling her overboard.

She held her breath and kicked, but whatever had hold of her wasn't letting go. She was dragged along at high speed, slicing through the dark like a torpedo. Her lungs tightened and the more she struggled, the more her body screamed for oxygen. How was this happening? Could she really drown in her own dream?

Then she remembered. This was *her* dream. So why did it feel like the gods were in control?

She gasped and inhaled a lung full of saltwater, sending her body into a series of violent spasms. The grip on her wrist tightened, and the water got colder. Darker. They were diving now. Diving into a deep, dark abyss from where she was sure she'd never return.

She squeezed her eyes shut and focused inward.

This isn't real. This isn't real. You can breathe . . . just breathe!

The hold on her wrist was released, and she felt herself spin. Round and round. Faster and faster. She was stuck in a vortex, getting tossed and turned by the centrifugal force. Her lungs screamed for air, and despite her mental and physical training, she was completely panicking.

No! No! This isn't real. Stop it. STOP!

She sat bolt upright, chest heaving. The little sailboat rocked, making subtle splashing noises in the calm water. She brought her hand to her throat, taking deep, slow breaths as she pulled herself together. When she finally looked around, she saw that the dreamscape hadn't changed. She was still in a bikini, floating on a tiny white boat in the middle of an imaginary ocean. The flock of seagulls still encircled something in the distance, and the sky was still a lovely shade of blue.

"Did I just have a nightmare inside my own dream?" she said aloud, needing to hear her own voice.

The water around her swirled, and a large hand emerged holding a trident. Poseidon tossed the trident onto the boat and heaved himself up. Hadley moved to starboard to make room. The vessel felt more like a toy boat beneath his ample frame but somehow stayed afloat. He took a seat and let his legs dangle over the sides. Then he pulled off his mask and flapped his flippers against the surface of the water.

"These are wonderful. What do you call them?" he asked, nodding to the flippers.

Hadley gripped the side ropes for support, still reeling from her dream's nightmare. "Flippers."

"Flippers," he repeated. "What an imaginative invention. My brother was right. Perhaps we will have something to gain from this new version of humankind."

The sun dipped behind the clouds, and a strong wind began to blow. The little boat began seesawing as the waves got bigger. Hadley tightened her hold on the ropes, and a feeling of nausea overcame her. Poseidon looked to the sky, curious.

"Why do you do this? I preferred the warmth of your sunny sky and the calm of your tranquil ocean." He looked annoyed and grumpy. Hadley did her best to calm the storm brewing in her mind, and hence the surrounding dreamscape.

"Your brother," she began carefully, focusing on the birds in the distance. Her nausea subsided, replaced by dread. "Which brother are you referring to?"

Poseidon's chest rumbled with laughter. Brightly colored fish leaped over the boat, wiggling their iridescent bodies in the air before plunging back into the water. He batted them away like pesky flies.

"This language we speak is strange, and yet I understand it. Even the nuances you believe me to be oblivious to. You wish to inquire if the brother I speak of is Hades, Lord of The Underworld."

Unable to answer yes, Hadley simply nodded.

Poseidon's gaze moved to the birds. The dark mass beneath them was getting bigger. "Hades has been banished to The Underworld, where he can do no more harm. He has been a barnacle in our sides for far too long."

Hadley gave him a disapproving look. Hades was far more formidable than a barnacle. But it was nice to know that Olivia was right—Hades *couldn't* visit them in their dreams.

"Well that's a relief," she said, squatting to take a seat beside him. "One less thing to worry about."

He regarded her curiously. "You fear Hades, yet you do not fear my brother Zeus? You do not fear *me*?"

She looked at his tight wetsuit and flippers, trying not to laugh. "Should I?"

"Yes, huntress. You should."

She straightened her posture, determined to appear strong. "I'm not scared of you. You're in my dream. These are my rules."

"But don't you see, child? This is no longer simply *your* dream. It is ours." Then he slipped on his mask, spun around, and fell backward into the water like he was going for a recreational dive. Hadley stared at the now frothy and churning sea, trying to make sense of what was happening. Above her, the birds squawked loudly, a frenzy of wings and screeching caws that made her hair stand on end. Something below them emerged from the water. A giant tentacle slapped onto the boat, tipping it sideways. Hadley fell forward and grabbed hold of the gunwale to keep from falling in. Her face was inches from the water, and just below its surface, a black eye regarded her malevolently.

This isn't real. This isn't real.

But even as she tried convincing herself, she felt the wood of the boat buckle and splinter beneath her as the giant squid squeezed.

"Stop!" she screamed. The sky had turned dark, and heavy sheets of rain were already falling.

Poseidon's head surfaced, eyes glowing in the darkness of her storm. "Find the Portal of Osiris, huntress. Or we will never stop."

Then the boat snapped in half, suffocating and crushing her before her broken body was pulled beneath the waves.

chapter 8

Hadley's eyes popped open. The cabin was still dark, and Soxie snored softly beside her. She looked to her left. Olivia and Alice were also asleep, and at least appeared to be having normal dreams. If that was the case, she couldn't wake them. Normal dreams were a treasured commodity these days.

She pulled her water bottle from her bag and drained it. Then she sat back and took a few breaths to calm her racing heart. It was a miracle she hadn't been thrashing about and screaming in *her* sleep. With shaky hands, she unbuckled her seatbelt and made her way to the bathroom at the back of the plane.

After locking the folding door, she closed the toilet lid and sat down. Then she let her head fall between her knees. She stared at the floor between her boots and focused on the ambient noise of the plane's air filtration system. It helped clear her mind, and she needed a clear head if she was going to get through this.

She clasped her hands behind her neck and closed her eyes. For several minutes she thought of nothing but her breathing. It succeeded in bringing her heart rate down and keeping the nausea at bay. She might be losing control of her dreams, but she was still in control of her body and mind, and there was no way she was getting sick in an airplane toilet.

Someone knocked on the door, and it nearly folded inward.

"Everything okay in there?"

"Yes," she called. "Be right out."

She stood and washed her hands, keeping her eyes down. When she opened the door, there was a man waiting with his hands in his pockets. He gave her a polite nod as he sidled past and closed the door behind him. Two steps into the aisle she heard, "What the hell?"

She stopped and pivoted around. The door folded open, and the man's head popped out. He looked at her with wide eyes.

"What's going on?" he demanded.

She gave him a puzzled look and stepped forward. "Excuse me?"

He moved aside and pointed into the small bathroom. She followed his gaze and tilted her head in to see. The mirror above the little sink was reflecting her image, but it was the wrong one. It was her profile from before, as she exited the bathroom, eyes cast down and hair billowing behind her. She gasped and shoved her way into the cramped room, immediately pressing her palm to the glass. The images fast-forwarded like a video, showing her leaving and her new friend entering. As soon as the mirror was back to normal, she glanced into the cabin, thankful to see most of the passengers in earshot were either sleeping or wearing headphones. One witness was bad enough. Multiple witnesses would have been a disaster.

"Is this a joke?" the man barked behind her, poking his head back in the bathroom. "Is there a camera behind that thing? Are we being *filmed*?"

She opened her mouth to explain, but quickly shut it. One witness or ten witnesses, how was she supposed to explain this?

"Uh . . ." she said, stalling. His dark eyes narrowed behind thick-framed glasses, and she noticed he had clenched his fists, the same way she did whenever she felt threatened. Crap, why was she so bad at lying?

"I-I wouldn't worry about it," she stammered.

He gave her a bewildered look. "You wouldn't *worry* about it? Are you kidding me?"

She started sidestepping away, wishing she could open the emergency exit and parachute out of the plane.

"I really don't know," she said as she lifted her hands in the air. "Sorry, I have to go back to my seat."

He frowned, and his head darted back and forth between her and the lavatory. "But—"

"Have a nice flight!" she practically sang, like some kind of lunatic. Then she whirled around and beelined back to her seat. Heat crawled up her neck as she sped down the aisle. When she sat down, she quickly buckled her seatbelt and leaned back, pulling her hair from her face.

"*I wouldn't worry about it?*" she whispered to herself, appalled. Did she really just say that? Of all the things she could say, that was probably the one thing that would ensure the poor guy *did* worry about it. She glanced over her shoulder, relieved to see he wasn't still standing by the bathroom or walking down the aisle toward her. With any luck, he'd forget about it by the time they landed and chalk it up to jetlag. She shook her head and couldn't help but chuckle under her breath.

Soxie stirred beside her and mumbled, "What's funny?"

She grabbed her sweatshirt off the floor and pulled it back over her. "Nothing, Sox. Go back to sleep."

When they landed in New York, Hadley ushered them off the plane as fast as possible.

"Slow down, Caldwell," said Soxie, tripping on her stiletto heels. "We're not boarding again for a few hours."

"I know. I just have a problem." She glanced over her shoulder as she speed-walked them through the bustling airport. Alice followed along without complaint, but Olivia just shook her head and grabbed Hadley's arm, slowing her down.

"It's not that big of a deal, Hadz. Nobody else saw, right? He can't prove anything. Let it go."

"What's she talking about?" asked Alice.

Hadley turned, scanning the sea of people swirling around them. The guy with the thick-framed glasses was nowhere to be seen. She exhaled and relaxed. Then she slowed her pace as they made their way to the international terminal, giving Soxie and her four-inch heels an opportunity to catch up. On the way, she filled them in on everything that happened on the flight, including her episode in the bathroom.

"Wow," said Soxie. "I'm sorry I slept through that. I could use a good laugh."

"You and me both," added Alice.

By now, they were sitting in an airport lounge, plates of half-eaten food sitting on the table in front of them. Hadley dipped a fry in mayonnaise and pointed it at Alice.

"That bad?" she guessed.

Alice pushed the food around her plate. Her white hair was tied on top of her head in a messy knot. With her slight build and brown eyes, she looked like an exhausted woodland faerie.

"Yes," she said, dropping her fork and pushing her plate aside. "I spent most of my dream with Demeter, and let's just say she's not my biggest fan."

"She blames you, doesn't she?" said Olivia carefully. "For Persephone."

Alice nodded. "The fact that I exist just reminds her that her daughter doesn't. She's never going to forgive me. And clearly, she volunteered to be my reminder last night."

Hadley placed a hand on top of hers. "Sorry. Looks like we all had a rough night. But yours feels personal. How do they expect us to make any progress if they keep messing with our heads like this?"

Soxie tsked. "I don't think they care. They want their Portal, and I don't remember any mythology books describing them as patient and understanding."

"At least they're leaving Margot and Janie alone," said Alice. "That's got to count for something."

"Let's hope it stays that way," Olivia said as she began consolidating their plates. "Last time I spoke with Margot, she told me she's on heart medication, and Janie has sleep apnea. The last thing they need is night terrors."

Hadley nodded, thankful the retired huntresses were being left to live their golden years in peace. They'd already done their part.

"My guess is the gods know we're more likely to find the Portal," Olivia continued. "So they're sticking with our dreams. But if last night is any indication, we have to assume the frequency is going to increase. Maybe there's a way to convince them to back off for a bit."

"How?" asked Alice.

"We need one of them on our side. Who's the most likely candidate?"

Hadley thought of her past dreams with Artemis. They'd hunted together many times in her makeshift forest and even had a few laughs. But Artemis seemed unbothered by their predicament, and Hadley had no reason to believe she'd help them.

Olivia shook her head. "No, I don't think it's Artemis."

"I sure as hell hope you don't think it's Dionysus," Soxie jumped in. "That dude is crazy. Like, mad-hatter crazy. He made me drink a barrel of wine. A *barrel*. Then he danced on my stomach until I was barfing up whole vineyards. I'm not kidding. It was wild, in the worst possible way."

Hadley wanted to laugh, but it wasn't funny. She remembered what it felt like to think she was drowning. She couldn't imagine what vomiting an entire vineyard would feel like, even in a dream.

They all stared at the table for a moment, digesting what Soxie had said. Finally, Alice leaned forward and rested her chin in her hands. "Who do you think it should be?" she asked Olivia.

"Just because I read minds doesn't mean I have all the answers," came her acerbic reply.

Hadley patted her back. "We know, honey. It's just a lot easier when you do."

A mild version of laughter rippled through their foursome. It wasn't joyful, side-splitting laughter, but it was something.

"All I can say is I vote no on Ares," declared Olivia, bringing them back down to earth. "He hasn't had a war to reside over in centuries, and I think his head is full of conflict versus resolution. He won't help us. Trust me. I know."

"What happened, Diaz?" asked Soxie. "He send you to war or something?"

Olivia closed her eyes and shivered. "Or something. I don't want to talk about it."

Hadley gave her a sympathetic smile. She understood; she didn't want to talk about her dip in the ocean with Poseidon either. She shoved another fry in her mouth out of habit.

"Then who are we talking about?" she asked, bits of potato flying from her lips.

"How about Athena?" suggested Soxie. "She's the goddess of wisdom, right? Sounds promising."

"And also warfare," added Olivia. "No, I don't think she's the one either."

Hadley chewed on the end of her milkshake straw. Hermes only delivered his message three days ago, and already the gods were losing patience. And what about the guy on the plane with the thick-framed glasses? The mirror glitch was low on their list of priorities right now, but she couldn't help but wonder if he was still thinking about it. Would he ever tell someone what happened, or would he take it to his grave?

"Hadley, focus," Olivia said, tapping her arm. "The guy will be fine. Besides, you're never going to see him again anyway."

"I know," she responded, shaking it off. "I just felt bad. When are these mirrors going to start behaving?" Then she turned to Alice. "Any luck with your projections?"

Alice glumly shook her head. "No. I don't know what I'm doing wrong. I bring up the image in my mind first, then I envision it in the mirror. It always worked before. But now, no matter how much I focus, nothing happens. It's giving me a headache just thinking about it."

Hadley rubbed her back. "Don't worry. I'm sure you'll figure it out. Is there anything we can do to help?"

"Thanks, but I don't think so," she replied. "I know it's there. Something's just blocking it."

Her emphasis on the word *something* was telling. Either she truly believed David was to blame, or there was another reason her power was being dampened. Time would tell. Speaking of the time, Hadley looked at her watch.

"We should head to the gate. So what did we decide? Which god do we ask for help?"

Olivia scooped up their stack of plates. "We didn't decide. And the more I think about it, I'm not sure it's a good idea. Asking for help means we might owe that god a favor. I don't want to owe any of them a favor."

"You don't think they'll help us out of the kindness of their immortal hearts?" asked Soxie.

"No. I don't."

Sixteen hours later, after navigating a chaotic customs scene at Cairo International Airport, they were in a car on the way to their hotel. Uncle Mayron may have skimped on the flights, but he insisted they have a private car and driver for their stay. His name was Sam, though Hadley suspected that wasn't his real name. He was friendly and boisterous, talking the entire way from the airport to the hotel. And because traffic in Cairo made rush hour in Phoenix look like the Autobahn, the drive took almost two hours.

By the time Sam dropped them off, Hadley was ready to drop. They all were.

"I'm sorry, guys," said Soxie. "I need to sleep. I don't care if Zeus sends a lightning bolt up my ass. I'm fading."

A man in the lobby gave them a dirty look, but they were too tired to care.

At reception they were greeted by a woman with a sparkling smile and lips painted the color of wild berries. Her skin was dark and flawless, and her hair was slicked back into a chic bun. In her smart hotel uniform, she made them feel like four hobos who'd just jumped a train from Philly.

"This hotel is nice," Alice said with a yawn, squinting as the morning sun streamed into the palatial lobby.

Hadley checked the time on her phone and reset her watch. It was almost nine in the morning Cairo time, but her body felt like it was 2:00 a.m. the day before. Her internal clock was all out of whack. She barely listened as the woman behind the desk rattled off hotel information.

". . . and from your adjoining rooms you will find a splendid view of the Nile River."

They would have oohed and aahed if they weren't half zombies at the moment. After checking their passports and explaining the hotel amenities, she gestured to the elevator bank to their right.

"You will find your rooms on the tenth floor." Then she handed Soxie four keycards and a sealed envelope. "We received this message for one in your party. A Miss Daniels."

Hadley glanced at Alice. She looked about as good as they all felt, though the purple bags under her eyes stood out more due to her white hair. Soxie handed her the envelope. She stared at it for a brief moment, then folded it in half and stuffed it in her back pocket.

"You're not going to read it?" asked Olivia.

"Not right now. I don't want to get upset. It might cloud my focus."

Hadley slung an arm around her. "If there was anything wrong, he'd call or text. I'm sure it's just a love letter."

"That's why I don't want to read it."

Hadley glanced at the others but didn't press any further. It was Alice's letter, and Alice's business. Besides, unlike the gods, a love letter could wait.

Their rooms were spacious and well-appointed. Hadley dumped her bag on one of the two queen beds and moved to the window. She pulled the heavy drapes aside and let sunlight flood the room. Alice walked up to stand beside her.

"That woman wasn't kidding," she said. "We're right on the river. Look at that view."

Hadley nodded in agreement. The Nile glistened in the morning sun. They watched as a set of eight-person rowboats glided past the hotel, coxswains shouting, and oars slicing through the water. It was a synchronized dance of movement that gave the scene a magical feel. Beyond the river, a brownish-gold haze settled over the city of Cairo.

"Have you been here before?" asked Alice.

"Once. We used the map to visit when we were fourteen, but we didn't see much."

"Really? Why?"

Hadley stared at the hazy view, eyes glazing over. "We didn't know what we were doing. You can't just walk up to the pyramids and have a peek inside. You need tickets, a guide, a driver—all the stuff we didn't have at fourteen. It was pretty intimidating."

"I'm sure it was," agreed Alice, her gaze still on the rowers. "I still can't believe we're in Egypt. I know we're here for the statue, but do you think the Portal is here too?"

"I don't know. It should have disappeared with the Realm. But if it's connected to Osiris, then it makes sense it might find its way back here."

"Or maybe the Realm didn't disappear at all."

Hadley felt a flurry of excitement at the thought. Despite the dangers associated with it, she missed the Realm.

"Then where did it go?" she prodded.

"Who knows?" Alice said as she made her way to her bed. She unzipped her suitcase and proceeded to unpack. "Maybe it's hiding in the place between."

Hadley cocked her head to the side. "The place between?"

"Yes. It's where I spoke to Philautia, when I was sort of dead. You know, after the thing with my dad."

She said it so nonchalantly, as if her father regularly got possessed by ancient gods. Then again, Alice had been through much worse with Hades. The "thing" with her dad probably felt like small potatoes.

"It's a good theory," Hadley said, unzipping her own suitcase. "But if being 'sort of dead' is the only way to get to it, that's a hard pass. Besides, right now I'm more interested in getting the gods to back off."

Alice nodded tiredly and yawned. Then she grabbed her toiletry bag and headed to the bathroom. Hadley finished unpacking and knocked on the door that connected their room to the one next door. Olivia opened it a few seconds later. She'd already taken off her makeup, and a toothbrush was stuck in the corner of her mouth. Without her heavy kohl eyeliner, her eyes looked bigger, despite drooping from exhaustion.

"Hey," she grunted.

Hadley greeted her in return and stepped into the room. "What time is Sam picking us up for the museum?"

"Three," Olivia replied, heading back to the bathroom. Hadley nodded and pulled the phone from her pocket to set her alarm for 2:45 p.m. Then she turned to Soxie, who was lying sideways on the bed, flipping mindlessly through channels on the flat-screen television.

"Anything good on?"

Soxie rested her head on her hand as she continued surfing. "No, not really, just—oh, wait. Here we go."

Hadley dropped onto the bed next to her. She'd stopped on a movie channel that was playing *The Matrix*. It was the scene where the main character must choose between a red or blue pill. She rested her head on Soxie's shoulder and yawned.

"Which would you choose?" Soxie asked.

Hadley stared at the screen, her eyelids growing heavy. "Between ignorance and the truth? The truth, obviously."

"Yeah. Me too."

They continued watching in silence as the character made his decision. Hadley couldn't help but compare it to the decision each of them had made when they were thirteen. Philautia didn't offer red and blue pills, but she still allowed them to make the choice. By accepting a piece of her soul, they were also shown the truth. But Philautia never accounted for a third pill, the one they were swallowing right now. The one where gods haunted their dreams and made them chase an ancient portal halfway around the world.

Olivia emerged from the bathroom. She crawled onto the bed, and Hadley scooched over to make room. "We always have a choice, Hadz," she said, eyes glued to the screen. "I just hope we're making the right one by coming here."

"What's the alternative? Letting the gods destroy our minds?"

"*Shhh*!" ordered Soxie. Hadley rolled her eyes, unaware the movie was so important. She heard Alice emerge from their bathroom and was about to head back when another character on the screen grabbed her attention. She felt Soxie and Olivia tense at the same time.

"Morpheus!" they shouted in unison.

Olivia leaped to her feet, face flushed. "Of course! I was so focused on the Olympian gods that I never thought to consider him."

"You think he would help us?" asked Hadley.

"He's the god of sleep and dreams," she said excitedly. "If anyone could, it would have to be him, right?"

Soxie flipped off the television and tossed the remote aside. "But how do we get in touch with him?"

Alice's head popped through the open doorway. "Did I just hear you say Morpheus?"

They quickly filled her in, and she made her way to the other bed and sat down.

"I don't know," she said, her forehead creased. "Didn't we decide it was too risky to owe a god a favor? Why would Morpheus be any different?"

"Well, they're encroaching on his world. Dreams are *his* domain," explained Olivia. "I'm curious to know if he has anything to do with what's going on. Couldn't hurt to find out."

"But *how*?" persisted Soxie. "What do we do? Dial 1-800-Sand-Man?"

Olivia's eyes lit up, then a smile slowly spread across her face. "That's exactly what we're going to do."

chapter 9

Hadley squinted at the sun reflecting off the Nile. It was almost 10:00 a.m., which meant they had a few hours to make this happen before Sam picked them up to take them to the museum. She snapped the curtains shut, plunging the room into darkness. Then she felt her way to her bed and climbed in. She heard rustling in the other bed.

"Are you nervous?" Alice whispered.

Hadley waited for her eyes to adjust. When they didn't, she turned on her side and spoke in Alice's general direction. "Maybe a little. But it's not like we have anything to lose at this point. We still have to sleep. I just hope we don't end up making a bad situation worse."

"Well, we agreed this is just a test. No one's asking for anything yet."

"Right."

A few seconds ticked by in silence. Hadley closed her eyes, saying a little prayer that her dream didn't turn into another nightmare.

"Night, Hadz."

"Night, honey," she said, then rolled over and waited patiently for sleep to come.

After a few minutes, soft snores came from the other bed. She lifted her head, envious of Alice's ability to fall asleep so fast. Hadley had been dead on her feet when they arrived, but now she felt like she'd just sucked down a double espresso with a cold brew chaser.

With a silent huff she grabbed the extra pillow and flipped over, desperate to get comfortable. But it was no use. One second she was too hot, the next she was too cold. She flopped around like a guppy, getting more and more agitated. The harder she tried sleeping, the harder it became. Finally, she gave up and grabbed her phone, ready for some mindless scrolling.

Her eyes widened when she saw the missed text from her dad.

She hesitated to read it, not wanting to disrupt the dream mission she was about to embark on—if she ever got to sleep, that is. But she couldn't help herself, and she opened it anyway.

Dad: *I'm sorry for the way things went down at the Boneyard. I never could get it right with you, could I? Even last year, when you were missing, the way I handled it was wrong. I was scared, and when Caldwell men are scared, we get angry. I'm not saying it's right. It just is. I thank god every day you turned out to be the smart and strong young woman you are. But that anger is still in you, Haddy. Don't let it destroy you the way it destroyed your brother.*

Below it was a much shorter text, encased in its own light gray bubble. She knew before reading it that it would demand more from her than she was willing to give.

Dad: *If you do decide to visit him, don't do it for him. Do it for you.*

Her eyes welled up, even as the acid in her stomach churned. Caldwell men get angry? That was a laugh. Caldwell men did more than get angry. Some of them got so angry they ended up behind bars. Or worse, six feet under.

She briskly typed her response.

Hadley: *I don't have time for this, Dad. Go see him if you want. I'm not interested.*

She locked her phone and threw it to the end of the bed. Then she closed her eyes, determined to fall asleep, if only to escape the reality of her waking life—gods and portals be damned.

She was sitting in a cheap motel room that smelled of old cigarettes and mold. She scanned the glossy pages of the magazine she was reading. An article about celebrities who recycle red carpet looks caught her attention. She'd read this article before. Soxie was on the bed across from her, filing her nails.

Just then, the door to the bathroom burst open. Alice flew out in a rage of white-and-brown hair. She slammed the door shut and leaned against it.

"Where are we again?" she asked the room.

Hadley lowered her magazine and looked up. "North Dakota," she answered because she knew she was supposed to.

"South," Soxie corrected her without looking up from her nails.

Hadley shrugged, not really caring where they were, but realizing she still had a line to deliver. Because the script of this particular scene had already been written.

"Okay, South Dakota," she conceded. "Why?"

Alice pointed with her thumb at the door behind her. "Just wondering if I'll get the electric chair when I murder him."

"Ha," Soxie said. "Get in line."

Alice groaned and fell onto the bed. Then she grabbed a pillow and shoved it over her face to scream into it. Hadley gave Soxie a look, but neither of them moved to intervene. They understood her frustration.

Alice pulled the pillow off her face. "Can we please, please splurge for a bigger room tomorrow? Or break into one?"

Hadley tamped down her irritation. Like it was that simple. "We can't break into anything," she proclaimed. "And it's not as easy as it looks, by the way." It amazed her how quickly they just expected her to break into random cars and houses, as if she didn't have to consider things like alarm systems, closed-circuit cameras, or nosy neighbors.

"We're down to our last hundred bucks as it is," Soxie said as she turned off the television. "We have to do a Realm jump for provisions."

Alice sat up. "What, tonight? No!"

Hadley gave her a crooked smile and tossed the magazine aside. "Sorry, honey, you're babysitting."

Alice fell back on the bed and covered her face again with the pillow. Then the bathroom door opened, and David stepped out. He shoved Alice aside and made himself comfortable on the bed.

"What's for dinner, witches?"

Hadley was about to rip him a new one, but Alice beat her to it. "For the millionth time," she hissed. "We are not witches."

He cracked open a beer and said, "Whatever. Like I give a shit."

Hadley stared at his smug face, feeling the rage build in her chest. How dare he treat Alice like that! But then something tugged at her brain, like she was standing in a long line and the person behind her had just tapped her on the shoulder, reminding her to move forward.

She took a moment to survey the scene. It was one of the motel rooms they'd squatted in last year, when they were on the run. When Alice's hair was only half white, when their peers still referred to them as the Wayward Sisters, and when David was the demon magnet they needed to clear the Realm and save Cithaeron's soul.

She leaned back and imagined giving herself a facepalm. Of course. This wasn't real. She was asleep, and this was only a dream. But why did she keep dreaming about the past? Were the gods mining her memories or something? She quickly scanned the room to make sure no gods were present. Satisfied, she moved her attention back to David. He was manically flipping through channels on the old television, occasionally pausing to take a swig of beer or belch. On the surface he looked the same, but somehow she could tell this was a different David. A dark energy clung to him like a heavy, odorless cologne. The "new" David—the one that now housed Cithaeron's soul—wasn't perfect, but his soul had had its comeuppance. It had paid for its sins and deserved happiness with its other half. With Alice.

Hadley sighed, then noticed the room had gone silent. She looked up. During her reverie, Olivia had entered the room and was now staring at her, waiting for her to take the papers she held.

"Oh, right," Hadley said, realizing she'd missed her cue. "Sorry. Thanks."

Olivia nodded and moved to deliver the other email printouts she'd collected on her Realm jump. Hadley quickly folded the two pieces of paper and was about to stuff them in her back pocket when they were suddenly snatched from her hand. She whirled around.

A woman who looked like she had a team of professional stylists on retainer stood behind her. Her white gown draped her body flawlessly, held together by a gold belt that matched her gold arm cuffs, necklace, and crown. She had dark hair gathered in loose curls at the nape of her neck, and eyes the color of emeralds. Her gaze narrowed as she examined the printouts in her hand.

"Tell me the meaning of these."

Hadley bristled at her superior tone. "Hello, Hera."

The Queen of the Gods stepped forward. Her face was sharp angles and hard lines, yet still beautiful. "Do not make me repeat myself, huntress."

The room grew silent again. Hadley stole a quick glance behind her. Olivia, Alice, Soxie, and David were all staring at them with blank expressions. They were no longer playing out the scene from her memory. Even the ambient noise—outside traffic, the hum of the television, the occasional bang of old pipes—had stopped. Hera's demanding presence had put her dream on pause.

Hadley glanced at the phone by the nightstand, remembering what she was supposed to do. But she hadn't counted on this particular dream visitor tonight. Hera's sometimes jealous and vindictive nature made navigating her a challenge.

"They're just old messages," she attempted to explain. "Nothing you'd be interested in."

Hera's eyes turned to slits. "Do not presume to know the desires of a goddess," she snapped. Then she waved the printouts at the wall behind her. It began to disintegrate, brick by brick, until it revealed what looked like a scene from an apocalyptic movie. Nothing but dry, cracked earth littered with rotting carcasses and animal skulls, all set beneath a sky that was devoid of clouds, sun, moon, and stars. It wasn't even a sky. It was just . . . nothing.

"This is all that is left of our world," she continued. "Your interests *are* our interests now, huntress."

Hadley stared at the dying landscape. It was so depressing, so desolate and bleak. An inexplicable sadness came over her. But why? Did she actually feel *sympathy* for the gods?

"I'm sorry," she said, squaring her shoulders. "But it's not our fault your world is dying."

Hera flicked her hand and the apocalyptic scene vanished. Then she moved to the chair by the window and sat down like she was sitting on a glass throne instead of cheap, ripped vinyl.

"You speak the truth," she said, albeit reluctantly. "The fault lies with Hades. But this changes nothing. The gods' salvation lies with the Portal of Osiris. You *will* find it for us."

Hadley glanced at the phone again, wishing there was a way to speed this dream up. "We're doing everything we can. I promise."

"Your promises mean nothing," she said dismissively. Then she seemed to remember the papers in her hand. She grinned deviously and threw them at Hadley's feet. "These *do* mean something, do they not? I see the angst in your heart. Tell me now, and perhaps I will show your dream mercy."

Hadley dropped her head in defeat. This was not something she felt like reliving, but if it placated Hera, it had to be done. She bent down to retrieve the papers and sat down on the bed. Soxie, Olivia, Alice, and David had vanished. She and Hera were alone in the room. Rather than explain the contents of the emails, Hadley decided it was easier to read them. She flattened the creases on the first printout and proceeded to read it aloud.

"*Haddy, what the hell is going on? Now the Martins are saying you kidnapped their son, David. Is this true? Why, Hadley? I didn't give up everything for you to turn into a low-life criminal like your brother. Whatever you're doing, stop and think about the consequences. I'm not ready to put you in the grave too. I'm just happy your mother isn't alive to see what you've become. You're better than this.*"

It was strange to read those words again. Their disappearance last year had raised a lot of alarms, and if it weren't for Uncle Mayron, they'd probably have ended up in jail. But in all the emails he wrote, her dad never once asked if she was okay, or said he was worried about her. She understood now that he was scared, but still. It would have been nice.

Eager to get this over with, she turned the paper over to read the email printed on the other side.

"*Hadley. Can you please talk some sense into Alice? I think she'll listen to you. I really do. I know I messed up, but what do you expect? You break into my dream and force me to tell you where the compasses are—and for what? So you can help Alice die? Because, make no mistake, that is what you're doing. Do you really want that on your conscience? I don't understand how you can be so ignorant. This isn't a game, Hadz. I know I'm not your favorite person, but I'm asking you to do the right thing. The Realm isn't worth her life. Please, Hadley. Please bring her home.*"

Despite her best efforts, her voice cracked at the end. She sat for a moment, staring at the wrinkled piece of paper. Cithaeron had typed these words when he was still Colin, when Alice believed she was doing what she had to do to save him. None of them liked it, but they were a team. Their bond wasn't something that could be explained. They would do anything for each other, including helping one of their own do the unthinkable. But Cithaeron never saw it that way. He only saw their loyalty to Alice as a betrayal to him.

"You did not do as he asked," Hera said, amused. "You were willing to let your friend die. Interesting. Perhaps you are not as weak as you seem."

As much as Hadley wanted to slap her across her royal face, she thought better of it. She let the piece of paper fall to the ground and braced herself for the last email. The one she had a feeling the queen sitting across from her was going to love.

"*Haddy Bear,*" she began, hating the sound of her old nickname. "*I hear you've gotten yourself into some trouble. Can't say I'm surprised. We apples never fall far from our trees. Pretend all you want, but you're still a Caldwell. We share the same blood, which means if I'm a monster, so are you. The sooner you face that, the better. Grandpa Frank wasn't the enemy. He was just trying to make sure we stood a chance in this fucked-up world. His old heart may have run out of beats, but yours still has plenty left. Are you really going to waste them? Going against your nature is just plain dumb. You don't want to be a dumb blond all your life, do you? So stop being one. I'm offering you my help. Take it or leave it. I'm done caring either way.*"

She finished reading and carefully folded the paper in half. It wasn't any better or worse reading those words the second time around. It was just draining. She let herself fall back on the bed, wondering why she wasn't more upset.

"Do you believe him?" Hera asked. "Do you believe you're a monster?"

"No," she said to the water-stained ceiling. "I've seen monsters. Real ones."

Hera laughed. It was a deep, guttural laugh that felt threatening. "Oh, huntress. I doubt that. But I am curious, do you believe *he* is a monster?"

Hadley closed her eyes, remembering the time she'd convinced Soxie and Olivia to help her break into Caleb's dreams. She'd been sure if they could just prove he was infected by a demon, then everything could be fixed. The dream hop was successful, but the outcome was disappointing. There was no demon. Only her brother and his anger.

"No," she answered. "He's not a monster. It would be a lot easier if he was."

Hera exhaled loudly. "*This* is the cause of the angst I see in your heart?" She made a *psh* sound and stood. "Perhaps you are as weak as you seem. I am no longer interested in this dream and have no desire to remain."

"You're leaving?" Hadley said, sitting up. It sounded too good to be true.

Hera looked like a dragon about to breathe fire. "A queen knows when to grant mercy. I will leave you to the rest of this pointless dream. But know this, huntress, if you do not produce the Portal soon, you *will* know my wrath."

A fierce cold settled on Hadley's skin. She did not want to be on the receiving end of Hera's wrath. She had a feeling it was worse than Zeus's.

"Understood."

Hera nodded, then like a cheap magic trick, she disappeared in a cloud of billowy white smoke.

Hadley dropped back onto the bed and took a moment to collect herself. Hera wasn't her favorite goddess, but she respected her. The fact that she'd decided to show her mercy only strengthened that respect. But they'd never be safe as long as the gods could come and go in their dreams at will.

She rolled over and swung her legs off the bed, taking a seat on the edge as she grabbed the phone off the nightstand. Cradling it in her lap, she lifted the receiver and dialed zero for the motel operator. She was surprised when someone answered.

"Front desk," said a bored voice. Hadley knew it was her own subconscious on the other end, but she still felt nervous about how this would play out.

"Hi. This is Hadley in Room . . ." She paused and looked around. When she spotted the room key by the window, she added, "Room 18."

"Yes?" came the curt reply.

Hadley shifted uncomfortably. "Can you please put me through to Morpheus?"

The voice on the other end was silent. Hadley held her breath, waiting. They'd agreed they would use whatever means they had in their dream stories to contact Morpheus. It just so happened Hadley had a phone in a roadside motel room.

After a few seconds, she began to second-guess herself. Maybe this was all a huge waste of time. Either way, she had nothing to lose.

"Hello?" she said.

Silence.

She was starting to get annoyed. Even if there was no way of contacting Morpheus, her subconscious didn't have to be so rude.

"Are you going to put me through or not?"

"Hold, please."

Hadley jerked to attention. She heard a click, then ringing on the other end. Her hand gripped the phone, heart racing. By the tenth ring, she started to lose hope. Did she come this far only to have him not answer? She was about to hang up when someone on the other end finally picked up.

"Morpheus," said a robotic voice.

She froze. The voice didn't sound like something her subconscious would create. It was both masculine and feminine, and completely devoid of emotion. But was it really him?

"Are you real, or is this just a part of my dream?"

"Only you can answer that question, huntress."

Her hand shook. It *felt* real, so maybe it was. "Okay," she said, fighting to keep her voice calm. "Then you're real."

"A wise answer."

She hugged the phone to her chest, choosing her next words carefully. "Do you know why I summoned you?"

"Do *you*?"

Her courage waned. She'd agreed not to ask for his help yet, so what was she supposed to say? She stared at the old television across the room, seeing her reflection in its gray glass.

"Not really," she finally admitted. "I just wanted to know if you were listening."

"I am now."

She bit her lip, unsure what to make of his response. Other than being associated with dreams, she didn't know that much about Morpheus. She popped to her feet as a thought suddenly came to her.

"Are you aware that other gods have been infiltrating our dreams?"

"Yes."

"Oh. I see," she said, wavering. She didn't expect him to answer that fast. "Doesn't this bother you?"

When he didn't answer right away, she knew she was onto something. Before he could reply, she added, "I thought dreams were *your* domain."

"Dreams belong to the dreamer. I am but the canvas on which they are painted. I cannot help you, huntress."

Her heart sank. "So you *do* know why I summoned you."

She heard what sounded like a sigh. But with a god, it was hard to tell. "Your dreams are all my world has left. They are not enough. We will not survive. Our salvation lies with the Portal of Osiris."

"So I've heard," she said drearily, her patience wearing thin. All of this was code, and none of it was helping. She knew she wasn't supposed to ask, but what if she didn't get another chance?

"Can you at least give us a few days? Let us sleep in peace so we can focus on finding your precious portal. The nightmares won't help. They'll just slow us down."

"I am the god of sleep and dreams, Hadley. If you seek to end your nightmares, you have summoned the wrong god."

Her stomach dropped, and hearing him say her name didn't help. It made her feel like he knew way more than he was letting on. She licked her dry lips. "Who should we be summoning?"

A light on the phone started blinking. She ignored it, determined to come out of this dream with something useful.

"Who should we summon?" she repeated.

"Find the Portal, huntress," was all he said. Then he hung up, leaving her staring at her warped reflection on the old television screen. Why didn't he tell her? Was he just playing games with her? She returned the phone to its cradle with a disappointed sigh. It immediately rang, making her flinch. She'd forgotten about the other line. She reluctantly picked it up.

"Hello?"

"Hadley? Hadley, wake up!"

"Alice?" she said, confused. "Where are you? What's going on?"

"You have to see this, Hadz. WAKE UP!"

Hadley opened her eyes to find Alice leaning over her, shaking her. She blinked a few times, feeling fuzzy and out of sorts. Then she pushed onto her elbows and looked around. The curtains were open, and sunlight streamed into their room.

"Finally!" Alice said, her eyes sparkling with excitement. "Hurry, you have to see this!" Then she hopped off the bed and ran into the bathroom.

Hadley rubbed the sleep from her eyes and sat up. Her mouth was dry, and her lips felt cracked. She took a quick drink from her water bottle, then groggily shuffled to the bathroom to see what all the fuss was about.

She found Alice standing in front of the mirror above the vanity, staring at her reflection. Only the reflection in the mirror wasn't hers. It was her cat, Boop. He was sitting on the counter with his usual haughty manner, tail swishing back and forth. Hadley's grogginess immediately dissipated.

"Oh wow, you did it. Your power's back! That's great!"

Alice nodded enthusiastically. "I was starting to think it would never come back."

Hadley stepped forward, happy that cat allergies didn't apply to mirror projections. She studied the image, marveling at how real it looked, as if Boop might step right through the glass and into Egypt. "Why do you think it came back now?"

Alice shrugged, eyes still on Boop. "I'm not sure. I just felt different when I woke up, so I decided to give it a try." Then she beckoned her closer. "But Hadz, there's more."

Hadley leaned back, eyeing the cat in the glass. "What do you mean?"

"You'll see."

The anticipation in her friend's voice got her attention. She'd seen plenty of Alice's projections, but she'd never seen her so excited about them. She watched closely as Alice folded herself over the sink and tapped on the mirror. Boop's head popped up and he meowed.

Hadley widened her eyes. Did that just happen? Was the projection *reacting* to Alice?

"Here, Boops," Alice called to him, pressing her nose against the mirror. The cat jumped up and tried pushing his nose into hers from the other side.

"What kind of projection is that?" Hadley reeled. It was one thing for Alice to project images onto mirrors. They'd seen her do it a hundred times. But the images had never interacted with her before.

Alice giggled as Boop meowed louder, pawing at the glass. Then he turned around and sat down with his back to them, tail twitching. A feline snub if Hadley ever saw one.

"Are you making him do that?" she asked, mesmerized.

Alice shook her head, her face flushed with pride. "No. And when it started moving on its own, I even wondered if this really *was* Boop."

Hadley had wondered the same thing. "How do you know it's not?"

"I called my mom and asked her to check on him. She said he was in the kitchen with her and the dogs. She'd just fed them breakfast."

Hadley turned back to the image in the mirror and called Boop's name to get his attention. His ears twitched in response. Needing to sit down, she lowered herself onto the edge of the tub. "This is wild."

Alice grinned and waved her hand in front of the glass. The image of Boop disappeared, replaced by her reflection. "Sorry I woke you up. But I needed one of you to see it."

"It's okay. I'm glad you did. My dream wasn't going well anyway."

Alice gave her a halfhearted smile. "You couldn't reach Morpheus either?"

"No, I did," she said, leaning her head back to stare at the ceiling. "He just didn't tell me what I wanted to hear."

chapter 10

Hadley watched the city of Cairo fly by from the back seat of Sam's Mercedes. The windows were tinted dark, and through her sunglasses, day appeared to be night. Yet it was just after 3:00 p.m., and while she didn't feel rested, at least they had all managed to get a few hours of sleep.

Olivia twisted around from the front seat, eyeing Sam's earbuds. He was listening to classical music at such a high volume that he'd be hard-pressed to hear a foghorn if they blew it in his ear.

"Morpheus had to be referring to Melinoë," she said grimly. "She's the only one that makes sense."

A hush fell over them. Hadley knew Olivia was right, but knowing was different from understanding.

"Then why didn't he just say her name?" she finally asked.

Soxie exhaled loudly. "She's the goddess of nightmares and madness. If you say her name, she probably pops up behind you like the Candyman."

"I'm sure it's more complicated than that," Olivia said with an eye roll. "But even so, none of us is stupid enough to summon Melinoë, and Morpheus knows it." Then she turned her attention to Alice, who sat in the middle. "Did Persephone ever mention her to you?"

Alice tensed. "No. I forgot she even had a daughter. Do you think they were close? 'Cause I'd hate to think Melinoë is helping the gods torture us for revenge."

"Is there a better reason?" asked Soxie.

"You know what I mean. Demeter already blames me for Persephone being gone. What if Melinoë does too? Do you think that's what this is really about?"

Olivia shook her head. "No. The gods want the Portal. That's what this is about. I'm disappointed that Morpheus can't help us, but at least you got your powers back. That's a win, right? Tell me again how it happened."

Hadley turned to look out the window as Alice walked Soxie and Olivia through the return of her powers, the one piece of good news they'd had in days. Morpheus was a bust, and Melinoë was a non-starter. But at least Alice's power coming back meant the mirrors would go back to normal—no more glitches. Or so they hoped.

Hadley lost track of the conversation as she let herself get lost in the changing scenery. One minute they were passing high-rise office buildings and fancy hotels. The next, modest structures made from concrete blocks and the occasional fruit stand. Most of the women she spotted were covered head to toe despite the mild temperature. It was a fascinating city, with so much to see. If they didn't have a portal to track down, it would have been nice to explore Cairo, maybe do some shopping in a nearby *souk*, or take a *felucca* ride on the Nile.

"Um, Hadley?" asked Olivia. "Are we boring you?"

Hadley pulled her gaze from the window and sat up. "Sorry. I think my brain is turning to mush. Yes, I agree. Or wait, what were we talking about?"

"We're talking about how Melinoë wasn't exactly the product of a happy home," Olivia informed her. "Zeus is her father *and* her grandfather. Think about that."

"That's so wrong," Hadley cringed. "Poor Persephone."

"Exactly. But they're gods. The myths are riddled with these kind of stories. It's dangerous to assume they share the same morals as we do. It's also dangerous to assume Morpheus was telling you the truth, Hadley."

"He didn't sound like he was lying," she argued. "In fact, he sounded kind of nice. At least compared to Hera. Though to be fair, she was nicer than she's ever been. Don't get me wrong, she still threatened me. But she didn't torment me. Not this time, anyway."

"Consider yourself lucky," scoffed Soxie. "I got Hephaestus, and let me tell you, legend had it right. That is one unfortunate-looking god. I was dreaming about my first Christmas with Mayron when that ugly SOB showed up. First, he lit the tree on fire, then he used the flames to forge a dagger just so he could brand me with it like a steer. After that, he stuffed me inside one of my own presents, wrapped me up with a bow, and reminded me that the clock is ticking. Ugly bastard."

"Yikes," said Olivia. "But if it helps, I had to take Artemis hunting, and she knows how I feel about animals. It was awful."

"Did she make you relive any bad memories?" asked Hadley.

"Just one. Pretty much the same one they all like to use." She stopped and turned back to face front. Hadley leaned forward and placed a hand on her shoulder.

"Hammacher?" she asked.

Olivia nodded, and Hadley turned back to the window. Other than the vicious brutes who used to guard the Boneyard, she'd never spent much time with dogs until she met the Roxland Dobermans, Hammacher and Schlemmer. Hammacher was a good dog, and she gave her life to save Alice. It was a sad day, for all of them.

"What about you, Alice?" Hadley asked, eager to change the subject. "Who did you get?"

She sighed wearily. "After I realized my powers were back, I wasn't going to say anything. I figured maybe our luck was changing. But now that I know Morpheus can't help us, I might as well tell you. You'll find out sooner or later."

"Find out what?" asked Olivia. "Who visited your dream?"

"Zeus. And he didn't even bother with a past memory. He just showed me our future if we don't comply."

They all looked at her. "And?" asked Soxie.

She took a breath. "It was a mirror image of our graves. The names were written backward, and even though we were supposed to be dead, I heard us screaming. It was a warning."

"A warning?" Olivia repeated, her voice pitched higher than usual. The car turned and came to a stop in front of a security gate. Sam pulled out an earbud and rolled down the window to speak to the guard.

Alice glanced at the exchange and lowered her voice. "I think he was telling us that not even death will save us."

"Okay, friends!" said Sam jovially, making them all flinch. "We are here! You are ready to learn about fine Egyptian history, yes?" Then he drove them inside the gate to drop them off at the museum entrance, as if they hadn't just been dropped on their asses by Alice's revelation.

The Museum of Cairo was housed in a massive building with upper and lower floors connected by a central hall. Hadley spotted several armed security guards stationed near the entrance, and she had no doubt there would be more scattered throughout the building. She assumed there were also plenty of cameras pointed at each antiquity from varying angles—similar to a Vegas casino. It made her nervous about what they were about to find. If the base of the statue wasn't visible, they were in big trouble. Stealing a priceless piece of Egyptian history was unethical, not to mention impossible.

"Don't panic until we have a reason to panic," Olivia whispered under her breath. "Besides, I think we passed unethical last year when we buried a body in the desert."

Hadley gave her a hard look before dumping her phone in the bowl by the metal detector and walking through. The rest of them followed without incident. Then they made their way to the central hall while Alice handed them each a folded museum directory.

"Here. This will tell us where the statue is. And remember, no flash photography. We're allowed to take pictures, but make sure your flash is off."

Hadley pulled out her phone and changed the settings on her camera. As she stuffed it back in her pocket, she took a second to look around. The central hall was two stories high with large columns and shallow levels of its own, separated by wide sets of stone stairs. Above them, she saw people walking on the second floor, some of them looking down on the hall from behind a gallery railing. The interior was palatial and grand, which seemed fitting. The artifacts housed within were, after all, priceless pieces of human history.

Hadley walked toward what had to be a sarcophagus. The lid was separated from the base, which was positioned a few feet away in the center of the hall. Both were made of stone, and the lid alone had to weigh two hundred pounds. It was ornately carved, with a figure lying on top in a perpetual state of repose.

Soxie walked up beside her. "These things creep me out."

Hadley frowned, wanting desperately to run her fingers along the cold stone, but decided it wasn't respectful, and probably not allowed. "Why?" she said as she inspected the carved face. "I think it's beautiful. Imagine the time it took for someone to make this and have it survive this long."

Soxie shivered next to her. "Exactly. This one is what—three, four thousand years old? Call me crazy, but I don't want strangers four thousand years from now staring at what used to be my coffin. Cremate me and throw me in the ocean if you have to. Just promise me I'll never be on display."

"You won't know the difference, so what does it matter?"

"Apparently I will, if we don't find the Portal. Now come on. This map says the Osiris statue is on the second level."

Hadley's stomach turned at the thought, and she let herself get pulled away without complaint. They had no way of knowing if Zeus's threat to Alice was real, but the idea that they could still be screaming in their own coffins four thousand years from now was reason enough to stay focused.

They followed Alice up the stairs to the second level, where they passed glass cases that housed everything from ancient pottery to intricate gold jewelry. The museum was organized by time period, and without a tour or audio guide, it was intimidating. Luckily, Alice seemed to know where she was going, until suddenly she stopped. The three of them nearly ran into her.

"Look at that," she said, pointing at a catlike sculpture.

Hadley moved forward to read the plaque, and despite the urgency of their situation, she grinned. "The likeness is uncanny."

"I'm sure Boop wouldn't mind if we worshipped him like Bastet."

Soxie chuckled. "It makes you wonder, though. What happened to Bastet? Or Osiris, for that matter? We know what happened to the Greek gods. We're living that nightmare right now. But what happened to all of *them*?" She stopped, pointing at the antiquities surrounding them.

Hadley couldn't help but wonder herself. It was a question they'd bandied about for some time. Up until a year ago, the only gods they encountered were those of ancient Greece: Persephone, Hades, the Furies. It wasn't until they learned that Alice's soul was stolen from an Egyptian god that they realized other gods existed too.

"Maybe they lost humanity the same way the Greek gods did," suggested Olivia.

Hadley pondered the idea. "You think—the comet? You think it took humanity away from them too?"

Olivia shrugged. "It makes sense. Why else would they have disappeared?"

Hadley turned back to the statue of Bastet. It was bronze with gold accents. Very haughty, and very Boop-like. But was she real? And did Ptah's Fire—or Bolle-Marin, as they knew it—take the ancient Egyptians away from her and her fellow gods? The comet only showed up once every twenty-five hundred years. If it was powerful enough to banish the Greek gods to another dimension, then it could have done the same to the Egyptian gods. And as they'd come to learn, gods don't do well when they no longer have mortals to worship them. Olivia was right. It was the only explanation that made sense.

"Let's just hope wherever they went, they stay there," said Soxie. "We've got our hands full with one set of gods as it is."

"Right," said Alice, nodding. Then she consulted her glossy map, all business, and continued to lead the way.

A few turns and several corridors later, she came to a stop and lowered her map. "Here it is."

They collectively held their breath as they gathered behind her. The statue looked exactly as it did on the website, though encased in glass, and maybe a little smaller than Hadley had expected. The placard said it was made of graywacke, whatever that was. But there didn't seem to be any other information available. No provenance, no dynasty, no place of discovery—nothing. It was like the thing just showed up one day, in all its imposing glory. The expression on the statue's face was a cross between happy and smug, like he had a secret he'd been dying to tell for centuries.

Alice stepped closer and lightly trailed a finger down the glass. "I don't feel anything," she confessed. "If my soul once belonged to him, shouldn't I feel *something*?"

"Maybe you never really belonged to him," Olivia speculated.

Alice's head spun around. "What do you mean? Zeus told us that Hades stole my soul from Osiris."

"Yes, but who's to say Osiris didn't steal it too?"

"From who?" asked Hadley. Soxie just nodded, equally curious.

Olivia gave the ceiling an exasperated look. "We're talking five thousand years ago. You can't expect me to have that answer."

Hadley looked at Alice. She'd started twisting a lock of her hair, deep in thought. The idea felt . . . big. Bigger than they had time for right now.

"Okay," Hadley said, pulling out her phone, eager to get what they came for. "We're here. Let's see what Osiris has to say."

They had a 360-degree view of the base, so getting a shot of the missing hieroglyphs was easy. But as they looked over the photos back at the hotel, their momentum came to a halt.

"It's a pyramid," insisted Olivia, hands on her hips. "How many times do I have to tell you?"

"One more time would be great."

She shot Soxie a dirty look, then marched to the desk and pointed at her laptop. Displayed on the screen were three symbols: one that looked like a falcon, an elongated oval with pointed edges, and a triangle atop a thin rectangle. Then she pointed at the close-up picture of the Osiris statue on Hadley's phone.

"They're exactly the same," she said. "It's a pyramid hieroglyph."

Soxie leaned back and crossed her legs with a sigh. "Fine. It's a pyramid. But we're in Egypt. What are we supposed to do with this information?"

Hadley walked over to the minibar and grabbed a bottle of water. She held the cold plastic to the back of her neck and asked the room, "How many pyramids are there?"

"Over a hundred," answered Olivia.

Soxie groaned. "Great. Now what? We can't search a hundred pyramids. I doubt we can search one!"

"We don't have to," Alice piped up. Hadley turned to look at her. She was sitting in the chair by the window, tapping away on her own laptop. She spun it around so they could all see the screen. On it was information for a tourism site offering private guided tours.

"The Osiris Shaft," Hadley read aloud. "What is that?"

Alice smiled. "It's not so much what, but where."

Soxie groaned again. "Well? I hate when you guys do this, by the way. When you have information, just—"

"It's beneath the Khafre Pyramid," Alice said loudly.

"Which one is that?"

"It's the second-largest pyramid on the Giza Plateau, right next to the Great Pyramid."

Hadley felt some hope rush back in. Now they were getting somewhere. "Okay, so can we get in? Is there a tour tonight?"

Alice turned the laptop back around and shook her head. "No. We have to arrange it privately. I'm emailing with them now; looks like they have an opening tomorrow afternoon, but it's not cheap." She paused and looked up.

They all turned to Soxie. She took a deep breath and said, "Piggy bank Roxland to the rescue again. How much?"

"Two thousand US," Alice said, grimacing.

Soxie laughed. "That's it? I thought you were going to say ten thousand."

"Wow. You're not exactly in touch with the common man, are you?"

Hadley and Olivia stifled laughs, but Soxie narrowed her eyes and stood. "It's a good thing I love you, Daniels," she said. "Otherwise, I might be offended." Then with a flip of her curls, she turned around and headed into the adjoining room.

"Sorry!" Alice called after her.

Soxie answered by slamming the door behind her.

Alice pulled the laptop up like a shield and peeked over the top. "Did I go too far?"

"No, don't worry about it," said Hadley. "She's always been a little weird about her money."

Olivia fell stomach-first onto the bed. "Yeah, we used to tease her about it too. It's hard not to. It's an obscene amount of money."

Alice set her computer back on her lap. It was after six, and the sky over the Nile behind her was dimming, making her white hair glow around her head like a halo.

"I don't even want to know," she said, then snapped the laptop shut and stood. "But I better go apologize. Why don't you guys head down to the restaurant? We'll meet you there."

They agreed and watched as Alice softly knocked on the door to the adjoining room and let herself in, closing the door behind her. Olivia rolled off the bed and joined Hadley by the window.

"Is Soxie really mad?" Hadley asked her.

"No. She's just cranky. Lack of good sleep does that."

Hadley took a drink of water and stared out the window. The sun set over the west bank, casting gold and silver flecks across the river's surface. The call to prayer sounded in the distance. It was calming and peaceful, which felt strange considering how chaotic their lives were at the moment.

"Well," she said, taking the seat Alice just vacated. "We can't get into this Osiris Shaft until tomorrow. Any chance we can stay up all night? I'm tired of reliving bad memories. I miss my old dreams, when the worst that happened was my teeth falling out or being late for Biology."

Olivia pursed her lips. "Those are anxiety dreams, Hadz. Your subconscious was already trying to show you something. The gods just found a way to pull back the curtain."

"And that's a good thing?"

"No. But I'm starting to think it's not the worst either. I know it sounds morbid, but reliving Hammacher's death has helped me let her go. I never really tried before because thinking about her was too painful. But that pain—that anger—it doesn't go away. We have to face it sooner or later."

Hadley turned back to the river. The call to prayer still chimed throughout the city, giving the golden sunset a magical feel. "But what if the anger is all you have left?"

She felt a hand close over hers. "You let it go anyway. And when you do, we'll be there to help you if you fall."

Hadley wiped away a rogue tear from the corner of her eye. "Thanks, honey. I appreciate that. And maybe you're right. Maybe reliving painful memories can be healing. But it should be *our* choice, not the gods'. We have to find a way to get them out of our dreams."

Olivia removed her hand and sat back. "Don't even think about trying Melinoë, Hadley. We've got enough problems as it is."

"I won't," she promised. "But speaking of problems, one of us has to call David and fill him in. He's left me three voicemails already."

Olivia pushed her chair back and stood. "I'll rock, paper, scissors you for it."

"Yeah, because that's fair."

She shrugged. "That's life."

Hadley shook her head and pulled out her phone. "Let's just fast-forward to when you read my mind and cover my rock with paper."

Olivia smiled wide, then skipped out the door. "See you downstairs. Say hi to David for me!"

chapter 11

Hadley never made it down to dinner. The conversation with David took over an hour, and by the time she hung up, she was too tired to join the others downstairs. Instead, she ordered a club sandwich from room service and ate it in silence as she stared out the window. It was dark, and she saw more of her own reflection than the river outside, but she wasn't in the mood to turn on the television or scroll mindlessly through her phone.

She dipped a soggy fry in ketchup and popped it in her mouth, thinking about her conversation with David. She'd tried being patient with him, but it was like telling a story to a toddler who keeps interrupting. He had to know every single detail, right down to the make and model of the car Sam was driving them around in. She knew it was hard for him to be so far removed from the action, but it was also his own choice.

The door behind her opened, and Alice walked in. "Hey," she said as she took off her jacket.

Hadley finished chewing and pushed her plate aside, wiping her hands on her jeans. "How was dinner? Where are Olivia and Soxie?"

Alice tossed her jacket on the bed and sank to the floor in front of it, leaning her back against it. "They're talking to the concierge.

One of the ballrooms downstairs has a mirrored ceiling—we spotted it on the way to dinner. They're asking if we can reserve it tonight."

"Why?"

"Olivia wants us to try dream hopping each other. She thinks if we can dream together, it'll be easier to handle what the gods throw at us."

Hadley rested her cheek in her palm, thinking. "But we don't have our compasses. How does she expect it to work?"

"Well, we've done it before, remember? With Coli—sorry. David." She paused, staring vacantly at the minibar in front of her.

Hadley nodded. Yes, she remembered that dream hop all too well. It was the catalyst to their three months on the run, when Alice was forced to destroy demons to save her soulmate.

"When you talked to David . . . how did he sound?" she asked. "Did you tell him what's going on?"

Hadley moved to sit on the floor next to her. "I told him about the hieroglyphs and our lead on the Khafre Pyramid. And he sounded just like you'd expect. Worried. He misses you, Alice."

She stared straight ahead. "Did you tell him I recovered my powers?"

"No," Hadley replied, hesitating. "I thought that would be better coming from you."

Alice looked down. "Thank you. I'd rather he didn't know. At least, not yet."

"Honey, he's your fiancé. He's your *soulmate*. Don't you think he has a right to know?"

She shook her head. "He'll think it's because we're not together. My powers returning now will only strengthen his argument. So yes, he has a right to know. But I have the right not to tell him."

Hadley took a breath. "Fine. I support you no matter what. But I know if the roles were reversed, you'd want to know. You'd believe you have a *right* to know."

Alice turned to her, accusation in her eyes. "That's harsh, Hadz."

"I'm sorry, but I'm not going to lie to you. David isn't my favorite person in the world, but you are. And I hate that you feel like you have to choose between him and us. It shouldn't be that way. You'll only end up resenting us in the end, and that would break my heart."

Alice gave her a small smile and took hold of her hand. "That's why we're here, so I don't have to choose. But no matter what happens, I'd never resent you, Hadz. I love you to the moon and back. You know that."

Hadley unfolded herself from the floor and pulled Alice to her feet, hugging her tight. Her white hair was soft beneath her chin and smelled of lavender and mint. Hadley breathed her in, happy for this simple moment.

"I love you too, silly. Now tell me more about this dream hop."

The room they reserved was on the smaller side and looked more like a dance club than a swanky hotel ballroom. The walls were dark, and the carpet was a garish crimson-and-gold design. Electric candles flickered on top of black cocktail tables, and in the center of the room hung a disco ball that was far too big for the space. As promised, though, the ceiling was paneled with mirrors.

Hadley helped Alice push some of the tables aside to make room while Soxie and Olivia created their makeshift beds in the middle.

"How long do we have the room for?" Hadley asked Soxie.

"Till eight a.m. I told them we needed it for a midnight group meditation."

A loud cheer erupted from down the hall, followed by the sound of drums and an electric guitar. They all turned toward the noise.

"Sounds like the wedding reception next door is just getting started."

"I've got it covered," Olivia assured them as she passed out earplugs.

Hadley glanced at her reflection in the ceiling as she stuffed the plugs in her ears. "I wish we had our compasses," she said.

"They only worked because they were connected to the Realm," Olivia pointed out, her voice now dampened. "But we're still connected to each other by Philautia's soul. If we can't stop the gods from invading our dreams, at least we can try facing them together."

Soxie kicked off her heels and dropped onto the pile of blankets. "Hear, hear."

Hadley followed suit and sat on the floor to unzip her boots. She was all for this idea because they were always better together. She just hoped her friends didn't have to suffer through her painful memories. It was bad enough reliving them herself.

Olivia shot her a compassionate look before busying herself arranging their pillows. Hadley set her boots aside and got up to dim the lights. She couldn't figure out how to turn off the disco ball, so it continued its slow spin, reflecting a thousand beads of light around the room. On her way back, she grabbed a few candles and handed them out. Even if the candlelight was fake, it would help them relax.

They took their spots on the blanket and linked hands. With their heads in the center, and their feet pointing outward, they formed a four-pointed star. Candles flickered between them, giving them just enough light to see. Their hair pooled beneath them, Alice's almost disappearing against her white pillow. The music next door didn't let up, but the bass consistently thumped through the floor in a rhythmic way, enhancing the short meditation Soxie guided them through. Once she finished, they met each other's eyes in the mirror.

"Okay," said Soxie. "Are we ready?"

They nodded, and she began. She started with breathing cues, waiting until it seemed they were all breathing as one. Then her cues got further and further apart. Hadley's eyes felt heavy, but she forced herself to keep them open, determined to stay focused. Their previous dream hops had been in other people's dreams, with the help of a compass and a piece of the dreamer's DNA. They'd never tried dream hopping each other. If this was going to work, they had to try and fall asleep at the same time. They had to be *that* connected.

Hadley kept moving her gaze methodically, making eye contact with each pair of eyes before moving on to the next. The bass thumped, and tiny squares of light floated over them with every turn of the disco ball. The result was surprisingly tranquil, as if they were lying at the bottom of a shallow Caribbean sea with sunlight breaking through the surface.

"Breathe in, breathe out," Soxie chanted.

They inhaled at the same time, then everything froze.

Hadley blinked, then frowned when her reflection didn't blink with her. It just lay there, mid-inhale, same as the rest.

"Seriously?" griped Soxie. "Not again."

They all sat up, craning their necks to see their reflections overhead.

"Why is it still getting stuck?" asked Alice. "I thought once my powers returned, the mirrors would be fixed."

"I thought so too," Olivia said, dejected.

Hadley ran her hands down her face and stood. She grabbed the nearest banquet chair and stepped onto it. But even balancing on her toes, she was too short to reach the ceiling. With a groan, she hopped off and started to drag one of the cocktail tables over.

"Can one of you steady this while I climb up?"

The three of them stepped forward and held the table as Hadley climbed. Once she felt balanced, she reached up and touched the glass. But the image didn't unfreeze. Determined, she rose onto her toes again, pressing both palms into the mirror. Their reflections remained stuck.

"Well this is new," said Soxie. "What now?"

Hadley dropped her arms and glanced at the double doors, only then noticing how quiet it was. What happened to the music?

"Guys . . ." said Alice, her voice tinged with fear. They all turned and followed her gaze. She was staring at the floor beneath the disco ball.

"Oh my god," exclaimed Soxie.

Hadley's mouth dropped open, and she nearly toppled off the table because she, Olivia, Soxie, and Alice were still lying on the floor in a four-pointed star, fast asleep. Hadley stared at her sleeping twin, wondering if this was what it felt like to have an out-of-body experience.

Dream Olivia suddenly let out a loud whoop, nearly giving them all a heart attack. "We did it! We're dreaming together!"

Hadley's eyes darted around the room. Everything looked the same. If it weren't for their actual bodies snoozing in the middle of the room, she'd have no way of knowing this was a dream. She hopped off the table and headed for the double doors.

"Hadley, wait," called Olivia. "We have to stick together. If we separate, we may not be able to find each other again."

She stopped and turned around. "Right. So what do we do? Just hang out in here until we wake up?"

Olivia eyed the doors warily. "I have a feeling those lead to our dreams."

"Then what is this?" Soxie asked, gesturing to the room they were standing in.

"An entry point?" suggested Olivia. "We've never done this before. Maybe the only way to connect our dreams is to first create a point of entry, which we just did."

"So if our dreams are out there," Alice began, pointing to the doors, "I vote we stay in here."

Hadley glanced at the doors, the urge to open them immense. But Alice was right. If their dreams were behind those doors, then so were the gods. They were safer in here. She made her way back to her body and took a seat next to it.

"Get comfortable, girls. This is going to be a long dream."

"I'm so bored," Soxie complained. She was lying on top of a table, legs dangling, staring at the mirrored ceiling. "Shouldn't we be able to conjure up some cards at least?"

"Doesn't look like it," replied Olivia. "Not in here, anyway."

Hadley finished braiding her sleeping doppelgänger's hair. She'd already done the same to the rest of her snoozing companions. Meanwhile, Olivia and Alice sat at one of the tables, chins in hands, staring into space.

"If only we could just sleep," Alice grumped.

Olivia nodded at the figures on the floor. "We are sleeping."

She snorted. "You know what I mean."

Hadley finished her work and stood. She agreed with Alice. Sleeping through their sleep would be so much easier. But they'd already tried it, and it didn't work. They couldn't fall asleep. This entry point felt like a waiting room at a doctor's office with no Wi-Fi and nothing to read. With wishful thinking, she pulled out her phone again. The screen refused to unlock. She shoved it in her pocket and started walking in figure eights because she couldn't think of anything better to do.

"How long do you think we've been in here?" she asked no one in particular. Then she glanced at her watch out of habit. The hands were stuck on the time they entered: 8:12 p.m.

"It's got to be three hours at least. Maybe four," mumbled Soxie. "What time did you set the alarm for?"

"Seven," Hadley answered with a sigh. Which meant they still had hours of mindless boredom to kill. She dropped her hands to the ground and kicked her legs up into a handstand. She walked forward a few feet, holding in her core for balance. Then a loud rap on the double doors sent her stomach into her throat. She tumbled over and shot straight to her feet, just as the rest of them did.

They all looked at each other. Olivia pressed her index finger to her mouth and shook her head, urging them to keep quiet. Hadley glanced at the doors. She'd never advanced past her junior black belt—being a huntress had taken priority—but she still knew how to defend herself. In real life, that is. But this was a dream, and the same rules never applied.

Rap. Rap. Rap.

The slow uniformity of the knock threatened to shatter her already brittle nerves. She lifted her hands up and mouthed, *What do we do?*

No one moved. Whatever was on the other side of that door clearly knew they were in there. She figured if it could get inside, it would have. Maybe it needed an invitation, like a vampire. If that was the case, all they had to do was wait it out.

BANG. BANG. BANG.

They jumped. If Hadley was still wearing her boots, she would have flown right out of them. They immediately closed ranks in the middle of the room, huddling next to their bodies. The last knock nearly blew the doors off their hinges. What happened if they opened? She glanced at their bodies, willing them to wake up.

Her phone buzzed loudly in her pocket, making her flinch. She pulled it out and stared at the screen, unable to believe what she was seeing. She looked up. The girls stared at her, eyes wide and expectant. She turned the phone for them to see.

Morpheus? Alice mouthed.

What do I do?

Olivia gestured to the phone. *Answer it.*

BANG. BANG. BANG.

The doors splintered and cracked, and terror wrapped itself around them like a cold blanket. Hadley fumbled with the phone, hands shaking. It continued vibrating, informing her simply that Morpheus was calling. She sucked in a breath and answered.

"Hello?"

"You cannot hide from dreams, huntress."

She swallowed, eyes locked with Olivia's. "Why not? We've been doing a good job so far."

"You are mistaken. You have avoided nothing."

Her blood simmered, despite her fear. "If the gods insist on tormenting us, then you can't blame us for finding a safe place to wait them out. So bang on the doors all you want. We've already lasted a few hours. We can last a few more."

He laughed softly. "No, huntress. The clock does not start until you pass through those doors."

She crinkled her brow. "What do you mean?"

"You have paused the hands of time," he said matter-of-factly. "If you do not leave this room, you never will."

Olivia's face turned white as she listened to the conversation in Hadley's mind.

"How do I know this isn't some ploy to get us to leave?" she asked forcefully. "Why should I trust you?"

"You should never trust a god," he said simply. And that's when she knew he was telling the truth. Because only a trustworthy god would say that. She closed her eyes and shook her head.

"I understand. Thank you for telling me."

When he didn't answer, she pulled the phone from her ear. The screen was locked again, as if the call never took place. She fell to the floor and put her face in her hands.

"What?" shouted Soxie. "What did he say?"

"It was a courtesy call," Olivia explained. "He was letting us know that we aren't waiting out anything. Time stopped when we arrived, and it won't start again until we leave."

"Wait, what? For everyone, or just us?"

"Does it matter?"

Hadley couldn't help but laugh. They'd been hiding in this room, thinking they found a perfect—albeit boring—loophole against the gods. But all they'd really done was park their subconsciouses in some kind of never-ending waiting room from hell. She pushed off the floor and stood.

"Well, I guess that settles it," she said, pulling on her boots. The rest of them exchanged resigned looks and readied themselves before moving to the double doors. A second later, they smiled with bravado, linked hands, and entered their dreams.

chapter 12

Hadley braced herself as the doors swung open, fully prepared to deal with whatever had been banging on the other side. But the hall was empty.

They looked at each other and tentatively stepped forward. Hadley swiveled her head back and forth. While it looked like a normal hotel hallway, it appeared to go on forever in each direction. It reminded her of the infinite hallways of the Realm, without the mirrors or side passages. But this one had doors. Many, many doors—and each was conveniently labeled. With no immediate threat apparent, they unlinked hands and spread out to investigate.

Hadley made her way to the nearest door and read the placard aloud. "'Falling.'" She scrunched her face and stepped back. "What's that supposed to mean?"

"This one reads 'Flying,'" said Alice. Then she turned to Olivia, two doors down. "What does yours say?"

"'Being Chased,'" she replied.

Soxie laughed. "This one says, 'Teeth Falling Out.'"

Hadley walked past a few more doors, reading their placards aloud as she went. "'Naked in Public,' 'Missing a Test,' 'Drowning.'" She paused, getting an eerie feeling. "This is so bizarre. So we just choose which dream we feel like having?"

"I think it's safe to say we're already dreaming," said Olivia. "But since we're linked, our collective subconscious came up with this system to organize our dreams. It's kind of cool, don't you think?"

"Sure, I guess," Hadley answered. It felt a little too good to be true. She passed another door, which said "Failing Brakes." An entire dream devoted to driving and not being able to brake? That didn't sound *too* awful. Better than drowning. She'd already had that dream, thanks to Poseidon.

"Aha! I found the door to our memories," Soxie announced. "At least we know not to open this one."

Hadley walked over to read the placard for herself. It said simply, "Memories." She frowned and peered down the hall. "I feel like this is some sort of trap. What happens if we don't choose?"

"Why wouldn't we?" countered Alice. "I've always loved dreams about flying. What if we all chose that one?"

"I could get on board with that," said Soxie.

Olivia was lingering by a door that said "Dogs." Hadley could tell she wanted to open it, but instead she nodded once and turned around. "Okay," she said with finality. "I'm good with flying too."

Hadley still had her reservations about opening any of these doors, but staying together was more important than choosing the wrong door. Once they were gathered in front of the door marked "Flying," Alice grabbed hold of the handle and turned.

The door remained closed.

She tried the handle again, jiggling it to be sure, but the door held fast. She stomped her foot like a frustrated child and turned to Hadley. "Do you wanna give it a try?"

Hadley nodded and stepped forward. But as she reached for the lock pick she kept in her boot, she stopped short of retrieving it. A closer look at the door told her there was no point. There was no keyhole or cylinder casing, nothing to insert her hook rake and turner into. They might as well be standing on the wrong side of an emergency exit.

"There's no locking mechanism," she said, pointing at the handle. "I can't pick a lock if there's no lock to pick—even in a dream."

"Well that sucks," Soxie commented, though she didn't sound surprised. "Guess we're not flying tonight. So which one do we try next?"

Hadley glanced down the long hallway, then at Olivia. "How about 'Dogs'?"

Olivia's eyes brightened, and she immediately moved to the door in question. They all crowded around her, decision made. She grabbed the handle and turned, but the door wouldn't budge. The rest of them sighed and stepped back. Clearly this wasn't going to be as easy as they thought. Olivia's shoulders slumped and she turned around, leaning her back against the door.

"Guys, I don't think—"

It happened so fast none of them had a chance to react. The door behind her suddenly opened, and she fell through. By the time Hadley registered what was going on, the door had already slammed shut.

"Olivia!" she shouted, leaping forward. She yanked on the handle hard, pressing her shoulder into the door. But like before, it remained locked. Finally, she gave up and turned around. Soxie and Alice were standing a few feet away, faces tight with worry.

"Now what?" she breathed.

Soxie shook her head. "So much for staying together. Do you think . . . Alice, what are you doing?"

Alice had moved away from them and was now walking slowly down the center of the hall, pausing to read each set of doors before continuing forward. It looked like she was searching for one in particular.

"Alice?" Hadley called after her.

If she heard her, she didn't let on. Instead she kept walking, stopping when she appeared to find the door she was looking for. Only then did she turn to look at them.

"It says 'David,'" she said blankly. "I have to open it."

Hadley's stomach rolled as she watched her reach for the handle. "Wait! What if it's—"

But it was too late. The door suddenly flew open, sucking Alice into another dream before slamming shut with a resounding bang. Hadley froze with her hand up in front of her, as if the gesture alone could stop what could no longer be stopped.

"What were you going to say—that it might be the wrong David?" asked Soxie.

Hadley dropped her hand, despondent. "Yes. But it doesn't really matter. None of this is a choice."

"Meaning?"

She swept her arm in a wide arc. "Our dreams aren't letting us choose just any door. They're waiting for us to choose the *right* door. And it's different for each of us."

Soxie looked down and stabbed the red-and-gold carpet with her heel. "So which door is calling to you?"

As much as she didn't want to admit it, the "Memories" door was calling to her. She feared it as much as craved it, which probably meant it was the only door that would open for her tonight.

"'Memories,' unfortunately," she answered.

Soxie looked up. "Me too."

"Really? Maybe we can still try it together!"

But their hope evaporated the moment they stepped up to the door, because the placard no longer read "Memories." It read "Serenity Lodge." Soxie's expression turned dark.

"Well now I know what I'm dreaming about tonight."

Hadley placed a hand on her arm. "I'm sorry, Sox. I wish I could go with you."

She took a breath and squared her shoulders. "It's okay. I'm still learning to accept the things I cannot change, right? Besides, as rehabs go, this one wasn't so bad."

Hadley smiled and gave her a fierce hug. "I'll see you soon," she whispered, her face buried in curls. Then she stepped back and watched as Soxie opened the door and disappeared. This time, the door closed softly behind her with a barely audible click.

Now that she was alone in the hallway, Hadley felt an overwhelming urge to run. She couldn't explain why; she just had to start running. So she did. She ran and ran, doors of dreams flying past her faster and faster. A strange sense of urgency pushed her forward, as if the door she sought might disappear at any moment.

Suddenly, there it was, lit from above by an unseen light. The placard read "Johanna Caldwell." Hadley didn't hesitate. She stepped right up and turned the handle.

Wind whipped through her hair as the convertible sped across the desert. The wings on the dashboard angel flapped like mad, making it look like a divine hummingbird. Hadley smiled and lifted her arms in the air.

"Woohoo!" she squealed. Her voice was immediately swallowed by the rushing wind.

Her mom laughed and whooped along with her before turning the radio up. It was a song from the '90s by a band named Oasis. Hadley didn't know the words, but she pretended to sing along anyway. She pressed her hands into the wind, pushing against it as the Shelby's engine roared.

There were no other cars on the road. It was just them, barreling down the highway at questionable speeds. For miles, the desert stretched in all directions. Dusty earth and rocks, saguaro cacti, and the occasional acacia tree dotted the landscape. Above them, the sun blazed against a sky as blue as her mom's eyes.

Hadley turned to look at her as she belted out the last verse. Her face was radiant and sun-kissed, and her light brown hair floated around her in slow motion as if she were singing underwater. But it was her smile that Hadley loved more than anything. It was warm and carefree. It drew people into her orbit, like her happiness alone was a bright, shining star. Hadley relished these times together when it was just her, her mom, and the open road.

The song abruptly ended. She turned to catch her mom looking at her.

"You know, honey, we never actually did this."

A painful longing ripped through Hadley's core. She preferred believing it was real, that this was a memory she shared with her dead mother. She glanced at the dashboard angel, wings still flapping like crazy. It all felt so real. The noise. The wind. The sun on her face. It made the truth feel unfair and cruel.

"I know," she finally said. "I just wish we had."

Her mom reached across and patted Hadley's cheek. "Me too."

"Touching, but unproductive," said a voice behind them. Hadley's head snapped around.

A man with long black hair sat in the back seat. His skin was ghostly pale, making his deep crimson eyes glow. He was clad head to toe in black, and shiny iridescent wings sprouted from his back, capturing the wind like sails on a sailboat.

She'd already known who he was before she turned around. His voice had given him away, yet his scent was surprising. It was difficult to place—a combination of burning leaves and rotting fruit—yet it was subtle and oddly pleasing.

"It's nice to meet you in person, Morpheus," she said.

The corner of his mouth lifted, and he glanced at the driver's seat. "You may go."

Her mom nodded and brought the car to a stop on the side of the road. Then she unbuckled her seatbelt and exited, leaving the keys in the ignition. Hadley pulled against her seatbelt, trying to unbuckle it.

"Mom! Wait!"

Johanna Caldwell turned around and smiled. "I love you, Hadley," she said, "but it's time to let me go." Then she blew her a kiss and walked away, her body silhouetted against the setting sun.

Hadley felt a fissure of sadness open up in her dream like a sinkhole. The ground beneath them rocked, and the car pitched forward as the road threatened to devour them. She struggled with her seatbelt, determined to free herself. But the damn thing was stuck. She turned to the back seat in a rage.

"Let me out of here!" she spat, convinced they were about to plummet into a bottomless pit.

"Very well."

In the span of a second she was sitting on the rooftop of her grandfather's warehouse. The Boneyard stretched before her; its carcasses of rusty vehicles creaked in the wind. She glanced at the old school bus. A crow was perched on top of it, eyeing her with its beady black eyes. It cawed once, then flew away.

"Please forgive my brother. Phobetor's crow has no meaning in this dream. He is only curious."

Hadley glanced up. Morpheus stood beside her, surveying the Boneyard dreamscape, his wings neatly tucked behind him.

"Curious about what?" she asked. She knew little about Morpheus, but even less about his brothers, Phobetor and Phantasus. She only knew that they appeared to mortals in their dreams—Phobetor in animal form, Phantasus as inanimate objects.

"Crows represent many things. Death. Rebirth. Transformation. But it has been a long time since we have walked in the dreams of mortals. So much has changed. Is it true, what this dream tells you? Is it time to let your mother go?"

Hadley hugged her knees to her chest and moved her gaze back to the Boneyard. "I don't see how I can let go of something I never had."

"Perhaps that is the message," he suggested.

She gave him a puzzled look. "What is?"

He looked into the distance, where his brother's crow disappeared. "You pine for a life you never lived. Would it not be more fulfilling to treasure the one you have?"

Her eyes burned, and even though she knew he was right, she wasn't going to give him the satisfaction of telling him so.

"Why are you here, Morpheus? Because, as you can see, a lot's happened since you've been away." She demonstrated by waving a hand at the Boneyard. It wasn't much to look at, but it represented humankind's progress, for better or worse. "We don't need you anymore."

"We are not here because you need us. We are here because *we* need *you*."

She rose to her feet. He was taller than her by a foot at least, but she craned her neck, determined to look him in the eye. "Did you ever consider *asking* for our help?"

He smiled knowingly. "Tell me truthfully, huntress. Would you have given it so freely?"

Her cheeks warmed as she considered the question. If the gods weren't threatening them, would they have trekked halfway across the world in search of the Portal? Would they have put their lives on hold for some supernatural scavenger hunt?

"No," she finally admitted. "We wouldn't."

"Then you see, I'm afraid you give us no choice."

The sky overhead turned black, and Phobetor's crow cawed somewhere in the distance. Hadley felt goosebumps rise on her arms. She turned back to Morpheus, but he wasn't there. The roof started buckling beneath her, and she tried outrunning it, but it fell out from under her, dropping her like a bag of bricks into the trunk of an old Buick. She tried getting out, but her hands and feet were tied. Her grandfather appeared above her, a chewed-up cigar sticking out from the corner of his lined mouth.

"Thirty minutes, Princess. After that, she goes in the compactor. You know what that means, right? Don't let me down." Then he slammed the lid shut, trapping her in the dark.

Her heart hammered in her chest. *No. No, not this memory! Please, no!*

"MORPHEUS, PLEASE!" she shouted. She wriggled and banged her head against the roof of the trunk, and her breath turned shallow as she sucked in too much air. She was hyperventilating, and it was making her light-headed. Could she pass out in a dream?

This isn't real. This isn't real. This isn't real.

But it felt real, and she didn't want to relive it. Even if she knew how it ended. No. No, she couldn't do it. She wouldn't.

"MELINOË!" she screamed.

The lid immediately popped open. She scrambled out of the trunk and fell to the ground, gasping for air. Her hands and feet were no longer tied, so she pulled her knees up and dropped her head between them. She took a few calming breaths until she felt the panic begin to subside. Then she felt a light touch on her head and looked up.

A ghostly woman stood in front of her. Or rather, floated. Hadley's throat locked, and she crab-crawled backward.

"It is unwise to summon me, mortal," the woman said with a smile. Her teeth came to little sharp points, and there was a strange duality to her appearance. Everything about her—her skin, her dress, her hair—cycled between light and dark. Even her eyes. One was milky white, like a corpse, and the other was black. Her jaw was sharp, and her features were hard to define. She was beautiful yet hideous at the same time.

Hadley pushed herself to her feet. "I didn't know what else to do. You're . . . you're Melinoë, right?"

Instead of blinking, her eyes switched colors. The black one was now white, and vice versa. The effect was chilling.

"You question a goddess?" she hissed. A loud crack of thunder rocked the dreamscape, shaking the ground. Hadley looked around. They were no longer in the Boneyard. They were standing on the banks of a dark river, and just past the shoreline was a wall of gray fog. It was impossible to see the other side.

"No. I didn't—I don't mean to offend you. I . . ." She paused. What now? She'd clearly done the one thing they weren't supposed to do. She'd summoned the goddess of nightmares and madness. Olivia was going to kill her.

"It was a mistake to summon you," she admitted. "I'm sorry."

Melinoë tilted her head to the side. "The lie drips from your tongue, huntress."

Hadley felt a sharp prick on her tongue and tasted something sweet and metallic. She licked her lips and brought her fingers to her mouth. They came away bright red, and her mouth filled with blood. Her eyes went wide as she gagged, spitting out blood. When it hit the ground, it turned into little red spiders that scurried up her legs, attempting to reenter her body by any means necessary. Her mouth. Her nose. Her eyes and ears. It was a horror movie times a thousand. She didn't just freak out. She. Lost. It.

She fell to the ground, writhing, shrieking, and retching as she swatted at her arachnid blood. Her mind was one snap away from a full psychotic breakdown, and she wasn't sure waking up would set it right.

"Okay!" she screamed. "I was scared! I summoned you because I was scared!"

The spiders vanished, and she found herself lying face down on the cold dirt ground. It was moist and smelled of sulfur, like the river it banked. She pushed onto all fours and took a second to catch her breath.

Wicked laughter echoed across the water. Hadley quickly leaped to her feet and looked around. Everything was dark and gray, and Melinoë was nowhere in sight.

"Morpheus may seek to know your desires, but I seek to know your fears, huntress," said her voice through the fog. "This dream does not frighten you, not truly. Tell me what does, and I will grant you what you wish."

Hadley brought her hand to her chest, still reeling from the spider bit. "I don't want anything from you!" she yelled.

"Tell me your deepest fear and I will grant you time, huntress. Time to find the Portal of Osiris."

Hadley felt the breath escape her body. "Time? You mean you'll leave us alone? You won't invade our dreams?"

"Your fear, huntress," the voice demanded.

Hadley looked around. She'd summoned an Underworld goddess and somehow ended up on the banks of the River Styx, or at least what her subconscious assumed it looked like. Melinoë was offering her a short reprieve from the gods' torment. If she shared her deepest fear, she had no doubt Melinoë would try to use it against her. But wasn't it worth the peace it would give them to focus on the Portal? And after they retrieved it, *they* would be the ones holding all the cards. For now, all she had to do was play along.

"Okay," Hadley agreed. "I'll tell you."

chapter 13

Hadley woke up an hour before her alarm was set to go off. She bolted upright, removed her earplugs, and took a moment to get her bearings. The ballroom was just as they'd left it, lights dimmed and electric candles flickering. Soxie, Olivia, and Alice were still fast asleep. She studied each of their faces, looking for signs of distress. But they all seemed to be sleeping peacefully, and she didn't have the heart to wake them.

Quietly, she folded her blanket, slipped her boots on, and used Olivia's face to unlock her phone and set another alarm. Then she texted her to let her know she was going for a run. On her way upstairs, she stopped by the front desk to inquire about running paths. They gave her a map with a route that crossed the river and looped back via another bridge a mile down. It was chilly out, so she dressed in a turtleneck and joggers, added an oversized jacket and gloves, and tied her hair in a bun, which she stuffed under a baseball cap. With sunglasses on, she could be anyone, which was the point. She needed to lose herself for a bit and simply run.

The brisk morning air was perfect for running, and it wasn't until she started feeling her lungs struggling and muscles fatiguing that she realized how much she needed this. To just tire out her body physically and give her mind a rest. She completed the first loop in twenty minutes, so she kept going until she'd been running for over an hour. By the time she got back to the hotel, the sun was well above the horizon and her phone had blown up with texts from the girls, wondering where she was.

She met them at breakfast in the hotel restaurant, still in her workout clothes. Every dish on the menu ladened the table: pancakes, waffles, eggs Benedict, yogurt, oatmeal, bacon, hash browns, and a basket of croissants and muffins. Hadley salivated just looking at it. When she sat down, she noticed each of her friends' eyes were a little brighter than they were yesterday. Even Alice, whose complexion was usually as pale as her hair, seemed to have a bit more color in her cheeks.

"There she is," said Soxie, looking up from her phone. "How was it?"

Hadley sat down and helped herself to a muffin. "My dream, or my run?"

"Since when do I care about your crazy workouts?"

"Touché," she smirked. Then she pulled the plate of waffles toward her. "Tell me about yours first."

"Not much to tell. It started out rough—you know, at Serenity—but then the dream story just ended, and I don't remember anything after that. I just woke up feeling more rested than I have in a while."

Hadley kept her eyes on her plate as she dowsed her waffles in syrup, avoiding eye contact with Olivia. "That's great! And what about you, Alice?"

"Same," she answered. "My door to David ended up being the old David, and that was no picnic, but then it switched to some random dream I can't remember either. Not that I'm complaining."

"Fantastic," Hadley said with a smile, before sparing a glance across the table. "Olivia?"

She was busy meticulously cutting her pancakes into bite-size pieces. "Well, it started out in an animal kill shelter, so I was bracing myself for something really awful, but next thing I knew I was in a meadow playing Frisbee with Fred and Ginger when they were puppies. It was really nice."

Hadley nodded and stuffed a large piece of waffle in her mouth.

"So," Soxie prompted her. "What about you? No gods, right?"

Still chewing, she managed to take a bite of bacon and a sip of orange juice, all the while keeping her eyes glued to her breakfast.

A fork dropped loudly on the plate across from her. "You didn't."

Hadley flinched and looked up. Olivia stared daggers at her.

"You summoned *Melinoë*?" she said incredulously. "What were you thinking?"

Alice's coffee cup froze halfway to her mouth. "Wait, you did what?"

Hadley finished chewing and swallowed. Then she took a quick drink of water and sat back. "It's not like I planned it. It was an accident."

"An accident?" Soxie asked. "What the hell were you dreaming about?"

Trying to hide it was pointless, so Hadley spent the rest of breakfast explaining to them what had happened in her dream. When she finished, they sat in silence while she devoured the last croissant.

"And Melinoë never mentioned Persephone," Soxie finally confirmed.

"Nope."

"But, your deepest fear?" Alice said quietly. "That's really all she wanted?"

Hadley tilted her head and stirred her tea slowly, trying her best not to relive the encounter in her head. Then she set her spoon down and looked at them. "You guys, this is a good thing. No more night terrors. Now we can focus on what we came here to do. Find the Portal."

"And what about later, when Melinoë expects something in return?" challenged Olivia.

"I already paid her for this favor."

Olivia narrowed her eyes, unconvinced. "You know you can't trust her, right?"

Hadley tossed her napkin on the table and stood. "Yes, Olivia. I know. Which is all the more reason for us to find this Portal. If the gods want it so bad, it must be powerful. If we have it, then *we're* the ones with the power."

"Can't argue with that," Soxie said, pushing her chair back. "Shaft of Osiris, here we come."

Olivia arched an eyebrow but chose to keep her dissent to herself.

Their private tour was scheduled for 2:00 p.m. After breakfast, Hadley took a nice long soak in the tub to loosen her muscles from her morning run. Afterward, while wrapped in a cozy terry bathrobe, she nibbled on a granola bar as Olivia read aloud some facts about the mysterious Osiris Shaft.

"This says it dates back to around 2200 BCE," she said, eyes focused on her laptop.

Soxie moaned, unimpressed. "Like I said before. We're in Egypt. Everything's old."

"Well it looks like there are people who believe it's even older than that—much older. Like twelve thousand years, which would mean the ancient Egyptians found it rather than built it."

"Oh, god," said Soxie. "Please don't start with the alien conspiracy theories."

Olivia ignored her and continued reading. "It's only been open to the public for a few years. There are three levels, connected by vertical shafts. The lowest is some kind of subterranean hall that used to be filled with water. But it's apparently pretty complex in design, not to mention it reaches a depth of almost sixty meters."

"It's two hundred feet *below* the pyramid?" confirmed Hadley. "What was its purpose?"

"Not really sure that's been officially determined. I'm guessing it's some kind of tomb. But if the Osiris statue is pointing us to a pyramid, the one that sits above a tomb named after him has to be our best bet."

Alice leaned in to look over Olivia's shoulder. "Why was it filled with water?"

"No idea. They found sarcophagi and human remains down there, yet people used to swim in it, like it was some underground pool."

"Gross."

Hadley grabbed a pillow and threw it at Soxie's head. "Don't judge. Maybe it was some kind of cleansing ritual."

"Whatever," she said, throwing the pillow back. "Just so long as we don't have to swim in it." Then to Olivia, she added, "It's dry now, right?"

"Looks like there's still some water on the lowest level. It's not deep, but I'd keep that in mind when you choose your footwear."

They all glanced at Soxie's feet, currently clad in four-inch-high stiletto booties. She rolled her eyes and headed for her and Olivia's bedroom. "Great. I hope the hotel gift shop sells Wellies."

Hadley got dressed and called the front desk. After learning that the gift shop did not, in fact, sell Wellies, they arranged for Sam to pick them up early and take them to a store that sold sports clothing and equipment. They weren't *technically* spelunking, but it didn't hurt to be prepared. They each found the necessary waterproof gear, and at the last minute, Hadley grabbed a small backpack, mask, and snorkel. The mask reminded her of Poseidon, and she decided it was a sign. Soxie gave her a look when she dropped it at the register, but thankfully kept her opinions to herself.

Sam took them straight from the store to the Giza Plateau, which, with traffic, meant they were fifteen minutes late. Their guides—a man named Youssef with thinning gray hair and kind eyes, and a younger man named Karim who seemed to be either Youssef's assistant or apprentice—greeted them. Karim nodded enthusiastically as

Youssef gave them a quick rundown of the tour and recited a list of instructions, which basically amounted to, "Respect that this is a site of archaeological importance, don't take anything or leave anything, and do what we say when we say it," or something along those lines, though said in a much nicer way, with slightly accented English. But Hadley only half listened. The surroundings interested her more.

Seeing the pyramids up close was intense. Jaw-droppingly intense. Even seeing them from a distance was magnificent—three massive structures standing in the middle of the desert, evidence of an ancient civilization lost to time. Hadley knew they consisted of hundreds of thousands of stones, each weighing god only knows how many tons. She'd pictured stones the size of a desk or couch. But standing near the base of the Khafre Pyramid, each block of limestone was the size of an SUV. They reduced in size closer to the top, but still. The idea that humans carved these and somehow stacked them to arrange perfect forty-five-degree-angled slopes, thousands of years ago . . . it blew her mind.

"Actually, 53.1 degrees," murmured Olivia. "But yeah. It blows my mind too."

Hadley nodded silently, and the four of them continued standing in awe and staring up at the towering Pyramid of Khafre. Its top was different from the others as it still had some of the original casing stones that had once made the sides look smooth. It sat between the Great Pyramid and the smaller Pyramid of Menkaure, but its position in the middle, directly behind the Great Sphinx, made it feel more important somehow.

At some point, their guides had stopped talking, giving them a moment to take it all in. The sun was still high in the sky, and the heat warmed their faces even as a cold wind blew sand through their hair. It was the middle of the afternoon, and the pyramid complex was packed. Hundreds of tourists meandered along the bases of the pyramids and up the long path from the Sphinx. The complex itself was massive, including not just the three main pyramids but also smaller pyramids, causeways, and satellite structures. It was hard not to admire the grandiosity of it all. Whatever these things were built for, they were built to last. And to be seen.

Youssef stepped forward and smiled. "It is beautiful, no? Okay, girls, we go now. This way."

Youssef and Karim led them away from the pyramid to a shallow ditch carved directly into the bedrock beneath the causeway. At the end of the ditch was an ordinary gate with mesh stretched over its metal bars. Hadley was expecting something more elaborate, like the temples carved into rock at the lost city of Petra. This looked more like a crude entrance to a storm cellar.

"So what's the plan here?" asked Soxie as Youssef and Karim busied themselves with the gate. "Are we just winging it? What exactly are we looking for?"

Hadley took off her sunglasses and stuffed them in her backpack. "No idea. I guess we'll know it when we see it."

"That's helpful."

"It's all we've got," said Olivia. "I just hope we find something. Otherwise . . ."

They all looked at each other. Olivia didn't need to finish that sentence. They all knew what "otherwise" meant. It meant they were dead in the water.

Just then, the gate swung open with a loud creaking bang. They turned toward the entrance.

"Okay, my friends!" Youssef said as he held the gate open, Karim smiling beside him. "Welcome to the Shaft of Osiris!"

Hadley shaded her eyes and peered into the darkness beyond the gate.

"Please let there be something in there," she whispered to herself, then walked through.

chapter 14

The air cooled the moment Hadley stepped inside. In front of her a long tunnel led to a secondary entrance on the other side of the causeway. To her left she looked over a metal railing, down into a deep hole. The hole was about the size of a freight elevator shaft and looked as if it'd been chiseled away with hand tools. The shaft extended at least thirty feet down and rose several feet above her head. Sunlight shone through a square opening at the top. It was covered in bars, either to keep people out or to keep them from falling in.

"This is the surface level," said Youssef. "Not much here, we see more below."

The others gathered around her while Youssef lowered himself onto a ladder adjacent to the railing. It was bolted into the bedrock and looked a little rickety, but it didn't creak or vibrate when he put his weight on the top rung. He turned and said something to Karim in his native tongue—Hadley guessed Egyptian Arabic—then he waved for them to follow him. Karim stayed just outside the entrance. He noticed Hadley looking at him and smiled.

"Don't worry. I wait here. There are many tourists around, but this is a private tour. Only for you."

Hadley relaxed a bit. She had no idea what they were going to find down there, but if they needed to get a closer look at something that was off-limits, one guide would be easier to distract than two. She also liked knowing there was someone standing guard up top in case anything went wrong below. She thanked Karim and waited for Soxie, Olivia, and Alice to make their way down the ladder before climbing down behind them. The ladder felt rough beneath her hands, like something from an old mine. But it held.

When she reached the bottom, she hopped off the last rung and wiped her hands on her pants as she looked around. The bottom opened up to a long rectangular room. At the far end, another shaft led further down. It was much smaller than the first, and positioned above it was some sort of winching system. In the middle of the room, an electric light made it easy to see that there wasn't much else to see.

"Relax," said Olivia as she scanned the ceiling and walls. "This is only the first level."

Hadley stepped up to the wall and ran her hand along the rough stone. She wasn't expecting a big arrow pointing to the location of the Portal, but this was just a cave-like room with a hole in the floor. They'd confirmed they were allowed to take pictures and videos, but there wasn't anything to document here. She looked at Soxie and Alice. They looked equally unimpressed.

"I guess we keep going down," said Soxie with a shrug.

One by one, they followed Youssef down the ladder of the next shaft. It was a longer climb down, and the air got slightly colder as they descended. While nothing felt particularly ominous about the shaft so far, they were still climbing deep below a pyramid built thousands of years ago, comprised of millions of tons of rock. It was hard not to feel a little nervous.

Bringing up the rear of the group, Hadley hopped off the final rung and pulled a flashlight out of her pack. She turned and shined it on the room before her. It was similar in size to the room above, only this one had six separate niches carved into the walls. In two of them were large black boxes that looked like sarcophagi, their lids pushed to the side. One electric lamp sat in the middle of the room, casting eerie shadows into each dark niche. Alice, Soxie, and Olivia had already branched out, their own flashlights in hand, scanning the walls for anything that might scream Portal.

"The shaft was first explored in the 1930s but not fully excavated until 1999," said Youssef as he took a spot in the corner of the room. "Human remains were found in two sarcophagi. Many artifacts were recovered as well, though it is likely the tomb was raided long ago."

"Grave robbers?" Hadley said as her heart sank. Youssef nodded and continued reciting his list of facts about the shaft, but her mind was already spinning. Of course. She hadn't thought of grave robbers, though it made sense. Many tombs in Egypt had been pilfered of their valuables long ago. What if what they were looking for had walked away with a thief three hundred years prior? Was this all a huge waste of time?

She swung the beam of her flashlight into a nearby niche and stepped forward. The lid of a large basalt sarcophagus was unceremoniously shoved to the side. She shined her light into the opening. There was nothing inside other than some dirt, bits of twenty-year-old trash, and a black, sticky-looking residue. It covered the outer side and lid of the sarcophagus as well.

"What is this black stuff?" she asked Youssef, pointing her flashlight at the stone.

"It is a mystery of the Osiris Shaft," he said casually. "One theory is oil leaked from a drum during excavation. Other is mixture of animal fats, beeswax, and oils used for burial ritual."

Soxie stepped closer to investigate and brought her nose close to the stone. "Smells weird."

Hadley crouched down and leaned in for a sniff. Her nose tingled with a combination of petroleum and something organic, like fungus or mold.

"Do you know if there are any carvings on the walls, or hiero-glyphs?" Alice asked Youssef.

Hadley stood and turned around. Alice was spinning slowly, shining her light on the walls and ceilings, inside the niches. All it revealed was a bunch of rough-cut limestone.

"No," answered Youssef. "No hieroglyphs. Remember, we sit below the water table. The tomb was filled with water for many years."

Hadley let her flashlight beam fall to the ground. This excursion was proving more and more hopeless by the minute. Even if whatever they were looking for wasn't stolen by grave robbers, it could have been washed away or eroded by water. Water had a fun little way of destroying everything in its path, especially evidence.

Olivia sidled up next to her. "We still have another level," she said quietly. "Don't give up yet."

With that, they let Youssef know they were ready to descend to the third and final level. He shined his flashlight on the top rungs of a ladder behind him and proceeded in climbing down. Hadley waited for Soxie, Olivia, and Alice before making the descent herself. The third shaft was roughly the same size as the second, though it was colder, darker, and damper. Even the air felt heavy and wet.

Hadley gripped the sides of the ladder, careful to take it slow. It was slick with moisture, and she couldn't afford to slip. If she fell and broke her leg, how would they get her out? She doubted Youssef or Karim could carry her up these ladders, and there was no way to know how long help would take to reach them.

She leaned her head back and looked up. None of the shafts were connected, so it wasn't one long two-hundred-foot drop. All she saw was the dim ceiling of level two. The hamster tunnel design prevented any light from the surface from reaching past the first level, which made for a very, very closed-off feeling. She took a breath and paused. She wasn't claustrophobic, but she was already looking forward to getting back up top to the fresh desert air.

A splash below made her glance down. The beam of a flashlight crossed over the surface of water, and the top of Alice's white head waded away from the ladder. It looked like the water reached her hips. Hadley felt her last shred of hope fray. If the lower level was filled with water, what could they possibly hope to find?

When she got to the bottom, she kept a firm grip on the ladder and gingerly dipped one foot into the water. She'd expected it to be ice cold, but it wasn't. Her waterproof pants kept her legs dry, but she felt the temperature just fine. It wasn't warm like bathwater, but it wasn't frigid, like it probably should have been.

She pressed her boot into the ground, searching for a good foothold, worried she might slip on something slimy. But instead of hard, slippery bedrock, her heel sunk into loose sand. She let go of the ladder and waded toward the others. There were no lights down here. Other than the light from their flashlights, it was pitch black.

Youssef was explaining how both excavations had tried and failed to pump all the water out of the shaft. For whatever reason, it refused to leave the lower level. Hadley turned and moved her flashlight along the walls of the room. It was smaller than the others, and the vertical tunnel dropped directly into the center of it. There were no niches, or places where sarcophagi would have sat. There was nothing carved into the walls, and no big aha moments. In fact, there didn't seem to be any purpose for the room at all. It was just a square cave with three feet of standing water and some wooden beams that, while old, were not original to the structure. They'd clearly been brought in during one of the excavations and left down here to rot.

"What was this room used for?" she finally asked.

"Ah, another mystery of the Osiris Shaft," Youssef mused. Hadley shined her light toward him, careful not to blind him.

"No theories?"

Youssef smiled wide, and his teeth almost glowed in the darkness. "Theories are not fact. It matters not what it could be, only what it was. And perhaps, girls, that is a mystery Osiris does not want solved."

"Great," Soxie grumbled. Alice and Olivia were less obvious, but their body language said it all. If this was it, they'd come down here for nothing.

Hadley tried not to let her disappointment get the better of her. Instead, she shined her flashlight into the water below her. She saw her new waterproof boots clear as day, even the little plastic ties on the ends of her shoelaces. Her eyes widened.

"Wow. Look at this water. It's crystal clear!"

The others shined their flashlights down. The light cut through the surface of the water, highlighting the ground beneath their feet. Other than a few slivers of floating wood, they could have been standing on a beach in the Caribbean. The water was that clear.

Hadley quickly scanned the corners of the room. Where was this water coming from?

"Where is this water coming from?" Olivia asked, echoing her thoughts.

"Groundwater," Youssef replied with a shrug. "Now I give you five minutes to explore, but then we go back up. Yes?"

Hadley frowned. She was hoping for something better than "groundwater." She needed to get a closer look. She needed to see what this pool of water was hiding.

She made eye contact with Olivia and relayed her thoughts, something she preferred not to do unless she absolutely had to.

Can you find a reason for him to take you up, and stall him for a bit? I want to see if I can figure out where this water is coming from.

Olivia nodded. Hadley could tell she wasn't thrilled with the idea, but thankfully she was willing to go along with it. A second later, she yelped and made a big spectacle of falling into the water. Naturally, Alice and Soxie rushed to help.

"What happened?" asked Soxie, grabbing hold of her arm to steady her. Alice grabbed her other arm.

"I don't know," she said, gasping. "I stepped on something sharp—I think it pierced through my shoe! I have to get out of here!"

"Let me see," demanded Soxie, already bending over to have a look.

Olivia batted her away. "No! Just get me out of here!"

Hadley feigned alarm as she peered into the water by Olivia's feet. "Oh no! Do you think it was a nail? Can you walk? Youssef, can you help get her to the surface? She might need a doctor!"

Youssef's face turned pale, which was not easy to see in the low light. But he obviously didn't like the idea of one of his tour group stepping on a rusty nail from 1933. He sprang into action, pulling a two-way radio from his belt.

"Yes, yes, I radio Karim and let him know to meet us on the first level. You girls follow!"

He shouted something into his radio, then took hold of Olivia's arm and slung it over his shoulder. Soxie and Alice helped him carry her through the water to the base of the ladder. Hadley hung back, waiting until he and Olivia were a few rungs up. Then she grabbed the back of Soxie's shirt and pulled.

"She's faking," she whispered into her hair. "You and Alice follow and keep them occupied. I just need a few minutes down here alone."

Soxie's back stiffened, and she glanced over her shoulder. Then she nodded once and waded toward the ladder. Hadley shut off her flashlight and slunk into the darkness behind her, praying Olivia's ruse bought her enough time.

Within seconds, Alice and Soxie were on their way up the ladder. Without their flashlights reflecting off the damp limestone walls, Hadley stood in the kind of darkness that wasn't just complete but suffocating. She waited until it sounded like they were a good way up before she turned her flashlight back on, making sure to point it away from the shaft.

The room seemed different now that she was alone. Without the other bodies, it definitely felt like a tomb. But it had to be more than that. She brushed the chills aside and quickly dug in her pack for her mask and snorkel. She strapped them onto her head, confirmed the seal was good, and dove into the shallow water.

She floated in the darkness, letting the beam of her flashlight lead the way. She was thankful she'd insisted they buy waterproof flashlights, otherwise she'd be swimming blind. She spun in a slow circle while she shined her light on every corner of the room. As she feared, there was nothing much to see. Just sand, and smooth rock where the sand met the bottom of the walls. She pushed forward, keeping her head below the surface. When she got to the nearest wall, she spit out the mouth of her snorkel and held her breath as she dove further under.

She got as close to the base of the wall as she could and inspected it with her flashlight. Nothing. Just rock and sand. She pushed along the wall and continued until she got to the first corner. She pressed her fingers into the rock, searching for a crack or current. Anything that would indicate where the water was coming from. But there wasn't even a seam. She surfaced for air, then quickly dove back under. She followed the base of the wall all the way around the room, inspecting every square inch she could. It required some fancy maneuvering around the wooden beam structure, but it appeared there was nothing hiding behind that either. She completed her underwater circuit of the perimeter in less than five minutes. There was just nothing to see.

She surfaced and yanked her mask off in frustration. No noise came from above, but she was sure they were close to the top by now. Soon, they'd discover she was missing, and one of them would come down looking for her. She was running out of time.

"Dammit!" she said, kicking at the sand beneath her. Her flashlight was still below the surface. It made the water in the room glow, casting an eerie blue-green light on the limestone walls. She dropped her head and was about to pull her flashlight from the water when she noticed something dark beneath the sand she'd disturbed. She shoved her mask back on and dipped her head under to have a look. Reaching down and pushing more sand away, she revealed a stone floor with black residue, similar to what they'd seen on the sarcophagus above.

Heart racing, she madly began scraping heaps of sand away, uncovering what looked like a solid line, about three inches thick. She pushed away more sand and followed the line to where it eventually stopped in the middle of the room, directly below the open shaft. There, it intersected with seven other lines, all evenly spaced apart. Where they intersected was a solid round circle, about a foot in diameter. She pulled her head from the water and shined her light in the direction of each line. Did the circle represent the Portal? And what was with the eight lines? Where did they go? What did they *mean*?

A sound above startled her.

"Girl! You must come up now!" bellowed Youssef.

Hadley closed her eyes and groaned.

Crap. Her time was up.

chapter 15

Hadley held the piece of paper up proudly. She wasn't much of an artist, but she'd managed to draw a rough sketch of what she'd uncovered beneath the sand.

"And you're sure the circle was the same size as the map?" confirmed Olivia.

Hadley nodded. "I think so. It's been a while since I've seen the map, but it looked pretty close."

Soxie emerged from the bathroom in a robe and slippers, towel-drying her hair. "Can we just call it the Portal from now on? Fair to say it's a hell of a lot more than a map."

Hadley teased her own damp hair to help it air dry and scooted her chair in. After returning to the hotel and cleaning up, they'd ordered a small feast from room service. Their little jaunt below the pyramid had left them famished, so now they sat at a table in Soxie and Olivia's room, helping themselves to quite the silver-domed spread. Hadley dipped a corner of her grilled cheese sandwich in tomato soup and blew on it before taking a bite. She spoke with her mouth full. "Okay, boss. Portal it is."

Soxie gave her the side-eye as she popped a mini spring roll in her mouth and sat down. "Names aside, what do we think that means?" she said, gesturing to Hadley's drawing.

Alice leaned across the table and picked it up. "Looks like a square pizza."

"You're just hungry," Hadley said with a laugh, though Alice had a point. Her crude drawing did sort of look like a square-shaped pizza cut into eight slices with a piece of pepperoni in the middle.

Olivia snatched the paper from Alice's hand and scowled at it. Alice looked about to protest, but then thought better of it and resumed eating. If anyone was going to figure it out, it was Olivia. The rest of them might as well enjoy their meals while she did.

No one said anything for several minutes, each of them keeping an eye on Olivia while they ate, waiting for her eureka moment. Eventually, Soxie's impatience got the better of her.

"Well?" she said. "You figure it out yet?"

Olivia gave her a reproving look, then palmed the drawing down on the table. "No. I didn't."

"Well that can't be right. Nothing at all?"

Olivia exhaled and ran her hands through her hair. "I was thinking maybe those were ley lines." She paused to point at the eight lines extending from the circle. "The Giza pyramids are located on a node. Same as Chichén Itzá and Stonehenge."

"What the hell is a node?" asked Soxie.

"It's the point where ley lines intersect. It's supposed to be a place of strong electromagnetic energy—some believe supernatural energy."

"That sounds promising."

Olivia shook her head. "Not really. I doubt Stonehenge and Chichén Itzá could have anything to do with the Portal. They're too young. Besides, even if those are ley lines, they're pointing us in eight different directions. That doesn't feel right to me."

"Okay, then if not ley lines, what else could they be?" asked Alice.

"I wish I knew," she answered. Then her eyes moved to the full-length mirror by the bathroom. "Why don't we try using your powers?"

Alice looked skeptical. "In what way?"

Olivia pointed to the mirror. "Project an image of Hadley's drawing onto that mirror. Maybe it'll reveal something we're missing."

"Good idea," Hadley chimed in, pushing the drawing toward Alice. "Can't hurt."

Alice stared at the symbol for a few seconds, then scooted her chair back and stood. They followed her to the narrow entryway where the mirror hung and crowded around her to watch. She took a shaky breath, then slowly lifted her hand toward the glass. Their reflections immediately became distorted, and the colors of their clothing and hair swirled together like paint. It was mesmerizing to watch, and they all stepped a little closer, eager to get a look at what would happen next. The swirling colors faded as their images disappeared, replaced by a black background with wavy white lines. Alice began moving her hand, rearranging the lines until they formed the symbol from Hadley's drawing.

"Okay," she said through a satisfied breath. "Now what?"

Olivia stepped up to the mirror, running her fingertips along the lines. "Can you move it around so we can see it from different angles?"

Alice furrowed her brow. "I'll try."

The image slowly spun as she twisted her wrist. Their heads all tilted to the side, following the spin. But the image looked the same from every angle. They could have held the drawing up to the mirror and it would have produced the same result.

"Try a 3D version," prompted Olivia.

Without missing a beat, Alice flicked her hand, and the lines broke away from each other, surrounding the center circle like a starburst. It was cool to watch, but it didn't offer much in the form of clues.

Olivia stepped back. "*Hmm.* I'm not seeing anything."

"Maybe they're some kind of star map, and the center circle represents the earth?" Soxie suggested.

Hadley stared hard at the 3D image. "Even if you're right, how would we go about confirming which stars it's pointing to?

My drawing is from memory; it's not mathematically accurate. We'd have to go back to the shaft and measure the lines."

"It's a good theory, Sox," said Olivia. "I just don't know how we could prove it. There are too many variables."

Alice's shoulders sank, but she kept her hand pointing at the mirror. "Anything else you want me to try?"

"As long as we're here, I want to see how your powers changed," said Olivia. "Show us what you showed Hadley."

"Wait, can we see something besides Boop?" Hadley entreated them. "No offense, Alice, but your cat and I aren't exactly on good terms."

She chuckled. "It's because you can't pet him. He resents you for that."

"The feeling's mutual, trust me. So can you project something else?"

Alice waved her hand and the lines disappeared, revealing four girls standing in front of a mirror. "All right, what do you want? Schlemmer?"

"So she can sneeze all over the glass?" laughed Soxie. "No, thanks. Why does it have to be an animal? How about a person?"

Alice's eyes lit up. "I haven't tried that yet with these powers. Who do you suggest?"

"I don't know. How about Barry? Or your mom?"

She squinched up her face. "My mom? I love her, but I'm kind of enjoying the current seven-thousand-mile buffer. How about Mayron?"

"Pass," said Hadley. "I feel like even his projection will find a way to interrogate me."

Soxie nodded. "Agreed. He's been on my case enough as it is. I don't need his projection judging me too."

"How about Molly?" Olivia said delicately.

Alice's eyes darted to hers in the mirror. "Molly? But, she's gone."

"Not here and here," Olivia said, pointing to Alice's head and heart. "Did you really never try before?"

"No. It felt too raw. Too soon."

"And now?"

Alice looked in the mirror and shrugged. "It would be nice to see her again," she admitted. "I guess I could try."

Once settled, they all stepped back to give her room, and watched as her hand changed the chemistry of the mirror, swirling it like a liquid until their reflections disappeared, replaced with the image of a woman with auburn hair and light brown eyes. She wore a royal-blue flight attendant uniform with a red silk scarf that matched the color of her lips.

Hadley knew how hard this must be for Alice. She placed a hand on her shoulder and said, "She looks perfect."

Alice half smiled. "She always did."

The image of Molly tilted her head, and Hadley could have sworn she was looking directly at them.

"Show us how this projection works," said Olivia. "I want to see it interact like Boop's did."

Molly's head swiveled in her direction. "I hope you don't expect me to chase a ball of yarn."

A collective gasp filled the tiny hallway, and they grabbed on to each other to keep from falling over. The image in the mirror smiled brightly.

"Girls, it's so nice to see you," she said. Then she turned to Alice and added, "I've missed you, Bunny."

The four of them huddled together, eyes wide with shock. This was way more than a simple projection.

"M-Molly?" Alice sputtered.

The woman in the mirror placed her hands on her hips. "Sweetie, you know my true name. I don't think it's fair to your aunt's memory to keep calling me Molly."

Alice swallowed. "Persephone? But how? Is this . . . Are you real?"

"I'm as real as your memory allows me to be."

"Wait," Olivia interjected, lifting her hands as if she could pause the proceedings. "Are you saying you're a *memory*?"

Persephone seemed to ponder the question. "More or less." Then she looked down and gave her uniform a disapproving look. "Though I wish you'd remember me in better clothes."

Hadley couldn't believe what she was seeing, and more importantly, hearing. Persephone's projection was throwing the entire playbook out the window.

"Memories don't have conversations," challenged Soxie.

"And how many memories of a goddess have you encountered?"

Soxie didn't answer, and Hadley didn't blame her. The memory of a goddess was definitely uncharted territory.

"Do you mean, I could have been talking to you this entire time?" asked Alice, her voice cracking.

Persephone smiled sadly. "Sweetie, you needed time to grieve. I just never expected you to take as long as you did."

"What do you mean?"

She fell into an invisible seat behind her. "Memories fade, Alice. I started to get worried your memory of me was fading too much. And I was right. Look at how you remember me—in my flight attendant uniform. What happened to my clothes? Please don't tell me Judy sold them."

Alice faltered. "I think she gave them to Goodwill."

"She *gave* them away?" Persephone cried, her face red. "The Valentino? The Armani? Not the Oscar de la Renta!" Then she stood and started pacing back and forth. "Did she at least give you the veil? I found that in Rome when you were two years old. I specifically left instructions for you to have it."

Alice looked down. "Yes, I got the veil. Thank you."

Talking about the veil meant talking about the wedding, and from the look on her face, Alice was uncomfortable with the subject. Hadley quickly inserted herself into the conversation.

"Why were you worried Alice's memory of you would fade?" she asked.

Persephone stopped and turned to look at them. "Because this memory of me is all that's left. You needed a little reminder of that."

Olivia sucked in a startled breath. "*You're* the reason the mirrors were getting stuck!" she said, pointing at the glass. "No wonder they never felt threatening. Why, though? Were you trying to send us a message?"

Her mouth twisted into a lopsided grin. "More like trying to get your attention."

"But, you're a memory," Hadley felt compelled to point out. "How could you manipulate the mirrors?"

"It wasn't me, silly," she clucked. "It was always Alice."

Alice looked more than a little surprised. "No, it couldn't have been me. I *lost* my powers, Persephone."

"You can't lose them, Bunny. They're a part of you now. They'll grow and change as you do, but they've always been there. If you thought they were gone, it's because you needed to believe they were."

They took a moment to digest her words. Hadley rewound the past few days in her mind, seeing the mirror glitches in a new light. They started happening after the bridal fitting when Alice voiced her concerns about David. And since then, their lives had been on fast-forward as they tried to evade the gods and find the Portal. Were the glitches really just a byproduct of Alice's mental distress?

"So I was the one blocking my power," whispered Alice, her eyes distant as she put it all together. "I'm such an idiot."

Persephone smiled. "We all get in our own way sometimes. Don't be so hard on yourself. Your power revealed itself when you were ready to wield it again."

Alice nodded as if she not only understood but had always known. Hadley couldn't help but relate. She'd gotten in her own way plenty of times. Her ordeal with Melinoë was proof of that.

"Speaking of," Olivia suddenly jumped in. "Persephone, what can you tell us about Melinoë?"

"Melinoë? Why would you ask about her?"

"Because Hadley summoned her, and we don't really know what that means yet."

Persephone's head snapped in Hadley's direction, eyes big and blazing like a five-alarm fire. "You summoned Melinoë? Why?"

Heat rushed to Hadley's face. She hated being put on the spot. "It was kind of an accident," she said weakly.

"Nothing with Melinoë is an accident. Tell me what's going on."

For the next ten minutes they told Persephone everything that had happened in the past few days. When they finished, she looked more like a ghost than a goddess.

"The Portal of Osiris?" she said, her brows knitting together. "But that . . ."

"What?" Olivia prodded.

Persephone's expression suddenly hardened. "Let me see the symbol again."

Alice lifted the drawing toward the mirror. Persephone stood and moved in for a closer look, her nose almost touching the other side of the glass. "I don't recognize it."

Hadley deflated. If Persephone didn't know what the symbol meant, how were they supposed to figure it out? Then again, she was just a memory—whatever that meant. The whole thing was making Hadley feel slow and confused, like her head had been turned inside out.

"We need to sleep on this," Olivia announced, picking up on everyone's exhaustion. Alice looked like she was about to drop, but she held the projection long enough for them to say their goodbyes. As Hadley turned to leave, Persephone called her name. She turned back to the mirror.

"Melinoë thrives on fear, Hadley," she told her. "If you face your fear, she can't hurt you."

Hadley smiled tightly and left the room.

Fifteen minutes later, she and Alice were tucked in their beds with the lights out, and Soxie and Olivia were already snoring next door. Hadley snuggled into the soft sheets, ready to succumb to a long, godless sleep. Then she heard a faint tapping and rolled over. Light from Alice's phone illuminated her face as she typed away on the screen.

"Who are you texting?"

"My mom. I promised I'd send pictures of our trip." She added air quotes to the last word.

Hadley propped herself up on her elbow. "Do you want to talk about what just happened?"

"What's there to talk about? She's a memory. She isn't real."

"She certainly felt real."

Alice kept tapping. "I guess. I'm just not sure what I think about it yet."

"That's fair," said Hadley, treading carefully. "It's too bad she didn't know what the symbol meant, though. Are you planning to text David, or do you want me to? He might be able to help."

She stopped typing and looked up. "Would you mind? I'm afraid if I pull his number up I'm going to call him, and then he'll just say he loves and misses me."

Hadley leaned over to turn on the bedside lamp, bathing them in soft yellow light. "I'm no expert, but that sounds like normal boyfriend behavior. Besides, Persephone just told us why the mirrors were getting stuck. It had nothing to do with David."

"Didn't it, though? What if the real reason my power came back is because I'm here, seven thousand miles away from him?"

Hadley shook her head. "I don't believe that, and neither do you. Your power is new, and you're still learning how to use it. Maybe it's like a caterpillar turning into a butterfly, or a snake shedding its skin. In order for it to grow, you have to adapt and grow with it."

"And when I didn't use it for months, I wasn't adapting. I was ignoring it," she yielded, her tone flat. "I was letting the caterpillar suffocate in its cocoon."

"Well, I wouldn't put it like that, but basically—yes. This thing with David, though . . . it's not just about the mirrors, is it?"

Alice dropped her phone in her lap and leaned against the headboard. Then she tilted her head toward Hadley and gave her a rueful smile. "Have you ever opened a bag of potato chips and eaten just one?

"Have you met me?"

She cracked a tiny smile. "Exactly. So you get it. David is sort of . . . all or nothing for me."

"Seems a little—"

"Unhealthy?" Alice suggested.

"Your word, not mine."

"But you know it's the right one."

Hadley wasn't sure what to say. Alice and David were soulmates. They belonged together, but Hadley never considered what kind of pressure that might put on a relationship. Were soulmates allowed to have problems? Were they allowed to have the same fears and doubts as the rest of them? Or was a perfect relationship the only option? Seemed like a bona fide recipe for failure, not that Hadley was an expert. She'd never been that interested in romance, but she'd seen plenty of movies about it.

"Okay," she said, sitting up. "I think I know the problem."

"Do tell."

"Yours isn't just a love story. It's a love-at-first-sight story."

"Like Snow White and Cinderella? Barf."

Hadley raised an eyebrow. "Am I wrong?"

Alice exhaled and looked down. "No."

"Okay, then. Here's the thing: You were never given a choice. The second your souls recognized each other, the choice was made for you. Maybe that's the problem. Maybe you need this time apart to finally, once and for all, *choose* each other."

Alice's head popped up. She looked equal parts relieved and frightened as she began twisting her butterfly ring back and forth. "Hadley, you're a genius."

"Thanks," she said with a satisfied smile.

"But, but what if . . ." she trailed off.

"What if what?"

The color drained from Alice's face, except for a tiny red splotch on the apple of each cheek. "What if he doesn't choose me?"

Hadley laid down on her side and reached her hand across the space between their beds. Alice took it.

"I think that's the point, honey. You're not supposed to know. But if it helps, I'd bet every last dime of Soxie's money that you've got nothing to worry about."

She laughed softly. "Thanks, Hadz. I hope you're right."

Hadley waited until Alice was asleep before gently releasing her hand and letting it fall limply back on the mattress. Then she sent a text to David, recounting their conversation with Persephone and their trip to the Osiris Shaft, along with an image of the symbol from the bottom chamber. She was tempted to tell him to call Alice, but she realized he deserved this time for himself too. But did she think there was a chance they *wouldn't* choose each other?

The thought made her laugh.

Alice fidgeted in her sleep and turned over. Hadley clamped her mouth shut and set her phone back on the nightstand. Then she closed her eyes and fell blissfully, fast asleep.

When she woke up, it was without a racing heart or clammy forehead. For the first time in a long time, she had slept like a baby. The room was still dark, so she leaned over to check the time on her phone. It was five thirty in the morning.

Careful not to wake Alice, she quickly pulled on a pair of sweatpants, shoved her feet into her sneakers, grabbed her jacket, phone, and keycard, and snuck out the door.

The lounge off the lobby was empty except for one early riser tapping away on her laptop. Hadley stopped at the continental breakfast bar and grabbed herself a large cup of coffee and a croissant. Then she took them onto the back patio and sat at the table closest to the water. The river looked inky black in the gray light of morning. She zipped up her jacket and pulled her knees up to guard against the chill. Then she took a bite of her croissant and chewed mindlessly as she stared into the coming day.

No bad dreams. It was nice to wake up like a normal person for a change, and to know that, at least for now, Melinoë was keeping her word. Hadley wondered if Morpheus had anything to do with it. He wasn't exactly on their side, but she had the feeling he *wanted* to be. Melinoë, on the other hand, seemed to be on her own side. Just picturing her haunting face gave Hadley an icy feeling that had nothing to do with the river's chill. She set down her croissant and cradled her hot coffee to her chest, letting the steam warm her nose. Her gaze settled across the river, where bright red streaks slashed across the morning sky, and the call to prayer traveled over the water.

She settled back in her chair and relaxed. The coffee was strong, and the croissant was a perfect blend of buttery and flaky. They were still a long way from solving the mystery of the Portal, and Persephone's memory showing up only complicated things. But for now, Hadley was going to enjoy this simple breakfast and breathtaking view. Moments like these were few and far between lately.

Her phone buzzed in her pocket, ruining her Zen moment.

When she saw who was calling, she considered letting it go to voicemail. But that would just be delaying the inevitable, so instead she answered.

"You're up late," she said. "Or is it early? What time is it there?"

"It's eight p.m. Did you get my text?"

Typical David. No small talk. Straight to the point.

"I just woke up," she lied. "What text?"

She put the phone on speaker and pulled up her texts. She hadn't expected David to get back to her so quickly, but sure enough there were several missed texts, starting at 2:00 a.m. Cairo time. Oops.

"Tell me more about this memory of Persephone," he said. "Are you *sure* it was her?"

She chose to ignore the accusation in his voice. "I have no way of proving it was her, David. But do I think it was? Yes. Or at least, the memory of her. Which is still messing with my head a little bit."

"Do you think this memory could be dangerous for Alice?"

Hadley let her head fall back and stared at the sky. It was too early to be grilled like this. "I don't know. Are your memories a danger to you?"

"Mine don't talk to me through a mirror."

"It doesn't mean they can't hurt you." She thought about her own memories, the ones she'd been reliving in her dreams. Memories didn't have to talk to remind you of the pain they caused.

"Just keep me posted if you notice anything strange, okay?"

"Don't I always?"

He brushed aside her sarcasm. "Anyway, that isn't why I called. I think I know what the symbol you found means, but you're not going to like it."

She took a deep breath and dropped her head to her chest. So much for a calm and peaceful morning.

"I'm sure I won't," she reluctantly agreed. "What is it?"

"It's the Great Pyramid."

She did a double take at her phone, unsure if she heard him correctly. "No, the Osiris Shaft was beneath the Khafre Pyramid. It has nothing to do with the Great Pyramid."

He laughed. "Hadley, of the two of us, only one has actually lived in Egypt. Can you just trust me that I know what I'm talking about?"

"You lived in Egypt? When?"

He sighed. "A long time ago. Does it matter?"

She wanted to say yes, it did matter. Every single one of his past lives mattered, just like every one of his huntresses mattered. He'd confessed that to her just days ago.

"Fine," she said, unwilling to get into it. "So tell me how you think a circle with eight lines has anything to do with a four-sided pyramid."

"It wouldn't, if the Great Pyramid only had four sides."

"Huh?"

"It has eight."

She sat up. "Wait. What are you talking about? I've seen it. We were right there; it looks like a regular pyramid."

"From the ground, maybe. But not from above."

The four of them crowded around Olivia's laptop, staring at the image on the screen. It was an aerial view of the Great Pyramid, and David was right. There were eight sides.

Soxie walked to the window, as if she could see the pyramid from their hotel. "What kind of pyramid has eight sides?"

"This one," said Olivia. "I can't believe I missed it. It's so obvious."

Hadley and Alice swapped eye rolls. It didn't matter that none of them had thought of it. Olivia would still rake herself over the coals for missing it.

"But why does it have eight sides?" asked Soxie.

"It's just the way it was built. This says it could have been for structural purposes, or maybe even a design flaw—though I doubt it. The pyramids were built with insane precision."

Hadley leaned in to get a better look at the screen. When viewed from above, there was a slight indentation on each side of the pyramid, running from peak to base. It was like taking a regular pyramid, drawing a central line down each side, and pushing it in just enough until four sides became eight. It reminded her of origami, as if the sides of the pyramid were simply folded in.

"It wasn't discovered until 1940, when a British pilot noticed it from above," Olivia continued. "Almost like it was meant to be an optical illusion."

Hadley stepped back and sat down on the bed. Their hotel rooms had become a makeshift base of operations, complete with food wrappers, discarded bottles, and at least two laptops plugged in and searching the web at the same time. It was a nice room, but she was getting sick of it.

"Okay," she addressed them all. "If the Osiris Shaft is pointing us to the Great Pyramid, now what? Do we schedule another tour?"

Olivia leaned in to her screen and shook her head. "No. There are no private tours available, and the public tours only get you as far as the King's Chamber. It's not high enough."

Hadley sat forward. Olivia had brought up an illustration of the inside of the Great Pyramid, or Pyramid of Khufu, as it read above the diagram. The picture showed three distinct chambers that rested deep inside the pyramid, accessed by narrow passageways with steep inclines. She noticed a cloud of red dots that sat above the highest chamber, just below the peak. If the Osiris Shaft was telling them to look at the top of the pyramid, this had to be it. She stood and walked over to point at the screen.

"What's that?"

Olivia stared at her laptop for a moment before sitting back. "It's not good."

"What do you mean?" asked Alice. "Why?"

"It's a chamber that was only discovered a few years ago, by cosmic ray imaging."

"Excuse me?" said Soxie, walking over. "Cosmic ray what?"

Olivia pushed away from the desk and stood. "Go ahead. Have a look." Then she turned and fell face first on the bed with a loud groan.

Soxie sat down in the seat she'd vacated, squinting at the text below the picture. "Some speculate about what is hidden in this 'Chamber of Secrets,'" she read aloud, then paused. "Are you fucking kidding me?"

Hadley prodded her to keep reading. Soxie tut-tutted but continued. "Some say it contains the remains of Pharaoh Khufu, while others believe it could hold a secret treasure."

"Secret treasure," Alice whispered. "You don't think that—"

"Yes," Olivia interrupted her, speaking into her pillow. "That's exactly what I think."

"Shit," said Soxie.

Hadley dropped her head into her hands. David was right. They were not going to like this.

chapter 16

Hadley sat staring at the screen of her phone. She really, really didn't want to do this, but after hours of deliberating, they'd all agreed this was the only option left. She looked up to see Alice, Soxie, and Olivia sitting on the far bed, watching her.

"And you're *sure* Uncle May can't help?" she whined.

"Oh, he probably can," Soxie replied with a laugh, "but he's made it clear he won't. He's not willing to tangle with the Egyptian government. This has to be off the books. Like, super off."

"Please. Like Mayron doesn't deal with this kind of stuff all the time. I don't understand why we have to involve Caleb."

"Because, unlike your brother, my uncle isn't a convicted felon. He might operate outside the law, but he prefers not to break it when possible. We need someone with criminal connections. Pretty sure your family fits that bill."

Hadley shot her a withering look. "Thanks."

"Hey. If the felony fits."

"Not exactly helpful, Sox," Alice reprimanded her.

"Sorry. That was out of line. Hadz, I didn't mean *you*, obviously. I just—"

Hadley waved her off. "It's okay, Sox. I know what you meant. And you're right. I just hate that you are."

Soxie stood and walked over to where Hadley was sitting. She grabbed hold of her chin and planted a firm kiss on the top of her head. "You know I love you, gorgeous. But stop stalling and get it done."

Hadley leaned back and flashed her a sarcastic smile. Soxie winked and headed for the door. The others stood to follow her, but then Olivia paused and turned around.

"Do you want us to stay?" she asked.

Hadley smiled, comforted by the concerned expression on her friend's face. Olivia already knew the answer to her own question, but Hadley appreciated the ask.

"Thanks, O. But I'd prefer some privacy."

Olivia nodded and followed Alice and Soxie out of the room. The door swung shut with a soft click. Hadley stared at it for a few seconds before sighing and bringing her attention back to her phone.

She hadn't seen Caleb since their grandfather's funeral. And other than the email he sent her last year, there'd been no communication between them at all. Her dad chose to bury the hatchet and let bygones be bygones, but it didn't mean she was willing to do the same. Some wounds ran too deep.

She swallowed hard, thumb hovering over the keypad. Asking Caleb for help felt like the worst kind of sin. She'd promised herself she'd never speak to him again. Yet here she was, four years later, calling him to ask for a favor. The thought put a sour taste in her mouth.

Her head swiveled to the window as she dropped her phone into her lap. The Nile flowed steady and true, just like it had for centuries. It was past midnight, and the lights of the city sparkled in its dark waters. Even at night, it was a view she'd never get used to, and one she'd probably miss. But it also reminded her of where they were, and the gargantuan task that lay before them.

The hidden chamber, or "Chamber of Secrets," in the Great Pyramid had never been opened. It was discovered thanks to cosmic ray imaging—whatever that was—which detected a void within the upper part of the structure, completely sealed behind meters of solid rock. There was virtually no way for them to access the chamber, not without heavy explosives. While none of them claimed to be saints, destroying one of the Seven Wonders of the World was a line they'd never cross. They'd be better off sacrificing themselves to the gods.

So what were their options? Not many, as it turned out. In fact, there was really only one.

And it was a doozy.

She took a deep breath, held it for a few seconds, then picked up her phone and dialed. After several minutes, a series of menu options, operators, and holds, her brother's gruff voice came through the line.

"Well, well, if it isn't my long lost Haddy Bear. To what do I owe this honor?"

Hadley cringed. His voice cut her to the bone, yet she relished its familiarity. It was like a bowl of hot soup she knew would burn her tongue, but she took a sip anyway.

"I'm nineteen years old, Caleb. I'm not your Haddy Bear anymore."

He chuckled. "I suppose that's true. My mistake. So what do you want, *sis*? I'm guessing this isn't a social how're-you-doing call."

Hadley's jaw clenched. Why did she feel guilty? It's not like it was her fault he was in prison. Yet somehow hearing his voice brought her back to her childhood, back to the time she worshipped the ground he walked on. Before he left her alone and ruined everything.

"You're right," she said, her voice full of frost. "This isn't a social call. I need your help, but if you don't want to give it, that's fine. I'll find someone else."

There was a pause on the other end of the line. She knew their conversation was being monitored, but there was no way around it. If he had a contraband mobile phone, she didn't know about it, so this mode of communication was her only option. She'd have to choose her words wisely.

"Hello?" she said.

"I'm here," he responded, his voice low. "I'm listening."

She took a moment to get her nerves under control. She hated putting him in this position, regardless of how she felt about him. But the girls were right. He was their closest bet to finding a solution to their little problem. She decided to start small.

"Do you know anyone in Cairo?" she asked.

"Egypt?"

"No. Cairo, Minnesota," she couldn't help but respond. When he didn't say anything, she added, "Yes, Egypt. Do you know anyone? Or have connections to anyone here?"

"So you're calling me from Cairo." It wasn't a question. Dammit, she'd never planned to offer her location, not that it should matter. Yet most things did when it came to Caleb.

"Maybe," she fired back. "What difference does it make? Can you help or not?"

There was another long pause, before he said, "I'm guessing you can't tell me what this is about."

"No."

There was an even longer pause, making Hadley wonder if the call had dropped.

"Okay," he said suddenly, startling her. "I'll see what I can do. I'll call you back in fifteen minutes."

"Wait, but don't you need—" she began, then stopped as a recording interrupted her, announcing the call had been terminated.

She pulled the phone away from her ear and stared at it. It had defaulted to her lock-screen photo—her and the girls smiling by the pool back home. She let it drop back in her lap and turned to the window. The city had grown quieter, most of its residents either asleep or lying in bed, trying to sleep. With the time change, this was the only time she could talk to Caleb, but there was something eerie about waiting for his call in a deserted hotel room at one o'clock in the morning.

She sent a quick text to Olivia, filling her in and telling her she needed more time before they came back upstairs. It was too embarrassing to talk to Caleb in front of them. She felt like she reverted to her preteen self in his presence—even over the phone—and she didn't want the girls to see that side of her.

With nothing to do but wait, she stood and paced the room, stretching her legs. She stopped to look at her reflection in the mirror by the door. The overhead light highlighted the worry lines on her forehead. She pulled her palm across it to flatten them, but to no avail. They popped right back up in all their stressful glory. She sighed and lightly tapped the mirror, relieved they no longer had to worry about their images getting stuck. Even though it had been Alice the whole time, it was nice to check something off their to-do list—because lately it felt as long as a drugstore receipt.

She made her way to the minibar and plucked a can of Coke from the fridge. She had just cracked it open when her phone buzzed loudly on the table. She nearly dropped the soda as she dove to answer it.

"Caleb?" she said breathlessly.

"Get a pen," he replied, all business. "Write this down."

She grabbed a pen and room service menu off the desk. "Ready," she said.

"Marwa Sayed. She'll meet you in the Khan El-Khalili *souk* tomorrow at eleven a.m. Wear a brown hat and a red scarf. Don't be late."

She scribbled the instructions down before realizing what she was writing. "Wait, how do I find her?"

"She'll find you."

"But," she began, without knowing what she wanted to say.

"But what? You asked for my help. This is it."

Her heart felt heavy. He'd helped her, no questions asked. Even after all this time, after all the hurt and pain between them, he'd come through. Part of her wished he'd just told her to drop dead. But deep down, she knew he wouldn't, because deep down, he was still her brother.

"Thank you, Caleb."

When he didn't respond, she felt the sting of her stubborn pride. "I mean it," she added brusquely. "I . . . This is really important. I wouldn't have asked otherwise."

"I know. Just do me a favor, okay?"

She nodded, unable to agree vocally. As if hearing her nod, he said, "Be careful, Hadley. I don't know this person. She's a friend of a friend—best I can do. I trust the guy who set up the meet, but I can't vouch for her, or anyone in her circle. Remember what we taught you. Be smart, kiddo."

She ignored the lump in her throat. "I will."

"Okay then," he said. "If you need me, text me at this number. I may not be able to respond immediately, but I'll check it as often as I can."

A smirk passed her lips. "A burner phone in prison. Why am I not surprised?"

"You know me, sis," he said. She could almost hear the smile in his voice. "I never did like playing by the rules."

"No," she said with a lazy sigh. "You never did."

There was a sudden rush of movement in the background, what sounded like gates opening or banging into one another. Caleb whispered something away from the phone. Hadley leaned forward, as if that would help her hear better. When he came back, his voice was hurried.

"I gotta run. Remember what I said. Be careful, Hadley." And then he was gone, and Hadley couldn't help wishing he'd said, "Goodbye, Haddy Bear," so she could pretend she hated it.

chapter 17

"I feel ridiculous."

"Good, because you look it."

Hadley gave Soxie a tiny shove, making her teeter on her five-inch platform wedges. "Give me a break. This is all they had in the gift shop."

She noticed Alice and Olivia look away as she adjusted the brown felt cowboy hat that balanced awkwardly on top of her head. It was a child's hat, with pictures of the pyramids printed on the band. She'd had to stretch it out to its max to get it to stay on her head, and with the oversized red scarf, Soxie was right. She looked ridiculous. If she was worried about this Marwa person finding her, she needn't be. She only hoped the woman didn't change her mind about helping them.

"So we have no idea what this Marwa woman looks like," Alice presumed as she scanned the stalls on either side.

Hadley shook her head in response, then stopped to admire a table full of gold-and-turquoise scarab beetle pendants. The man behind the table smiled kindly at her, waving her further into his stall.

"No, *sukran*," she said, not wholly sure that was the correct response, but he seemed to understand and gave her a friendly wave as they moved on.

The Khan El-Khalili *souk* was a famous bazaar located in the historic center of Cairo. A major tourist attraction, it was already packed with people at ten forty-five in the morning. Vendors sold everything from classic Egyptian statuettes to spices, jewelry, T-shirts, gold and silver bowls, belly-dancing costumes, and more. It was a medieval-looking maze of brick-and-cobblestone alleyways, each filled with treasures that would take weeks to sift through. The energy was high, with tourists haggling over prices while vendors pretended to be offended at their first offers. It was a customary dance taking place before their eyes, the buying and selling of market wares. The smells, the colors, all of it was intoxicating and full of tradition. Hadley could spend days wandering this *souk*, if only they had days to spare.

A man at a stall with beautifully embroidered shoes was waving them over. Since none of the shoes had five-inch heels, Soxie wasn't interested, but the rest of them couldn't help but stop.

"Yes, you try!" he said, all teeth behind his sun-weathered skin. Hadley looked at her watch. They still had ten minutes, and it's not like she knew who they were looking for, or even where in the market they were supposed to meet. They might as well enjoy a little retail therapy while they waited for Marwa to find them.

Alice and Olivia each chose a pair of pointy flats with intricate designs stitched on the sides. Hadley pulled off her boots and tried on a pair of sandals that laced up her ankle. They were soft and supple, and smelled of fresh cowhide. She walked to the full-length mirror positioned just outside the stall, then did the thing people do when trying on shoes—she moved back and forth as if that mimicked walking in real life.

"Very nice," the proprietor of the booth said. "You buy, yes?"

Hadley nodded and smiled. She reached into her bag for her wallet when something in the mirror's reflection caught her eye. There was a woman standing behind her, on the other side of the alleyway. She was dressed in a stylish cream-colored suit, high heels, and a black hijab that covered her hair and neck. The dark sunglasses she wore made it hard to tell if she was looking in Hadley's direction, but it *felt* like she was.

Soxie sidled over to look in the same mirror. "You see her?" she said, pretending like she was admiring Hadley's shoe choice.

"Yes. Let's keep walking and see if she follows us."

They paid for their shoes and kept their pace slow as they wandered out of the stall. Every couple of minutes, Hadley would find a reason to angle her body until she spotted the woman's suit in her peripheral. She was definitely following them. It was either Marwa Sayed, or someone who worked for her. Whoever she was, she was keeping her distance, observing before making contact. It gave a sinister feel to the excursion, one Hadley hoped ended better than it was starting.

The further they ventured into the *souk*, the busier it got. Vendors consistently beckoned them as throngs of people meandered out of shaded stalls and into the warm Egyptian sun.

"Can you get a read on her?" Hadley whispered to Olivia as they passed a woman selling beaded handbags.

"Trying," she said out of the side of her mouth. "There are too many people here, and every one of them seems to be noticing us because of that stupid hat. I can't pinpoint which one is her."

Hadley tugged at the brown felt hat. At least it was shielding her from the sun, but she was ready to toss it in the trash or give it to the next child she came across. With a huff, she flung one end of the red scarf around her neck, hoping it was the universal sign for "I'm the American you're looking for."

It must have worked, because a few steps later, the woman in the cream suit was suddenly in step beside them. She kept her gaze straight ahead and walked casually, with her hands in her pockets, like she was strolling through the park on a Sunday afternoon. Her lips were stained a deep scarlet red, and her light brown skin, though covered in makeup, looked dewy and fresh. The sides of her sunglasses sported big gold C's, and every inch of her screamed designer and expensive, including her perfume—floral with a hint of spice. The woman was all class, and very intimidating. Even Soxie had to be impressed.

"At the end of this alley, you'll see a stall with a man selling ornamental birds," she informed them. Her accent was hard to place. She sounded British, except her vowels and consonants were more precise, leading Hadley to believe that despite the perfect enunciation, English was not her first language.

"Just past the stall," she continued, "you'll see a gray door. Wait five minutes, then knock twice. You will come alone. Your friends can wait outside."

"She goes nowhere without us," growled Soxie.

The woman just smiled and kept walking. "Then perhaps no one will answer. We do not seek your help. It is you who seek ours." And with that, she turned down a side alley and ducked out of sight.

They all stopped in the middle of the *souk*. People continued walking past, flowing around them like they were rocks in a stream.

"You're not going in there alone," said Soxie, before turning to Alice and Olivia. "Guys, back me up."

Olivia had that focused look on her face, the one she got when she'd been diving into someone's mind. "I don't know. I think it might be okay."

"You think?" said Soxie, flabbergasted. "That woman was straight out of a James Bond film. I think we're getting in over our heads here."

Hadley plucked the child's hat off her head and fanned herself with it. Despite the chill in the air, it was hot standing in the sun.

"Sox, your uncle is more James Bond than she is. Besides, she's right. We need her more than she needs us." Then, to Olivia, she asked, "What did you see in her head?"

Olivia lowered her gaze to the ground. People continued moving around them, as if the four of them were now a part of the bazaar. "I didn't get much, except that she's not happy about being on the hook to help us. I get the feeling that we're payment for a debt she owes someone else." She paused and looked up. "Your brother must know some interesting people."

Hadley pulled off her scarf and stuffed it in the hat. "He sure does."

"So what does this mean?" asked Alice. "If we don't let her go by herself, the woman will just call it off?"

Olivia nodded. "Yep. From what I can tell, she's looking for any excuse *not* to help us."

"But she doesn't even know what we want!" Alice whispered fiercely.

"She knows enough to know it's illegal. We wouldn't be seeking her help if it wasn't."

Hadley shoved her hat, scarf, and bag into Olivia's hands. "Here. We can't stand here arguing about it all day, and we can't afford for her to pull back the favor. You guys stay here. I'll be fine."

They all looked at her with varying degrees of doubt. But time was running out, so all she could do was give them a reassuring smile before turning around and heading toward the end of the alley. She felt their eyes boring into her back, but she kept her stride confident, her head held high. She was a Caldwell. If any of them could handle this, it was her.

She stopped when she spotted the stall with the ornamental birds. There were a few people standing next to it, examining carved wooden birds with plumes of real feathers and sparkly jewels for eyes. Birdsong played through speakers mounted atop the booth, making it sound like an aviary. As she took a few steps past the stall, she noticed a nondescript door with peeling gray paint tucked in snugly between the bird booth and a stall selling clay pottery. It was attached to a stone building so drab in comparison to the colorful *souk* that she would have missed it if she wasn't looking for it. A glance at her watch showed the five minutes was almost up. After giving herself a quick mental pep talk, she ducked into the narrow passage and gave the door two swift raps with her knuckles.

She counted the seconds as she waited, wondering if they were watching her through a hidden camera. Then she heard a lock unlatch from within, and the door slowly swung open. A young man with dark features and spiky jet-black hair ushered her inside. She darted through the opening and felt a whoosh of air as the door slammed shut behind her. A hand pushed her from behind.

"Go," he said. So she went.

The inside of the building was as drab as the exterior. There was nothing but gray stone walls and threadbare area rugs, with the occasional bare bulb lighting the way. The man pushed her through the front room, down a long hallway, and into a back room with a single window that looked out at the other side of the *souk*. Hadley wondered what this building was used for, if it used to be an office, or someone's home. Now it was run-down and cold, and the back room was empty except for a desk and a few folding chairs. Two more men stood against the wall by the window. One of them was smoking, and the other was focused on his phone. They both, however, had military-grade assault rifles slung across their chests. Hadley's back stiffened. The man smoking gave her a bored glance and nodded to the desk, where the woman in the cream suit was perched, one leg crossed over the other, her manicured nails tapping impatiently against the wood.

"Miss Caldwell," she said, gesturing to the chair in front of her. "Please, sit."

Hadley glanced at the man behind her. He was now leaning against the doorjamb, blocking the entrance to the hall. She didn't see a rifle, but she guessed he was carrying somewhere on his person. A quick scan of her surroundings revealed the window and door to be the only escape routes, and they were both blocked. If this went down badly, well, at least she tried.

With as much courage as she could muster, she walked to the chair and took a seat facing the woman. By perching on the edge of the desk and making Hadley sit lower than her, the woman was asserting her dominance. It was a classic power move. But Hadley had no choice but to play along. So she settled herself in her seat and looked up to meet the woman's gaze.

"You must be Marwa Sayed," she said. "Thank you for meeting with me."

The woman's eyes flashed with amusement. "Do not thank me yet. I am not in the business of helping silly American girls who wear silly cowboy hats."

"I was told to wear a brown hat!" she protested, a little too loudly. Movement behind her made her freeze; it sounded like one of the men by the window had taken a step forward. The tension in the room was palpable. She needed to defuse it, and fast.

"I'm sorry," she said quickly. "I didn't mean to yell. You're right. I am a silly American girl, and I was wearing a silly hat. I'll own that."

Marwa Sayed stared at her, unblinking, as she continued to drum her nails on the old desk. "Do not patronize me, Miss Caldwell. My time is valuable, and I have no interest in unnecessary chitchat. Tell me what you want."

Hadley swallowed. Here went nothing.

"I need to get to the top of the Great Pyramid."

Nails stopped drumming on wood, and a hush fell over the room. Marwa Sayed glanced over Hadley's head at the men behind her, as if confirming they heard what she just heard.

"This is why you've contacted me?" she said, her voice low and threatening. "To dishonor one of my country's greatest treasures?"

Hadley felt panic build in her chest. "No! Of course not. We would never! I just—I promise it's nothing like that. But it's very important that I get up there."

"Why?"

Hadley heard the men in the room step closer. They were either angry or curious. Either way, what could she say that would convince them to help her? God, she wished Olivia was with her right now.

"I'm waiting, Miss Caldwell," Marwa said, resuming her incessant nail drumming.

Hadley took a shallow breath and spoke slowly, choosing her words with care. "We have reason to believe there is something hidden in the upper chamber. Something . . . valuable. We can't get to it from inside, so I need to climb to the top to see if there's another way in."

Marwa stared at her for a moment, dark eyes reflecting the exposed lightbulb hanging from the ceiling. Then, out of nowhere, she burst out laughing. It was so loud and sudden that Hadley nearly jumped out of her skin. Then the men behind her started laughing, until the whole room was having a real knee-slapper of a time at Hadley's expense.

Hadley knew the less she said, the better. So instead of explaining further, she waited patiently for the laughter to die down. Eventually, Marwa wiped the tears from her eyes, pushed herself off the desk, and walked around to have a seat on the other side. Then she scooted her chair forward and steepled her hands.

"It is illegal to climb the pyramids of Giza without permission," she said, straight-faced. "You must obtain special authorization from the Ministry of Antiquities."

Hadley nodded. They'd already looked into this, ad nauseum. The paperwork alone would take weeks, and with all the restrictions and oversight, it would be impossible for them to search the pyramid with any semblance of privacy.

"We'd prefer to bypass the proper channels," she said carefully.

Marwa pursed her lips. "I see. So you are treasure hunters."

"Well—"

"Give me your phone," she interrupted, reaching her hand out expectantly. Hadley hesitated, then pulled her phone from her pocket, unlocked it, and handed it over. She felt the menacing presence of the men behind her. They were whispering to each other, no doubt still laughing at her.

Marwa swiftly typed something into Hadley's phone, then slid it back across the desk.

"You will receive instructions from the number I just messaged," she said, glancing at the phone. "My people can get you as far as the base, but if you are caught, you face heavy fines and up to three years in prison. Do you understand?"

Hadley nodded, terrified at the thought. If they got caught, would Mayron help them? *Could* he help them?

Marwa smiled and leaned back. "And do not bother mentioning my name. I'm sure you've already concluded it is an alias. Even so, it would be best for you to keep your pretty American mouth shut. Do you understand?"

Hadley swallowed uncomfortably. "Yes, I understand. Thank you. What do you require for payment?"

Marwa—or whatever her name was—simply smiled. As scary as she was, Hadley couldn't help but like her. She was a real badass boss bitch if Hadley had ever seen one, and honestly, she kind of respected that.

"It has been taken care of," she said with a flick of her hand. "Have fun on your little treasure hunt."

She snapped an order at the man by the door and he stepped forward, gesturing for Hadley to rise. She stood to follow him out of the room, but just before leaving she couldn't help but stop and turn around. Marwa's face was already buried in her phone.

"You're not worried about me damaging the pyramid?" Hadley heard herself ask.

Marwa looked up, surprised. "Do you intend to damage it?"

"No, but I just told you I'm looking for a way into the upper chamber. I'm curious as to why that doesn't concern you." She wanted to slap her hand across her own mouth. What was she thinking? Was she *trying* to ruin this deal?

One perfect eyebrow lifted, and the woman called Marwa set down her phone. "Miss Caldwell, the Great Pyramid of Khufu has been standing for thousands of years. It has survived far more than silly American girls like you. Am I worried that you will find this secret chamber? No. But if your people wish to pay me so you can embark on your little adventure, well, I am a businesswoman after all. Now go. *Our* business is done."

chapter 18

They spent the next couple of hours exploring the *souk*. Alice bought some aromatic spices for her mom, Olivia found hand-made leather collars for Fred, Ginger, and Schlemmer, and Soxie spent twenty minutes haggling over a garnet amulet that matched the color of her hair. The price wasn't the issue, it was just that Soxie had never haggled before, and she seemed to really enjoy the process.

By 2:00 p.m. they were beat, so they stopped at a teahouse in the heart of the bazaar for a cup of the best coffee Hadley had ever tasted. It was a charming establishment, with large, gilded mirrors, crystal chandeliers, and a bunch of small café tables that spilled into the alleyway. For a while, they sipped their coffee in silence, watching the menagerie of tourists and locals as they went about the business of buying and selling.

"I could sit here all day," Hadley mused, her eyes heavy despite the caffeine pulsing through her veins.

"Me too," said Alice.

"Three," Soxie and Olivia said together.

Hadley took another sip and glanced at a mirror to their left. It was high on the wall and tilted to reflect the tables beneath it. It reminded her of the mirror they fell through last year in Lyon, France. That had been one hell of a day, yet somehow this one put it to shame. She picked up her phone for the seventh time in as many minutes.

"Anything?" Alice asked.

She sank further into her seat and set the phone back down. "No. Nothing."

"I'm sure we'll hear from them soon," Alice offered, always the optimist. "It's not like we can climb up in broad daylight. I'm sure it'll be a nighttime job."

Soxie coughed, nearly spitting out her coffee. "Nighttime job? You make us sound like a gang about to knock over a 7-Eleven."

"If only," said Hadley, wishing it were that easy. Not that she'd condone robbery of any kind, but stealing a pack of Twizzlers and a Gatorade sounded a lot less intimidating than scaling a 450-foot-tall ancient pyramid. "By the way, that reminds me," she added. "We need to decide who stays and who goes."

Olivia narrowed her eyes. "We? Like you haven't already decided. You don't get the final say, you know. This is a democracy."

"What do you mean?" asked Alice, her eyes flitting back and forth between them. "I thought we were doing this together."

"No, Ali," said Soxie, knocking the rest of her coffee back like a shot. "Hadley's right. It's too dangerous to risk all of us getting thrown in prison. Two of us climb, and two of us stay behind."

Alice turned to Hadley. "It's you and me, right? I need to be there because of my powers and my connection to Osiris. And you, you're . . ." she trailed off, as if unsure of what Hadley was.

"Related to a criminal? Have criminal DNA?"

"No!" she said, slapping her palm on the table. Cups rattled in their saucers. "You know I didn't mean it like that."

Hadley grinned and leaned over to ruffle her white hair. "I'm just messing with you. Of course it should be me. First of all, I made the deal. Marwa's people will be expecting me. Second, I'm the only one with any climbing experience."

"You've climbed the rock wall at the gym," said Soxie. "That's hardly climbing experience."

Hadley shrugged and finished her coffee. "It's better than nothing."

The text came in around four o'clock that afternoon. It read: *30.124020, 31.301580, 01.00.*

Hadley stared at it for several seconds. They were back in the sporting goods store, purchasing the necessary items needed for their upcoming expedition. Olivia walked up with a pair of night-vision goggles in her hands.

"These were the cheapest I could find, but—" She stopped when she caught sight of Hadley's expression and leaned over to have a look at her phone. "They're latitude and longitude coordinates," she concluded, not missing a beat. "For one a.m."

Hadley dropped her phone to her side, annoyed. She would have gotten there, eventually. Olivia giggled and placed the goggles in Hadley's basket.

"I know you would have," she teased. "It's just more fun when I beat you to it."

"For you," Hadley deadpanned. Then she threw a nod at the goggles. "They didn't have two pairs?"

"They're six thousand apiece. I don't even know if we can afford one."

Hadley looked over Olivia's head to where Soxie and Alice were standing, examining ropes and carabiners.

"It sure was a lot easier when Uncle Mayron wasn't so tight with the purse strings."

"You can say that again," agreed Olivia.

Hadley hung back as Olivia brought their items to the register, hopeful that Soxie's credit card didn't laugh in their faces. Then she sent a quick thumbs-up emoji to the mysterious number. She had tons of questions, but if they were sending latitude and longitude coordinates, she had the feeling they weren't interested in answering over text.

She joined the others at the register, where Soxie was already fuming over the cost of the goggles. But she eventually agreed that a flashlight's beam was too limiting. If they made it inside the pyramid, they'd need all the sight they could get.

When they got back to the hotel, Hadley sent the girls to the room while she went in search of a city map. There was no way of predicting what they might find at the strange coordinates, but even a rudimentary lay of the land was better than nothing. And even though the internet was bound to navigate them successfully, sometimes she liked the feel and comfort of an old-fashioned paper map.

The concierge provided her with a few pamphlets that included maps, and as she unfolded one of them, the others slipped from her hands and fell to the floor. As she bent over to pick them up, someone knelt down to help. She looked up and found a familiar pair of green eyes staring back at her.

"What are you doing here?" she said, rising to her feet.

David grinned his oh-so-David grin. It was a combination of Cheshire Cat and Puss in Boots. Mischievous, yet somehow adorable. If "schmaltzy" were a smile, basically. He stood and lifted his arms as if to hug her, but she stepped back, just out of reach. His face fell, and his arms dropped to his sides.

"It's nice to see you too."

Chastened, she stepped forward to give him an obligatory hug. It was more of a lean-in-and-pat-on-the-back, but it counted.

"Sorry, I just didn't expect to see you here," she said, easing back. Then she glanced at the elevator bank, and added, "Does Alice know you're here?"

He shook his head. "No, and I'd prefer she didn't. For now."

"I don't understand what's going on with you two," she confessed. "It makes no sense."

He planted his gaze on the floor. "It's been hell not being with her, Hadz. But—and please don't ever repeat this—I've needed this time. It's been hard switching to another person in the same life. I have all of Colin's memories, and none of David's. Yet I have to *be* David. It gets confusing, and sometimes I forget who I am. If this is the man I am, the one I'm offering her, I need to embrace who that is, so she can too."

It was the kind of circular logic that made her skin crawl. Then again, she'd never had to live in someone else's body. She'd never had to be someone else. Maybe there was more sense to his logic than she was giving him credit for.

But still.

"Listen, for what it's worth, I don't think Alice cares if you never figure out who or what you are. She loves you, no matter what. But she needs her space too, so I get it."

His eyelids fluttered. "She said that?"

Hadley pulled her hair from her face. Of all the things she had to worry about, Alice and David's love life was probably number 194 on the list.

"I really don't have time for this. I have a pyramid to climb and an ancient portal to uncover. Your identity crisis will have to wait."

His expression soured, and he stuffed his hands in his pockets. A stoic mask slid across his face, and the old, overbearing David returned.

"Fine. That's actually why I'm here." He stopped to dig something out from the bag slung across his chest. "I thought you might need this."

Her breath caught. It was wrapped in a thick velvet sheath, but the oblong shape made it easy to identify.

"You came all this way just to bring us the dagger? How did you get it past security?"

His lip curled slightly. "I may have flown private."

Her jaw dropped. "Um, Soxie's going to kill you. Mayron made her fly coach!"

"What can I say? I'm more charming than she is."

She snatched the dagger from his hand. "You're a pain in the ass is what you are."

He laughed. "Believe me. I know."

An awkward silence ensued as they stood in the middle of the lobby, waiting for the other to say something. A few travelers walked by, their roller suitcases making subtle clicking noises on the marble tile. Eventually, Hadley glanced at her watch. It was just past six, and they still had a lot of planning to do.

"I really need to get upstairs," she said at last. "They're probably wondering where I am. Are you staying in the hotel?"

He stuffed his hands back in his pockets, making himself small. It was strange to see him so unsure of himself.

"No, I'm a few blocks away." Then he shrugged. "You know. Space, and all."

She lifted the dagger. "How am I supposed to explain this?"

"Just say it was delivered via messenger."

"Right. Because Olivia doesn't read minds or anything."

He sighed impatiently. "Hadley, please. You know I was talking about Alice. I don't want to be the one who screws this up. If she needs her space to focus, I'm giving her that. Just promise me you won't say anything, not until we're on the other side of this thing. Soxie and Olivia will play along."

"Okay," she grumbled, swatting an errant hair from her face. "I promise. But then you have to promise me something."

It took a moment before he nodded.

"Promise me you'll figure this David crap out. You're David. That's who you are now. Deal with it and live your life. Otherwise, what's the point of all this?"

His jaw jutted out and she sensed him struggling not to blow his top. But then, as if by some miracle, he let it all go. His shoulders sagged and his chin dropped to his chest.

"You're right. I'm an idiot."

She thought about it. "Sometimes, yes. But right now, you're just an idiot in love. There's a difference."

He looked up and smiled, eyes twinkling. "I'd say be careful, but I've never needed to say that to you, Hadz. You're the strong one. You always have been, and I know you'll take care of her for me."

"No, I won't."

He blinked, and she slapped him on the shoulder.

"I'll take care of her for *us*."

chapter 19

Hadley adjusted the straps on her backpack, making sure it was nice and snug. Sam was grumbling in the front seat, appalled by the address they gave him. He didn't like that particular area of town, and he didn't understand why they wanted to go there. When they'd confirmed the coordinates via Hadley's maps and Olivia's laptop, they'd been just as surprised. It was nowhere near the pyramids, and according to Sam, it was not a desirable neighborhood. They told him they were meeting a friend and not to worry, but he was clearly worried. And that, in turn, made Hadley a little worried.

Alice took hold of her hand and squeezed. They were both dressed in black with knit caps covering their white and blond hair. The nightly sound and light show at Giza would be over by now, but there were still powerful spotlights trained on the pyramids, lighting them up like lounge singers on a desert stage. Hadley and Alice would have to stick to the shadows if they were to climb unnoticed, and light-colored hair didn't fit well with that plan.

"I still can't believe David sent the dagger through the mail," Alice wondered aloud, more to herself than to Hadley. "He spent centuries protecting it. Why would he take this kind of risk now?"

Hadley gave her a sidelong glance. She didn't want to lie, but if Alice knew David was here, she'd be too distracted, and tonight they needed their heads in the game. Hadley schooled her face and said, "I don't know. But who cares? We have it if we need it."

Alice nodded absently, then turned to look out the window, gnawing on her thumbnail. Hadley would have done the same, but she'd already chewed hers into oblivion.

They turned onto a rough and gravelly road, and the car slowed to a crawl. Hadley leaned forward and pressed her face against the tinted glass.

Most of the buildings on the street were dark, with the exception of two or three dim lights flickering through drawn shades. They passed a heap of smoldering garbage, its embers still glowing deep within the pile. Even through the car's closed windows, Hadley's eyes stung with the smell of burning plastic and rotting vegetation. Sam waved his hand in front of his face and mumbled something under his breath in Arabic.

"Is that where we're going?" Alice inquired, pointing to a light further down the road.

Hadley peered into the darkness ahead. Halfway down the street was what looked like an outdoor café. A few chairs and tables were scattered haphazardly in the roadway, making it impossible for any normal-sized vehicle to get through. Strings of lights hung across the road, and candles burned lazily on the tables. Considering the time, and the dark streets they'd been driving through, this little patch of dirt road was bustling with people. As they got closer, she noticed most of the seats were filled with men and women drinking tea or smoking hookahs. An older gentleman with a beard as white as Alice's hair sat on a rug in front of the café, playing the lute. The music was calming, yet lively. It made for a festive and cozy scene.

"This looks all right," observed Hadley, her anxiety easing.

Sam harrumphed but said nothing. Unable to get through the street, he stopped the car and did a three-point turn until he was able to park on the side of the road, facing the opposite direction.

"Okay, girls, you go. I wait."

Hadley and Alice looked at each other.

"Oh, Sam, that's so nice," Alice hurried to say, putting an extra ounce of sweet in her delivery. "But we can't let you wait. We haven't seen our friend in a long time, so we might be a while."

His reply was curt. "That is fine. I wait."

"We'll probably be spending the night," Hadley blurted out. Sam's head snapped around, his eyebrows nearly climbing to his hairline. Hadley realized her mistake and quickly rushed to fix it.

"It's just, our friend, she has a new baby, and we promised we'd help her. You know how it is, right? Babies can cry all night, and she really needs some help. But don't worry, she'll bring us back to the hotel in the morning."

His posture relaxed, and he smiled. "Ah, yes, babies cry too much! You go, help your friend. You are good girls. Maybe one day you have babies of your own!"

Hadley and Alice exchanged another glance, trying not to laugh. Then they thanked Sam and quickly exited the car, pretending to wave at someone sitting at a far table. As the car pulled away, they slowed their pace and stopped beneath the first string of lights at the edge of the café. A few people glanced in their direction, some giving them a good once-over before going back to their conversation and tea. A woman smoking a hookah seemed quite interested in their clothes, while the man playing the lute nodded and managed to wave hello without missing a note. It felt like a scene out of a movie—a secret coffeehouse in the heart of the city where locals gathered to chat the night away. It was a different side of Cairo, one Hadley felt lucky to experience.

"This is pretty cool," said Alice as she looked around in awe. "I wonder why they sent us here. Do you think this is the right place?"

Hadley scanned the tables, looking for anyone who could be their contact. She spotted an empty table near the center of the street with what looked like a reserved sign, and as she took a few steps closer, she realized she was right.

Alice moved next to her, and read the sign out loud. "'Silly American Girl.' What's that supposed to mean?"

Hadley couldn't help but laugh. She was really starting to like this Marwa woman.

They sat down at the table, and within seconds an older man appeared with two cups of steaming-hot aromatic heaven. They tried to pay, but he just waved them off and scurried back to his kitchen, which looked like it was part of his home. She wondered if he made anyone pay, or if this was some kind of shared community situation. Everyone seemed at ease and comfortable with each other. Perhaps it was a family affair.

A man, probably in his early twenties, suddenly materialized out of nowhere, like he'd been waiting in the darkness just outside the café's circle of light. He flipped a chair around and straddled it backward, resting his elbows on the back. It was the sort of thing guys like him did to look cool. And in this case, it worked. He was as handsome as they come, maybe even more handsome than David, but with darker skin and dark eyes, and teeth that nearly glowed as he flashed them a dimpled smile. His black T-shirt and tight jeans completed the look in a very rakish way.

"So," he began. "The silly American girls want to climb the Pyramid of Khufu. I love it!"

Laughter rippled through the other tables as if they were all in on the joke. Hadley felt her face grow hot. His sarcasm was about as subtle as his eye-watering cologne.

"Yes, we would like to climb the pyramid," she confirmed. "I take it you're our contact?"

He stared at her for a moment, then burst out laughing. The other patrons laughed with him, and the whole thing really did start to feel like a movie. One that involved two silly American girls lost in the *Twilight Zone*.

Hadley squared her shoulders and sat up straight, pulling the straps of her backpack taut. "I'm assuming Marwa sent you? We'd like to get going now if that's okay."

He smiled even bigger—if that was possible. "Marwa," he repeated. "No, no, American girl. Marwa sent *you* to *me*."

Alice stiffened next to her. The last thing they needed was to panic. If they panicked, they were in trouble. Remaining calm and confident was the only way through this. Hadley squeezed Alice's thigh, then leaned back casually and tented her hands in front of her chin.

"Did she?" she said, giving him a long, measured look before continuing. "Then she must have also told you that her people would give us access to the pyramid. The deal has already been made."

He began to drum his fingers on the back of the chair, just like Marwa. "Yes, but that deal was not made with me. You and me," he gestured between them, "we make our own deal."

Hadley focused on keeping her voice steady and her face expressionless. "Okay then," she hedged, "let's make a deal. What do you want?"

He pulled a toothpick from his pocket and began to pick his shiny white teeth with it. "That depends, American girl. What do you have?"

Thirty minutes and one pair of six-thousand-dollar night-vision goggles later, Hadley and Alice were crammed in the trunk of a car while their contact, whose name was Ibrahim—or so he said—drove them to the Giza Plateau. He never mentioned how he was planning to get them past security, but Hadley assumed he either knew one of the guards or worked as a security guard himself. The less they knew, the better.

Alice was a jangle of nerves in Hadley's arms, the little spoon to her big one. But her nervousness somehow quieted Hadley's own. If it wasn't for Alice, she would never have been able to get inside this trunk.

"Hadley?" Alice whispered.

"Yes?"

"Tell me about your brother."

Her limbs tensed. "Why?"

"Well, I'm locked in the trunk of a stranger's car—a stranger he put us in touch with. I know you don't like to talk about him, but I could use the distraction right now."

Hadley sighed and readjusted her position. The car accelerated, and soon they heard a rhythmic *thump, thump* as the vehicle moved onto a paved roadway. If need be, they could kick out the brake lights and wave down another motorist, but Hadley didn't think it would come to that. Ibrahim was an opportunist, but he still answered to Marwa, and as cold as she was, Hadley trusted her. So if Alice wanted to talk, then Hadley might as well oblige. It's not like they had anything else to do.

"What do you want to know?" she said at last. "Why he's in prison?"

Alice shrugged in her arms. "I assume it's for stealing cars."

Hadley laughed to herself. "That's the simplified version, but yes. Caleb was running the entire organization."

"But your dad got out. Why didn't he?"

"He didn't want to get out. He chose that life over us."

Alice turned her head as if trying to see Hadley behind her. "I'm sorry. It must have been hard to ask for his help."

"It was."

A long stretch of silence followed, nothing but the hypnotic hum and thump of the car's tires as they sped through the night. Hadley's thoughts naturally went to the place she preferred they didn't—imagining what life would have been like had her brother chosen differently.

"After the divorce, I was angry at my dad for a long time," Alice suddenly said, her voice thin, cutting through the quiet. "I lived and breathed that anger, and eventually I came to depend on it. I didn't want to try and understand him. I just wanted to hate him."

Hadley closed her eyes. She wasn't in the right mindset for this kind of talk.

"But the thing is," Alice went on, "when I finally did let it go, I realized my anger wasn't just hurting him, it was hurting me. It takes a lot more energy to hate someone than it does to love them."

Hadley choked back tears that suddenly threatened to spring forth. She appreciated what Alice was trying to do, but she couldn't afford to get emotional right now. They had a job to do. A big one.

"You're right, honey," she said, patting her on the leg. "You should think about getting that stitched on a pillow."

That earned her a sharp elbow in the rib.

"Ow!" she laughed. Then the vehicle suddenly slowed, and she hushed, listening. The car door opened and closed, and she heard muffled voices. A few seconds later, the door opened and closed once more, and they were moving again.

"What was that?" Alice whispered.

"Probably a security checkpoint. We must be close."

Neither of them said anything as the car bumped along at a snail's pace. Hadley reached down to grab the switchblade she had stashed in her boot. She didn't know what they were driving into, so it was best to be prepared. When the car finally came to a full stop, she flipped it open and held her breath. She sensed Alice holding her breath as well.

Footsteps crunched on gravel, and there was a quick knock on the trunk before it popped open. Ibrahim's face was masked in darkness, with only the white of his teeth reflecting the ambient light from a crescent moon.

"Okay, girls. Out."

Hadley breathed a sigh of relief and quietly folded her switchblade, stuffing it back in her boot. Then she crawled out of the trunk behind Alice and lifted her arms overhead to stretch her body.

She squinted into the dark to see where they were when Ibrahim suddenly yanked her backpack off her back.

"Hey!" she cried out, attempting to snatch it back. He held it out of reach, unzipped it, and rummaged inside. Her temper flared.

"We already gave you the goggles. What more do you want?"

He pulled out the length of rope they'd bought at the sporting goods store, and tossed it in the trunk, along with her flashlight and climbing gear. Then he shoved the bag into her chest and motioned for Alice to hand over her pack as well.

"We need those," Hadley pleaded, gesturing toward the trunk.

Ibrahim ignored her and searched Alice's pack, repeating the process. Then he looked up.

"This is not Everest, American girl. You free-climb, or you don't climb at all."

Hadley glanced at Alice. They weren't in a position to argue at this point, but she couldn't help it.

"What about our flashlights?" she persisted. "How are we supposed to see?"

"This is not my problem," came his clipped reply. Then he extended his hand and added, "Give me your phones."

Part of her was itching to pull out her switchblade to prove she wouldn't be bullied, but she tamped down the urge and handed him her phone. Alice did the same.

"You'll get these back when you return. You have two hours."

He slammed the trunk shut and walked toward the driver's seat.

Hadley spun in a quick circle. She didn't see anything, other than darkness and a few city lights twinkling in the distance. Where the hell did he take them?

"Wait!" she called after him. "You were supposed to take us to the base of the pyramid!"

He stopped and turned around. Then he leaned back and pointed at the sky.

"Use your eyes, my friends. You are here."

They looked up. What she'd thought was darkness wasn't darkness at all, but the shadow of a megalithic structure towering over them, blocking out the sky. As she craned her head, Hadley saw a corona of light as it bent around the top of the pyramid, making the side they were standing on so dark it almost disappeared.

"It's so dark," whispered Alice, echoing her thoughts.

Ibrahim laughed. "Only for two hours. Better hurry!" Then he jumped in his car and sped away, leaving his headlights off so that all they saw was the faint glow of his brake lights as he turned and disappeared.

"Two hours?" Alice repeated as she stared after him. "Is that going to be enough? What happens after that?"

Hadley turned back toward the pyramid. "I think it's normally lit by ground spotlights, but it looks like they arranged for them to be off for two hours. If we're not down before then, we'll be exposed, and our ride will leave without us."

"Great."

Hadley dropped her pack on the ground and knelt down to dig in the side pockets. She found the false seam she'd sewn in earlier and ripped it open to confirm the dagger was still there, safely hidden in the lining behind her water bottle. She kept digging until her fingers gripped the penlight she kept on hand for emergencies. She stood, stuffed it in her pocket, slung her arms through the straps of her backpack, and turned to Alice.

"Okay. Let's go."

Ten minutes in, she realized why Ibrahim had taken away their equipment. It would only have slowed them down. The pyramid consisted of meticulously carved rectangular blocks stacked on top of each other and positioned so that they narrowed at the top. It was a simple yet precise design. Climbing the blocks didn't require anchors, ropes, or carabiners. But it was physically challenging, like climbing a stone staircase with five- to six-foot-tall risers.

Hadley pulled herself up onto a limestone block, then took a breath before lying on her stomach and reaching down to offer Alice her hand. Once she pulled her up, Alice then helped boost Hadley onto the next block. Together, they slowly made their way up, block after block. Occasionally, there were smaller blocks they could use as steps or footholds that allowed them to scramble up. With only a sliver of moonlight to guide them, it required a lot of concentration. But the higher they got, the smaller the blocks became, until soon they were able to climb without each other's assistance and quicken their pace.

About three-quarters of the way up, Hadley suggested they stop and rest. She sat back against the cool limestone, letting her feet dangle over the side. Alice, breathing heavily, dropped down beside her and pulled a water bottle from her pack. She took a long drink, then handed it to Hadley. After quenching their thirst, they sat for a few moments, catching their breath, and staring at the city in the distance. It was a moment that deserved its moment, so they sat in silence, appreciating it. Then a cool wind blew up the side of the pyramid, bringing with it fine granules of sand that stuck to them like glitter.

"It's so quiet up here," observed Alice.

Hadley nodded and pulled off her cap to wipe the grit from her face. It was true, there was a hush up here that felt unnatural, as if some sort of noise-canceling technology was being deployed. The further they climbed, the quieter it got. And it wasn't just quiet. It was *muted*.

"I feel like this is what they'd say in a horror movie," Alice prefaced, "but . . . don't you think it's a little *too* quiet?"

"Yes," Hadley admitted. "I do."

There was a sudden vibration in the stone beneath them. They both jumped, staring at each other with wide eyes. Then, as if the limestone itself was absorbing light from the tiny crescent moon, Hadley could swear it started to glow.

"What's happening?" Alice rasped.

Hadley cautiously placed her palm on the rock. It was no longer cool, but warm. She moved her gaze upward. They were still at least ten minutes from the top. Was this a warning, or an invitation to keep going? She turned to Alice.

"We must be close. Unless that was an earthquake, I think the Portal is here, and it knows we are too."

Alice's face looked pale in the dim light. She looked up, then down, as if trying to decide their next move. "Okay, but now what? Do we climb to the top, or try to find a way in here?"

Hadley thought for a moment, then hopped down a couple of steps. The strange glow she'd seen disappeared, and the stones at this level were cool to the touch. She returned to where Alice was waiting and confirmed the stone there was still warm. Next, she climbed two steps higher. The rocks got brighter and warmer. She grinned and turned back to Alice.

"I can't believe it, but I think we're about to play a game of hot and cold."

Alice moved up the pyramid to stand next to Hadley. She pressed her hand to the rock and seemed to come to the same conclusion. Then she stood to look out over the Cairo desert.

"Listen," she said, her voice hushed. "It's even quieter. And is it me, or is it getting darker out there?" She pointed toward the city, which, only a few minutes before, had been lit up like any other modern metropolis. But now, to Hadley's shock, it looked like someone had just pulled the plug. On everything.

"Is it a blackout?" she wondered, unable to fathom what else it could be. She peered into the blackness, then lowered her gaze. There should have been light coming from the base of the pyramid—from the spotlights trained on the other antiquities in the complex, including the Sphinx. But there was nothing. It was as if someone just drew a blackout curtain over the world.

Alice took a hesitant step toward the edge. "This is really weird."

Hadley grabbed her penlight to check the time on her watch. "We only have a little over an hour. We need to keep moving."

Alice fell in step beside her, and they continued climbing. When the blocks grew cold and dull, they changed direction, and with each set of warmer stones, it got quieter, and the world around them darker. Despite their zigzag pattern, they were getting closer to the top, and their progress was much faster. The steps got smaller, and it started to feel like they were climbing up a normal set of wide stairs.

Hadley crouched to feel the temperature of the block she was standing on. It was slightly cooler than the one she had just left, so she changed directions and made a diagonal hop onto the next step. As she did, she slipped and frantically flung her body forward, grabbing on to anything she could. But her hands couldn't find purchase, and she felt herself begin to slide. But how? What was happening? She heard Alice yelp behind her, and she turned just in time to see her falling as well.

It didn't make any sense! They were sliding down a solid, smooth slope. The steps were gone.

"Hadley!" Alice screamed.

Hadley clawed at the smooth limestone as she continued to slide, faster and faster. Panic took over and she heard herself scream. And then suddenly there was nothing to claw at. She was falling in empty space, arms and legs windmilling as she tumbled through the air. When the darkness came, it suffocated her like a thick blanket, swallowing her whole.

chapter 20

When she came to, Hadley was lying on her back at the bottom of a deep shaft, with only a square of night sky visible above. Even so, the stars shone brighter than she'd ever seen them, even in a planetarium.

"Argh," Alice grunted beside her.

Hadley sat up, disoriented, as her vision swam with tiny little dots. She turned to Alice, swaying.

"Are you okay?" she managed.

Alice nodded, wincing as she pushed herself up. "I think so. You?"

Hadley did a quick scan of her own body. Other than a few scrapes from sliding down the pyramid, everything seemed to be working properly. She looked at the square opening above them. Judging from the height, neither one of them should be talking right now. Or breathing.

"That's got to be fifty feet," she deduced, craning her neck to judge the distance. Then she glanced at the ground. It was packed earth with a fine layer of sand—certainly not enough to break their fall. "We should be dead, or at the very least, really, really hurt."

Alice peeled herself off the floor and kept her gaze upward. "I didn't feel my body hit the ground. Did you?"

Hadley thought about it. "No," she said, bewildered. "I didn't." Then she stood and dusted herself off before turning to take in the rest of their surroundings. They were standing in the only patch of light provided by the stars far above. At the edge was total darkness, the kind that felt more like a wall than empty space. The temperature was cool, and the air was damp and musty. Without realizing it, they had both moved to the center of the light.

"I think we found the chamber," Alice said, gesturing from the wall of black to the opening above. "But how did we end up in here, and more importantly, how do we get out?"

Hadley closed her eyes and considered their situation. She couldn't explain it, but the steps they'd been walking up had suddenly transformed into a smooth rock face. She remembered learning the pyramids were once covered in casing stones, making the sides smooth. But the casing stones were removed centuries ago and used to build the city of Cairo.

Her eyes popped open, and a cold feeling seeped into her skin. Her bones. *Now* it was starting to make sense. The city lights going out. The ultra quiet. They hadn't just climbed up a pyramid. They'd climbed into another time.

She relayed her hypothesis to Alice, whose face turned as white as her hair. Then they turned to peer into the darkness surrounding them, suddenly wary. Before, it was just a lost chamber in a pyramid. But now? Well, it could be anything.

Hadley pulled out her penlight. "Well, at least we know we have more than an hour to make it back."

Alice chuckled nervously, then moved in, wrapping an arm around Hadley's waist. "Yeah. I'm guessing Ibrahim won't be waiting at the bottom for a few thousand years."

Normally Hadley would laugh, but even humor wasn't making their predicament any less grim. What if they were stuck here, in another time, forever? She quickly dashed the thought aside. Panic caused people to make rash and stupid decisions. They had to stay focused and sharp. She took a long, deep breath, flipped on her penlight, and pointed it at the dark.

Alice's fingers dug into her flesh but relaxed once the light revealed what lay beyond the darkness. It was just a simple rectangular room, carved straight into the limestone. Together they slowly spun in a circle as Hadley trained her light along the rough-cut walls, looking for a passage of some kind. But there was nothing. She moved the light toward the center of the room, expecting a sarcophagus, or maybe even a treasure chest full of gold. Marwa had accused them of being treasure hunters, after all. But other than a small puddle of water, the room was empty. And from what Hadley could tell, the only way out was fifty feet up.

She felt Alice sag beside her. "This isn't good."

"No need to panic just yet," she reasoned. "Check the walls. Maybe there's a lever or something that will open up a passageway."

So for the next few minutes, they meticulously ran their hands along every crevice of the room they could reach, from the highest corners to the edges where the stone met the floor. They pushed and prodded, but nothing moved to reveal a secret tunnel with lit torches like they'd find in a movie. It was nothing but an empty room with an opening fifty feet above their heads. Hadley blew out a shaky breath and examined the walls. They were rough-cut but lacked any sort of handholds, making a free-climb impossible. If they didn't find a passage down here, they were stuck.

Alice kicked at the ground in frustration, sending a cloud of dust into the air. "We should try the dagger," she suggested.

Hadley looked at her and nodded. The dagger was dangerous because it was unpredictable. It could hurt them as easily as it could help them. But they were quickly running out of options. So with shaky hands, she pulled the dagger from her pack, unwrapped it, and handed it to Alice, handle first.

"Be careful," she urged her.

Alice gripped the handle and walked to the closest wall. Hadley kept her light trained on her and waited with bated breath as she lifted her arm and stabbed the rock.

"Ow!" she cried as the knife ricocheted off the stone and bounced out of her hands. She flicked her wrist a few times, smarting from the pain.

Hadley hissed in empathy, then bent over to pick up the dagger. She moved it into the square of light from the vertical shaft. Although old and tarnished, the dagger looked undamaged. When she shined her light on the wall, it revealed a small scratch in the limestone, but nothing more.

"That clearly didn't work," Alice remarked, still wiggling her wrist.

Hadley felt real fear begin to gnaw at her gut. If the dagger was useless, they really were in trouble. But to be sure, they spent the next several minutes *carefully* running the tip of the blade along the walls. It was good to be thorough, but the result was the same. No secret passageways or escape tunnels.

They were in a sealed chamber that seemed to have no purpose whatsoever.

Eventually, they both crumpled to the floor. Hadley flipped off her light to conserve the battery, and they sat in the dark, their breathing ragged from exhaustion and fear. Starlight from the shaft opening continued to cast a column of light on the floor where they'd landed, in what Hadley was starting to think was less of a chamber, and more of a grave. She tried communicating with Olivia telepathically, but the effort was futile. Olivia's gift might occasionally cover short distances, but how could it cover time? The horrifying truth was that it couldn't. They were on their own.

"What are we going to do?" Alice sniffed. "I don't want to die here."

Hadley's eyes pricked. She didn't want to die here either. Suddenly angry, she scrambled up and jumped into the square of light.

"HELP! HELP! CAN ANYONE HEAR US? WE'RE DOWN HERE!"

Alice joined her, and together they screamed bloody murder up the shaft that, for all they knew, opened up on a world that no longer existed. But they didn't care. If an ancient Egyptian from three thousand years ago heard them, they'd take it.

But no one came, and it wasn't long before their throats burned raw from the effort. Again they collapsed to the floor, spent. Their desperation was quickly morphing into hopelessness.

For hours they sat in the square of light, leaning into each other's backs and occasionally nodding off. They took turns taking sips of water, doing their best to conserve their supply, but the exertion of climbing and falling down the pyramid proved to be too much. Their water had run out, and their luck wasn't far behind.

Alice dropped her empty bottle on the dirt floor next to her and lazily pushed it away. It rolled into the darkness, where it would no doubt remain for thousands of years. Hadley wondered if an archaeologist would one day come across it, unable to explain how a stainless steel thermos from the twenty-first century ended up in a four-thousand-year-old tomb. But then she remembered—this chamber had never been opened, at least not in her time.

Her time.

Tears fell down her cheeks in fat, heavy drops. Her time. Their time. Were their bodies nothing but dust now? Had they been gallivanting around Cairo for days with no concept of how close they were to their own graves? She sucked in a breath, unable to mask her sob.

"Don't," said Alice. "Don't give up yet, Hadz."

Hadley wiped her eyes and sniffled. She felt Alice shift behind her, but she didn't turn around. "I'm sorry. I just don't know what else to do."

Alice inhaled as if she was about to say something. When she didn't, Hadley reached back to grab her hand. Their fingers intertwined, and Hadley couldn't help but feel thankful they were together. She didn't want Alice to die, but she didn't want to be alone either.

"I'm glad you're here," she whispered, squeezing her hand. "Is that selfish?"

"No," answered Alice. "I'm glad you're here too. I'm sure Soxie and Olivia feel the same."

Something between a sob and a laugh erupted from Hadley's mouth. She felt a silent giggle behind her.

"Sorry," Alice said. "Couldn't resist."

Hadley nodded into the dark. She'd much rather laugh than cry, even if the occasion was more suited for the latter. But laughter couldn't diminish the thirst already gnawing at her throat, soon to be followed by hunger. They'd die of dehydration before they died of hunger, but neither was a fun way to go. She glanced in the direction of the lone puddle of water, wondering how long before they succumbed and drank it. It was standing water from a different time. The bacteria would likely make them sick, speeding up the dehydration process. Eventually, they'd be too mentally crazed and weak to talk, so if there was anything left to say, now was the time to say it.

"You know," she began, her voice surprisingly even. "That wasn't my first time locked in the trunk of a car."

"It wasn't?"

"No. When I was eight years old, my dad served ten months for felony theft. This was before he quit the business," she explained, taking a second to collect herself before trudging on. "Anyway, Caleb and I had to go live with my Grandpa Frank, and Frank wasn't exactly fond of kids, especially girls. In his eyes, Caleb could at least help out in the warehouse and learn the business, but not me. I was a liability."

"You were eight years old! What kind of man thinks of his eight-year-old granddaughter as a liability?"

She laughed softly. "Frank Caldwell, that's who. He was battling a rival organization for territory and was convinced they'd try to use me against him. I was never his granddaughter. I was just a problem he needed to solve. So he decided to teach me how to handle a kidnapping situation, because—and I quote—'I'm not giving up the East Valley for a weak little girl whose own mother was too weak to survive her birth.'"

Alice gasped. "Oh my god, Hadley. That's horrible! Your grandfather sounds like he was a misogynistic asshole. I'm so sorry."

"It's okay. I learned how to navigate him early on, and the other guys in the garage let me help out when he wasn't watching. I learned a lot in that place, despite my shitty grandfather. But Frank's way of preparing me was to tie my hands and feet and throw me in the trunk of a car. He told me I had thirty minutes before the car went into the compactor—whether I made it out or not." She paused as bile rose in her throat. "For those thirty minutes, I really believed I might get crushed, because Frank was crazy enough to let it happen. I almost passed out from hyperventilating. That was the dream I was about to have when I summoned Melinoë. I just—I couldn't go through it again. I panicked."

"Hadley, you're not a robot. Of course you panicked," said Alice. "It's called PTSD. Why didn't you say anything when Ibrahim ordered us into the trunk?"

"I didn't need to. I had you."

Alice chuckled. "I'm pretty sure you were the one comforting me."

"Trust me. I would have lost it if you weren't there."

Hadley could almost hear Alice smile. "Well? Did you manage to get out of the trunk on your own?"

"No. Caleb found me, and when he opened the trunk, he said, 'You know the secret to getting out of a locked trunk? Don't *ever* let yourself get put in one.'"

Alice shrugged behind her. "It's not bad advice. Right now I wish we'd taken it."

"Me too," she said with a tiny laugh. "Caleb had his moments, even if most of them were bad."

A few seconds passed in silence. Hadley had never repeated Caleb's words from that day out loud. She was surprised she still remembered them yet knew in her heart of hearts it was verbatim. Later, she learned Frank had told Caleb where she was, and never really intended to crush her like scrap metal. But in her mind, her brother saved her life that day.

"Do you forgive him?" Alice said, interrupting her thoughts.

Hadley wavered. "After my dad got out, we cut ties with Frank. I never saw him again, not until his funeral. And by then I tried not to think of him at all. He was just a mean, miserable old man. We were never going to be close."

"I'm talking about your brother."

Hadley felt something snap deep inside, threatening to shatter her into a million pieces.

"Why would you ask me that?"

"Why shouldn't I?" she said gently.

Hadley tried desperately to blink back the tears that were already falling. "Because . . . that was my biggest fear, the one I admitted to Melinoë."

She felt Alice twist around behind her. "What was?"

"That I would never be able to let go," she croaked, the words nearly dying in her throat. "That I would die, or he would die, and I would take my anger with me. But even being here now . . . knowing this might be the end, I still don't know if I can do it. What does that say about me?"

Alice exhaled. "It's not that simple, Hadz. All it says is you're human."

Hadley wasn't letting herself off that easily. "But you did it. You forgave your dad. So why can't I forgive Caleb? The really messed-up thing is, I know you're right—what you said before. Love *is* a lot easier."

There was a faint sniffle behind her. "No, Hadley. You know what's really messed up? The letter from David, the one that was waiting for me at the hotel."

Hadley's ears perked up, wondering why Alice was bringing it up now. "Why? What did it say?"

"That he trusted me to come back to him," she replied with a hoarse voice. "And that no matter what happened, he'd wait for me—until the end of time if he had to. And now look at us." She stopped, her breath hitching. "We're literally lost in time. He's going to spend the rest of his life wondering what happened, why I *didn't* come back. I shouldn't have called off the wedding. Love *was* the easy choice, but I still chose fear. I ruined the only time we had left."

"No, honey. You didn't. He's in Egypt right now. Well, not right now, but—you know what I mean."

Alice's back straightened. "He is?"

"Yes. He brought the dagger himself, but I think he really just wanted to be near you. I'm sorry I lied. He asked me to. He wanted you to have your space."

Hadley waited tensely for a response. She wasn't sure if she was about to get yelled at or not, but then Alice gripped her hand tight.

"Thank you for telling me. It helps. And for what it's worth, even if you never forgive your brother, I'm glad you got to speak to him again."

Hadley felt a sob crawling up her throat. "Me too."

"I love you, Hadley."

Tears fell down her cheeks like a faucet. She didn't bother wiping them away.

"I love you too, Alice."

They quieted, and the silence of an ancient time resumed. A few moments passed before Hadley had to ask, "Do you think Olivia and Soxie will be okay?"

"I hope not. They better be miserable without us."

Hadley snorted. Alice snorted. Maybe even the pyramid snorted. And the next thing she knew they were both doubled over, cackling so hard her side hurt and her stomach cramped into a pretzel. But she couldn't stop laughing, because tears of joy instead of pain were all that were left.

When one of them stopped, the other started again, until Hadley laughed so hard she kicked her legs out and sent her own water bottle sailing into the darkness. It landed somewhere with a deep, resounding *plunk*.

Their laughter immediately died in their throats. They looked at each other, then back at the dark. Hadley quickly grabbed her penlight and shined it into the room.

Alice's water bottle was on its side next to the far wall, but Hadley's was nowhere in sight. They shot to their feet and stepped forward, the light from the penlight darting back and forth as Hadley scanned every inch of the floor, just to be sure.

"Where did it go?" asked Alice.

Hadley moved the light to the puddle in the middle of the floor. It was the size of a manhole, and up until now, she'd assumed it was just leftover standing water from ancient rainfall. But if her bottle landed in it and disappeared, then it wasn't just a puddle.

They moved closer and knelt down beside it. The water was thick and oily black. It reminded her of the tar-like substance they'd seen on the sarcophagus beneath the Khafre Pyramid. She leaned down and sniffed. It smelled the same too.

"What do you think?" prodded Alice. "The dagger?"

Hadley nodded eagerly and pulled the dagger from her backpack. But after a few minutes of sticking the point into the water, they gave up. As before, nothing was happening. Hadley sat back on her heels.

"Now what?" she said.

Alice leaned forward, the penlight illuminating her reflection in the black water. "We need to see how deep it is."

Hadley stared at the water. Of course! It wasn't a puddle—it was a hole! *This* was the passage they'd been searching for. She grabbed the penlight and held it between her teeth. Then she threw off her cap and quickly tied her hair back with a band from her wrist.

Alice gave her a worried look, then pushed the dagger toward her. Hadley nodded, zipped it in her side pocket, and looked up to meet her friend's eyes.

"I'm just going to see where this leads. Don't do anything until I get back, okay?"

Alice nodded, eyes shining. "Be careful, Hadz," she begged her. "Don't let me die here alone."

Hadley leaned over, pulled the penlight from her mouth, and pressed her lips to Alice's forehead. "I won't. I promise." Then she scooted forward and lowered her body into the hole. As black and oily as it appeared, the water felt like normal water—cold and wet against her skin. She kicked her feet around, feeling for the bottom, but as she'd expected, there wasn't one. She lowered herself further until she was up to her neck, one hand still holding the penlight, the other holding the edge. Then she gave Alice one final smile, took a deep breath, and went under.

chapter 21

Hadley pressed her hand into the sides of the hole, pushing herself further down. After several feet, she felt the pressure on her ears beginning to build. She opened her eyes, hoping the water didn't burn them, and was pleasantly surprised. It stung a little, but no more than a lightly chlorinated pool. What really surprised her, however, was that she could see. The further down she went, the clearer the water became. Her penlight illuminated the rough limestone all around her as she continued descending. Then, suddenly, her feet hit something solid. She moved her light down and saw that the hole emptied into a bigger tunnel that moved laterally rather than vertically. She quickly maneuvered around, stuck the penlight in her mouth, and started swimming.

Like the hole leading into the chamber, the tunnel was completely submerged. She swam hard, scanning the limestone above her for any sign of an air pocket, or another passage. Her lungs were starting to protest, but she'd already come too far. If she tried going back now, she wouldn't make it. She had to keep swimming until she found the other side.

Assuming there was one.

She felt like a free diver lost in a Yucatán cenote, searching for the way out. Her legs and arms began to fatigue, and the lack of oxygen was making her light-headed. But she kept pushing, swimming as hard and as fast as she'd ever swum in her life. She refused to drown in this water-filled hamster tube. She refused to let Alice down.

And then she saw it. It was nothing but a dull blue glow at first, but the closer she got, the brighter it became. It was light. Not angelic, divine light, but actual glimmering *sunlight*, shining through the water at the end of the tunnel. Never mind that it was impossible. She didn't care. Her lungs had used up everything they had. She was seconds away from her body insisting she breathe, and if she inhaled before surfacing, she was doomed.

Her chest convulsed as her body fought against her. The penlight fell from her mouth, floating away. But she was so close. The light was only a few feet away. In one last burst of will, she planted a foot against the floor of the tunnel and pushed off with all her might. She sailed through the water, past the lip of the tunnel opening, then shot through the surface with a gasping cry of release.

She made a loud, horrible wheezing sound as her lungs gulped in fresh, clean, beautiful air. It took a moment for her to do anything but try and breathe. She floundered a bit, slapping at the water until she came to her senses, breathed deeply, and let herself float.

It was then that her brain finally caught up. She had emerged in a natural pool of some kind. It was small and surrounded by sand and palm trees, their leaves rustling quietly as the wind blew in from the surrounding desert. She paddled toward the edge of the pool, and when her feet touched the bottom, she waded forward, dropping to all fours when the water got shallow. She clawed her way toward the tiny beach, letting herself fall with a thud on her back, sopping wet, but alive.

She stared at the sky. It was a bright, almost royal blue against the green leaves of the palm trees. Sunlight fell in beams through the fronds, warming her face and blinding her. She turned her head. In the far distance, she saw the pyramids, only they looked shiny, smooth, and white, and they nearly sparkled.

She slowly sat up, mesmerized by the sight. They stood solemnly and alone. There was no city built around them, no civilization that she could see. From here, in this desert oasis, all she saw were three incredible feats of humanity towering over the desert landscape, viewed as she imagined they were meant to be viewed. As awe-inspiring, magical, and almost otherworldly.

It took a moment for her to realize what was happening. The pyramids were at least a mile away, maybe more. There was virtually no way she swam through a mile-long limestone tube. Maybe a dolphin could do it. Maybe. But not a human. So how did she get here?

A twig snapped behind her. She shot to her feet and whirled around.

Standing at the edge of the pool was a boy of no more than thirteen or fourteen years old. His skin was dark, and he wore a head covering and a threadbare linen tunic tied at the waist with a strip of raw leather. His shoes were not so much shoes as cowhide strapped to his feet. His dark eyes studied her with an expression that belied more curiosity than fear.

He said something to her in a language she'd never heard before and couldn't begin to place.

She shook her head and lifted her hands. "I'm sorry. I don't understand."

He frowned and stepped forward, gesturing to the pool she'd just been swimming in. He repeated his first phrase. She shook her head again and shrugged, the universal sign for "I have no idea what you're saying." He seemed to understand, or at least pretended to. He sighed and beckoned her forward.

"You want me to follow you?" she guessed, then immediately chastised herself for saying something so dumb. She glanced at the pool, hoping Alice was okay, and praying she didn't try to come after her. Hadley was the better swimmer, and she barely made it. Without a light to guide her, Alice's chances were zero.

The boy barked what sounded like an order, making her flinch.

"Okay, okay, I'm coming," she grumbled as he turned and led the way.

She'd been right. They were in a desert oasis. Beyond the watering hole and cluster of palm trees, the desert stretched for miles—sand dunes on one side, pyramids on the other. She wondered where the boy came from, and why he was out here alone. She couldn't see the Nile, but it couldn't be that far. Maybe he lived along the river. But was he planning to take her across the desert? She didn't have that kind of time. Not with Alice waiting back inside the pyramid. She was just about to catch up to him and somehow communicate that she couldn't follow him, when he suddenly halted and dropped to the ground. She stopped and took a step back as he started to dig.

The urge to ask him what he was doing was immense. But she held her tongue and watched as he pushed deeper into the sand, flinging mounds of it to the side. He'd dug about two feet when he let out a satisfied grunt and sat back on his heels. In his hands was a bundle of cloth tied together with frayed rope. He dusted it off and set it on the ground beside him. Then he turned and shot Hadley a worried look. She realized she'd been leaning over his shoulder, crowding him, so she muttered a quick apology and shuffled to the side to give him room.

From a less claustrophobic distance, she watched as he untied the bundle and carefully unfolded layers of fabric. When he lifted the last flap to reveal what was hidden inside, Hadley felt the world tilt beneath her.

For a brief second the sun felt hotter, and the air thicker. She wondered if anything was real. The boy. The desert oasis. The pyramids in the distance. Was all of this just a trick of her dying brain? Did she drown in that tunnel after all?

The boy stared at her with narrowed eyes, gauging her reaction. Without realizing it, she'd stumbled backward, as if he'd just pulled the pin on a live grenade.

But it wasn't a grenade. It was the dagger. It was Philautia's dagger!

Her pulse raced as she stared slack-jawed at the weapon in his hands. The leather handle was slightly less weathered, and the blade was a little less tarnished, but there was no mistaking it. She'd know that dagger anywhere, especially since the same one was currently zipped up in her side pocket. She felt the outside of her thigh to be sure, both comforted and flummoxed when her fingers brushed against the bulge made by the hilt.

The boy didn't miss a beat. He pointed the tip of his dagger at her thigh, then barked another order of some kind that immediately put her on the defense. Despite not understanding a word he said, there was a familiar tone to his voice that, coupled with the dagger in his hand, made it all too easy to get annoyed. Because she'd been taking his orders since she was thirteen, and old habits die hard.

She licked her dry lips and whispered, "Cithaeron?"

His eyes went wide. They changed color for a few seconds, from dark brown to a slightly darker brown. It was subtle—nothing like when David's green eyes clouded dark—but it was a change, nonetheless. Hadley felt tears clouding her own eyes. She wasn't sure if they were tears of fear or joy, but she didn't care.

"Oh my god," she couldn't help but say. "I can't believe this. It's really you."

He blinked hard a few times until his eyes resumed their previous brown color. Then he gestured at her pocket and said what she could only assume was "Show me what's in there." So she unzipped her pocket and pulled out the dagger.

Neither of them said a word as their eyes darted back and forth between the identical objects in their hands. But they weren't identical, were they? They were the *same* object, separated by time. The thought made Hadley's head start to spin. Here she was, standing in front of a boy who was the past version of the man she knew as David. Processing what this meant would take time, but time wasn't something she had right now.

She dropped the dagger to her side. "The Portal. Do you know where to find the Portal of Osiris?"

He shook his head, indicating he didn't understand. She looked around for something that might help. Then she knelt on the ground and drew figures in the sand, what they'd seen on the statue in the museum. A man, a half-moon, a sphere, and an ankh. It might have a different meaning for Egyptologists in her time, but the fact that she was here meant it was exactly what they thought it was. It was the symbol for the Portal. She stepped back to give him room to study the image. But there was no recognition in his eyes, only confusion.

"You have to know what this is!" she snapped, pointing at the sand. "Otherwise, why am I here?" She'd been gone too long. Alice would be out of her mind by now.

The boy Cithaeron knelt down and brushed his hand through her drawing, erasing it. Then he placed his dagger in the sand with the hilt facing Hadley and gestured for her to do the same with hers. With no other ideas, she placed her dagger next to his, the pointed end facing her. She wondered briefly if it mattered if they touched. Could two of the same objects from different times come in contact with each other? Or would it create some kind of world-destroying paradox?

She sat back and waited for something to happen. Cithaeron looked up and smiled. She didn't know the face, but she recognized the smile. It was the same one she'd seen Colin, then David, flash whenever he was feeling extra smug and bossy. When he was getting his way and enjoying it.

Before she knew what was happening, he snatched the dagger—her version of the dagger—and took off running in the opposite direction.

"Hey!" she yelled. "What the hell?"

She scrambled up and ran a few steps in his direction, but he was too fast. He'd already cleared the edge of the oasis and was running full tilt into the desert. And not just any desert, an ancient Egyptian desert that no longer existed. She couldn't go chasing after him. There was no telling what she'd find, or how dangerous this time could be for a lone woman from the twenty-first century. Her dad and Caleb certainly never prepared her for this.

With a sigh, she bent over and picked up the other dagger. She shoved it back in her pocket and zipped it shut. Then she turned in a circle as palm leaves rustled above her.

"Now what?" she thought out loud.

A bubbling sound in the pool behind her caught her attention. She whirled around and saw something bobbing in the water. She waded in to get a closer look, frowning when she recognized one of the straps of her backpack. But how—

A jolt of panic ripped through her chest as she noticed something else floating in the water.

"Alice!" she screamed as she frantically splashed through the shallows and dove in. Within seconds she had Alice's head out of the water and was dragging her to the edge. She pulled her onto dry sand and was about to start mouth-to-mouth resuscitation when Alice suddenly spat up a mouthful of water and began coughing.

"Oh, thank god!" Hadley sobbed.

Alice coughed for several seconds, hacking the way people do when they've just breathed in a lungful of water. Hadley held her shoulders and turned her on her side, pushing her hair back to soothe her as her body expelled the ancient H_2O. When the color returned to her face and her skin felt warmer to the touch, Hadley helped her sit up and flung her arms around her.

"What were you thinking?" she cried into her wet hair. "Why did you come after me?"

Alice coughed a couple more times and answered with a raspy voice.

"I'm sorry," she said, "I didn't know what else to do."

Hadley pulled her closer and nodded. It was dumb, but the truth was she would have done the same thing. She pulled back and cupped Alice's face.

"I'm sorry I left you for so long."

It was then that Alice finally took a moment to look around. Hadley watched her take in the palm trees and the surrounding desert. The pyramids in the distance.

"Where are we?" she finally asked.

Hadley closed her eyes and let her head fall forward, exhausted. "You mean *when*."

chapter 22

It took a few minutes for Hadley to bring Alice up to speed. The hardest part was convincing her that not only was a past version of Cithaeron here, but she'd just missed him. There was no sign of him, just miles of desert baking in the unrelenting sun. But after agreeing it was too dangerous to go looking for him, they decided to head back to the pyramids. Neither of them could explain it, but somehow they knew the Portal wasn't here after all. It was a disappointing revelation, to say the least. But at this point, their priority was getting back to their own time. They couldn't, however, go back the way they came. According to Alice, the second she made it to the bottom of the first passage, a current pulled her sideways and swept her away. She'd been moving so fast she lost consciousness. If there was a current running through the tubes, it might explain how they got here, but they'd never be able to swim against it. Besides, even if they did get back to the chamber, they'd still be trapped. At least on the outside, they had options. So as the sun moved closer to the horizon, they started hoofing it toward the pyramids.

It took longer than expected. Even as dusk approached, it was still hot and arid, sucking away all moisture and slowing them down. Hadley's throat was dry, and her lips were cracked. Alice's water bottle, which she'd been smart enough not to leave in the chamber, had already been drained of oasis water. The further they walked, the more they had to stop and rest. It didn't help that gusts of wind kept blowing sand in their faces, making it difficult to breathe. By the time they reached the base of the Khufu Pyramid, it was dark, and the temperature had dropped at least thirty degrees.

Hadley sat down and shivered as she attempted to wipe the grit from her nose and mouth. Alice dropped beside her, teeth chattering.

"N-n-now what do w-we do?" she stuttered, huddling into herself.

Hadley peered into the darkness. At least they were alone. Whatever time they had wandered into, no Egyptians from the past were camped out at the base of the pyramids. She turned and craned her head to look at the steep slope behind them. It looked as daunting as it did in their time, only worse. There were no steps to climb. The pyramid still had its casing stones, and each seemed to be fitted with such precision that nothing but thin grooves were visible. She stood and flattened herself against the stone. If she remembered Olivia correctly, the Khufu Pyramid had a 51.5-degree slope. It wasn't impossible, but it would be tough.

"We're g-going to have to sc-scale it," she managed.

Alice just nodded and stood up, her entire body shaking. She was clearly too spent to argue.

"D-do what I do," Hadley said as she dug the tips of her fingers into the first groove and pressed the edge of her boot into the rock, making sure her body was flush with the cold stone. Then she took a deep breath and started shimmying up. One hand, then one foot. Other hand, other foot. It wasn't graceful, but it seemed to be working. After a few feet, she paused to ensure Alice was following. To someone on the ground, they would have looked like a couple of geckos scaling an angled wall. The casing stones were smooth, but thankfully not slick. There was still some texture and grip, which made traversing the spaces between grooves possible. Dicey, but possible.

"Keep flush-sh with the wall, and use your legs," she told Alice, even as her own foot slipped. Every once in a while she'd hear a slip behind her, and her heart would stop. But Alice was holding on, and together they were doing it. They stopped to rest a few times, but not for long. The higher they climbed, the colder it got. They couldn't afford to stay still. The exertion was the only thing keeping them from hypothermia.

Hadley gritted her teeth as the wind howled in her ears. She glanced up. The sky around them was awash with stars. So many stars. And they were *bright*. Almost blinding. The light helped them see where they were going, at least, even if it was a treacherous sight. Around the halfway point, Hadley's body shook with fatigue, so much so she was almost vibrating.

"Do you feel that?" called Alice, her voice nearly swallowed by the wind.

Hadley paused and pressed her cheek against the stone. It wasn't ice cold anymore. In fact, it felt a little warm. She closed her eyes for a second, relishing the warmth.

"Hadley!"

She lifted her head at the alarm in Alice's voice, and her body began shaking even more. Then she realized it wasn't her that was vibrating, it was the pyramid. Excitement gripped her.

"We must be close. Keep climbing!"

Adrenaline kicked in, and they went from lazy geckos to clumsy spiderwomen. They slipped and slid as they ascended, too eager to worry about being careful. The higher they got, the warmer the stones got, and the brighter. Soon the rocks they scaled glowed with a white, luminescent light.

They were almost there; Hadley felt it. She reached out to grab hold of the next groove, when suddenly her hand slapped through empty air. She fell forward onto her stomach with a smack, and the air flew from her lungs in a big whoosh.

By the time she got her breath back, she was crying with joy. Alice crawled over and collapsed next to her, crying similar tears of relief. They were still on the pyramid, but the casing stones had disappeared. The lights of Cairo twinkled in the distance, and light bled up from the ground spotlights trained on the rest of the complex.

They were perched on the edge of a block at least four hundred feet from the ground, but they were back. They were back!

The lights on their side of the pyramid were still out, but they made good time as they descended, even in the dark. When they reached the bottom, they dropped to the ground, and Hadley could have kissed it. But headlights flashing nearby caught her attention.

"Welcome back, girls!" Ibrahim whisper-yelled. "Only two minutes left. Hurry!"

Hadley and Alice looked at each other, smiled, and ran through the dark toward the car.

Ibrahim was kind enough to drop them back at their hotel. He didn't even make them ride in the trunk. Apparently, once the crime had already been committed, there was no reason to keep them hidden. In fact, he was quite jovial, chatting up a storm and offering to take them to dinner and a club that evening. They politely declined.

"Suit yourselves, my friends!" he said, before returning their phones and peeling away.

They watched as his car disappeared down the road. It was still dark, and traffic was light. Hadley checked the time on her phone. It was 5:15 a.m.

Of course, her watch told a different story. It also read 5:15 a.m., but the calendar number was ahead by one day. They hadn't been lost in the past for two hours. They'd been lost there for twenty-four.

Twenty-four hours in the past, and all they had to show for it was the same dagger they started out with. Well, maybe not *exactly* the same.

"I need a shower, food, and sleep," Alice said as she shuffled toward the hotel entrance. Hadley followed, and noticed the doorman give them a strange look. She spotted their reflection in the glass and saw what he saw. Two bedraggled, roughed-up girls covered in dust and grime. He must have thought they had quite the evening. She shot him a weary smile, and they made their way upstairs.

Soxie and Olivia were up, waiting for them. After showering and ordering breakfast, they sat down and walked them through everything. When they were finished, Hadley could barely keep her eyes open, and Alice was already nodding off.

"You guys get some sleep," ordered Olivia. "We'll figure things out when you wake up."

Alice was out before her head hit the pillow. Hadley climbed under the covers and turned out the light. The last thing she heard was Soxie and Olivia pulling the curtains shut and closing the door behind them.

When her eyes opened, the room was pitch black and the air was still. She didn't have to confirm the time to know it was late. But nature called, so she begrudgingly left the warmth of her hotel bed and carefully felt her way to the bathroom. When she got there, the door was closed, a yellow strip of light shining beneath it. She rubbed her eyes and yawned, then leaned against the wall to wait for Alice to finish. Her eyelids grew heavy, and she decided to close them for just a few seconds.

". . . don't know why, but he must've had his reasons."

Hadley's head popped up. She blinked hard, confirming she was awake. Did she just dream that? She lightly pressed her ear against the door, listening.

". . . have to go. Talk to you soon."

The toilet flushed and the water turned on. Hadley immediately stepped back and waited for the door to open. When it did, Alice jumped in shock.

"Oh!" She reared back, hand flying to her chest. "Sorry, I didn't know you were waiting."

Hadley looked past her into the bathroom. "Is everything okay? Were you on the phone?"

"Yeah," she said, squeezing by. "It was just my mom. You know how she gets when I don't check in."

"Gotcha," Hadley said, eyeing her friend curiously. Alice gave her an awkward smile and rushed back to her bed. Hadley stepped into the bathroom and shut the door behind her. Looking around, her gaze fell on the giant mirror above the sink.

She stared into the tired, bloodshot eyes in her reflection. If Alice wanted to keep her conversation to herself, Hadley would respect her privacy. The only problem was, she didn't see a phone in her hand when she left the bathroom.

With a heavy sigh, Hadley turned around and went about her business. Whatever was going on, Alice would tell her when she was ready.

Hadley woke up thirsty, and her head felt like it might split open like a watermelon. With a groan, she flung off the covers and wiped the crust from her eyes. Then she sat up, staring at Alice's empty bed. She glanced over to see the door to Olivia and Soxie's room ajar, but she didn't sense movement on the other side.

"Hello?" she called.

"They're downstairs," said a voice behind her.

She twisted around. David sat in one of the chairs by the window. The curtains were open, revealing a gray sky with hints of gold.

"What time is it?" she asked. "How long was I asleep?" She felt sluggish and groggy, which usually meant she'd slept too long.

He glanced at the window. "Almost a whole day. I'm guessing you needed it."

Her mind began defogging, and she noticed the dagger sitting on the table in front of him. Everything came rushing back, including the image of the boy from the desert in his linen tunic grinning and running away from her.

She sat up, wincing as her head pounded. "Why?" she managed to ask. "Why didn't you tell me?"

He pulled a packet of Advil from his pocket and tossed it on the bed next to her. She gratefully tore it open and swallowed the pills dry. Then she leaned against the headboard and pressed the heels of her hands into her forehead, waiting for the pills to take effect.

A few seconds passed before he spoke. "You've seen *Back to the Future*, right?" he said at last.

The throbbing in her head began to subside. She glanced up and gave him a bored look. He knew she'd seen it. They'd watched it together when they were fourteen. "What's your point? You couldn't tell me because knowing the future can lead to dire consequences? No wait, Doc Brown called them catastrophic. Good to know we're taking time travel advice from a movie."

He leaned forward and rested his elbows on his knees. "It makes sense, though, doesn't it? What if you had known, and made one tiny decision based on that knowledge? And what if that tiny decision led to you *not* finding me in that desert? What then?"

"I have no clue," she admitted.

The answer seemed to satisfy him, and he sat back. Then he carefully picked up the dagger and balanced it on his palm.

"After hundreds of years, I started to think it never happened— that you were some kind of hallucination. When you live as many lives as I have, they eventually start blending together. It gets harder to decipher what's real and what isn't."

"When did you decide it was real?"

"The first time we met. Well, I guess it was technically the second," he laughed dryly. "Even after sixteen hundred years, there was no mistaking those cornflower-blue eyes."

Her mind grew cloudy again. She grabbed the glass of water on her nightstand and drank it down in three gulps. Then she wiped her mouth with the back of her hand and turned back toward the window.

"All right. I get why you couldn't tell me. But why did you switch the daggers?"

A shadow crossed his eyes. "Honestly? I really don't know."

She couldn't believe her ears. "What?"

"You have to understand," he said in a rush, shooting to his feet and pacing. "I'd just woken up as Cithaeron, and it was only my second life after Philautia brought me back. Everything was still new to me. I was only there that day to retrieve the dagger from where I'd hidden it in my first life. And suddenly there you were, shooting out of the water like a siren. I knew you didn't belong, that you had to be there for a reason."

She couldn't help but picture what it must have been like for him to see her emerging from that pool, dressed in black, speaking a strange language.

"So you tested me," she said, her eyes following him as he paced back and forth like a caged lion. "You tested me by showing me *your* dagger."

He stopped and looked at her. "Yes."

She winced, not expecting such a blunt reply. "Okay . . . so why did you steal mine? I still don't get the point. Aren't they the same thing?"

"I used to think so, but not anymore." He carefully placed the dagger back on the table. "Now I know it wasn't just a gut instinct. I was always supposed to switch them."

She scooted forward as her adrenaline flipped into overdrive. "Wait, are you telling me I brought back something else?" She pointed at the table. "That's not Philautia's dagger?"

He sat back down and took a moment to collect his thoughts. "No, it *is*. It's the same weapon she used to create the Realm. But there's a big difference now." He glanced at the table. "This one never saw the *destruction* of the Realm."

Her headache flared back up. "What are you saying? This dagger still believes the Realm exists? Wouldn't that mean the dagger I left in the past knows it doesn't?"

"Yes, but you're forgetting something. The Realm still *did* exist back then. It wouldn't matter what the dagger did or didn't believe. It couldn't stop the Realm from existing."

She was about to go cross-eyed trying to make sense of it all. "Yes, but—"

"Wouldn't the dagger I stole be the one I already had," he said robotically. "That's what you were going to say, right?"

"Yes, if you'd let me say it," she snapped. "The logic doesn't work. They'd keep getting swapped, over and over again."

"Maybe, if you think time works like that."

"Don't you?"

He shrugged. "I have no idea. Maybe time isn't linear, or circular, or anything we can begin to understand. Maybe it's comprised of millions, trillions of separate realities, where every possible thing is happening at the same time. We don't have to understand it. We just have to work with what we've got. And what we've got is a dagger that you brought back from fifth-century Egypt."

Her mind reeled. She needed coffee. Bad. "Okay, assuming everything you're saying is true, what does this have to do with the Portal? The statue, the Osiris Shaft, the secret chamber . . . we've been following clues to the Portal. Why would . . ." She stopped as her question suddenly answered itself.

He nodded with approval and smiled. "Exactly. The Portal is still in the Realm, and *this* dagger," he gestured to the table, "is the key."

chapter 23

They said goodbye to Egypt the next day, and much to Soxie's delight, they were not flying commercial. Hadley sat in the back of the private plane with Olivia while Soxie and David played cards up front, and Alice napped in the chair opposite them.

Every few seconds, Hadley noticed David's gaze move to Alice, as if confirming she was still there. The tension between them had eased, but not completely. Hadley wasn't there when they reunited in Cairo, but from what she could tell, they weren't back to their normal lovebird selves. They seemed a little fragile and unsure of each other.

"I know what you mean," said Olivia, glancing up front. "But I'm sure they'll be fine. It's not like they can stop being soulmates. They're stuck with each other, so let them work it out. I'm more worried about you."

Hadley fidgeted in her seat and turned to look out the window. "Don't. You know I hate when you do that."

"What, worry about you? That's one of the dumbest things you've ever said."

"Thanks."

Olivia kicked her in the shin.

"Ow," she yelped, reaching down to rub her leg. "Okay, fine—I get it. I'm worried too. Does that make you feel better?"

"Yes, actually. At least it means you're taking this thing with Melinoë seriously."

Hadley couldn't help but laugh. "By *thing*, I assume you mean my deepest, darkest fear. So yes, I am taking it seriously, but what difference does it make? Even if she tries using it against me, there isn't anything I can do to stop her. Either way, better me than all of us."

Olivia gave her a disapproving look. "You're acting like Alice did last year, pretending that the weight of everything falls on your shoulders. That's not how we operate. One of us goes down, we all go down."

"Are you trying to make me feel better or worse?"

She leaned forward and placed her hand on Hadley's knee. "Neither, dummy. I'm just telling you the facts. You made a deal with a goddess, and that's never a good idea. If there are consequences, we'll face them together. But once we have the Portal, we'll have our bargaining power."

Hadley wondered. "Are we messing with stuff we don't understand? What if the gods are using us, hoping we'll do exactly what we're doing?"

"Of course they're using us," Olivia laughed curtly. "That's what they do, Hadley. They either use us or discard us. They don't give a shit about us either way."

It was rare for Olivia to curse. Even Soxie's red head popped up from her seat in the front.

"Are you guys fighting?" she called.

"No!" they shouted.

"Whatever," she mumbled. David gave them an apologetic look and resumed shuffling his deck of cards. Alice stirred across from them, burrowing deeper into her blanket.

Hadley turned her attention back to Olivia. "What about Persephone? You can't lump her into that same category."

"Actually, I can. She was just like the rest of them until she lived the life of a mortal. She had to be one of us first in order to care about us."

It was a hard point to argue. The truth was, Persephone had come here to help Hades steal back Alice's soul. She'd changed her mind, but her intentions were not originally good ones.

Hadley shrugged and grabbed a bag of pretzels off the cart beside her. She tore it open and popped one in her mouth. "Problem solved, I guess," she said, crunching loudly. "We get them all to live as mortals."

Olivia sat forward and helped herself to a pretzel. Instead of eating it, she tapped it against her bottom lip. "It's not the worst idea."

Hadley inhaled a stray crumb and coughed. "I was kidding," she said, eyes watering. "The last thing we want is a bunch of gods running around as mortals. Don't forget, Hades lived as Colin for a while, and that did nothing for his moral compass."

"I suppose," Olivia said faintly. Then she sat back and nibbled on her pretzel, deep in thought.

With a sigh, Hadley leaned her head back and closed her eyes as she mindlessly munched on pretzels. If she knew Olivia, she was going to mull this over and turn it inside out until she proved, without a shadow of a doubt, that turning gods into mortals was a good idea.

It's not, Olivia.

That thought earned her another swift kick in the shin.

Forty-eight hours later, Hadley walked the perimeter of the Roxland property in joggers and a T-shirt, Schlemmer happily trotting along behind her. It was dusk, her favorite time on the estate, when the sky was streaked with vibrant purple, red, and orange, and the mountains nearby reflected the sun's hazy golden light. It was the in-between hour—the gloaming—when daytime creatures retreated to their burrows and the night came out to play.

Schlemmer's ears suddenly perked up, and she started barking. A second later, Hadley heard the sound of hooves and turned to see

Soxie riding up on Max, the big black gelding who everyone agreed was the sweetest horse in the Roxland stables. Soxie expertly brought him to a halt a few feet away. In her tailored riding outfit, she could have been on a fox hunt in the English countryside.

"Hey, it's getting late," she said. "Are you heading back soon, or do you need a ride?"

Hadley looked up and smiled. "Sorry. Lost track of time. It's just really nice to be home."

Max snorted and pawed the ground, eager to get going. Soxie patted him on the neck while Schlemmer ran circles around them, hoping for a race back to the barn.

"Yeah," Soxie nodded. "It's good to be back on our own turf. I wouldn't have wanted to do this in Egypt. Nothing against Cairo or anything. Just feels better here."

Hadley agreed and turned back toward the mountains. Crickets had started chirping, filling the air with their evening song. There was no wind, but the moment the sun dipped below the horizon, the temperature would drop considerably. She'd been walking out here for over an hour, enjoying a lazy, normal, no-gods kind of afternoon. Since their return from Egypt, the mirrors were still working properly, and their dreams had been simple, boring old dreams. It felt like a stalemate. The gods knew they were close, and they didn't want to risk pushing them off course.

It was the calm before the storm, but they couldn't live in it forever.

Soxie turned Max to the side and reached down to offer Hadley her hand. "Come on. We're meeting in the ballet studio at seven."

Hadley grabbed her hand and Max took a few steps forward, his momentum helping pull her up. She settled in the saddle behind Soxie, and they galloped back to the house, Schlemmer racing alongside, barking, and occasionally nipping at Max's heels.

Soxie dropped her off at the front door and headed to the stables. Hadley let herself in and made her way upstairs to change. But halfway up, she remembered leaving her phone in the library. She spun around and hopped onto the banister to slide the rest of the way down. Unfortunately, Mayron stepped out of the parlor as she was descending, startling her. She flew off the side and landed with a splat on the cold marble floor. It was only a few feet, and her butt took the brunt of it, but it still hurt. Not as much as the look on Mayron's face, though.

"Oh good. I'm glad the slides I installed are to your satisfaction."

She blew the hair from her face and sat up. "I'm fine, Mayron. Thanks for asking."

He was wearing his casual clothes, which were more business casual than casual: dark slacks and a beige crew-neck sweater with a starched collar peeking out from the top. He narrowed his eyes as if trying to make sense of her. Then he nodded and motioned to the parlor room.

"If you wouldn't mind, a word, please."

"Just one?"

He paused and shot her an icy look before walking through the door, expecting her to follow. She considered ignoring him and going upstairs, but this was still *his* house. With everything else going on, she didn't want to risk getting kicked out of the only home where she truly felt at home.

She took a deep breath and grabbed the stair railing to pull herself up. When she walked into the parlor, he was sitting in his usual spot by the fire. No scotch or stack of mail this time, just a cup of tea and his usual unpleasant demeanor.

"Hey, so I'm sorry about the stairs. It won't happen again."

He sipped his tea and stared at her. "Do you know what I do for a living?"

"Not really."

"Not really," he repeated. "Well then, let me enlighten you. I'm what you might call a truth finder. I make it my business to know when I am being lied to. Can I count on you to tell me the truth, Hadley?"

She glanced at the hall, hoping someone might come along to rescue her. "Um. Sure."

"Alice's Aunt Molly. Is she still alive?"

The question didn't surprise her because his obsession with Molly was starting to become a thing. "Well . . . I don't know how to answer that," she stalled.

"It's a simple yes or no," he fired back. "Is she alive or not?"

She squirmed, glancing at the doorway again. How could she lie without lying? Then the loophole revealed itself like a lightbulb above her head. He was asking about Molly, not Persephone. "No, Mayron," she said with confidence. "Molly is no longer alive."

He took another sip of tea and gently set the cup in its saucer. "I am also very good at spotting half-truths. Tell me what you are *not* telling me."

"I-I don't know what else to say," she floundered. "Molly *is* gone."

His expression did not change. Not one tiny muscle—nothing. The man was unnervingly good at being still. "Then perhaps you can tell me why I heard Alice speaking to her just this morning."

Her eyes opened wide. "What?"

"In the meditation room," he went on, casting his eyes toward the ceiling, in the general direction of said room.

"I'm sure you misunderstood. Why do you think she was talking to Molly?"

"I don't think she was talking to Molly—I know she was. But what I'd really like to know is why she referred to her as Persephone."

Hadley opened her mouth to respond, but she didn't have the right words for this interrogation.

"It's okay, Hadley," said someone behind her. She turned around. Alice was leaning against the doorway with her arms folded, staring at the floor. "He's right. I was talking to her. I've been talking to her every day."

Mayron exhaled. It sounded like a sigh of relief. "So she *is* alive."

"No," Alice shook her head. "She's not. One day we can explain it to you, but you have to trust me that she really is gone, and she's not coming back."

Hadley sidestepped out of the line of fire. This felt very much like an Alice-and-Mayron conversation, and she was happy to see herself out of it.

"I'm just gonna go," she said, pointing to the door as she made her escape.

Neither of them looked at her as she darted out of the room.

After running a brush through her hair and throwing on a pair of jeans and a clean tee, Hadley found Soxie and Olivia in the kitchen, rummaging for food. She checked the hall and nearby rooms—including the parlor room—to make sure Alice wasn't still downstairs, then took a seat at the island.

"Hey," she whispered, leaning over the granite counter. "Did you guys know Alice has been talking to Persephone?"

Soxie stopped digging in a box of cereal and looked at her. "What do you mean, talking to her?"

"I mean exactly that. Your uncle just gave me the third degree about it. Apparently, he overheard them in the meditation room this morning."

Olivia had just pulled out a carton of almond milk. She spun around, letting the refrigerator door slam shut behind her. "She's been speaking to Persephone alone?"

Hadley glanced nervously at the door and nodded. "Is it—should we be worried?"

"That she's talking to the memory of an ancient goddess?" asked Soxie. "I mean, she was her aunt. I'm sure she just misses her."

Olivia set the milk carton on the counter. "Every day?" she confirmed, catching up to Hadley's thoughts.

"Yes. She just admitted it to me and Mayron, and I'm pretty sure I overheard her in Cairo." Then to Soxie, she added, "By the way, you should know your uncle is kind of obsessed with this—there's no way he's letting it go."

Soxie dropped the cereal box to her side. "Great. Like we don't have enough problems right now. He's still pissed about the night-vision goggles we *lost*." She emphasized the last word with an eye roll. "But I'll talk to him."

They heard dogs barking in the foyer as someone entered the front door. Hadley glanced at her phone. It was a few minutes before seven.

"That'll be David," she predicted, grabbing a banana from the fruit bowl as she slid off the stool. "Should we tell him?"

Soxie and Olivia exchanged wary looks.

"Not yet," Olivia decided for them. "Let's wait and see how tonight goes first."

The mood immediately shifted as reality sank in. Their short reprieve was over. If David's theory was right, they would have the Portal in their possession tonight. If he was wrong, well, they were back to square one. And that didn't bode well for their relations with the gods.

A few seconds later, David popped his head into the kitchen. He seemed taken aback to find them already looking in his direction.

"Oh. Hey. Are you guys ready? Where's Alice?"

Probably talking to Persephone, Hadley thought as she finished her banana and tossed the peel in the trash. But what she said was, "Probably in her room. I'll get her. We'll meet you guys in the studio."

On her way upstairs, she stopped by the mirror on the second-floor landing. She'd been diligently checking her image every day, challenging it to misbehave. But her reflection just stared back at her with the same cornflower-blue eyes David said he'd know anywhere. She lifted her fingers to the glass and lightly brushed them against it. Could the Realm still exist behind this? Would she really have the chance to see it again? Despite all the unknowns that lay ahead, the thought brought with it an element of excitement.

Then she thought of Alice, standing in front of a mirror like this, talking to the memory of her lost aunt. Were they really in a position to judge? On the surface, it didn't sound healthy. Mourning the loss of someone required first admitting they were gone. But this wasn't exactly the same thing. Besides, if the Realm could still exist, didn't that mean Persephone could too?

Her mind was still flitting through all the possibilities when she knocked on Alice's door. When she didn't immediately answer, Hadley leaned in and pressed her ear against the wood. She heard faint whispering on the other side.

"Alice?" she called, knocking again. "Are you ready? Everyone's waiting in the ballet studio."

"Just a second!"

She tried the door, but it was locked. Alice never locked her door.

"Alice? It's me. Can you open up?"

A moment later, the door swung open. Alice's face was flushed, and she looked a little frazzled. Hadley stepped back and studied her.

"Are you okay?"

She smiled tightly and nodded before stepping through and closing the door behind her. It was obvious what was going on, but rather than press her on it, Hadley followed her silently to the ballet studio.

"I'm sorry about earlier, with Mayron," she said over her shoulder. "I should have told you."

Hadley waved her off. "We'll talk about it later."

Alice nodded and kept walking. When they got to the end of the hall, she pushed the heavy double doors open. Hadley entered the room behind her and stopped.

"Where's the piano?" she said, pointing to the corner where, for as long as she could remember, a grand piano had sat, most of the time gathering dust.

"Mayron donated it to charity," replied Soxie as she click-clacked across the polished wood, her reflection following in all the mirrors. "He keeps doing stuff like that to punish me. It makes no sense because I never played the damn thing."

"I think he's punishing me with that one," said David. He was leaning against the wall of windows that overlooked the back grounds. "Colin played the piano. David doesn't. So."

Hadley looked at the others. When he was Colin, he didn't play that often, but when he did, he played so masterfully it sometimes made her cry. She didn't know exactly what Mayron knew—more every day, it would seem—but if he had any inkling of who David really was, he'd make certain no one else outside their circle ever did. Even if it meant David would never play the piano for the rest of his life. Not in this house, anyway.

"I'm sorry," said Alice shyly. She moved to where he was standing and placed a hand on his arm. He smiled at her and kissed the inside of her wrist.

"Okay," Soxie commanded their attention, stopping beneath the crystal chandelier in the middle of the room. "O, can you dim the lights?"

Olivia nodded and made her way to the switch by the doors. As she brought the lights down, Hadley felt a charged energy in the air. None of them had stepped foot in this room for months. It used to be their go-to place for entering the Realm. The three walls of mirrors ensured an easy access point and an even easier return point. It was their de facto antechamber to the Realm. If it still existed, this could be the place to find it.

David kept hold of Alice's hand as they walked to the center of the room. He handed Soxie the dagger, handle first, then leaned over to kiss the side of Alice's head.

"I'll be right outside that door," he said, pointing to the entrance. "If you need me, just shout. Okay?"

Alice looked up at him and smiled. "Yes, of course."

It looked like he was about to bend down and kiss her, but she pulled him into a hug instead. Hadley found it a little cloying, but sweet. Then he looked up and said, "Compasses?"

Everyone but Alice nodded and patted their pockets to confirm their compasses were on their persons.

"Okay, then," he said, then with one last look at Alice, he strode out of the room and shut the doors behind him.

Once it was just the four of them, they took a moment to settle in. Alice turned in a slow circle, examining her reflection in the surrounding glass.

"Which one should we try?" she asked.

Hadley motioned to the east wall of mirrors. "Might as well use the same one we always did. The more familiar everything is, the better."

Alice nodded, and Soxie handed her the dagger. Her fingers slowly curled around the hilt. Her hand shook as she gripped the handle, but she didn't seem nervous. Which was good because Hadley was plenty nervous for the both of them. She stepped forward and placed a hand on Alice's shoulder. Soxie and Olivia did the same.

"Remember," said Olivia. "We move slow, and we don't break contact."

Alice met their eyes in the mirror. "Got it. Are we ready?"

They moved closer together, making sure there was some part of their bodies touching. They'd proven that being physically linked helped their connection, but for something like this, they needed to be more than linked. They needed to be one.

"On the count of three," said Soxie, as she pulled her compass from her pocket. Hadley and Olivia already had theirs at the ready.

"One, two . . ." she paused, meeting each of their eyes in the glass, ". . . three!"

They popped open their compasses, and Alice aimed the tip of the dagger toward the glass. A hush fell over the room as they held their breath, watching. Waiting. Staring hard at their reflections, reflections that should have disappeared. But they didn't. They were still there.

Nothing was happening.

Alice's knuckles turned white as she gripped the dagger, willing the Realm to appear. Sweat dripped down her brow. After several moments of nothing, Soxie let out a loud groan and snapped her compass shut.

"Well, shit."

Alice dropped her head while Olivia sank to the floor, stretching her neck. Hadley just leaned back and stared at the dim lights of the chandelier. It was only their first try, but the failure was demoralizing.

"I think this is going to take a while," Soxie muttered.

chapter 24

Soxie was right. For over an hour they failed to find the right combination that would open the doorway to the hidden Realm. They tried holding the dagger together, four hands overlapped at the hilt. They tried turning it clockwise, then counterclockwise. They set it on the ground and spun it like a top. They even pressed it, albeit very carefully, against the glass. Still nothing. There was a time the dagger opened all mirrors, but that was within the Realm. They'd never tried using it on a mirror outside of the Realm. It had felt too dangerous, but the more they experimented with it, the less tentative and more frustrated they became. Hadley was beginning to wonder if David was wrong. Maybe what she brought back from Egypt was nothing but a dud.

Soxie stomped her foot like a toddler. "Argh! Just stab the damn thing already."

"Are you sure?" asked Alice.

They all looked to Olivia for confirmation. Philautia had created the Realm by stabbing a slab of smooth obsidian, one of many surfaces that qualified as a mirror at the time. Doing it again seemed like a risky move.

"I think we have to," Olivia said, exasperated. "I don't see any other option. But we'll do it together."

So together, and rather awkwardly, they held the dagger, counted to three, and stabbed the mirror. Hadley squeezed her eyes shut at the last second, expecting to get worm-holed into another dimension. Instead, she felt an unpleasant vibration as the blade ricocheted off the glass and threw them all backward. They landed on the floor in a heap of tangled limbs, dropping the dagger like it was a radioactive hot potato. It bounced on the hardwood, making an innocent clanking sound like it was just another knife and not a supernatural *thing* that was clearly working against them.

"Ow, motherf—" Soxie began, but ended with a hiss.

Hadley sat up and clutched her throbbing hand to her chest. "That. Hurt," she said through clenched teeth. She might as well have stuck her hand in a pool of electrified bleach. Alice and Olivia grunted in agreement, each of them tending to their own injured appendages.

"Okay. Let's not do that again," advised Soxie.

Olivia grimaced. "I should have known better. We're not immortal. We're not demi-goddesses like Philautia. We shouldn't assume it will work the same for us."

Hadley flexed her fingers as the stinging sensation subsided. She eyed the dagger with contempt.

"What good is a key to the Realm if we can't use it?"

Alice crawled over and grabbed the dagger with her uninjured hand, then she pushed herself up and looked at them. "I'm throwing it."

"Go for it," huffed Soxie.

Hadley expected Olivia to object, but she didn't.

"Agreed," she said. "Just do it."

So Hadley made her way to her feet and demonstrated to Alice the correct way to throw the dagger. When she was ready, they stood back and watched as she held it by the blade, pulled her arm back, stepped forward, and let it fly.

For a beginner, it was a pretty good throw. The blade hit the mirror at an angle. If this was a knife-throwing contest, she would have received a decent score. But the dagger simply pinged off the mirror and fell to the floor, leaving nothing more than a hairline crack in the glass.

"Dammit!" Alice yelled, staring at the useless lump of metal and leather. "What now?"

They each took turns throwing the dagger at the glass. The result was the same. No Realm, more cracked mirrors. There was no method to their madness, and their patience stretched from thin to nonexistent.

Before they started stabbing each other, they agreed to a fifteen-minute break. When they opened the doors, David leaped up from his seat on the floor, blinking rapidly. They'd been at it so long, he'd fallen asleep.

After washing her hands, Hadley splashed water over her face and leaned against the sink, staring at her reflection. Her eyes were red and puffy, and her skin looked sallow. She hated to admit it, but they had run out of options.

When she got back to the ballet studio, Alice was sitting in the center of the room, staring at the dagger in her hands. David was kneeling next to her, speaking low. They looked up when she entered the room.

Alice appeared calm and determined, but David's eyes were fire. He stood and stormed out of the room, almost slamming into Soxie and Olivia as he blew past.

"What the hell's wrong with him?" Soxie asked.

Hadley shook her head, then turned to Alice and knelt down beside her. "Honey, what happened?"

She looked up and smiled sweetly. "Oh, girls. He'll be fine. It's nothing to worry about."

Hadley leaped back as if she'd just touched a live current. Alice was looking at her with the same face she'd looked at her with a thousand times. Yet, right now, Hadley wouldn't be able to spot her in a police line-up. Because, despite the same brown eyes, white hair, and heart-shaped face, this was not Alice.

"Alice?" she still whispered, not knowing what else to say.

"I'm sorry to barge in like this," she replied as she slowly peeled herself off the floor. "But it felt like you needed my help."

Soxie and Olivia gasped, and the three of them stepped back. Hadley found herself between them, gripping their arms for balance. "Persephone? Is that you?"

Not-Alice stepped toward the mirror to inspect her reflection. Her eyes met Hadley's. "I think you know it is, sweetie." Then she glanced back at her image and frowned, brushing her fingers lightly across her cheeks. "Before I forget, will one of you make sure Alice is wearing sunscreen? I don't remember her having this many freckles."

Olivia took a tentative step forward. "Persephone, what are you doing here?"

"I told you," she said, fiddling with her hair and puckering her lips. "I'm here to help. I told Alice it would come to this, but well. You know Alice. She can be so stubborn."

Hadley was floored. She'd suspected something was up, but never this. "Does she—does Alice know you're here?"

She laughed. It was Alice laughing, but the pitch was slightly higher. Less Alice, more Persephone. "Don't be silly," she said. "Of course she does. How else would I be here? I'm just a memory, remember?"

"This is too weird," Soxie said under her breath.

Olivia aggressively shook her head. "Wait. How can you help us? Don't we need Alice to open the Portal?"

"*Shhh*!" she hissed, leaping forward and nearly baring her teeth. They all jumped back. "Do not say such things! The Portal must *never* be opened. Do you understand?"

Hadley felt more lost than she had in a while, and that was saying something. "But hang on. We used it all the time. We traveled the world through that thing."

"Yes," she said, dropping her head and planting her hands on her hips like a disappointed schoolteacher. "You *used* it. You didn't open it. Those are two very, very different things."

The room felt like it got smaller all of a sudden. They'd been so fixated on finding the Portal for the gods that they never stopped to think why they wanted it so badly. "Why?" she asked. "Why can't it ever be opened?"

Alice—or rather, Persephone—swallowed, letting her gaze drift between them. "Because it's not just a portal. It's a universal reset. It's your Great Flood, on a much, much bigger scale. The entire scale."

Hadley felt a distant fear pooling in her stomach. "Are you . . . Is that why—"

"Yes," she interrupted. "The gods want it so they can turn back the clock. It's the only way to get back the world they lost."

"A universal reset?" Soxie parroted her. "Do you mean end-of-days stuff?"

"No. It's much worse than that."

Olivia's face paled. She glanced at Hadley nervously before saying, "You don't mean like, *Big Bang* kind of reset, do you?"

Persephone's eyes turned fierce. Unyielding. "I don't know about your big bang theory, but essentially, yes. It's a do-over. And this time around, you can bet the gods won't allow our worlds to be split apart. Which means the world as you know it will never exist."

"Holy shit."

Hadley agreed with Soxie's assessment. She was having a hard time breathing because of it. "But if it resets, how would they even know?" she asked.

"They wouldn't, unless they happened to be in possession of the Portal at the time it was opened."

"Oh my god," whispered Olivia. "It's the Great Flood *and* Noah's Ark."

Persephone gave her a thin smile. "That's right, sweetie. Destruction and salvation. It's the source of creation. It *is* creation."

"And Alice's soul—"

"Is one of its first."

Hadley felt dizzy from the enormity of it all. She all but floated to the ballet bar and clung to it as she slid to the floor. What if they had done what the gods had asked? Would they have just blinked out of existence? They'd be none the wiser, though, so would it even matter? The idea was mind-blowing, and not in a good way. Because it did matter. It wasn't a perfect world, but it was their world. The gods had their chance, and they blew it. They didn't deserve another one.

She grabbed the bar and nearly growled in anger as she pulled herself back up. "Okay. We don't give them the Portal, and we definitely don't let Alice open it. So now what? We just let them torture us for the rest of our lives?" It wasn't ideal, but it was better than the actual end of days. Or in this case, the beginning.

Persephone smiled slyly. "Not if I have anything to say about it." Then she turned and made eye contact with each of them. "Do you trust me, girls?"

They looked at each other. Persephone had proven herself time and again. There was no reason not to trust her now.

"Yes," Olivia spoke for the group. "Alice trusts you, so we trust you."

"Thank you," she said with a tiny smile. Then she took the tip of the dagger and pressed it into Alice's palm. Hadley stepped forward to intervene, but Olivia held her back.

"We're trusting her, remember?"

Hadley's stomach turned, but she said nothing as blood pooled in Alice's palm. Then the three of them watched as Persephone coated the blade in Alice's blood and made her way to the cracked mirror. She met their eyes and spoke to them through the glass. "She won't have a compass. You know what that means, right?"

Hadley's brain function stalled. *Wait. What?*

"I'm counting on you to get her out," Persephone said.

When realization finally dawned, it was a split second too late. Hadley had just started running toward her when Persephone lifted the bloody dagger and stabbed her own reflection. Hadley felt her eyes burn as a flash of light suddenly flooded the room. It had the strength of a nuclear blast, knocking her back and momentarily blinding her. She writhed in pain for a few seconds until her vision returned. Then she slowly sat up, wiping her watery eyes.

The ballet studio floor was covered in glass shards. She quickly checked herself to make sure she wasn't cut, then turned to Soxie and Olivia. They'd been blown to the corner of the room where the piano used to sit. Hadley said a silent *thank you* to Mayron for getting rid of it.

"Are you guys okay?" she asked as she stood and dusted herself off.

Olivia nodded and did the same. "I think so. Sox?"

Soxie grunted and stood halfway up, leaning her hands against her knees. "I'm fine. But what the hell happened?"

Hadley turned toward the mirror. Or rather, the spot where the mirror used to be. In its place was nothing more than torn drywall. On the floor below it, in the middle of the broken glass, lay the dagger.

Dread formed in the pit of her stomach. The dagger was there, but Persephone was gone. And so was Alice.

chapter 25

Alice blinked a few times, waiting for her eyes to adjust. Birds chirped, and sunlight warmed her face. Her hand stung and the ground beneath her felt strange, but also familiar. It was spongy in a way—sort of there and not there at the same time. Like the ground in a dream.

She inhaled sharply and sat up. The blood rushed from her head, and her vision swirled with little white stars. When they cleared, she found herself sitting in the middle of a sun-dappled forest. The trees were enormous, stretching so high she couldn't see where they ended and the sky began. In fact, she couldn't see the sky at all, yet rays of golden sunshine peaked through the branches, casting beams of light that illuminated the forest floor. But that wasn't all that was illuminating it.

She gasped and scrambled to her feet, vaguely aware of the squishy ground as she tilted her head back to see. A slight breeze moved through the giant trees, making their leaves sparkle and shimmer. They tinkled melodiously like a million windchimes dancing in the wind.

She stepped forward, toward the closest tree. Its trunk was the width of a small house, and its bark seemed to move and change in the shimmering light. She reached up and pressed her hand against it. It sank in, as if she were pressing it into a pile of thick dough. It gave a little but held. She looked up, letting her gaze move over the hundreds of branches towering above her. Leaves of gold and silver swayed back and forth, bouncing sunlight off each other. A few of them blew off in the breeze, windmilling through the air in slow motion before landing softly on the ground a few feet away.

Except they weren't leaves. They were mirrors.

Her pulse quickened and she stepped back, spinning to take in the rest of her surroundings. The forest floor was strewn with mirrors of every size and shape, with frames of silver, gold, black, white, and everything in between. They were everywhere, but not just on the ground. Some of them floated in mid-air, as if hanging from the trees by invisible string. She took another step back and felt her heel sink into the dough-like earth. She glanced down to see what looked like grass, but upon further inspection she realized was the same material as the trunks of the trees. It was the squish.

She laughed out loud even as a lump formed in her throat. The squish. It used to be the blackish-gray substance that made up the cracks between the mirrors in the Realm. But now it had transformed into grass and trees. She even saw sprigs of flowers popping up here and there, creating the vision of an enchanted forest with mirrors reflecting each other as far as the eye could see.

She sank to the ground next to a large oval mirror with an ornate silver frame. Bright pink and yellow flowers she couldn't name were growing along the sides, as if holding the mirror in their springtime embrace. She leaned forward to touch the petals of one, but her fingertips pushed straight through them. The flower disappeared and popped back up, just out of reach. It wasn't real. It was just another version of the squish, but it was spectacular. She sat back and took it all in, smiling as a beam of sunlight crossed her face, warming her cheeks.

Persephone had done it. She'd brought the Realm back! She'd assured Alice it was possible. They'd been meeting in secret for days, and while Alice hated keeping it from the girls, she didn't want to risk them not letting her do what needed to be done. Persephone told her it wouldn't be easy, and Alice's hand was proof of that. She glanced at the thin line of red already crusting over. It stung, but no more than a bad paper cut—a small price to pay for what they'd accomplished. Perhaps the trial and error in the ballet studio was a waste of time, but she'd had to try. After all, didn't she have powers? What was the point if she didn't start using them? But it turned out those powers did not extend to creating Realms. Persephone taking over had been their last resort.

"Hello, Last Resort," she whispered, leaning back. She stared at the hundreds of thousands of mirrors hanging around her. It wasn't the Realm she remembered, but that had been Philautia's Realm. This one was Persephone's.

The beauty surrounding her was stunning, like a vivid painting come to life. A small mirror slowly floated through the air, catching her eye. She reached out and snatched it. It was tiny, nothing more than a pocket mirror. Instinct made her bring it to her face to check her reflection, but it wasn't there. Like the old Realm, these mirrors only reflected each other, making for a dizzying spectacle. She tossed the pocket mirror aside, and it floated through the air before settling onto a patch of green grass. Wildflowers immediately sprung up around it, welcoming it into the fold.

"Persephone," she said aloud. "You did it!"

On cue, birdsong erupted around her. She looked up, searching for the source. When she spotted it, she couldn't help but laugh with delight. They weren't real birds, of course. They were projections of birds being displayed in a cluster of mirrors on the branches above her. They hopped from branch to branch—from mirror to mirror—before taking flight and disappearing into the forest of glass beyond.

A smile stretched across her face. Not only had Persephone managed to bring the Realm back, but she'd also done it in her own image. She was, after all, the goddess of spring.

Alice pulled herself to her feet. Rather than let her shoes sink into the squishy grass, she stepped onto the surface of the silver-framed mirror. Plenty of mirrors littered the forest floor, making it easy to avoid the squish. With a grin, she hopped onto the next mirror, a round decorative one that probably hung in someone's powder room. She stared at her feet, picturing what might be on the other side of the glass. Was there someone looking into this mirror right now, washing their hands, or fixing their hair?

These were questions she hadn't asked in a long time. But this was the miracle of the Realm. She spun in a slow circle, staring at the endless forest that stretched before her in every direction. Millions of mirrors glinted and sparkled in the faux sunlight, reminding her of what they were. They were windows to the world, each connected to a real mirror somewhere on the planet. The question was, which one would bring her home?

The thought made her freeze. The dagger. Where was the dagger?

Her heart leaped into her throat as she frantically scanned the mirrored forest floor, searching. She dropped to her hands and knees, crawled over mirrors, and slid her hands beneath the frames, letting her fingers dig through the squishy grass, hoping they'd brush against the hilt.

After a few minutes of fruitless searching, she sat back, breathless and resigned. The dagger wasn't there. Which meant she wasn't going anywhere anytime soon.

Her thoughts drifted to David, and a small pain took hold in her chest. He was the last person she spoke to before she let Persephone take over. She'd promised him it would be okay, that Persephone knew what she was doing. He'd been angry, but she'd dug in her heels and, as usual, he gave in. His last words to her before storming out of the ballet studio were clipped and hurried, but the message was crystal clear—and it wasn't even for her.

"Don't fuck this up, Persephone," he'd said.

It was rare for David to curse. Even as Colin, she couldn't recall him ever using the F-word. He was scared, and right about now he'd be learning she was stuck in the Realm without a compass. The last time he thought she was lost, he ended up in a coma. Her mind raced with all the horrible possibilities. She had to get out of here, if only to stop him from doing something stupid.

She shot to her feet, chose a direction, and started running.

Hadley found David in the stables standing in front of Max's stall. He had a hold of his halter and had pulled his head down so that their foreheads were touching. She wondered how long he'd been out here, talking to a horse. But she couldn't judge. Max was one of the best listeners on the Roxland estate. They'd all stood in front of his stall at some point, pouring their hearts out.

"Hey," she said softly, careful not to startle the horse.

David didn't turn around but offered a quiet "hey" in return.

"You okay?" she asked. It was a dumb question, but sometimes those just flew out of her mouth.

"Do I look okay?"

"No."

He patted Max on the neck and stepped back. The horse immediately ducked into his stall, as if he knew a heated conversation was about to take place.

"Why?" he spoke up unexpectedly, raking his fingers through his hair. "Why does this keep happening? She needed her space, so I gave it to her. I thought I was doing the right thing. But now look where we are! She's stuck in the Realm, and there's not a fucking thing I can do to help her!"

Hadley flinched at his choice of words. "First of all, it's not about you, David," she said calmly. "And you gave her space because you needed it too. This isn't about that. It's about the Realm and the Portal."

His expression softened, and he ran his hands down his face before dropping onto a bale of hay.

"I know," he relented. "I just hate feeling helpless. It's not a good look for me."

She walked over and took a seat beside him. "Honestly? It's better than obnoxious and rude, your normal go-tos."

"Shut up," he said, bumping his shoulder into hers.

She bumped him back. "Listen, I came down here to tell you we've gathered all the mirror fragments and put them in the library safe."

"Good," he said, nodding. "Did you add a piece to each of your compasses?"

"Yes."

"Okay. Take the dagger with you too. If Persephone succeeded, you're entering a new Realm. It may not look the same, but it should still function the same. I think."

She raised an eyebrow. "You think?"

"It's not like I've been through this before," he spat, pulling on the back of his neck. "I've told you what I know. There's nothing more I can do."

Hadley bristled and stood. "Fine. I've delivered my message. We'll see you when we get back." She turned to go.

"Wait."

She whipped around, hair smacking her in the face. "What?"

His eyes were dark and pleading. "Find her for me, Hadley. Please . . . find her for us."

The desperation in his voice caught her off guard. Vulnerability had never been David's strong suit. It was out of character. Or was it? Suddenly, she saw him through different eyes, and in that moment he reminded her of her brother. Caleb had spent most of his life scared too. His behavior, his anger, it all stemmed from fear. Fear of failure. Fear of things he couldn't control. But she had her own fears too, didn't she? Fear of abandonment. Fear of letting go. Her fears were no better or worse, they were just part of who she was—a flawed human being. But she was also a huntress, which meant it was her job to protect humans like herself, regardless of their flaws. David might be far from perfect, but guess what? So was she.

Before realizing it, she'd stepped forward and thrown her arms around him. It was something she'd never done, and he stumbled a bit, losing his balance. His body was rigid, as if unable to process what was happening. But a second later, he returned the embrace.

"We'll bring her back," she promised. "And for the record, you're not helpless."

He laughed into her hair. "Liar."

She pulled back and held him by his shoulders. "I still think you're a pain in the ass, but I was wrong when I said Alice was the only reason you're still here. You're here because you care what happens to us, and I'm sorry I never gave you credit for that."

He gave her an arrogant smirk. "Is that right?"

"Ugh," she groaned, shoving him. "You really don't want me to like you, do you?"

He smiled and lightly pinched her chin. "Of course I care what happens to you, Hadz. I'll always care."

It was the damndest thing, but her eyes started to well up, as if this was a tender moment or something. She acknowledged it the only way she could, with a fierce nod of her head. Then she turned around and marched toward the house, eager not to let her feelings show. Maybe eventually she would, but not today.

"Bring our girl home, Hadley," he called after her. "I'm counting on you."

She threw him a backward wave and kept walking, steeling herself against her emotions. *I said not today, dammit.*

"I love you, Hadz," came the three words she'd never heard him say. Her shoulders stiffened and she trudged on, but the corner of her mouth lifted, and she couldn't stop one treasonous tear from slipping down her cheek.

chapter 26

Running full speed through the mirrored forest didn't feel much different from running through the old Realm. The faster Alice ran, the further she could leap from mirror to mirror, eventually turning and running sideways up tree trunks, or along the surfaces of mirrors hanging like gigantic Christmas ornaments. The laws of gravity didn't apply, and when she changed direction, so did the world around her. It was gravity playing by her rules, and not the other way around. She leaped and flew through the air, reveling in the familiarity of the Realm. It felt good to be back, even if her primary goal was to find a way *out*.

Occasionally, she'd spot a break in the trees and speed toward it. The first clearing she came across was a small meadow with several mirrors lying in the grass. Clusters of daisies sprung up between them. There were also a few larger mirrors floating in mid-air, projecting images of dragonflies and bees buzzing about. The sound was as intense as the images themselves.

The next few clearings she discovered were equally impressive. One had hundreds of mirrors lying side by side, projecting the surface of a koi pond. The water was crystal clear, and dozens of brightly colored koi swam from mirror to mirror, just going about the business of being fish. It was so realistic she hesitated to walk across, lest she fall through. Another clearing had mirrors projecting a small creek complete with river rocks and boulders, and yet another had a wall of levitating mirrors that did nothing but project a springtime rain shower. Alice could almost feel the damp as she made her way past.

There was so much to see. The forest, like the hallways of the Realm, was endless. She even tried getting to the top of the tree line, to see if she could get a bird's-eye view of Persephone's Realm. She climbed for what felt like hours, leaping from branch to branch, and even running straight up the trunk. But she never reached the top. She still couldn't figure out exactly *how*, but somewhere along the line, she was no longer climbing—she was descending. The switch was almost imperceptible. One second she was leaping up, and the next she was leaping down, as if the entire world had turned upside down. Once she realized what was happening, she changed direction, thinking maybe she was just confused. But again, the world flipped. There was no top. The top *was* the bottom, and that was that. Like the topsy-turvy hallways of the Realm, it was an Escher painting, forestry edition.

Eventually, she gave up and sat down on a thick branch somewhere in the middle of the madness. Hundreds of mirrors hung all around her, swaying back and forth the way giant leaves would. It was bizarre and surreal and everything she expected something like this would be. Beams of sunlight bounced from glass to glass, giving the entire world a golden glow. When she looked out at the neighboring trees, she saw more of the same, only from her vantage point, she was looking at a million more mirrors, sparkling in eternal sunshine. The magnitude of it all made her feel very small, and very alone.

She was also beginning to feel tired and thirsty. There might be plenty of mirrors here projecting streams and rainstorms, but it didn't mean there was real water for her to drink. There was a reason no huntress ventured into the Realm without a compass. Alice never had a compass of her own, but at least with the dagger, all she'd have to do was pick a mirror, exit through it, and hope for the best. It might be a house in Lençóis, Brazil, or a restaurant in Lyon, France, but it was better than being trapped and dying of dehydration.

The thought spurred her to immediate action. After everything she'd been through, she wasn't dying here now. This was Persephone's Realm. She had to be here, in some form, right? And then she gave herself a facepalm for being so stupid. She'd been running through this place like a madwoman when she should have been calling for help. She scrambled up, took a deep breath, and screamed at the top of her lungs.

"PERSEPHONE! IT'S ALICE!"

Her voice carried through the forest in surround sound, bouncing off millions of mirrors, sounding like millions of Alices screaming into the void. She tried again.

"PERSEPHONE, PLEASE! I NEED YOUR HELP!"

Her echo traveled through the neighboring trees. It was loud and clear, making her wonder how easy it would be to pinpoint her location. Because it really did sound like she was yelling back at herself, over and over again.

"Persephone, please! I need your help!
Persephone, please! I need your help!
Persephone, please! I need your help!"

The effect was unsettling and brought goosebumps to her arms. She sat back down and shoved a floating mirror aside. It spun like a top, coming to rest a few yards away, hovering in the air and taunting her with its uselessness. She stared at it, wondering what would happen if she just rammed it with her fist. Then something in the glass caught her eye.

She sat up and leaned forward. There it was again—a flash of green. She shot to her feet, grabbing the branch above her for balance. She heard the sound of a bird chirping behind her and spun around. Another flash of green shot through one of the mirrors to her right. She leaped forward, catching sight of feathers just as the image left the mirror's frame. She stopped and scanned the surrounding mirrors until she spotted it again. It was hovering in a mirror two branches down, waiting for her.

It was a bright green parakeet, the same one her Aunt Molly bought her when she was five years old. The one she eventually set free.

"Keetie!" she yelled.

The bird flapped its wings vigorously, then flew out of frame, appearing in the glass of an adjacent mirror, where it zipped back and forth, chirping. Alice laughed at the sight. Persephone had heard her after all, and she'd sent Keetie, Alice's childhood pet, to guide her. The chase was on!

The little bird led her on an intense sprint through the forested Realm. It was similar to chasing compasses in the old Realm, only this was a projection that moved from mirror to mirror. Alice lost track of it a few times, panicking when she thought it was gone for good. But then she'd see a spot of green in a distant mirror, and leap across the trees to reach it before it disappeared again.

Her breath was ragged by the time Keetie's image finally stopped and hovered in a floating mirror at the edge of a clearing. She stepped up to the glass and placed her palm against it. Keetie's image blurred a bit, sang a happy little tune, then vanished. Alice said a silent *thank you* to the imaginary bird and turned toward the clearing. It was empty, save for one large oval mirror hovering in the center. Alice felt her feet sink in the soft "grass" as she made her way over to it.

The mirror spun slowly, both sides reflecting everything around it except for Alice. It had no frame or fancy beveled edge. There was nothing special about it. She watched it slowly spin for a few seconds, waiting for something to happen. When it didn't, she lifted her hand and stopped the mirror's revolution. Again, nothing happened, so she let go, allowing it to continue its slow rotation. Then, for no other reason than to give it a try, she grabbed an edge and pulled as hard as she could. It was like yanking the cord on an old lawn mower. The mirror suddenly sprung to life and started spinning much faster than it should have.

She waited to see if it would slow, but it didn't. It kept gaining speed, spinning so fast that within seconds it no longer resembled a mirror. It morphed into a bright white light that somehow absorbed everything around it. Soon, it was just Alice and the bright, pulsating light.

She stared into the light. It was warm and soothing. It beckoned her in a way that felt familiar and safe, like an old blanket or a favorite chair. There wasn't time to think things through. The Portal of Osiris was calling to her, and its siren song was strong.

She stepped through.

Hadley's compass felt different. Heavier, somehow.

"I know," said Olivia. "Mine too."

Hadley stared at the silver compact in her hand. Inside was a piece of jagged obsidian and a piece of ballet studio mirror, two very different types of mirrors, separated by thousands of years. Each were used to create a realm. The question was, would they work well together?

"Feels like something's moving in there," added Soxie.

Hadley instinctively pulled her hand away from her. Soxie had a point. It did sort of feel like there might be two tiny snakes inside, coiling around each other. She didn't love the analogy, but it was the one that came to mind.

"We have to trust these to guide us," said Olivia, even though she looked a little wary herself. "If you don't feel a connection, then something's wrong."

Hadley and Soxie looked at each other.

"I definitely feel a connection," Hadley assured her. "I know this one is mine. It just feels . . . different."

"Yep. Way different vibe," agreed Soxie.

Olivia looked satisfied. "Well, we're not jumping into the old Realm, so we can't expect it to feel the same." Then she turned toward the wall of mirrors that was absent one panel.

They were standing in the ballet studio, ready to cross over. It would be their first Realm jump since the Realm disappeared. But it didn't feel like riding a bike. It felt like they were thirteen again, about to enter for the first time. Hadley glanced at the drywall where the previous mirror panel had been. David had insisted they gather the fragments and lock them in the safe, but it seemed like a waste of time. A huntress was more than just the mirror fragment she possessed. She also contained a portion of Philautia's soul. Now, Persephone? That was another story. As a goddess, she didn't have a soul. She wasn't even supposed to exist, yet her memory had managed to possess Alice, and create a new Realm.

Hadley felt a shiver run up and down her spine. Now that she thought about it, David was probably right. Maybe it *was* a good idea to keep those mirror shards safe.

"Are you guys ready?" asked Soxie, demanding their attention. Hadley nodded, and the three of them gathered in front of the still-intact mirrors. Soxie counted down from three, and they popped their compasses open.

The room remained the same, but their images in the mirror disappeared. It happened in the blink of an eye, and they all immediately let out huge sighs of relief. It worked. They were back!

"Yes!" whooped Soxie.

Hadley turned in a circle. Without the piano as a reference, it was hard to determine whether they were in the Backwards Place—the name they'd given their preferred entryway to the Realm. It wasn't the only way to enter, but it was the more agreeable way. In the Backwards, they didn't just enter the mirror's reflection; they *became* the reflection.

Hadley looked around and spotted an old piece of sheet music lying in the corner. She walked over to study it. It was covered in dust and the top read "ɘnul ɘb ɘɿiɒlƆ." *Claire de lune*, one of her favorite pieces of classical music. She nodded once and stood.

"It reads backward," she confirmed. "We're good."

"Okay then," said Soxie. "Let's get—" She stopped short. "What is it, O?"

Hadley looked up. Olivia stood in front of the mirror Persephone had shattered. Only, here, in the Backwards, it was still intact. Hadley shot to her feet and pointed at the glass panel.

"Why is that still here?"

Olivia shook her head slowly. "I have no idea. Sox, can you check the hall?"

Soxie hurried to the doorway. It was strange not to hear her heels clacking on the hardwood floor or see her reflection in the mirrors. She rounded the corner and disappeared. They waited. And waited. Hadley called out to her, wondering what was taking so long. The entrance to the Realm should be right outside. It should be anywhere that wasn't in a direct line of sight to the mirrors.

"Sox!" Olivia called this time.

She sailed back into the room a second later, looking flummoxed.

"It's all—it's all backward," she stammered. "All of it. Every-where."

Hadley's eyes grew big. "What do you mean, all of it?"

"Just what you think I mean. It's like the whole world has been turned inside out. And the dogs are clueless—like they're frozen or something. I walked right up to Schlemmer, and she didn't budge. Pretty sure she didn't even know I was there."

"Frozen?" Hadley repeated, struggling to comprehend. How could the dogs be frozen? And how could the entire *world* be back-ward? She was already moving toward the hall to see for herself when Olivia snapped her fingers.

"No, we don't have time to investigate. We have to get to Alice."

Hadley shook her head to clear it. "Right," she said before throwing a nod at the hall. "But if that's not the entrance anymore, then how do we get in?"

Olivia glanced at the mirror that shouldn't be there. "I think it's through here. Look."

They watched as she lifted her hand and pressed her finger against the glass. It sank straight through. The "ghost" mirror was the door.

Hadley slowly made her way back to Olivia's side. She gave the dagger strapped to her thigh a quick pat for good measure. They'd been prepared for things to be different. The dagger, their compasses, and now the Backwards—all of it had changed in some way. Was it better or worse? Right now, it didn't matter. She'd promised David she'd bring their girl back. So that was what she would do.

Soxie sidled up next to them. Then, with one last look at each other, they held hands and stepped into a new world.

chapter 27

The floor beneath Alice tilted as she made her way down the Jetway. It was drafty, as usual, so she reached for the sweater in her bag, only to discover she wasn't carrying a bag. She stopped and looked down, confused. What happened to her carry-on bag? Or her roller suitcase? This was weird. Did she leave them in the terminal? She turned around. The tunnel behind her stretched on and on, its artificial lights fading into eventual darkness. There were occasional seams in the walls, and the floor was dark and rubbery, with black-and-yellow caution lines running along the sides. Otherwise, it was empty. She whirled back around, realizing she was alone on the Jetway. Where were the other passengers? What was happening?

A sound up ahead caught her attention. She moved toward it, eager to find someone who could help. The tunnel bounced ever so slightly as she hurried along. Eventually, the passageway came to a sharp left turn. When she rounded the corner, she saw that the plane was connected to the Jetway, and the cabin door was still open.

Phew, she thought as she dug in her back pocket for her boarding pass. But her hand came up empty. She frantically patted the rest of her pockets, spinning in circles as she searched for it.

"Don't worry, Bunny. You're the only passenger on this flight."

She froze and looked up. Her Aunt Molly stood on the other side of the cabin door in her crisp royal-blue uniform, complete with silk scarf and stylish, yet sensible pumps. Alice stared at her, convinced there was something wrong with all of this, but unable to grasp what it might be.

Molly gave her a dazzling smile, ushering her forward. "Hurry up now, we're taking off soon."

Her voice carried a sense of urgency that Alice couldn't ignore. Before she realized it, she was on the plane and buckled into a first-class seat. Molly closed the cabin door and disappeared into the galley, giving Alice a moment to settle in. She clasped her hands in her lap and looked around. She was seated in the third row, middle aisle. Empty seats surrounded her on all sides. She twisted around and saw that the rest of the plane was empty too. Rows and rows of empty seats, just waiting for passengers who would never come. It was a big plane for just one passenger. And then a thought wormed its way into her brain. Why was she on this plane to begin with? Where was she going?

"Welcome aboard, Bunny."

Alice turned to face front. Molly was standing in the aisle with her flight attendant props, ready to give the safety demonstration. Alice gripped the armrests as the engines roared to life and the plane began to taxi onto the runway.

"Where are we going?" she blurted out, happy to finally find her voice.

Molly shushed her. "Not now!"

Embarrassed, Alice slunk down in her chair. Even though there was no one else on the flight, she didn't want to be an unruly passenger. So she sat silently and watched while Molly went through her entire spiel, even using the safety card from the pouch in front of her to follow along. When Molly finished, she pressed the intercom and spoke through the plane's PA system.

"Flight attendants, prepare doors for departure and cross-check."

Alice felt her brow tighten as she looked around again. There were no other flight attendants. Was Molly okay?

Before she had a chance to ask, the engines roared louder, and Molly strapped herself into her jump seat. Alice frowned and turned to the windows, hoping for a clue as to where they were. But the windows were closed. She scanned the rest of the plane. Sure enough, every single shade was drawn.

Well, this sucked.

With no other option, she leaned back and closed her eyes as the plane took off. She felt her stomach drop as the wheels left the ground, but that part always gave her anxiety—more so when she was flying alone.

Her eyes popped open, and she stared at the back of the seat. Alone. Why was she alone? Where were the girls? Where was David? And then something clicked into place in her brain. Finally.

The plane leveled out, but the captain didn't inform them they'd reached cruising altitude, because there was no captain, and none of this was real. Alice flung off her seatbelt and stormed up front. She found Molly in the galley, preparing the drinks cart. She glanced up and smiled wide.

"Can I get you something, sweetie? I'm making chocolate chip cookies in a bit. I'll save you a couple."

"What are you doing, Persephone?"

A look of sheer disappointment crossed her Molly-like face. With a sigh she abandoned what she was doing and grabbed a mini bottle of white wine from the bar cart. She downed it in one go, then wiped her mouth with the back of her hand.

"Damn," she said, tossing the empty bottle in the trash. "I was hoping you'd at least make it through dinner service. You would have had the choice of lobster thermidor or chateaubriand."

Alice glowered. "What's going on? Where are we?"

"Oh, sweetie, don't be so dramatic. You've been on a plane before. There's quite a few in your memories to choose from."

The cabin suddenly rattled with unexpected turbulence. Alice glanced toward the cockpit, wondering if it was empty. She'd never been in a cockpit before, so she dared Persephone to conjure one up from her memories.

"Why am I here?"

Persephone grabbed two more bottles of wine and opened the cockpit door. "Come on," she said. "I'll show you."

With an impatient huff, Alice ducked through the door. There was no cockpit. The door led straight into her childhood bedroom. She stood in the doorway, stunned. It was just as she remembered it. The white dresser with the butterfly pulls, the pale-yellow canopy bed, her favorite stuffed bunny propped up against the pillows. She half expected to see her five-year-old self lying on the floor, drawing pictures of houses with chimneys and lines of curly smoke.

Persephone moved to stand next to her. She was no longer in her flight attendant uniform. Instead she was wearing a chic silk jumpsuit with expensive-looking jewelry. She stared at the room while she knocked back another drink.

"I see you still love your wine," Alice said, her tone filled with snark.

Persephone glanced at the empty bottle and tossed it aside. "Oh, right. Sorry. It's just that, in most of your memories of me, I'm drinking. I find myself still gravitating toward it. I wasn't the best role model, was I?"

"No," Alice agreed with a laugh. "Maybe not the *best*. But you were a goddess living as a mortal. I think we can cut you some slack." Then she turned back to the room. "But what is this about?"

"This is one of my favorite places in your memories," she said wistfully as she took a seat on the tiny bed. "When you were little, I used to love curling up with you here and singing you to sleep. I'd never had that before. Melinoë . . . well, she was never much of the cuddling type."

Alice stiffened at the mention of Melinoë's name. As curious as she was about Persephone's relationship with her daughter—or lack thereof—she had the feeling her time here was limited. She stepped to the bed and took Persephone's hands in hers.

"Please, Persephone. I don't know if you're real or a living memory or something I can't even begin to understand, but we need your help. We need the Portal. It's here, right? I can feel it."

Persephone lifted her hand and cupped Alice's chin. "Of course it's here. It's been waiting for you."

"It has?" she asked, taken aback. "What does it want with me?"

"Bunny, it belongs to you."

Alice felt reality as she knew it begin slipping through her fingers. "What?" she whispered. "How can the Portal of Osiris belong to *me*?"

Persephone tucked one leg under the other, getting comfortable. "The Portal has existed since time began. Time itself only exists because of it. But it still requires a protector. Osiris was once its protector, but he failed, bringing about his own destruction."

"He failed," Alice repeated, "because Hades stole it from him, along with my soul."

She smiled. "Smart girl."

Alice needed a second. She grabbed the bedpost for support and sat down on the edge of the mattress. "How did the Portal end up in the Realm? If Hades had it, why would he let it go?"

"Because he didn't know he had it. Osiris hid the Portal *within* your soul, Alice. When your soul was stolen, so was the Portal. For hundreds of years it lay unprotected in The Underworld, hidden inside your soul until it found a new protector in Philautia. But now that Philautia's gone, the Portal has chosen you. It used the clues Osiris left behind to help you find it."

If Alice were made of glass, she'd have shattered by now. It was too much to follow, too much to comprehend. "How do you *know* all this?"

"*I* don't," Persephone replied. "But *you* do. Your soul's memory holds so much more than you realize."

Alice didn't even want to touch that. "But, who had the Portal and my soul *before* Osiris?" Even as she asked the question, she wondered if it was better left unanswered.

"Oh," Persephone said, shooing the question away with a wave of her hand. "I can't answer that. Your soul's memory is too long. Your mortal brain can't accept all of it, which means I can't either. It wasn't anyone from this world, I can tell you that much."

"This world?" she gulped.

Persephone grabbed hold of Alice's arms, giving her a look that meant business. "Alice, pay attention! The Portal is as old as *time*. It's been around for billions of years, and as one of its first creations, so have you. I'm telling you this now because you're finally ready to hear it."

If it was possible to lose consciousness while still being awake, Alice felt like she'd just watched her own body fall to the floor. Yet somehow, she was still sitting there, staring at a memory of the woman she once knew as her aunt, trying to comprehend the incomprehensible. Billions of years? No. These questions *were* better left unanswered. She didn't want to know any more. She stood, walked to the dresser, and idly tugged at a butterfly pull.

"Just tell me what I'm supposed to do," she pleaded. "I need to get back." *To the girls*, she wanted to say. To David—Cithaeron. They were what was important. The people in *her* world. The universe and creation? She didn't have the headspace for that kind of burden. One world at a time, thank you very much.

"Look at me, Bunny."

She looked up and met Persephone's gaze in the mirror above her dresser. "I never asked for all of this," Alice said, feeling the words get stuck in her throat. "I don't want this responsibility."

"The chosen ones never do," Persephone mused. "But you are powerful, Alice. You have a magic in you that has only yet scratched the surface. The Portal is no longer safe in the Realm. I can't protect it, but you can." Then she stepped forward and placed a small silver locket on the dresser. It was an oval design with a hinged clasp that hung on a thin silver chain. Alice's eyes rounded.

"Is that it? Is that the Portal?" She'd been expecting the old portal, the one they used to call the map—a simple round mirror about the size of a dinner plate. She hesitantly picked up the locket and let it rest in her palm. The thin chain slid slowly through her fingers.

"It has chosen this form for you, which means you have the ability to open it."

Alice stared at the delicate locket. She didn't know why, but something told her that opening it would be bad. Really, *really* bad. Like getting-sucked-into-a-black-hole kind of bad. Before she could stop herself, she flung it back on the dresser and leaped away, nearly knocking Persephone over.

"No!" she hissed, spittle flying from her mouth. "I can't open it! I won't!"

Persephone grabbed hold of her shoulders and turned her around. "And that," she said with a knowing smile, "is exactly why you were chosen."

The locket felt strangely comfortable against her chest. She rubbed it with her thumb and forefinger as she stared blankly at the airline seat in front of her. The smell of freshly baked chocolate chip cookies wafted through the air, and her stomach grumbled in anticipation.

"Now, these might taste amazing," said Persephone as she scurried over with a tray, back in her flight attendant uniform, "but remember, you aren't really eating. So you need to get back as soon as possible. You've been here too long already."

Alice gratefully plucked a warm cookie from the tray and shoved it in her mouth. Her tastebuds screamed with delight. It was chocolatey, buttery, gooey perfection. She greedily gobbled it up and sat back, closing her eyes as she chewed.

"Eating with no consequences? Persephone, this isn't the Realm. This is heaven." She felt a light slap on her arm and opened her eyes.

"Very funny," Persephone said as she sat down across the aisle, balancing the tray on her legs. Alice reached over and grabbed two more cookies, shoveling them in her mouth.

Persephone lifted an eyebrow. "You're still hungry, aren't you?"

Despite going through the motions of chewing and swallowing, Alice had to agree. Her stomach felt just as empty. Her throat just as dry.

"Yes," she admitted. "I guess it's time for me to go. But, I did have an odd question for you."

Persephone cocked her head to the side. "You can ask me anything. You know that."

Alice bit her lip, wondering if this was a good idea, but decided she had nothing to lose. "What happened with you and Mayron?"

Persephone gave her a puzzled look. "Mayron? Soxie's uncle?"

"Yes. He . . ." She paused, wondering how best to describe it. "He seems a little fixated on you. Or, I guess, who he thought you were—you know, Molly."

She looked down and stared at the cookies in her lap. "I'm not sure. My existence is tied to your memories. If you don't hold that specific memory, I don't think I can help."

"That's disappointing."

She shrugged. "What can I say? Being a memory is strange."

"So is talking to one."

A ripple of laughter passed between them. It reminded Alice of the chummy rapport they'd once had when Persephone actually existed. This—well, she didn't know what *this* was. But she was still glad for the moment. Once the moment passed, she sat up and looked around the cabin.

"How am I supposed to get out of here? I don't have a compass."

Persephone pointed at the locket hanging around her neck. "You can never open it, but you can use it. It knows the Realm, even better than I do. It can help."

Alice dipped her chin to look at it. "It can? How?"

"I suspect it will reveal its uses to you when *it* chooses. But for now, the girls are looking for you. They just entered the Realm."

Alice leaped to her feet. "They did?"

Persephone nodded, set her tray aside, and stood. "Yes, and I've given them the power to find you. But Alice, they're not alone."

"What? Who's with them?" she asked, her voice catching as a feeling of dread overcame her. "It's not David, is it? Please tell me he didn't try to enter the Realm!"

"No, sweetie. It's not David."

"Then who?"

Persephone bowed her head slightly. "This is why I can't protect the Portal. I'm the memory of a goddess, the Queen of The Underworld. I can't change that."

Alice blinked a few times, attempting to understand. "Do you mean demons can access the Realm again?" It wasn't the best news, but demons they could handle. They were huntresses—hunting demons was literally their job.

"Not demons."

She took a second to let those two little words sink in. "The gods?" she whispered. "Are you saying they now have access to the Realm?"

"Yes."

"Which ones?"

"All of them."

All of them? Alice couldn't believe it. If the gods had access to the Realm, what did that mean for them? For the world?

"Even . . . Hades?" she asked, barely able to get the words out. His name sliced through her brain like a jagged piece of glass.

Persephone took a breath before answering. "I'm not sure. We would both feel it if he was here, so I don't think so. Not yet anyway. But that doesn't mean you shouldn't fear the other gods. They can be just as ruthless. Some, even more."

"I have to go," Alice heard herself whisper. Hades was a problem, but Persephone was right. *Any* god in the Realm was a bad thing.

Without thinking, she ran to the exit door, grabbed the handle, and yanked hard. The door made a loud popping noise and shot out like a rocket. Wind from the pressurized cabin nearly blew her out with it. This wasn't a real plane, and they weren't really flying at thirty thousand feet. But it seemed like the logical way out, and she needed to find the girls and warn them.

"Alice!" Persephone yelled over the whooshing noise. Alice turned around. Masks had dropped from the ceilings, and random papers were flying about the cabin. She could barely see as her own hair whipped wildly about her face.

"I'm sorry, Persephone!" she screamed over the din. "You know I have to go!"

"Be careful!" she yelled back as the plane bucked back and forth. "I love you, Bunny!"

Alice planted her feet and gripped the sides of the cabin doorway. She looked out into the rushing wind. There was no ground or sky—nothing to indicate she'd be jumping to her death. There wasn't anything indicating she wouldn't be, either. But the time for guessing was over. She looked back, flashed Persephone a thankful, tear-filled smile, closed her hand around the locket, and jumped.

Hadley sat on the branch of a giant tree, staring at the forest of mirrors that stretched out in front of her. Everywhere she looked, glass floated and sparkled, spinning, or swaying in a supernatural breeze. Beams of golden light cut through the shadows, bouncing off the mirrors, creating a view that was equal parts stunning and intimidating. Soxie sat beside her, glancing up every few seconds and huffing with impatience.

"What's taking her so long?" she whined.

Hadley looked up through the dense, reflective "foliage." Occasionally, tiny mirrors would break off a branch and float toward the ground, catching rays of sunlight on their way down. It brought movement and a toy-piano-like sound to the forest that made it feel alive. But it also made it very hard to navigate. They'd been leaping through the trees for hours, like a scurry of flying squirrels or a murder of crows, searching for an end they had yet to find.

"It's only been a few minutes," Hadley replied, craning her neck as she searched for her friend's signature all-black clothing. Olivia had volunteered to climb to the top of the canopy while Soxie and Hadley scanned the forest for Alice.

"She might get lost. We don't know how this Realm works yet."

Hadley kept her eyes skyward. "If she stays on this tree, she should be fine."

"We'll see. Just hope she doesn't run into any demons."

A flicker of unease passed between them. Hadley hadn't thought of that. In the old Realm, when a demon was present, Philautia would alert them by sending a warning sound through the mirrors. But there was no way of knowing if Persephone's Realm worked the same way.

"Demons?" she said, anxiously eyeing the surrounding trees. "I thought Alice destroyed them all last year."

Soxie shook her head. "We don't know that for sure." Then she pulled out her compass and flipped it open. It did nothing but sit in her hand, as if waiting for her to use it to powder her nose. She snapped it shut.

"Well," she said, standing. "At least our compasses don't seem worried."

Hadley quickly pulled out her compass and repeated the process. Like Soxie's, hers did nothing. If there was a demon in the Realm, it would have been spinning into a ball of silver light. But again, that was the old Realm's rules. They had yet to learn the rules of Persephone's Realm.

With a sigh, she pocketed her compass and removed the dagger from the sheath on her thigh. Then she grabbed a floating mirror and gently placed the tip against the glass.

"How many times are you going to try that?" asked Soxie.

Hadley pouted like a petulant child when the dagger refused to show her what was on the other side. "Maybe this dagger hasn't learned how to open mirrors yet. It *is* sixteen hundred years younger than the other one. Do you think time has something to do with it?"

"Probably," Soxie answered, continuing to scan the trees. "You did go back in time to find it."

"Don't remind me. That logic still messes with my head." She sheathed the dagger just as movement in the distance caught her eye. She grabbed onto a mirror for balance and leaned forward. "Did you see that?"

Soxie followed her gaze. "See what?"

Hadley squinted, wishing she'd brought a pair of binoculars. "It was like a bright flash or something."

"Could have been light reflecting off a mirror," Soxie proposed.

"True," agreed Hadley, but her spidey-sense was telling her otherwise. Something was out there. Hopefully, it was Alice. She continued peering into the trees when a noise above startled her. Her head snapped up just in time to see Olivia's black-clad figure floating down. She landed on the branch next to her and sat down with a scowl.

"Well, that was a waste of time," she said, shoving a mirror aside. It broke off the branch and floated away.

"Why?" asked Hadley. "What did you find up there?"

"Nothing. There is no 'up there.' Past a certain point, you just find yourself climbing down instead of up. I tried switching directions, but it doesn't matter. This entire place is mirroring itself."

Hadley looked up, then down. "So you always end up back at the bottom?"

"Yup," Olivia answered. Then she plucked a hand mirror from the branch above her and started fanning herself with it. "I see you've had no luck with the dagger or compasses."

"No," confirmed Soxie. "Nothing yet."

Olivia nodded but flipped open her compass anyway. "Find portal," she said to it. Nothing happened, so she tried again. "Find Alice." Still nothing.

"Do either of you know what the definition of insanity is?" Soxie asked.

Hadley shot her a look. Maybe it was insane to keep trying the same thing over and over, expecting different results, but Alice was lost somewhere in this never-ending forest of glass. They had to keep trying. In solidarity with Olivia, she pulled her compass out and gave it an order.

"Find Persephone," she said. When nothing happened, she rattled off a series of orders, the equivalent of throwing spaghetti at the wall. "Find portal. Find Portal of Osiris. Find huntress. Find Alice. Find something. Find anything!" If the compass could laugh at her, she had a feeling it would. Instead, it just sat in her hand like a useless compact with two pieces of glass tucked inside.

"That's not fair," said Olivia. "They're not useless. They got us here."

"They just won't help us find Alice," Soxie felt the need to add.

Hadley reluctantly agreed, snapping her compass shut. Then she grabbed hold of the branch above her and screamed into the dense woods, "ALICE! ALICE, CAN YOU HEAR ME?"

Her voice echoed through the trees, bouncing off the mirrors in a way that made it sound like a song getting carried away by the wind.

"Alice! Alice, can you hear me?

Alice! Alice, can you hear me?"

Soxie and Olivia immediately joined in.

"ALICE! ALICE, WHERE ARE YOU?"

"YELL IF YOU CAN HEAR US!"

"Alice! Alice, where are you?

Yell if you can hear us!

Alice! Alice, where are you?

Yell if you can hear us!"

They waited and listened until their voices faded into the distant trees. If this Realm was truly infinite, Hadley wondered if their voices would be bouncing through it for the rest of time. The thought was mildly unsettling.

"Now what?" she said, looking to Olivia, as she always did.

Olivia sat down and put her head in her hands. "I don't know."

For several seconds, nobody said a word. They knew finding Alice wasn't going to be easy, but right now it was starting to feel dangerously close to impossible. With a shaky hand, Hadley pulled the dagger from the strap on her thigh.

Soxie eyed her with suspicion. "Now what are you doing?"

"Persephone used Alice's blood to create the Realm," she reasoned, holding the pointed end above her palm. "Maybe we need ours to find her."

Olivia's head popped up. "Hadley. You're a genius!"

"I am?"

She scrambled to her feet. "Yes! Alice's blood. Persephone was all but showing us how to find her! Here, give me that," she said, snatching the dagger from Hadley's hand.

"Hey!" she protested. Before she could stop her, Olivia ran the blade directly across her palm, drawing a thin line of blood. Then she pulled out her compass, flipped it open, and carefully squeezed a drop onto its contents.

Hadley and Soxie quickly repeated the process with their own compasses. When they were finished, Hadley wiped the blade of the dagger on her jeans and stuffed it back in its sheath.

"Okay," she said, meeting her friends' eyes. "Who wants to do the honors?"

Soxie and Olivia looked at each other. "You," they said together.

Hadley straightened her shoulders. "Here goes nothing," she said. Then she pointed her glass-and-blood-filled compass at the mirrored world and said, "Find Alice."

chapter 28

The spinning mirror spit Alice out like a nail from a nail gun. One second she was jumping from Persephone's airplane, the next she was prostrate on the spongy grass, gasping for air. It took her a minute before she was able to flip onto her back. The fake blue sky above mocked her. She stared at it with contempt, picturing all the other ways she could have exited the mirror that didn't involve an undignified faceplant.

"Thanks, Persephone," she grumbled as she pushed up onto her elbows. She was at the edge of the clearing, just outside the tree line. The floating mirror continued spinning slowly, reflecting everything but her. She scowled at it, hoping that next time—if there was a next time— Persephone might grant her a different way in and out of her memory.

She sat up and brought her hand to her chest, clutching the locket. Was it safe, hanging on her neck like this? She reached behind to feel for the clasp when a faint sound caught her attention. She dropped her hand and looked up.

"... *are you?*

... hear us!"

Scrambling to her feet, she rushed to the edge of the trees, listening.

"Yell if you can . . .

. . . where are you?

. . . Alice!"

Tears sprang to her eyes. The girls! She darted into the thick wood, and the voices rang out louder.

"Alice! Alice, can you hear me? Alice! Alice, where are you? Yell if you can hear us!"

She spun in a circle, trying to pinpoint where the voices were coming from, but it was impossible. The mirror-covered trees stretched on forever, in every direction. She walked backward and tripped over the thick frame of a mirror lying in the grass. As she fought to regain her balance, she stumbled into a floating mirror, banging her elbow on the glass. She kicked and cursed at it, sending it flying across the path. It settled in the air a few feet away, glistening just as prettily and innocently as it did before.

She took a second to compose herself. Spinning in circles and yelling at the mirrors wasn't going to help her find the girls. She turned back toward the clearing, but it was already gone. The forest of glass had swallowed it up.

". . . are you? Yell if you . . . Alice!"

The voices were fading. She could almost see the sound traveling through the mirrors, making them wobble as it passed, like a breeze blowing through the trees. But it was getting weaker, which meant it was simply passing through. For all Alice knew, she was miles from the girls' location.

She looked down and fingered the locket. "Help me find them," she asked the Portal. "Help me find the girls."

When nothing happened, she tried a different approach. "Show me the girls."

A mirror to her right suddenly broke from the branch and floated toward her. It was round, and roughly two feet in diameter. It stopped in front of her and hovered. She clutched the locket tighter and repeated her request.

"Show me the girls?"

A picture suddenly emerged on the mirror's surface, warped at first, like the reflection in a funhouse mirror. She watched with bated breath as the image came into focus. It was Hadley, then Soxie, then Olivia, leaping past. Then the image switched, showing them leaping past a different mirror at a different angle. It switched ten more times in the span of a few seconds, as if motion-detector cameras were tracking and recording their progress in real time throughout the Realm. Alice looked up into the trees and let out a small laugh. The mirrors were the cameras, and they were sending their feeds directly to her!

But where were the girls running? And how did she get their attention?

"HADLEY!" she screamed.

A second later, she saw Hadley stop and put her hand up. Alice couldn't hear what she was saying, but it was clear she'd heard something.

"I'M HERE!" Alice screamed again.

She watched as Hadley's eyes went wide, and she turned toward the mirror. Alice waved her hands wildly. "I'M RIGHT HERE!"

Hadley's face got closer to the glass. She peered into it, but her eyes weren't focusing. She was listening more than looking. Soxie and Olivia peeked over her shoulder, curious. Hadley mouthed something that looked an awful lot like, *"Alice, is that you?"*

"YES! YES! PLEASE, I'M HERE!"

Soxie said something and pointed away from the mirror. Hadley responded. Alice shook her head, trying desperately to read their lips. It looked like they were arguing about what to do. Then Hadley stood and took a step away. Alice panicked and slammed her hand into the glass.

It went straight through.

Something tugged on Hadley's jeans, making her slip and nearly fall off the branch. She yelped and looked down. A hand was poking through the mirror, and it had a death grip on her pant leg.

"Alice!" She quickly grabbed hold of the hand and pulled. Alice popped through the glass, using the frame to climb through. She fell on top of Hadley in a mess of laughing, sputtering tears.

"Hadz!" she cried, hugging her tight. Hadley laughed and grabbed hold of a nearby mirror to keep them from falling out of the tree.

Soxie and Olivia shouted with glee as the four of them piled on top of each other, hugging and laughing. Hadley couldn't stop them from rolling off the branch. But instead of falling, they floated gently down to a cluster of branches below.

After the euphoria of their reunion passed, Hadley reached out her hand to call her compass back. It had been leading them through the Realm to find Alice until, as luck would have it, Alice found them. With no other occupation, the little spinner of silver light bounced around them, joining in on the celebration. But she'd neglected it too long and was forced to coax it back like one would a shy dog, using endearments and high-pitched tones. When it finally gave in, it hovered over her palm until she was able to pluck it from the air, snap it shut, and stuff it in her pocket.

After dusting herself off, Alice walked them through everything she'd been through since she'd disappeared in the ballet studio.

Hadley leaned in to get a closer look at the locket. It didn't look like much, and it certainly wasn't *her* style. But it suited Alice. In fact, if she hadn't pointed it out, Hadley would have sworn she'd always been wearing it.

"And Persephone really thinks it's better off with you?" asked Soxie, before adding, "No offense. It's just—you know what it is, right?"

Alice barked out a nervous laugh as she absently pulled the locket back and forth on its chain. "Yes. She explained everything, but I knew before touching it that I could never open it."

"But why now?" asked Olivia. She was seated above them, boots swinging back and forth as she attempted to work something out. "We used the Portal to go to Bora Bora last year. Shouldn't it have recognized you? Why didn't it make you its protector then?"

"Because Philautia was its protector, and it was safe in her Realm," Alice replied, dropping her hand, and letting the locket rest against her chest. "But after the Realm disappeared, it was stuck in the place between. Everything was off-balance. If we didn't bring the Realm back, the Portal could have been lost forever."

"But, would that be the worst thing?" Soxie asked. Alice slapped her hand over the locket, offended. Soxie rolled her eyes and added, "I just mean, if it was lost forever, then it wouldn't need protection. If no one can find it, no one can open it, right? Problem solved."

"Yes, but you're making the assumption that the Portal doesn't care about being lost," Olivia jumped in. "That it's purely selfless and would sacrifice its existence for the greater good. I'm not sure that's the case. If anything, it's the opposite."

Alice looked down at the locket, face paling.

Really, Olivia? Hadley said through her mind. *She's wearing that thing around her neck.*

Olivia dipped her head. "Sorry. I didn't mean for that to come out the way it did. I just think we should be . . . careful about how we label the Portal. We can't assume it's all-loving and benevolent. It has the power to reset *everything*, to just scrap it all and start again. What kind of benevolent being would do that? Which begs the question: Has it been done before? And if so, how many times? Hundreds? Thousands? *Millions?*"

"Jesus, Olivia," said Soxie. Her face turned paler than Alice's, and Hadley was certain there was no color left in her own.

"Are you saying we've already *been* reset?" she barely managed. "Multiple times?"

Unlike the rest of them, Olivia didn't seem upset by her own revelation. "You guys, I'm not saying this to scare you. I have no idea if we've been reset—that's the point. We *wouldn't* know. But the Portal would. And maybe it likes to keep tabs on what's going on, in case it doesn't like what it sees."

Alice had both hands on the locket now, as if to keep it from popping open. "Do you think it could choose to reset on its own?"

Olivia shrugged. "I don't see why not. Maybe that's the real job of the protector. To keep things in balance so the Portal doesn't feel the *need* to reset."

Hadley knew Alice well enough to know she was about to lose it. She had reached up and was trying to unclasp the locket from her neck.

"I don't—I can't . . . dammit," she said, tugging harder. "Please. Somebody get this thing off me!"

Hadley fired a look at Olivia that said, *We need to work on your delivery skills.* Then she hopped over to where Alice was still struggling with the chain.

"It won't come off!" she insisted, yanking so hard that welts were forming on the back of her neck.

Hadley grabbed her forearms firmly, steadying her. "Honey, stop." Alice froze, locks of white hair falling across her face. Hadley continued. "You're panicking because you think you're in this alone. But it's *we*, remember? And if what Olivia's saying is true, we did what we had to do. We *had* to retrieve the Portal. There was no other option."

"There wasn't?" she rasped.

Hadley glanced at Olivia, then said, "No. Because if we didn't succeed, it might have restarted everything—simply because we failed."

"See, that's all I was trying to say," Olivia concluded.

Hadley laughed inwardly, then placed her hand over the locket, on Alice's heart. "It may not be all-loving and benevolent, but it's giving us a chance, so it must believe this version of us is worth holding on to."

Alice took a deep breath and nodded. Her lips were trembling, but she was pulling it together. "You're right. So it's up to us to prove we're worth it, which means the gods—" She stopped, and her eyes grew wide. "Oh shit. The gods! We have to get out of here, now!"

Hadley pulled back. "Wait, what about the gods?"

Alice was frantically scanning the trees around them. "They can get in the Realm now!"

Worried looks shot between them. Soxie immediately stepped forward and flipped open her compass. "Find ballet studio mirror."

The compact rose in the air and started spinning, faster and faster, until it was a silver ball of whirling light. It shot forward through the trees, then stopped a few branches away, hovering.

"Let's go!" Soxie shouted, then charged after it, the rest of them hot on her heels.

They flew through the trees at breakneck speed, leaping, flipping, and at times, almost flying. Soxie's compass led them through random clearings they'd missed before. One was filled with mirrors that appeared to be floating in some kind of Stonehenge formation. Another was just a bunch of mirrors lying on the ground next to each other, projecting a moss- and pebble-filled stream. Persephone had really outdone herself with this world. It was too bad they didn't have more time to explore it. But if the gods were here, they were already out of time.

The compass took a sharp turn, heading directly down the trunk of a tree. One by one, they turned onto the massive trunk, sprinting after it. Hadley brought up the rear behind Alice, watching as her friend leaped onto the tree and ran directly down it. But as soon as Hadley followed suit, the world rotated, and instead of running down a tree, she was running across it—like a giant log felled over a river. The gravity switch was nothing new, but dodging floating mirrors and branches was. It made their progress slower than it would have been in the old Realm.

When the compass reached the forest floor, their speed improved. It started zipping them along paths between the trees, some narrow and full of shadow; others wide and spacious, with beams of sunlight shining through. Getting out of the trees made for faster progress, but it also made them easier to spot.

Hadley kept eyeing the trees above, waiting for an ambush. It was difficult keeping Alice in her line of sight. Plus, she was getting tired. She suspected they all were.

Up ahead, the compass made a left turn. Hadley dug in and pumped her arms, hoping the ballet studio mirror was right around that corner. Then she spotted movement in her peripheral, a small flash of light. She turned her head, doing her best to scan the forest as it blurred past. The next thing she knew, she was flying backward, landing with a splat on the squishy forest floor.

She clutched her head in pain. *Ow.* That was going to leave a mark. She lay there for a few seconds, waiting for the spots in her vision to fade. Then with a groan, she pushed onto her elbows to get a look at what took her down. It was a large, rectangular mirror with beveled edges, most of it fogged up from steam—probably from someone's shower. She rubbed her forehead and glared at the mirror. Did it really have to be floating *in the middle* of the path?

With a throbbing head, she climbed to her feet just in time to see Alice disappear around the bend. She was about to yell after her, but a sudden wave of nausea overcame her, and she doubled over, falling to her knees. She dry heaved, then flipped onto her back, giving herself a moment. It was probably only a mild concussion, and she'd be fine in a minute or two. She closed her eyes and took a few slow, deep breaths.

The girls would notice she was gone any second. And even if they didn't, it was okay. She had her own compass. She could get back on her own, once her body allowed it.

She kept her eyes closed, focusing on the sounds of the forest. It was amazingly close to what a real forest sounded like, though more metallic than organic. She focused on the tinkling sound, imagining she was lying on the grass on the Roxland estate, with Schlemmer sunning her sleek black body beside her.

"Hadley! Hadley, where are you?
      Hadley! Hadley, where are you?"
Olivia's voice echoed through her pounding head.

I'm here, she could only yell through her mind. *Sorry, I ran into a mirror like an idiot. I just need a minute.*

She had no idea if Olivia was close enough to read her. The echo of her voice was already fading. In the real world, the girls could backtrack and find her. But this was the Realm, and it wasn't always that easy.

Don't try to find me. Just get Alice and the Portal out of the Realm. I'll be back soon.

Again, there was no reason to believe Olivia heard her, but it was worth sending the message. After a few minutes, she started to feel less queasy. She opened her eyes and gazed up at the trees surrounding her. Like Jack's famous beanstalk, they climbed all the way to the sky. Rays of sunlight crisscrossed between them, with no rhyme or reason to their pattern. There could be seven suns shining. It wasn't accurate, but it was still a nice touch. Dark and gray would have been far less spring-timey.

She brought her hand to her forehead. There was no blood, but a small lump had already formed over her left eye. Maybe next time she'd suggest they wear helmets. This Realm, like its creator, was equal parts beauty and chaos.

Feeling a little better, she pushed herself up, wincing only slightly at her throbbing head. She blinked a few times, refocusing her eyes. The guilty mirror still floated in front of her. She rolled away from it and slowly brought herself to her feet, clutching her head and swaying as another wave of nausea came and went.

"Get it together, Hadley," she said to herself. Then she pursed her lips and inhaled like she was breathing through a straw. It helped. Steadier on her feet, she dug in her pocket and extracted her compass. She smacked her dry lips a few times, then flipped it open.

"Find ballet—"

The compass flew from her grasp, as if an invisible hand had suddenly snatched it away. She stumbled back, dizzy and disoriented, landing on the surface of a mirror with a hard, painful thwack.

Ugh, this place is not childproof, she couldn't help but think as she rubbed her behind. Her brain felt muddy and thick. What happened to her compass? She looked up, searching the surrounding forest.

She spotted it stuck to the trunk of a nearby tree, an arrow sticking straight through it. Her adrenaline spiked, trumping the ache in her head. She dashed to her feet and whirled around. Artemis was standing at the edge of the path, another arrow armed in her bow. The tip of it shone like a diamond, catching the light with an almost blinding flash, confirming Hadley wasn't imagining things earlier. There *had* been something in the forest, and that something now had her diamond-tipped arrow pointed directly at Hadley's head.

"Hello, huntress," Artemis smiled, her eyes shiny with the exhilaration of the hunt.

Hadley lifted her hands in surrender as fear coursed through her veins, threatening to paralyze her.

"Hello, Artemis," she said, struggling to keep her voice steady. "How are you? It's been a while."

The goddess stepped forward, her bow and arrow poised and ready. She wore what Hadley assumed was traditional Greek-goddess-of-the-hunt garb. Sandals that laced to her knees. A drapey white dress gathered by thin pieces of gold rope. Garlands of gold leaves woven through her long dark hair. Her violet eyes didn't leave Hadley's as she silently closed the space between them.

"I am well, thank you," she answered, coming to a stop with the arrow's point mere inches from Hadley's face.

"If you're here for the Portal, I don't have it."

Artemis's mouth twitched. "I see. And do you know where it is?"

Hadley dropped her arms. Her head still ached, and her mouth was dry. If Artemis wanted to kill her, she'd already be dead. "It doesn't matter where it is. We're never going to give it to you."

"'Never' is a bold choice of word," she cautioned. "I would be careful how you use it."

"Okay, then," she laughed, "how about this? You can have the Portal when you pry it from my cold dead hands."

Violet eyes regarded her curiously. "Are you not afraid to die, mortal?"

Hadley groaned as another wave of nausea passed through her. Then she stepped forward, letting the tip of Artemis's arrow touch her clammy forehead.

"Of course I'm afraid to die," she retorted. "That's part of being a mortal. But I'm also a huntress, and it's my job to protect other mortals." She paused as bile rose in her throat. "So kill me if you want. Just please hurry because I think I'm about to throw up."

Artemis's eyes narrowed, and she dropped the bow to her side, tucking the arrow back in her quiver. Just in time, too. As soon as the bow dropped, Hadley leaned over, braced her hands on her knees, and vomited.

"I knew you would not relent," Artemis stated with a satisfied sigh. "You are too strong. Too much like me."

Hadley coughed and retched, dumping the contents of her stomach onto Persephone's carefully designed grass. At one point, Artemis gathered her hair and held it from her face. It was a very sisterly, human-like thing to do. Hadley managed a warbled "thank you" between heaves. It seemed appropriate.

When there was nothing left in her stomach, she spit and wiped her mouth with the back of her hand. Artemis released her hair and stepped back.

"Are you finished, or do you have more fluids to expel?"

"No," she groaned, spitting again. "I'm finished."

"Very well."

Hadley managed to stand, feeling better, but not much. She watched Artemis make her way to the tree where her compass was still pinned. She pulled the arrow out, letting the compass drop into her hand. She then turned around and tossed it in Hadley's direction. She caught it easily, frowning at the hole in its center.

"You killed my compass."

"I could have killed you."

Hadley stuffed the ruined compact in her pocket. "Fair point. So what now?"

Artemis tilted her head back and looked into the trees. "There is no game to hunt in this forest. I preferred the forest in your dreams."

Hadley thought of the last time she'd hosted Artemis in her dreams, when she'd been chasing down white stags and Hermes turned their world upside down. Was it really only a couple of weeks ago? It felt like centuries. She didn't want the gods in her dreams anymore, certainly not if they were going to torture them. But if it kept them happy—and more importantly, away from the Portal—maybe it was the only solution.

"Fine. You can hunt in my dreams, but can we limit it to two times a week? Three, tops."

Laughter spilled from Artemis's mouth. "Huntress, your dreams no longer interest the gods."

"They don't?"

"Your world is far more interesting."

Hadley did *not* like the sound of that. "My world," she repeated. "What do you mean by that?"

Artemis turned to look at the bathroom mirror responsible for Hadley's concussion. It was no longer fogged up by shower steam. She touched the glass with the tip of her finger and peered into it. "He looks promising, though his physique is not to my liking. And I would prefer a female, but I suppose he will do for now."

Hadley rushed to her side to see what she was seeing. Right before Artemis's finger left the glass, Hadley saw a middle-aged man with a towel around his waist, shaving. She slammed her hand on the glass, but the image had already disappeared. Artemis laughed behind her.

"You are a huntress, but so am I." She paused, giving Hadley an unnerving smile. "So from one huntress to another, I wish you luck with *your* hunt."

Hadley didn't have time to process Artemis's words. One second she was there, the next, she'd reached through the mirror and vanished—arrows, quiver, and all.

The forest grew quiet, as if the Realm knew something was wrong. Hadley stared into the mirror that refused to reflect her image. She imagined Artemis on the other side, grinning. Only now she was a middle-aged man with a towel around his waist. This was a disaster, on a global, possibly world-ending scale.

She dug in her pocket for her compass and flipped it open. Despite being damaged, it still had glass and blood inside. She pointed it at the mirror. It hovered for a second, then fell back in her palm, as if it was just too exhausted. Dammit. The bitch really broke it.

"Artemis!" she screamed at the mirror.

A hand suddenly reached through the glass, making her jump. A second later, Alice's head followed. Hadley brought her own hand to her pounding heart.

"Oh, honey, thank god it's you. You scared me half to death! You don't know—"

"C'mon, we have to hurry!" Alice said, cutting her off. Instead of climbing through, she was bracing herself on the frame of the mirror, like she was holding herself up through a trap door.

"Hadz, please," she said, beckoning her. "The door keeps moving. We have to go now!"

Hadley didn't know what she meant, but now wasn't the time to ask. So she took hold of Alice's hand and climbed through.

chapter 29

Alice pulled Hadley through the mirror, thankful to the Portal for helping them find her.

"Got her!" she called. Olivia was standing in front of the ballet studio mirror, her and Soxie's compasses on their last legs trying to keep it in place. The mirror was currently hovering at the edge of a clearing, but they expected it to move any second. It had already disappeared twice since they lost Hadley.

"Hurry, go!" yelled Olivia, waving them through.

Alice dragged Hadley through. They fell on the floor of the studio just as Soxie and Olivia dove through after them. The mirror disappeared with a snap that sounded like a static charge. One of the lights in the chandelier above them popped, sending shards of glass flying. They all covered their heads.

"Jesus!" Soxie yelled, curling in on herself as another overloaded bulb popped.

The lights flickered for a few seconds, then resumed their normal steady illumination, sans two bulbs. Alice carefully avoided the glass as she pushed herself to her feet. The rest of them did the same, though Hadley looked a little worse for wear.

"Hadz, how are you feeling?" she asked, eyeing her forehead. "Olivia said you ran into a mirror. I'm so sorry—you were right behind me. I should have noticed."

Hadley smiled and tenderly patted the bump on her forehead. "It's okay. It was a dumb accident. Thank you for coming back for me."

"Like we'd leave you behind," said Soxie. "But why didn't you use your own compass?"

Hadley shook her head, then dug into her pocket and pulled out her compass. There was a big hole right in the center of it. They all gaped.

"Because Artemis shot it with one of her arrows. Then she dove through a mirror and infected an innocent man through his reflection. Pretty sure she's walking around in his skin right now. So yeah. I was a little busy. Also, will you excuse me, please? I have to throw up again."

Speechless, they watched her run out of the room.

After Hadley dry heaved over the toilet, Soxie insisted she lie down and wait for Mayron's physician. She did, at least, let her brush her teeth first.

As expected, the doctor deemed it a mild concussion and prescribed her Advil, fluids, and rest—but not before bandaging her hand and confirming she'd had a tetanus shot in the past ten years. She'd completely forgotten about the cut on her hand, but Mayron's doc was nothing if not thorough.

The girls sat at her bedside with bandaged hands of their own as she recounted what happened in the Realm. They managed to let her tell most of it without asking too many questions. Even Olivia stayed silent, despite being able to see everything in Hadley's mind. When she was done, Alice and Olivia left to find David, but Soxie pulled up a chair and propped her heeled feet on the mattress, getting comfortable.

Hadley tried shooing her away, but her eyes were already drooping.

"I'm not going anywhere, Caldwell," she said, head already buried in a book. "Deal with it."

Hadley managed a weak smile. "Thanks, Sox." And then her eyes closed, and she was out.

When she opened her eyes, the chair beside her was empty. Frost covered the windows, yet the air inside was warm and fragrant. A tall dark figure stood at the end of the bed, firelight glinting off his shiny black wings. Hadley sat up, the scent of burning leaves and rotting fruit tickling her nose.

"Morpheus," she greeted him, albeit grudgingly.

His wings fluttered ever so slightly. "Huntress."

She wanted to cry from sheer exhaustion. It was like playing whack-a-mole. One god goes away, another pops back up. "What do you want?" she nearly exploded.

"You know what we want."

The urge to throw her pillow at him was strong. Instead, she hugged it tightly to her chest. "It's over, Morpheus. We can't let you start over just because you don't like the way things turned out. We won't give you the Portal."

He stepped out of the shadows, eyes burning red. "But you do have it."

Her back went straight. She could lie, but he'd probably know. "Yes," she admitted. "We have it."

The redness of his eyes dulled, and his shoulders relaxed. "And you will keep it safe?"

"Of course," she replied uneasily. "But why do you care?"

His wings snapped shut behind him. Then he moved with purpose toward the window. The frost evaporated, revealing a sky with enough stars to rival the Milky Way. "The gods may no longer need the Portal, but our existence still depends on it."

Hadley threw her pillow aside and jumped off the bed, unable to mask her excitement. "You don't want the Portal anymore?"

"We no longer *need* the Portal, but we will never stop wanting it. It would be safer in our hands, but for now, yours will suffice."

She frowned at his back. "Thanks. But you're not getting it, now or later." Then she moved to stand beside him, unable to tear her gaze from the magnificent starlit sky. "I'm curious, though. Why do you no longer *need* it?"

"Because you have given us this," he said, sweeping his hand across the window. The stars disappeared, and images of the world began rushing past. A traffic jam. A city full of skyscrapers. A crowded theater. Children on a playground. A moving sidewalk with travelers gliding back and forth. He was showing her a world teeming with people, full of promise. She hugged herself and stepped closer to the window.

"We didn't give this to you," she whispered, hoping against hope she was right.

He chuckled under his breath as the scenes vanished into the starlit sky. "The Realm, huntress. By bringing it back, you have reconnected our worlds. You have given us back our purpose."

Her head snapped toward him, and she grabbed the windowsill for support. "Are you telling me this was your plan all along, to send us after the Portal so we could bring back the Realm?"

"Huntress, we are gods. We have infinite plans, and each of them ends with you. *Humanity* is our salvation."

Hadley felt like a greyhound at the dog track, chasing a stuffed rabbit she would never catch. "No. I don't believe you. Persephone wouldn't do that to us."

"Ah, yes. My insufferable mother," said a voice from across the room. Hadley whirled around. Melinoë stood in front of the fireplace, her lithe appearance cycling between black and white. "Persephone's memory served us well, did it not, Morpheus?"

Morpheus nodded, though Hadley noticed he looked annoyed.

His wings had popped out again and were vibrating like the tail of an agitated cat. With an impatient sigh, he turned back to Hadley.

"Persephone's memory did not betray you. It behaved as it was destined, as did you. This world was always meant to be ours."

The earth might as well have stopped turning on its axis. Nothing was as it seemed. Olivia was right. The gods would never do anything but use them. Hadley dropped her head in her hands. "Oh my god," she whispered. "What have we done?"

"Do not fret, huntress," Melinoë cooed, her slithery voice almost maternal. "If it helps your weak, mortal heart, I bring nightmares to those who deserve them. You will find there is more to us than simply light or darkness. We are both."

Hadley dropped her hands and looked up. "Is that true?" she asked Morpheus. She still trusted him more than she did Melinoë.

He nodded solemnly. "I simply embody what mortals need and desire," he added. "Dreams are my domain, and they have been left unattended for far too long."

They were watching her like she was a child who just learned Santa isn't real. But their pity only pissed her off.

"Why are you here?" she yelled. "To gloat? Well, congratulations. You win. Now get out. Get out of my dream!"

Melinoë glanced at Morpheus, then floated to his side. Her corpse-like eye somehow sparkled in the dim light. "You misunderstand, huntress. We are not here to torment you. We are here to thank you. You have given us a gift, and we wish to give you one in return."

"I don't want anything from you," she snarled.

Morpheus stepped forward and gently took her arm, turning her toward the window. "You will want this, Hadley."

She was about to rip his wing off when the starry night sky disappeared, replaced by something new. Her eyes lit with recognition.

The window no longer looked outside, but in. It was the kitchen of her dad's house, the one where she spent her childhood burning grilled cheese sandwiches and sneaking extra cans of Dr Pepper. The yellowed linoleum, the lime-green laminate counters, the fluorescent overhead light—no detail was spared. But her dad had renovated it years ago. Why was Morpheus showing her this now?

Before she could ask, a figure walked into the room, a large duffel bag slung over his shoulder. She pulled back, surprised. It was Caleb, six years ago, on the night he left. She turned to Morpheus.

"What is this?"

"*Shhh*," he said, putting a finger to his lips. "Watch and see."

Hadley frowned but turned back to the window. Caleb had just pulled an envelope from his pocket. He stared at it for a second before gently propping it against the toaster. Then he turned around and left through the door to the garage. Hadley leaned forward. In big, bold Sharpie, the envelope read, "HADDY BEAR."

She stared at it, confused. This wasn't right. He never left her a note. What were Morpheus and Melinoë playing at? She was about to turn on them and rage when her dad walked into the room. His face was red with anger. He stood in front of the door, staring at it. Then he ran his hands down his face and shuffled to the fridge. He pulled out a bottle of beer, and as he slapped the refrigerator door shut, he noticed the envelope.

Hadley watched him pick it up, glance in the direction of her bedroom, and tear it open. His eyes moved back and forth as he read her brother's words—words meant for her. When he was finished, he dropped his head, gripping the paper in his hands. Then without warning, he crumpled it up and stuffed both it and the envelope deep inside the trash, the same trash her thirteen-year-old self would put in the dumpster the very next day.

The scene got blurry as her eyes filled with tears. "What did it say?"

One of Morpheus's wings settled lightly around her, like a warm feather cape.

"That is not for us to reveal. Our gift to you is the knowledge that it existed. It is up to you to decide what you do with such knowledge."

Hadley swallowed the apple-sized lump in her throat. "How did you get this?" she asked, pointing at the window. But as she did, her childhood kitchen vanished, replaced by the bright night sky.

Morpheus smiled. "Do not ask questions you know the answers to, huntress. It is unbecoming."

She cringed, but he was right. It was a stupid question. Morpheus was the god of dreams, the equivalent of the Sandman. And now, thanks to her, both he and Melinoë were loose on their world.

"We must go now," he said, tucking his wing back to his side. "But should you ever need me, you will find me in your dreams."

"And should you ever need me," added Melinoë with her shark-teeth smile, "I will find you in your nightmares."

Hadley shivered. *No thanks.* The goddess flashed her another toothy smile and vanished in a crack of white light. When she was gone, Hadley rounded on Morpheus, surprised by how betrayed she felt.

"I thought you were different. I thought maybe you cared what happened to us."

He closed his eyes briefly and sighed. "I care what happens to dreams. Without mortals, there are no dreams."

Hadley dropped her head and shuffled back to the bed. She sat down and stared at the floor. "This world doesn't need you anymore. It's not *meant* for you. I don't want to be your enemy, Morpheus. But you're not leaving us much choice."

"You always have a choice."

She looked up. His wings were stretched to their fullest, nearly spanning the length of the room. He waved a hand over the window, and it flew open. Then he turned to her and smiled. "Good luck, huntress."

A second later, his body split into a swarm of black crows that shot into the night and out of her dream.

chapter 30

They searched the entire house, but David was nowhere to be found.

"Do you think he went home?" Alice asked Olivia.

"Not a chance," she answered, shaking her head. "He's around here somewhere. Why don't you check the stables, and I'll check the garage?"

Alice nodded, ignoring the pit that was forming in her stomach. What if he'd left for good? And if so, could she blame him?

"Text me if you find him," she said, then headed to the barn.

It was dusk, a beautiful time of day on the Roxland estate. The light had a hazy yellow, dreamlike quality, and cicadas filled the air with their desert song. Nearby, red mountains faded into the darkening sky, soon to be swallowed by the upcoming night.

She followed the stone path toward the stables, letting the rhythmic sound of the cicadas calm her racing heart. The locket bounced against her chest with each step, reminding her of the monumental responsibility that lay ahead. She loved David with everything she was, but this was bigger than the two of them. She couldn't afford to make choices based on her own happiness anymore. The fate of literally *everything* now rested on her shoulders. Or in this case, around her neck.

She approached the entrance to the barn, more nervous than she expected. Would he be angry? Upset? Or worse, apathetic? But when she rounded the corner, she found the wide hallway between the stalls dark and empty. She flipped a switch by the door, bathing the barn in soft white light from the rafter chandeliers. Max's head immediately poked out of his stall, ears twitching. Aggie's head popped out from the stall opposite, followed by Oscar's. Well, the horses were here at least.

Alice gravitated to Max's stall, earning her snorts and agitated hoof stomps from the other equines. But she and Max went way back. David—Colin at the time—taught her how to ride on Max. Their trip to the desert together had been short, but it was one of the happiest times in her life. It was why she and David planned to move to Sedona. The desert had become a symbol of their love—beautiful and unyielding, despite the ravages of time.

But how could she move to Sedona now? Or even get married? In the span of a moment, her life's trajectory had been drastically altered, and the path ahead was now full of uncertainty. Her priorities would have to change.

Max shook his head and neighed as she approached. She smiled and patted his neck heartily, then leaned her forehead against his velvety soft muzzle.

"Hi, boy," she whispered. "You haven't seen David, have you?"

He snorted in response, and she gave him a half smile.

"I know. I've missed him too."

Her phone vibrated in her pocket. She stepped away from the stall to read the incoming text.

Olivia: *Found him. We're in the garage.*

Alice stared at the screen, unsure how to respond. She could run and be there in as little as two minutes, but maybe it was better if she let Olivia relay everything that happened. She wasn't sure she had the energy to walk him through it right now. With shaky hands, she texted back her response.

Alice: *Thx. I'm in the barn. Just need a second—will be up shortly.*

Olivia responded with a thumbs-up emoji, and Alice stuffed her phone back in her pocket. When she looked up, Max was staring at her with gentle but judging eyes.

"What, you disapprove?" she asked him.

He blinked but said nothing—because he was a horse that couldn't talk. But it didn't mean he couldn't listen. She sidled up to him and wrapped her arms around his neck, letting her head rest against his cheek.

"I wish you could tell me what to do, Max," she said, her throat nearly closing up as the words came out. "How can I ask him to wait? He's waited sixteen hundred years for me. What if he doesn't want to wait any longer?"

Max inhaled and sighed a big horse's sigh. It made her feel like he understood what she was saying and was maybe even annoyed by it.

"I know it's silly," she went on. "I know there's no reason we *can't* get married. But it feels selfish and wrong somehow. The girls need me, and I need them. I can't just ride off into the sunset and live my happily-ever-after now. There's too much work to do."

Other than some chomping of oats in another stall, the barn remained silent, and Max remained still. She let out a sad laugh and wiped a tear from her cheek.

"You're right. I know there's no such thing as happily-ever-after. But it sounds nice, doesn't it?"

Max shifted his weight from one hoof to the other, and she decided it meant he agreed. She closed her eyes and pressed her cheek into his neck, comforted by his sheer mass. He could flatten her like an empty cereal box, but he chose to stand still and listen because she needed him to.

"He's my soulmate, Max. We're *supposed* to be together. I know that. But sometimes I wonder if we did something wrong. Did we take our love for granted?"

"We're soulmates, not angels. No one said we'd get it right the first time around."

Her eyes popped open, and she spun around, releasing her hold on Max's neck. He whinnied and ducked back into his stall.

David stood at the entrance to the barn, his breath short and ragged, probably from running all the way from the garage. Their eyes locked, and he flashed her one of his brilliant, megawatt smiles. Her heart nearly burst, and the butterflies in her stomach started flapping like mad, the way they always did when he was near. Before she knew it, she ran down the hall and leaped into his arms. He held her for what felt like ages, burying his head in her neck. Her hair. Pulling her as close as a person could get. When their lips met, she felt the weight of all her worries flutter away, like leaves in an autumn breeze. She closed her eyes and let them.

Eventually, he pulled away and cupped her face in his hands. "Are you okay?"

"I am now," she breathed.

He smiled and ran his thumb across her cheek, tucking a stray hair behind her ear. Then his gaze dropped to the locket around her neck.

"So this is it," he said, lifting the locket from her chest and studying it. "The universe, in the palm of my hand."

She shrugged uneasily. "Something like that."

He stared at it for a few more seconds before placing it gently back against her heart. "I guess Persephone came through. I'm sorry I doubted her."

"And I'm sorry I didn't tell you about her before," she said, looking down. "If it helps, I didn't tell the girls either. It's just . . . it's been a strange couple of weeks. I know I've been distant, and I know it wasn't fair to—"

He pressed his mouth to hers, silencing her with another kiss. His lips were demanding, and his fingers dug into her waist, igniting a fire deep within her. She snaked her arms around his neck and balanced on her toes, getting closer, raking her fingers through his hair, and breathing him in—saying all the things he wouldn't let her say.

He suddenly broke away and pressed his forehead into hers. His breath was heavy, but his voice was even. "I'm sorry too."

"For what?"

"For all the same things you are."

She pulled back and laughed. "I think our communication needs some work."

"We have the rest of our lives."

She gave her ring a nervous glance. "Even if we don't get married?"

His expression darkened, and he drew her hand to his heart. "You're my future, Alice. You're my everything. Do I want to get married, raise a family, and grow old together? Do I want a house, white picket fence, dog-in-the-backyard life with you? Hell yes. I want that more than anything. But I don't *need* any of it. All I need is you."

Her eyebrow lifted. "You didn't mention a cat."

"Sorry," he chuckled. "Figured you and Boop were a package deal."

She smiled and stepped into his arms. "I want all of that too," she whispered. "I just—"

"I know," he cut in. "You need to save the world from the gods first. Boy, if I had a dime for every time I've heard that one."

She buried her face in his chest and laughed. It wasn't really funny—the gods were never a laughing matter. But if they didn't find a reason to laugh about it, the weight of it all would crush them.

When her laughter died down, she took a second to consider her next words. "I know it doesn't make sense," she finally began, "but I like the idea of taking things a little slower. Despite the gods."

He leaned back and lifted her chin, forcing her to meet his gaze. "Me too."

Her heart skipped a beat. She wasn't sure if it was a happy skip or a frightened skip. "Really?"

A soulful look crossed his face. "This is my last life, Alice. Up until now, they've been expendable. I know our souls will be connected forever. But if this is our only life together, I want to do it right. Rushing into marriage now, with everything going on . . ." He paused and glanced at thc locket. "It doesn't feel right."

She nodded and leaned into him. "You weren't the reason I lost my powers," she said softly. "It was my decision to stop using them."

"I know," he replied. "But I supported and encouraged that decision, even though I knew better. I started to believe the past could be changed, but I was wrong."

Her head flew up as she stepped back. "What do you mean?"

He seemed to take a moment to gather his thoughts before he cast his eyes down and said, "I lied when I told you the first time I saw you was in a dream. It was in Egypt, with Hadley."

"What?" she exclaimed, her voice slightly barbed. "You saw me?"

He nodded. "I was hiding behind a palm tree when Hadley pulled you from the water. I didn't understand what I was seeing. I thought you must be dead, but then your eyes opened, and I saw *you*," he paused as his voice faltered, "and I swear it was like witnessing the birth of a star—from nothing to everything in the span of an instant. You were this explosion of light that I couldn't begin to comprehend, and it scared me. I didn't know whether to run to you, or away from you. So I did nothing and watched you disappear into the desert like you were never there. You became a dream I clung to in every life afterward, because admitting you could be real—and that I'd never see you again—it hurt too much."

Her heart broke a little for him. "Why didn't you tell me?"

"I couldn't risk you knowing something that hadn't happened to you yet," he explained. "I was worried I'd overstepped when I told Hadley about the Great Pyramid, but I rolled the dice that I was *supposed* to tell her. Turns out, I was. But it's dangerous to mess with time."

Alice couldn't help but glance down at the locket around her neck. "How dangerous is it to wear it?"

He cracked a faint smile. "I don't care what you do with it, as long as you don't waste it. I don't want to be the reason you waste *your* time, Alice."

Her eyes stung as she stepped back into his arms. "Life without you would be the waste, Cithaeron. We don't have to have it all figured out right now. All that matters is that we figure it out together. No more secrets."

His arms wrapped tightly around her, pulling her close. "No more secrets," he whispered.

She let him hold her for a few moments, relishing the safety and warmth of his embrace. Then with a light snort she said, "Hadley thinks we suffer from love at first sight."

"Damn straight we do."

She giggled and tightened her grip around his waist. "So what do we do now?"

He caressed the back of her neck and sighed. "We keep the Portal safe, and you go back to doing what you do best. If the gods are here, there's work to do. You're a huntress, Alice. You'll hunt."

"And you?"

Laughter rumbled through his chest. "Are you kidding? The Realm is back. I get to order you all around again, just like the good old days."

"The girls are gonna love that," she teased.

He kissed the top of her head and pulled her closer. "Well, as the saying goes, your locket works in mysterious ways."

She smiled and closed her eyes, cherishing the moment. "I love you, Cithaeron."

He pulled her face to his and answered her with a kiss so powerful, so full of love, that she doubted even the Portal could erase it from time.

chapter 31

Hadley gripped the steering wheel as she stared at the prison. The buildings were drab and colorless, nearly blending in with the desert landscape and mountains beyond. A chain link fence with barbwire surrounded the property, and imposing guard towers flanked the interior buildings. She'd never been to a state prison before—her dad served his time in a county jail—but it looked just like she'd imagined it. Isolated and sad.

"Are you sure you don't want us to come in with you?" asked Olivia. Hadley turned to the passenger seat of Mayron's Shelby. Or, as she was still having a hard time admitting, *her* Shelby—a gift from Mayron that she was still trying to process. Apparently, it was his way of apologizing without really apologizing. It was an apology Hadley was willing to accept. She just hoped Caleb was willing to accept hers.

She reached over and grabbed Olivia's hand.

"Yes, I'm sure. This is something I have to do on my own. But you already knew that."

Olivia harrumphed. "Sometimes I still need to hear you say it."

A smile tugged at the corner of Hadley's mouth. She glanced at the bobble-headed angel on the dash, giving it a light tap on the head, setting its wings aflutter as she said, "Then I might as well tell you my dad didn't deny that he destroyed Caleb's note. He said he did what he thought was best. I just wonder if my mom would have done the same."

Olivia squeezed her hand. "I'm sure he *did* do what he thought was right at the time. It must have been hard for him, raising you on his own. It's not fair to compare his decision to one your mom never had to make."

"I know," she relented. "And I don't blame him. But it explains why he's been trying to get me to come here. I think he feels responsible for my rift with Caleb."

"Is he?"

She took a breath, ready to finally face the truth. "No. I am. I'm the one that couldn't let my anger go." Then she turned to Alice and Soxie in the back seat. She made eye contact with Alice and said, "I'm ready to let it go."

Alice smiled, and Soxie leaned forward, her mound of red curls popping through the front seats. "We're proud of you, Caldwell. I know this isn't easy."

Hadley unbuckled her seatbelt and twisted around to face them all. "Thank you, guys, for being here. But I feel guilty. We should be chasing down gods, not visiting my brother in prison."

"Relax, we will," said Soxie. "But it's been three days and the world hasn't ended yet. Besides, if they're infecting humans the way demons did, we can't do anything until Persephone figures out how to warn us *before* they enter a reflection."

"She's right," agreed Olivia. "And we don't even know if they can take over a body yet. Maybe they can only observe and influence."

"Isn't that enough?" Hadley challenged them all. "What about Hades?"

Alice visibly stiffened at the sound of his name, her hand flying to the locket around her neck. But she didn't look scared. If anything, she looked determined. Maybe a little angry.

"If he shows up, I'll be ready for him."

Soxie leaned back, appraising her. "Damn, Ali. I like this side of you—there's a fire in your eyes. Hades better watch his back."

Alice's shoulders relaxed as she chuckled and released the locket. It fell back against her chest as if it were magnetized. "It's not that I don't still see him as a threat. But I'm not going to live my life in fear. Besides, he's not the only god that can do damage. Every one of them is a potential threat."

"True," Soxie shrugged. "Although they can't be any worse than some of the evil bastards already roaming this planet."

Alice gave her a look. "I'm sure they *could*, Sox. But Persephone is working on a way to help us track them. I spoke to her memory this morning."

"Good to know," said Soxie, "but please don't let my uncle overhear you talking to her again. He's starting to freak me out with all his questions."

"That bad?" Hadley empathized.

"Worse."

Olivia turned to face front, propping her chunky boots on the Shelby's dash. "Yeah, I've heard some crazy theories rattling around in his brain. We're probably going to have to tell him everything at some point. Alice's mom too."

"Um, can we put a pin in that for now?" begged Alice. "She's still reeling over the wedding being called off. I don't think she's ready for anything else."

"But what about all her comments about you being too young to get married?" asked Hadley. "I thought she'd be happy."

"Not when non-refundable catering deposits are on the line."

"Ouch."

Soxie placed a hand on Alice's shoulder. "Well, look at it this way, Daniels. When you and David *do* get married, you can always have Judy do the cooking."

They all looked at each other and laughed. Then they hooked hands like a team about to head into the final play.

"Well," said Hadley, glancing at the prison entrance. "I guess I'd better get going." She paused, taking a moment to look each of her friends—her sisters—in the eye. Their support was everything, and she felt blessed to have them in her life.

"I love you guys."

"Love you more," they sang back, faces flushed with love.

The visiting area wasn't what she was expecting. There weren't stations with glass partitions and telephones on either side. Instead, she found herself in a sterile cafeteria-style room with round tables and flimsy plastic chairs. Two vending machines stood at the back of the room, one that promised coffee but had a big "Out of Order" sign taped to it and another with various snacks, though half of the slots were empty. Fluorescent lights buzzed overhead, and the only natural light came from small windows set high in the wall. Armed guards stood at both ends of the room, watching every exchange with eagle eyes and permanent scowls. It was as hopeless and depressing as a room could be.

Hadley was directed to the only empty table near the vending machines. Her escort rattled off instructions in a drone-like fashion, even though Hadley had already been briefed before entering the room.

"You're allowed a short hug hello and goodbye, but holding hands and prolonged touching is restricted. Failure to comply will result in termination of your visit."

Hadley nodded and sat down as the guard walked away, yelling, "No touching!" to a couple attempting to do just that. They pulled apart and kept talking without missing a beat. Hadley had the feeling this wasn't their first rodeo. She, on the other hand, felt more nervous than she had in a long time. She crossed and uncrossed her legs, then folded her hands on the table before pulling them into her lap, all the while trying not to stare at the other inmates and their visitors. There was a woman with a toddler, speaking in low whispers to a man Hadley guessed was her husband or boyfriend. An elderly couple speaking to their son. Cousins and sisters. Friends and brothers. There were a myriad of visitors from every walk of life, doing their best to bring a slice of happiness to the incarcerated.

She heard a buzz and looked up. A light next to a door up front turned green, and the guard standing next to it pulled it open. Her heart hammered in her chest as Caleb walked through.

He was thinner than she remembered, and his floppy hair had been shorn into a buzz cut. It made him look edgy and mean, like a typical hardened criminal. The standard-issue tan uniform and white sneakers, coupled with the angry way he carried himself, completed the look. The guard pointed in her direction, and Hadley felt her stomach clench as Caleb's eyes found hers.

His mouth turned into a thin line, and he made his way across the room, throwing a nod at another inmate on the way. Hadley took an uneven breath and stood. When he got to her table, he didn't walk around to give her a hug like he was allowed. Instead, he pulled the plastic chair back. It made a loud screeching noise as it scraped across the concrete floor. Then he sat down and leaned back, keeping his eyes glued to hers the entire time. Feeling like a fool just standing there, she quickly took her seat.

"Nice to see you, sis," he said. "What do you want now?"

She dropped her hands to her lap and looked down, uncomfortable meeting his accusing glare. "I don't want anything, Caleb. I just thought . . . I wanted to see you."

He laughed. "Well, you've seen me. Anything else?"

Her eyes shot up. "This isn't easy for me."

"Oh, right. I forgot. Because it's always about you, isn't it? Well, gee, Hadley. I'm so sorry. What can I do to make your visit to this fine institution more bearable? Should I ask the guards to order pizza? Get you a cozy blanket and cushion for your chair?"

She tamped down her rage, knowing that fighting would only make things worse. He was protecting himself the same way she had for so long. She straightened her back and clasped her hands on the table, leaning forward.

"You're right," she said, looking him in the eye. "This isn't easy for either of us. But I'm here, Caleb. I'm trying. Can you give me that much, at least?"

His expression softened an infinitesimal degree. Then he leaned forward and clasped his hands on the table, too. "Fine. If you'll tell me why you're really here."

She steeled herself, trying to remember all the things she'd rehearsed in her head the past few days. All the things she'd planned to say. But they'd somehow flown from her head and out the tiny windows of the visiting room. The only thing she could think of saying had nothing to do with the letter.

"That time in the attic," she blurted out. "When you found me trying on Mom's wedding dress. Why did you say I would never get married?"

His brow furrowed, and he leaned back. "What are you talking about? I never said that."

"Yes, you did," she insisted. "I asked you if I had to wear a dress when I get married, and you said, 'What makes you think you're ever getting married?'"

He blinked a few times and shook his head. "No. You're remembering it wrong. That's not what I said."

"Okay, then what did you say?" She was pretty sure she remembered it correctly but was curious to see how he wormed his way out of this one.

"I said, 'What makes you think you ever *have* to get married.'"

She looked past him, trying to remember. Had she been holding on to something false all these years?

"For what it's worth," he continued, "I saw what losing Mom did to Dad, and even though I sometimes blamed you for it, I know it wasn't your fault. But I was just a kid, too, Hadley. I didn't always say the right thing. Except in this case, I think I *did*."

"Why?"

He looked down. "I never wanted you to be that dependent on

someone for your happiness. I knew you were stronger than that, and seeing you in Mom's dress . . . it bothered me. You weren't that girl."

A mixture of emotions threatened to overtake her, but she couldn't allow them. Not when there was so much left to say.

"It's not a bad thing to depend on someone, Caleb. There was a time I depended on you."

"Yeah, well. We all make mistakes."

She laughed despite herself. "You helped me in Cairo. That wasn't a mistake."

"I called in a favor," he said, waving her off. "It was no big deal."

"It was to me."

A muscle worked in his jaw as he threw a glance behind him. "Is this really what you came here to talk to me about? Something I said twelve years ago?"

"No," she said quietly. "I want to talk about something you wrote. The letter you left for me six years ago."

His face hardened. "What about it?"

She closed her eyes for a second, fighting back tears she knew would only anger him. "What did it say?" she finally managed.

His chair squeaked as he leaned forward. "What do you mean? You never read it?"

"No. Dad found it first and threw it away. I only learned about it a few days ago."

"I can't . . ." He paused, looking flustered. "I don't really remember what it said."

"Liar."

He dropped his elbow on the table and drew a hand through his buzzed hair. "It doesn't matter anymore."

She leaned over and grabbed hold of his wrist. "It does matter, Caleb. Tell me what it said."

"No touching!" barked a guard. Hadley flinched and withdrew her hand.

Caleb shot the guard an annoyed look, then turned back to her, eyes penetrating. "You called me a coward that night. I was angry . . . because you were right. I was scared of ending up like Dad, living in a shit house selling used cars, focused on the past. Grandpa Frank promised a different life."

"And look where it got him. Look where it got you."

"I know."

She pushed her hands into her lap. "What did the letter say, Caleb?"

He closed his eyes, and she watched the energy drain from his body. "I was sixteen years old, with no money to my name. I didn't want to leave you alone with Dad, but I knew you'd never agree to come with me, not if I was going to Frank. I knew how you felt about him. So I . . ." He stopped, taking a breath before opening his eyes to look at her. "I wrote that you could come live with me when I turned eighteen. And I promised I'd stop working for Frank when you did. All you had to do was say the word. But you never did."

An alternate version of the past six years ran through her head like a video on fast-forward. She saw herself leaving her dad and moving into a tiny apartment with Caleb. She saw him putting his life on hold, struggling to provide for her. She saw her dad angry, broken, and alone. It wasn't a better version. It was just different.

"You really would have quit?" she whispered. "You would have left Frank?" A sudden wave of guilt threatened to drown her. If she'd said yes, maybe they wouldn't be sitting here today. Maybe Caleb wouldn't be giving up the next ten years of his life.

A deep chuckle came from his chest. "The truth is, I don't know. By the time I turned eighteen, I was in pretty deep. Then Frank died, and . . . I'm not sure I would have been able to leave. And even if I did, how was I supposed to take care of you? I didn't graduate from high school. I was a car thief with a record. Frank's organization was all I had. It wasn't just the money. It was feeling like I belonged. That I meant something to the people around me."

Hadley stared at her older brother, the same one that had pulled her from Frank's trunk. The one that had made sure she was fed and got to school on time when her dad was away. The one that had also lost a mother, one whose loss he grieved just as much—maybe even more. Because he actually knew her. Hadley had been holding on to a specter for too long. It was time to hold on to what was real.

"You meant something to me, Caleb. You still do."

He shifted in his seat and swallowed. "I'm sorry for what I said at Frank's funeral. I'm sorry . . . for a lot of things."

"Me too."

"Caldwell!" shouted a guard by the door. "One minute. Say your goodbyes."

Hadley looked at Caleb, the man she'd been angry at for so long. All this time, she'd thought he'd abandoned her. Would she have been better off with him? Probably not. But he hadn't wanted to leave her. Knowing that was enough. If only Melinoë had made her face her fears years ago.

They pushed their chairs back and stood.

"Well," she said awkwardly. "It was good seeing you, Caleb."

He smiled. "You too, Haddy Bear."

Her eyes filled with tears, and she stepped forward, throwing her arms around him. "I love you, you big jerk."

"Love you too, sis," he said, hugging her back.

"That's enough," called a guard. "Time's up, Caldwell."

Hadley pulled away and wiped the tears from her face. "I'll come back," she said. "I can visit every weekend, if you want."

He sniffed, then glanced around to make sure none of the other felons caught wind of him having emotions. "No, I don't want you upending your life. I won't be here forever. In the meantime," he stopped and lowered his voice, "you have my number."

She shot him a crooked smile and nodded, then stuck out her thumb and pinky finger, making a phone gesture with her hand. *I'll call you*, she mouthed.

He gave her a wink and a smile, then strode out of the room, head held a little higher than it was when he arrived.

Hadley walked through the front prison gates feeling lighter. Caleb was a convicted felon, and he deserved the time he was serving. But he was still her brother, and forgiving him felt like a good first step in repairing their relationship. She was already thinking of the ways she'd help him when he got out of prison. Maybe he could move into the room above the garage at Soxie's, or Mayron could help get him a job. Hell, maybe he could *work* for Mayron. She ventured to guess that some of the people on Mayron's payroll had records of their own. It could work, and she was starting to feel giddy with the possibilities.

She stopped and scanned the visitors' parking lot, putting her hand up to shade her from the sun. The girls said they might hit the coffee shop a couple miles down. When she didn't see the car, she sent a quick text to Olivia to tell her she was out. Olivia responded immediately, saying they were on their way.

She stuffed her phone in her back pocket and walked over to a stone bench near the front gate. Cigarette butts lined the gravel beneath it. She brushed a few of them aside and took a seat. Then she leaned back, letting the sun warm her face.

She sat for a few moments, clearing her mind. It felt good to sit and just exist. There were plenty of worries waiting for her, but for now, she relished the peace she found in the most unlikely of places. A prison.

A smile formed on her lips, and she kept her eyes closed, enjoying the nothingness of the moment. She heard the crunch of boots on gravel and opened her eyes. A man in a guard's uniform was walking from the parking lot toward the front gate. She acknowledged him with a friendly smile, then closed her eyes again.

His footsteps got louder as he passed her bench, then they abruptly stopped.

"Excuse me. Do I know you?"

Her eyes snapped open, and she turned toward him. He was about her height, with a decent build and dark hair. Mirrored sunglasses covered his eyes. She sat up and shook her head.

"Sorry, I don't think so."

He tilted his head to the side and took off his sunglasses. Then he pointed them at her.

"Yes. I do know you. You're that girl from the plane, the one that messed with the mirror."

Hadley's back went ramrod straight. She didn't recognize him because of the sunglasses and uniform. But it was him—the guy who saw her reflection get stuck in the airplane bathroom. The same guy Olivia promised her she'd never see again. Yet here he was. A guard in the prison where her brother was serving time. What were the odds?

She laughed, convinced the universe had a strange sense of humor. The man frowned.

"It's not funny. That really freaked me out. I couldn't look in a mirror for days." Then he paused and glanced at the prison behind him. "Were you visiting someone?"

"My brother."

He nodded, then took a seat next to her. She studied his profile. He had a sharp jaw and long eyelashes. His hair was black and disheveled, and his complexion was golden brown. Hadley guessed it was a combination of genetics and the Arizona sun. A glance at his nametag told her his last name was Santiago. He was cute, in a nerdy, prison guard sort of way. She wondered if he knew her brother but decided not to ask. It was too early to share that information. And then she wanted to laugh at herself. Because "early" meant there would be a later. And suddenly, she kind of wanted that with this guy—this stranger. She wanted a later.

"Santiago," she said, throwing a nod at the nametag. "Got a first name?"

"Adrian. You?"

"Hadley," she answered, offering him her hand. "Hadley Caldwell."

He took it. His hand was dry and callused, but warm. "It's nice to meet you, Hadley Caldwell."

"Likewise, Adrian Santiago."

They stared at each other for a moment, then turned to look at the mountains in the distance, as if they met up on this bench all the time. "About the mirror thing," she said, surprising herself. "I'm not sure I can ever explain it. Is that going to be a problem?"

He shrugged. "Not for me. I'm over it."

"You are?" She turned to him, impressed. "How'd you manage that?"

"When I saw you sitting here," he replied. "I never would have had the courage to talk to you otherwise. Must be a sign."

She liked the way his smile carried to his eyes, to his whole face. It intrigued her.

"So you believe in signs," she surmised.

"Only when they're as pretty as you are."

She rolled her eyes and shoved him on the shoulder. "Boo! And you were doing so well, Santiago."

"Damn," he laughed. "Anything I can do to redeem myself?"

"That depends."

"On what?"

"On how fast you answer the following questions," she said, folding her arms.

He angled himself toward her. "Hit me."

She narrowed her eyes as she considered him. Caleb was right. She never wanted to end up like her dad, dependent on another person for her happiness. Marriage wasn't her style, and never would be. But a date? Maybe.

"How old are you?" she asked.

"Twenty-two."

"Why were you flying to New York?"

"To visit my mother."

"Is that where you're from?"

"Brooklyn," he specified. "But yes."

"Siblings?"

"Two younger sisters."

She pointed her thumb at the prison behind her. "Does it bother you that my brother is in there?"

He sighed and looked toward the prison. "Only if you helped him get there. Otherwise, no. It doesn't bother me. People make mistakes. I hope your brother learns from his."

She was liking him more and more. "One last question."

"Phew," he said, pretending to wipe sweat off his brow.

"I like my privacy, and I'm not interested in anything serious right now."

He looked amused. "That's not a question."

"I haven't asked it yet."

"Fair enough."

She cocked an eyebrow. "Are you single?"

He mimicked her and folded his arms. "I wouldn't be sitting here if I wasn't."

"Good answer."

The sound of a car horn got their attention. She looked up to see the Shelby turning into the lot.

Hadley stood. "Well, that's my ride."

Adrian quickly leaped to his feet. He was about an inch shorter than her, but if she'd been wearing flats instead of her biker boots, they'd be eye to eye. She'd have to remember that.

"Hey, don't I get to ask you some questions now?" he said, feigning offense.

She dug her phone out of her pocket, unlocked it, and handed it to him. "No. Save them for our first date."

"I like the sound of that," he said, wiggling his eyebrows.

"Calm down, Santiago. I was thinking dinner, but now it might just be coffee."

He brought his hand to his heart. "You wound me, Caldwell. But I'll take it." Then he added his information to her phone and handed it back to her. She stuffed it in her pocket as the car pulled up next to them.

Soxie leaned out the driver's side window. "Everything okay, Hadz?"

She nodded, then turned back to Adrian. He'd slipped his sunglasses back on, and when she saw her reflection in the mirrored lenses, she couldn't help but grin. Sure, they had some gods to catch and a portal to protect, but what was the point of fighting if not for moments like these?

"Yes, Sox," she said. "Everything's great."

Adrian walked backward a few steps and flashed her a dimpled smile. Then he did the same thing she'd done to Caleb twenty minutes prior. He mimed a phone at his ear and said, "Call me."

She laughed as he spun around and disappeared behind the prison entrance. Then she hopped in the car and marveled at the chain of events that had brought her here. Did she believe in signs? Sometimes. But she trusted her instincts more. And her instincts told her this could be the start of something good.

the delivery

Hadley studied her reflection in her bedroom mirror. She wore a V-neck tee with her favorite leather leggings, a cropped jean jacket, and pointy ballet flats. She turned back and forth, trying to get a feel for the shoes. Alice walked up behind her.

"They look great," she said, pointing at the shoes. "What's the problem?"

Hadley shrugged and kicked them off. "They're just not me." Then she went to her closet to grab her motorcycle boots.

"Who cares if he's shorter than you?" said Soxie. She was lying on the bed with Olivia, idly scrolling through her phone. "It's good to look down on a man once in a while."

Hadley dropped onto the chair by her bed to pull on her boots. "It doesn't bother me. I just thought I'd try something different, that's all."

Alice looked crestfallen as she picked up the discarded shoes. "Do you want me to return them?"

"No, honey," she said, feeling guilty for not liking them. "I really appreciate you getting them for me. I'm sure I'll find a reason to wear them."

"Where? To a funeral?"

Hadley shot Soxie a bitter look, and Olivia elbowed her in the ribs. But Alice just laughed and threw one of the shoes at Soxie's head. She caught it with ease.

"Not cool, Ali!" she said, pointing the shoe at her. "You could poke someone's eye out with this thing."

Alice giggled and tossed the other shoe aside. Then she crawled onto the bed with Olivia and Soxie. Hadley finished buckling her boots and stood.

"Well, how do I look?"

They smiled.

"You look perfect, Hadz," said Olivia, her eyes shining. Then she hopped off the bed and proceeded to straighten the gold necklaces that were always getting tangled in Hadley's hair.

"I'd lend you this one," Alice said, lifting the locket from her chest. "But apparently it's never coming off my neck. You'll be burying me in this thing."

Soxie slapped her arm. "Not funny."

"I'm kidding! Geez. Tough crowd."

Hadley gave her a sympathetic look. "But really, no luck at all?"

Alice shook her head. "No. I can't get it over my head, and the clasp won't budge. David even tried cutting the chain with wire cutters."

"Well, maybe it's for the best," Olivia offered as she finished with Hadley's necklaces. "There's no reason to believe it would be better off in Mayron's safe."

"The dagger is," Soxie pointed out.

"Yes, but the gods might actually want the dagger. They no longer want the Portal."

"So they say," said Alice.

Hadley was about to apply her lip gloss when she stopped and turned around. "Wait. You think they're lying?"

"Persephone's memory seems to think so."

Soxie tossed her phone aside. "No. No more god talk. Not tonight. Tonight is Hadley's night."

Hadley rolled her eyes. "It's not *my night*, Sox. It's just a date. It's no big deal."

"Tell that to David," Alice said with a laugh. "He's already been cyberstalking this guy. He's worse than Olivia."

"Hey! All I said was I'd read him for her," argued Olivia. "I never said I'd go internet snooping." Then she turned to Hadley and stage-whispered, "But I will, if you want me to."

"You did just meet the guy two days ago," Soxie joined in. "What's the rush? I can get Mayron to do some digging if you want."

Hadley threw her hands up. "Guys, stop. I've got this, I promise." Then she turned back to the mirror. It felt good to be doing normal things again, like trying on shoes and going on a date. But they still had so much left to explore behind this glass. She pulled her new compass from her jacket pocket.

"Don't worry. You'll get to test it soon," said Olivia. "Alice says Persephone's getting close. Our blood is the key. She's using it to find a way to guide us."

Hadley nodded and stared at the compass. She'd transferred the contents of her old one to this one—including a new drop of blood—and even though it was the same style of compact, it felt different. She was both nervous and excited to try it once they got the green light to reenter the Realm. And then there was the new Backwards, the one Soxie claimed was an entire world turned inside out. Hadley was very curious about that one.

The doorbell rang, followed by the usual insanity of dogs freaking out and barking like mad. A flutter of excitement ran through her body while her friends leaped off the bed and ran to the window. She laughed.

"You guys are as bad as the dogs. You can't even see the front door from here."

Soxie turned and flashed her a mischievous grin. "That's okay. We'll watch the whole thing on the security feed after you leave."

Hadley grabbed her things and headed for the door. "Whatever. Bye, ladies. If I'm not back by sunup, wait longer."

"Atta girl," said Soxie, winking.

By the time Hadley got downstairs, the dogs were about to lose their minds. She quickly wrangled them into the library and shut the door. They wouldn't maul Adrian, but they might lick him to death. She figured she'd spare him this go around.

She checked her image one last time in the foyer mirror, then opened the door.

"You're early—"

It wasn't Adrian.

"Oh, I'm so sorry," she said, momentarily frazzled. "I thought you'd be someone else. Here, I can sign for that."

The man in the UPS uniform smiled wide and handed her the box. It was small and weighed almost nothing. She checked the shipping label. It read simply, "HUNTRESS."

Her heart seized, and she stepped back. On cue, the dogs snarled and scratched up the library door behind her.

"Do not worry, huntress. I mean you no harm. I am, after all, but a messenger."

She didn't know whether to laugh, scream, or cry. The man looked to be in his late twenties or early thirties, lean, but fit. She wondered if he knew what was happening, if he was watching this exchange take place, powerless over his own body and mind.

"What do you want, Hermes?"

He nodded toward the box. "Think of it as a peace offering."

She glanced at the box in her hands. There was nothing the gods could offer that would make up for what they were doing.

"We don't want your peace offering," she spat, shoving it into his chest.

"You will want this," he said, gently pushing it back. "I promise."

With an angry sigh, she tore the box open. Inside were several police reports for a man named John Taylor. She shook her head in confusion. Of all the things she could think to find in a box from the gods, this was not one of them. She scanned the contents of the papers, her eyes trained to find pertinent information after years reading her dad's and brother's. According to the reports, John Taylor had been arrested multiple times for domestic abuse, but each time the charges were dropped. Hadley's blood boiled. Whoever this guy was, he deserved a black eye of his own, or worse. But why was Hermes showing her this? She looked up to find him watching her closely.

"What is this?" she asked.

He tapped the plastic employee badge clipped to his uniform pocket. She gasped. John Taylor was standing right in front of her.

"Did you do this?" she demanded, curling the papers into her fist.

He recoiled in shock. "Of course not! The mortal John Taylor has been committing sins for a good portion of his pathetic existence."

Hadley checked the dates on the reports. Hermes was right. John Taylor had been a bastard for at least four years, but chances were, it was a lot longer than that. The reports looked real enough, but she'd be sure to confirm them later. She dropped them to her side.

"How is this a peace offering?"

He lifted his hands as if he himself were the gift. "When I am through with this body, I will dispose of it."

Her heart flew out of her chest. "What? No! You can't do that!"

He frowned. "Huntress, this mortal has sinned. He has brought the wrath of the gods upon himself. I thought you would be pleased."

Hadley felt the promise of the past two days disappear in the span of a second. Everything suddenly felt very heavy, and very real. She racked her brain for something to say. Anything.

"Listen, Hermes. You can't—you can't just go around killing people. Even if they're bad. That's not how it's done."

He angled his head to the side. "Then how do you punish mortals for their crimes?"

She waved the papers in his face. "You figured out a way to print these. You must know what they are. We have laws. A justice system." She stopped and thought of her brother. In a world where the gods were judge, jury, and executioner, she shivered to think what would have happened to him. "Maybe John Taylor doesn't deserve a second chance, but that's not for you to decide. Not anymore."

"The items you hold were among the mortal's possessions. He feels no remorse regarding their contents. He feels nothing but anger and rage, and he will commit these sins again. I see it in his heart."

Hadley sent a mental *SOS* to Olivia. This wasn't a moral dilemma she wanted to handle on her own.

"I'm sure he will," she said carefully. "But you know we can't let you do this. You know we'll be coming for you."

He smiled. "Artemis mentioned you were difficult. That is probably why she likes you."

The telltale sound of the front gates opening carried down the drive. Crap. Adrian. So much for a fun, carefree first date. She shoved the box back into Hermes's hands.

"Message received."

He nodded and tucked the box under his arm. "Until we meet again, huntress." Then he skipped down the steps and climbed into his dark brown truck. He seemed like the happiest delivery man in the world. She was surprised he wasn't whistling.

She watched his truck as it passed Adrian's car in the drive. He honked and waved, and Adrian waved back.

"How does he know how to drive?" asked Olivia behind her. She was out of breath, most likely from sprinting down the stairs.

Hadley handed her the police reports. "Apparently, he knows how to read too."

Olivia skimmed the papers, eyelids fluttering and pupils dilating. "This is bad."

Hadley glanced up and forced a smile on her face as Adrian got out of the car. "I'll meet you in the library in a few minutes," she told Olivia through her teeth.

Olivia nodded absently as she made her way back into the house, her nose buried in the police reports. Hadley turned and walked down the steps to meet Adrian.

He wore jeans with cowboy boots, a white button-down, and a black suit jacket. His hair was damp from a recent shower, and his smile was as warm as it was the last time she saw it.

"Hey," he said before leaning in to give her a kiss on the cheek. "You look really nice."

"Thanks. So do you."

He grinned bashfully, tugging at the sleeves of his jacket. "I hope you're hungry. I wasn't sure what you like, so I made reservations at five different places, but they're all about the same distance from here. Nice house, by the way."

She gave him a moment to take it all in. The Roxland estate never failed to wow.

"Listen, Adrian," she finally began.

"Uh-oh. I know what that means."

She smiled sadly. "I'm sorry, but I'm going to need a rain check. It's just that things are complicated in my life right now, and I—"

"Like your privacy," he finished, placing his hands on his hips and dipping his head. "I get it."

"I really am sorry. I was looking forward to this."

"Me too."

She wasn't upset. Disappointed, maybe. Bummed? Definitely. But it motivated the hell out of her. They *were* going to beat the gods. It wasn't a matter of if, but when. In the meantime, she'd give herself, and Adrian, a taste of what's to come. Before she could second-guess herself, she slipped her hand behind his neck and drew his face to hers.

There weren't fireworks or proverbial doves flapping in the air. In fact, it was probably one of the most awkward kisses she'd ever had, not that she'd had many kisses. But when he put his arms around her waist and gave into her, it was nice.

It wasn't love, but it was the promise of something. And that alone was worth fighting for.

acknowledgments

Thank you, reader, for embarking on this journey with me. I had so much fun bringing Hadley's story to life, and I hope you enjoyed her adventure as much as I did. She and her huntress sisters continue surprising and inspiring me. Sharing their stories with you is a true gift.

To my friends and family, thank you for your unwavering support. I couldn't have done it without you!

To my editor Susie and the team at SparkPress—you nailed it again. Thanks for giving the Realm the best home she could have.

A special shoutout to Cleveland D, my Golden Girls, and all my early readers. As always, your input was invaluable. But mainly, you just ROCK.

To my cat Maximus, who inspired the feline character of Boop, thanks for knocking the journals off my desk and napping on my mousepad. As a writing accountability partner, you stunk. But your cuddles kept me going.

To my patient, kind, loving, and supportive husband. My impostor syndrome has no chance against the strength of your encouragement. No matter how often I doubt myself, your belief in me never wavers. I'm forever grateful for your love and partnership.

And finally, to all the gals out there, inspiring and lifting each other up every day. You may not be battling gods and demons, but you're fighting the good fight and supporting the sisterhood. Stronger together. Sisters forever.

Hadley and the girls would approve.

about the author

Lenore Borja grew up in Phoenix, Arizona, and attended Arizona State University before moving to New York City to study acting at the American Academy of Dramatic Arts. After a brief acting career, she spent several years working in executive search and human resources in New York and San Francisco. She now resides in Fort Collins, Colorado, with her husband and two cats. When she's not writing, she enjoys adventure travel and anything that gets the heart racing, whether it's hiking, running, or getting lost in a good book.

Author photo © EJimmyD

Looking for your next great read?

We can help!

Visit www.gosparkpress.com/next-read
or scan the QR code below for a list
of our recommended titles.

SparkPress is an independent boutique publisher
delivering high-quality, entertaining, and engaging
content that enhances readers' lives, with a special
focus on commercial and genre fiction.